THE BIG BAD WOLF

BOOK 2: INSTINCT AND RAGE

13 PITCH BLACK CATS

PROLOGUE: HEAVY IS THE HEAD
THAT WEARS THE CROWN

R amos, the king of Rophmna, sat alone, an extravagantly decorated stone hall sprawling out before him. During the daylight, hordes of people clamored for his attention. Many wanted him to settle their disputes in their favor. Others wanted some measure of authority granted by him. King Ramos wasn't ignorant of the fact that some sought any sign of weakness to dispose of him and replace him with a ruler more suited to their dark desires. But today, before the sun rose, he made sure there was only one person to meet him.

From one of the many side doors, a man walked in. He was well-dressed with bright-colored clothing. Every detail of his appearance, from his perfectly combed hair to the shine of his leather boots, declared that he settled for nothing less than full control of everything. His gray hair was slicked back and trimmed short, and his face was gentle while showing his battle scars and wrinkles proudly. Even in the king's presence, he walked with a surety that few could claim.

"You wish to speak to me, my lord?" The elderly man's voice was clean and flat. No flourishes, no hint of an accent, just the words as they were.

"You've been busy." The king gave a knowing smile to the elderly gentleman. "Tell me, Midas, what is so important that you need to use my royal messengers so frequently?"

"You know of the sin of wrath that was summoned five years ago in Aquittemia?" Midas replied unapologetically. He continued without waiting for a response. "I looked into it because Nora Storm-leaf slew the demon. The summoners targeted one of her charges specifically. It was an odd case simply because the child was a beastkin."

"Yes, if I remember correctly, you investigated it rather thoroughly." The king leaned forward on his throne. "You called for the arrests and executions of dozens of cultists. But what does that have to do with what you're doing now?"

"It's unfortunate, but we did not get all of them, Your Highness," Midas said emotionlessly. "I'm seeing signs that match what happened five years ago occurring again now. So I've been trying to pinpoint their end goal. All I know is that they're not targeting the city again. It could be that they're targeting the tournament."

"Why do you never have good news?" The king leaned back and closed his eyes. "It will be my son's sixteenth birthday soon. Tradition dictates that we hold a tournament for any potential knight prospects." He let out a heavy sigh. "What do you recommend? Do I call off traditions because of some terrorists?"

Midas waved his hand and shook his head. "Unfortunately, I would say that is a bad idea. That would tip them off. We don't want them to know we're watching them. I want to use this opportunity to catch as many of them as possible." Midas shrugged. "Besides, the people have been looking forward to the tournament for a while now. I also know that all the other kingdoms, including The Wild King-dom, have asked for representatives to spectate."

"More headaches," the king groaned. "I request that you refrain from reading my personal messages in the future," King Ramos said, knowing the only way Midas could have that information was to have read all the messages in and out of the castle. "Now, on to more personal matters. How is my nephew doing since you've taken to educating him?"

"He is quite a charming boy." Midas smiled. The first genuine emotion appeared on his face. "He needs to stay away from all those books about fantasies where the hero saves the princess and slays the dragon and focus on military strategy."

"Ha! He's a dreamer, isn't he?" The king laughed. He loved his nephew, and when he fell ill five years ago, everyone thought he had died. But it was a miracle that he woke up just before they pronounced him dead. His personality had changed some, but everyone attributed it to the fever he'd had. And now that he was growing up, he was shaping up to be a fine man. "I've got to know. What brings the hero of the kingdom to show so much interest in a single boy?"

"Truth be told, I've had my eye on many children for some time before that." Midas had returned to his monotone voice. "He was the one who was able to catch and hold my attention."

A single word came from the king's lips. "Why?"

Midas smiled again. "He reminds me of myself when I was that age."

1

SLEEPLESS IN CENTARI

The frantic cracking of wood striking wood rang in my ears as the sounds reverberated off the training room walls. My frustration grew as I beat the stationary wooden dummy, and I panted from the exertion of having swung a practice sword around for most of the night.

This is supposed to calm me down, not make things worse. I growled as I struck the wooden mockery of a man. When I paused for a moment to catch my breath, I heard someone walking up the stairs to the training room.

Great, now I'm in trouble. With a scream, I swung the wooden practice sword at the dummy's fake head with all of my might. The crack left my ears ringing while the dummy's head went flying into the wall across the room and half of my practice weapon went soaring off in the other direction. The door opened, and a familiar motherly figure walked cautiously into the room.

"Trouble sleeping again?" Nora asked softly. "It's getting worse, isn't it?"

"What do you think?" I snapped. *Stop. Get a hold of yourself. It isn't her fault.* "Sorry. It's getting worse."

I turned to the tall elven woman, my ears and tail drooping. She was in a simple long black nightgown that nearly reached her stockinged feet with an additional layer of a long-sleeved shirt underneath. *It's the start of the water season, and things are warming up. How can she still be cold? Oh right, she's not covered in fur like me.*

"You know you can talk to me, right?" Nora walked up slowly to me.

"I have." I threw the broken piece of wood into the pile of other broken practice swords from earlier in the week. "But nothing's helped. I have so much energy that I can't sit still. I can't help myself but burn it all off until I practically pass out. And if I do sleep, it's only for a short time before I'm back to having an unreasonable amount of energy."

"I gave you permission to use this room at night, hoping it would help." Nora then looked at the pile of broken wood. "But that has become a costly decision. I also didn't expect you to be this loud, either."

"It would be better if I could just run around the streets at night, but you already vetoed that." I crossed my arms and scowled before quickly deflating. "Who am I kidding? That probably won't work anymore. I don't know why I have all of this energy and why it started at the beginning of the wind season last year." I stared at my claws. "It's got to be my recovery aptitude." *Salien, our local expert on the recovery aptitude and my doctor, has told me a lot about my recovery aptitude.* "Every time I hurt myself, I'll heal faster. With all this exercise and tiring myself out, my body must treat it similarly to when I hurt myself. Every time I exhaust myself, I recover faster. The more I exercise until I can't anymore, the more I need to."

Nora had a thoughtful look on her face. "You may be right, but I have a feeling there might be other factors contributing to it."

"Really?" I flicked my ears towards Nora. "Like what?"

"I had a feeling about it last season, but now it's undeniable." Nora stood, smiling at me. "With your growth spurt and now much more obvious developments, I can say with confidence that it's because you're now at an important stage of your life."

I looked at her, confused. "What developments?"

She pointed to my chest. *It's a little puffier than it used to be, but what does she mean?* The realization of what she was pointing out hit me hard. "You can't be serious. I'm too young for that."

"You're a little on the early side, but nothing unreasonable." Nora tried to suppress her giggling. "Don't worry, what you're experiencing is completely natural."

"Nope!" I covered my ears. "La-la-la-la. I don't want to hear it."

"You've seen all your sisters go through it. Now it's your turn." I could still hear Nora even after covering my ears. *This is the one time I wish my hearing wasn't as good as it is.*

I ran out of the room and down the stairs. After I left the classroom, I dashed to my room and barricaded the door, even though I knew full well that wouldn't stop Nora. My mind spiraled out of control as I paced back and forth. An unending nonsensical stream of uncontrolled thoughts tumbled in my brain before I slapped myself back into reality. *Mom's right; this is completely natural. I'm just over-reacting again.*

I went to the corner of my room where I had been marking my height over the years. *I've grown six inches in the last year. If my measurements are correct, that would make me sixty-six inches tall.* I walked in front of my personal mirror, which was hanging in a corner.

I scrutinized my appearance. The same silver fur covered my entire body as it had my entire life. *It's nice and thick while being a little longer from the recent ice season. My hair stopped growing once it passed my shoulders by an inch. It's as thick as my fur and almost as fluffy as my tail.* I smiled and admired all of my teeth. Forty-two sharp white teeth sat ready to sever flesh from bone. *I bit my tongue one time and punctured a hole through it. It stopped bleeding by bedtime, but it took the next day to heal fully.* I moved my gaze downward. *My tail is long and fluffy, about twenty-one inches long. I always take really good care of it. Is my butt getting bigger?* My furry fingers and digitigrade feet were tipped with sharp claws. *Over the years, I've become quite reliant on them, haven't I?*

I then turned my attention to the area Nora had mentioned. I wore a gray nightdress that I'd bought recently because I outgrew more of my clothes again. The lack of jewelry on my neck still left a satisfying feeling. *It's been a little more than a year, but it still feels liberating to be free of that collar. Now I can get angry without going blind and deaf as if a lighting bolt struck the ground in front of me.*

My chest had two slight bumps, the telltale signs of female maturity. *My breasts are growing. Right... puberty. I knew it was coming, but I never prepared myself for it. So Mom believes my excessive energy is due to me going through puberty. Is she right, or is it just a coincidence?*

I started pacing again, trying to get my thoughts under control. *Female puberty—isn't that mostly like male puberty, with some exceptions? I don't have to worry about growing extra hair. I'm covered in fur. So, a little extra height, breasts, and what else?* I could feel my eyes bulging as yet another realization hit me. *Periods... What do I do about them? Should I ask Mom about them?* I stopped my pacing and racked my brain to think of a way to talk to Nora about it. *I can't come up with anything other than asking bluntly.* A growl escaped my lips. *If she tries anything funny, I'll... I'll... I don't know what I'll do, but I'll be livid.*

I cleared the door of the barricade. When I opened the door, I saw Nora standing in front of it with her arms crossed, tapping her foot.

"Are you done?" she asked.

When did she get there? Was I so distracted that I didn't pay attention to her walking to my door? Fine, if she wants to play it that way...

I looked down each hallway, and when I didn't see anyone else, I grabbed Nora's wrist and pulled her to my room with almost no difficulty. She bit back a yelp of surprise. Once she got her feet back under herself in the middle of my room and I closed the door, she turned to me and said, "I forgot how strong you've gotten recently. Your physical aptitude really is something special." I couldn't suppress my grin.

"Tell me everything I need to know." I crossed my arms and glared at the elven woman. By flexing a muscle in my foot in just the right way, I started tapping a toe claw on the floor. *It's harder than it looks, but boy does it intimidate everyone.* "Now."

"I'm glad you've calmed down enough to accept that you're growing up, but you still need to remember your manners." Nora stood up straight and used her mom voice. *It intimidates everyone, except for her.* The air rapidly became harder to breathe.

I gave up all pretense of rebellion and caved. "Sorry." I walked tentatively to my bed. As I sat on my bed, I flattened my ears and curled my tail around my leg. "I'm just... I just... I don't know how to handle all this."

Nora sat on the bed next to me. "I know, honey." She wrapped her arm around me and pulled me in for a hug. "Your body is going through a lot of changes. I might not completely understand what you're going through or what you will go through, but I want you to know that I am not your enemy."

Red flag!

I pushed Nora away from me. "Hold on. What do you mean? What will I go through?" I was on the verge of tears a moment ago, but something about what she'd said irked me. *She knows something and hasn't told me yet.*

Nora had that look on her face that told me she knew exactly what I was thinking. She smiled and tried to hug me again. I caught her arm and held it away from me. She sighed as she lowered her arm. "You know how I inherited all of those books in the classroom?" *The ones Phan owned before they found him dead.* I nodded. "Well, I found some books that had more information on beastkin a little more than a year ago."

"And when were you planning on telling me this?" I bared my teeth and growled. *She's been holding out on me!*

"Stop that!" Nora flicked her wrist and used her magic to force my mouth shut. "Behave!" She pointed a finger right between my eyes. "I fully intended to tell you everything I learned in those books. I was just waiting until you were mature enough to handle the information."

Fine. I relaxed as I calmly brought my hands up to my mouth. I grabbed hold of the hardened air and pried it apart. It took every bit of strength I could exert, but I felt the magic lose out against my strength.

"Are you going to behave?" Nora was grimacing, but she still used a commanding voice.

"Yes," I said with a sigh, reining in the desire to slap her with my claws. "You remember I know the general information about puberty, right? I just don't know anything about beastkin."

"Yes, but you were having so much fun being a kid that I didn't want to ruin it for you." Nora was smiling again. "I'm glad I don't need to tell you how babies are made." A look of concern covered her face. "That conversation always leads to everyone avoiding me for at least a week." She shook her head. "But I digress."

I asked, "Do you know about human women bleeding every four weeks?"

Nora nodded. "It's known as a period."

It's a little more complicated than that, but let's keep things simple. I gave her a worried look. "Is that going to happen to me too?"

"Nope," Nora said, a little too gleefully. "That's a thing only human women have. You, as a beastkin, are going to have something a little different." *Okay, this pause isn't helping my nerves.* "Once a season, you are going to look to mate with the one that attracts you. Also, beastkin often bear two children at a time."

I stared at her, dumbfounded. "Did you just tell me I'll go into heat once a season?"

"If that's what you call it, then yes. But I should mention that it only happens once a male beastkin has been imprinted on you. Apparently, beastkin mate for life because for a male to be imprinted on you, they have to earn your approval. Or something like that." She sounded like she was questioning the words as she said them. "There were almost no details on that part."

"Is 'imprinted' really the right word?" I asked doubtfully.

Nora threw her hands up. "I don't know. I'm just using the vocabulary the book used. Also, you will be a fully grown adult at fifteen, too. That's different from every other race. Elves, dwarves, dragoons, and humans are all fully mature at age nineteen. Orcs and goblins aren't even worth mentioning."

"So am I going to go into the army once I'm fifteen?" *I believe the contract specifically said seventeen, not when I had become an adult.*

"Do you want to leave me that badly?" Nora looked hurt by my question. "Not unless we make arrangements otherwise. The contract you signed when you first arrived says once you turn seventeen. Why?"

"No, I just wanted to know. Do these books mention the average lifespan of a beastkin? If I'm going to be an adult at fifteen, do I live until I'm forty?"

"It did mention it. But I don't know why you think that. You'll live just as long as a human." Nora stared at me with concern. "If you're worried about having to live your entire life in the military, don't. So far, since you've been getting food from your apprenticeship with the trappers, it cut down your needed stipend considerably." She smiled at me. "Even if you keep breaking all the practice equipment at the same rate you have been until you're seventeen, you'll need to serve about six years. But that's only a rough guess." Nora stood up from the bed. "Now, you have a big day tomorrow, correct? Aren't you going on your first hunting excursion at sunrise?"

"I completely forgot!" *I've been so worked up that I completely forgot about that.* My tail wagged behind me.

"There's still some time before sunrise. Try to get some sleep. It is a big day, after all." Nora slowly walked towards the door. She smiled as I curled up in a blanket, then walked out and closed the door behind her.

We just had a conversation about puberty, and now you want me to go to sleep? I'm so excited that I'm finally able to hunt something now that it's the water season. Yeah, sorry, Mom. Sleep's not happening tonight. I'll take a nap later and be just fine. I lay down and stared at the ceiling, impatiently waiting for the sun to rise. The anxiety of the future kept my heart and mind racing throughout the night.

A HUNTING WE SHALL GO

A door opened and closed, disrupting the silence. It had to be Melody walking into the dining room from the back door. *Finally, it's almost sunrise. Melody's internal clock is one of the most consistent ones I know. She always walks in the back door just before sunrise to cook breakfast.*

It was easy to learn that because of my irregular sleeping schedule. I got up and performed my usual morning routine of brushing all my fur and changing for the day. Since I hoped I was going to be running a lot, I wore light clothing. Besides, it wasn't cold enough to bother me. It never was.

The halls were still dark as I walked down them. I walked into the kitchen just as Melody was finishing getting everything set up. She turned around and jumped a bit when she saw me. "You need to stop that," she whined as she put her hand over her heart.

I giggled. *So long as you aren't throwing knives at me again, seeing your reactions never gets old.* "You should be used to it by now. Good morning, by the way."

"We need to get you something so I can hear you when you walk up behind me like that. There was a time when you knocked when you entered a room. Can we go back to that?" She relaxed as she went to the meat chest. "I don't know why you have so much fun scaring me. But if you give me a moment, I'll have your breakfast ready soon."

I tried to put the feeling into words. "I get this rush when I sneak up on someone. It kinda feels like a mission accomplished. It's not my fault that my natural footsteps are silent."

"Well, you can save it for the animals you're going to hunt today." She sounded both lighthearted and grumpy at the same time. She opened the meat chest and pulled out two slabs of jerky. "This is for you."

"No eggs? I'll take it." I snatched the meat from her hands and effortlessly tore apart a piece with each bite. *Yay, meat!*

"We still can't figure out why you can't taste eggs." Melody smiled as she watched me devour my breakfast. I had a blissful look on my face.

"What I don't understand is that after all these years, you still feed them to me." I took a moment away from another bite to express my annoyance.

"Because they're cheap." Melody's tone made it sound like that was an obvious fact. "Today is different because you need to get going to meet Marigold and Zane at sunrise."

I bounced on my toes. "Yup, I'm going hunting today!"

"Off you go then. You don't want to be late." Melody waved her hand towards the door. "I'm sure you're going to catch something big today." She couldn't hold back her mirth.

I'm not coming back empty-handed, that's for sure.

I finished the first piece of jerky and made my way out through the front door, then took off for the south gate. There was almost nobody out on the streets so early in the morning. The sun was just about to rise, making the horizon a reddish-orange color as the light crept into sight.

I ran to the gate with energy to spare. I stopped right behind a guard, who stood there bored because nobody was entering the city this early.

"Surprise." I tapped the man's back with my claws. I didn't worry about them piercing through his leather armor.

"Ah!" he shouted. "Seriously, Lucia, do you have to do that every time?" He turned towards me.

"Yes, it's so much fun." I giggled at his expense. "Besides, Martin, it's good practice."

Martin gave me a sour look. The same look he gave me every time I teased him while he lived at the orphanage with me. "Trust me, you don't need it. But, wow, you're getting taller. How much have you grown lately?" He changed his expression to a more friendly one.

"I'm sixty-six inches tall now." I stood up as straight as I could. "You're just really tall yourself." *I'm still a good eight or nine inches shorter than he is.* "How much more time do you have to spend as a guard?"

"I still have six seasons left." He sounded bored. "So, do you want to tell me why you're out so early? Going for another run because you couldn't sleep again?"

"Not today," I chirped. "Today, I get to go hunting." My tail wagged.

"Ah, that *would* put you in a good mood, wouldn't it?" Martin smiled. He turned his head back in the direction he should have been looking the entire time. "It looks like your chaperones are here."

I turned to follow his gaze and found that both Zane and Marigold were slowly walking this way. "Well, I guess it's time to get going. See you around."

"Do me a favor and stay safe," Martin called out after me as I walked to meet my two employers. I waved to him to let him know I'd heard him and took a bite from the second piece of jerky for my breakfast.

"Still eating breakfast, are we?" Zane glared at me when I stopped in front of him. "Maybe you should have gone to sleep earlier so you wouldn't be eating your breakfast on the run." He stood up straight, with his hands on his hips and feet apart, though he never adjusted his head to look at me because we were almost the same height.

"I couldn't sleep last night," I said nonchalantly. "In fact, I haven't slept through the night in the last six weeks." I finished the last of my jerky.

"Are you going to be alright?" Marigold asked with skepticism in her voice. "Maybe we should do this another day once you've slept."

"No, please don't," I hastily pleaded. "I was so excited that I couldn't sleep last night." *That, and I had a wonderful conversation with Mom about puberty.*

"It'll be fine. I don't expect to see much today." Zane, with a carefree attitude, pointed in the direction of our destination with a small wave of his hand. He'd planned for us to go to his tried-and-true hunting spot. "Since you have so much energy, Lucia, lead the way. Let's see how much you've learned." He'd lightened up over the years as I'd studied under him and his wife.

I jumped at the task. We spent most of the morning heading to the place Zane directed us to. We walked through the fields around the town to the southwest. The town walls were no longer in sight once we reached the beginning of the forest. There was a noticeable temperature change once we entered the trees, and the two humans following me didn't hold their heavy cloaks as tightly as they had been. The foliage was thick, but most of it was still dormant.

I followed Zane's directions and pointed out any tracks I spotted. If I missed any, Marigold or Zane pointed them out to me. There was a time when Zane wanted to see if I could learn to track using my sense of smell. It went as well as anyone could imagine. Originally, I'd called Zane insane and refused to try it. Eventually, I gave it a try and learned that it was extremely difficult. Within some margin of error, I could tell how many smells were in a small area, but not how old they were or where the owner of the smell went afterward. The biggest hurdle was that I would smell everything: plants, people, animals, excrement, and anything else. Trying to sort out all the smells took a long time before I could figure out which one I was looking for.

As we walked, it looked like parts of the forest were waking up from the ice season. The trees didn't have many leaves on them, so the only major obstructions to our view were all the tree trunks.

Zane stopped us just outside of a small clearing. It was strange to find a small section of flat ground with no trees in the middle of the forest. The two humans discovered a clump of bushes that were strategically placed to provide ample cover for hiding.

After we settled in the bushes, Marigold grabbed my attention. "If there's any trouble, either run or climb a tree." Her tone was as stern as her expression. It was a rare look on her face, one she saved for important topics.

"Is there anything special we need to look out for?" I asked innocently.

"Just the usual dangers. Orcs, some wild animals, and dire animals," Zane answered. "Nobody's seen a dire animal in these parts for a few years now, so it's unlikely we'll need to worry about that."

"It's unheard of to see orcs this far south at this time of year," Marigold interjected.

"So that leaves wild animals," I finished. "But aren't we out here to kill wild animals?" *What are they worried about?*

"Yes, we are, but there are some predators that can hunt us." Zane had a sorrowful look on his face. "And there are some animals, like boars, that will require a bit more work to bring down. But if you see anything like a bear or a wolf, don't keep that information to yourself."

"Ah, those kinds of animals." *I get it now. We're not the only predators in these woods.* "So, what's the plan of attack?"

"We're going to sit quietly, looking for any sign of an animal that walks close enough for us to kill." Zane removed the bow from his back and took out three arrows, holding them in his hand. Marigold did the same thing.

"That sounds boring," I complained. "And I don't have a bow. What am I supposed to do?"

"Watch us and learn," Marigold said in a hushed tone. "Besides, I have a hunch that you won't want to use a bow when you hunt." She gave a slight smirk.

I sat down with a huff of frustration. *This is not what I thought it was going to be like.* I didn't sit quietly as I scratched at the ground. Both Zane and Marigold looked at me like I was a spoiled child who had been told they couldn't go out and play.

We sat in our little hiding spot, waiting. And we kept waiting. Zane and Marigold were sitting quietly while taking turns watching the surrounding area. I fidgeted with anything I could get my hands on. *This is worse than reading! I don't know what I should have expected, but I didn't think it would be this dull.* I kept drawing on the ground with my claws, playing with small rocks, or shredding up small plants. Because I didn't make any noise, Zane and Marigold couldn't scold me for anything more than not paying attention, though Zane was getting visibly annoyed with me for slowly peeling the bark off of a small branch.

"Why did we even let you come if all you were going to do was play around and not take this seriously?" He was quiet, but the anger was still there.

"I didn't think it would be this boring." I was a little louder than he was. "There's nothing even close."

Marigold put her finger to her lips. "Shh, quiet."

"Trust me, there isn't anything close." I rolled my eyes. "There hasn't even been anything close enough for me to hear except for a few birds chirping over in that direction." I pointed towards them.

"How long have you heard the chirping?" Zane sounded even more annoyed.

"A little while. Why?" I turned to him, confused. "I thought we were hunting for something worth our time."

"Birds can be worth our time," Zane snapped back. As soon as he said that, I heard a twig snap in a different direction. Just as he was about to stand up, I put my hand out to stop him. He looked like he was about to explode. I put my finger to my lips and pointed behind me, in the opposite direction of the birds. *Please tell me he can understand that there's something behind us. I just don't know how far away it is.*

Marigold crept up to the bush behind me and slowly peered above it. She lowered herself and whispered, "Giant toad."

Zane's eyes grew wide, and I could have sworn that his pupils turned into coins.

Giant toad? I've got to see this.

I poked my head over the bush. A large, bright-green frog with an uncountable number of small black spots on its back was hopping slowly through the forest. I estimated it was at least thirty arcs away from us, which was nothing more than an educated guess. Arcs were a measurement I struggled to get a feel for. Each arc was one hundred and fifty inches. Their distance was based on something involving magic, but I could never remember what. One or two arcs I could guess with some certainty, but anything more than that was tough. *Aren't frogs and toads cold-blooded?*

As I watched the amphibian continue its path through the trees, I couldn't take my eyes off it. *I know this feeling; my instincts are pushing me to hunt this toad.* The sensation was so strong, I couldn't stop myself from following them even though I didn't want to.

I didn't inform Zane or Marigold of what I was intending. The soon-to-be frog-leg dinner was hopping away from us.

What are toads' strongest senses? Taste? Smell? I should have watched more nature documentaries. Then again, I would never have guessed that I would die and have a second life in a fantasy world where I would be stalking a giant toad through a forest, ready to kill it with my claws. There are some things you just can't plan for.

I left the cover of the bushes, much to the dismay of the two humans behind me. The toad's movements were slow, yet methodical and purposeful. I circled around to the back of the creature and confirmed that the wind was blowing perpendicular to us.

The toad gave no sign that it knew that I was stalking it. My instincts kept pushing me to rush at it, but I held back, picking my steps quietly and gradually. I could hear both Zane and Marigold trying to keep up, but I moved much more freely. My small footprint and naturally soft step made it too easy to stalk my target. I gained ground slowly but steadily. Once I got close enough, I readied myself to pounce on my prey.

Carefully, I lowered myself into a crouching position and then into a four-point stance. Just before I was about to take off and charge the oblivious toad, I heard a crack that sounded like a branch breaking.

You can't be serious! Who did that?

Without breaking my stance, I turned to look at the person who'd broken the silence with a poorly placed step. My gaze landed on Zane.

He was still looking at the offending stick. He looked at me, and I mouthed, "Really?" at him. The sound, unfortunately, caught the attention of a certain toad. I heard two thumps and then returned my attention to my prey.

I stared at the giant toad, and it stared at me.

3

A WILD RIDE WITH MR. TOAD

I have to commit now. I took off towards the giant toad. With each step I took, my vision gradually turned red. Even with my element of surprise nullified, I had to try. Its eyes, an unblinking pool of darkness in a sea of red, followed my movements. Its mouth slowly opened as I closed in on it. *Are those teeth?* I was still some distance away when something shot out of its mouth. I dove to the side as a long, pink spear struck where I'd been only a moment before. *Is that its tongue? Why does it have a point at the end?*

Almost as quickly as it shot out, the tongue retracted. *Why does a toad need a spear for its tongue? Aren't they just long and sticky? Don't tell me toads eat meat too!* I scrambled to my feet. *This thing's movements are slow, so if I can get behind it, I should be fine.*

I stood up and started running around it, trying to use the trees as cover. I had almost made it behind another tree when a shower of splinters flew into my face.

The tongue had speared through the trunk.

This thing just punctured a tree twice as thick as me with its tongue, and it came out the other side. The tongue didn't retract immediately; it struggled for a few seconds before it returned to its owner. I turned to watch the toad more carefully. *I was lucky. Lesson learned: never take my eyes off of it.* Then two arrows buried themselves in the toad's face.

"What are you doing? Stay away from it!" Marigold shouted as she nocked another arrow.

"Just keep it busy while I get behind it." I turned back to the now-distracted amphibian.

"What do you think you're doing, girl?" Zane loosed his arrow. "Listen to her. Don't get close to it."

I just can't do that. I don't know why, but I need to kill this thing. The toad turned its attention to the two humans, and Zane's arrow embedded itself just under the creature's jaw. *Okay, now's my chance.* I dashed around to its backside.

The toad tried to skewer Zane with its tongue, but he fell to the ground before it reached him. *How long can this thing stretch its tongue? That was even further than before.*

Instinctually, I let out a low growl before I jumped on its back. It must have heard me because its body vibrated and started inflating. I sprang off the ground and landed on the center of the giant toad's back. I dug all of my claws into its wrinkly and slimy skin. *Gross. I'm going to need a bath when I get home.*

The toad didn't find my impromptu mounting an enjoyable experience. Its body kept inflating as it ran forward, straight towards Marigold and Zane. Zane stood up and looked shocked when he saw me. Marigold's face was bright red as she ran up to Zane and pulled him along with her out of the path of the runaway toad.

"Get off that thing right now! It's dangerous!" Marigold's screech grated on my ears.

I don't see how it's dangerous. It can't get me with its tongue. I released my right claw and held on tighter with my remaining claws. *Let's see if I can find your heart, Mister Toad.* I dug into the beast's back with my claws, tearing flesh, fat, and muscle. The toad never stopped inflating.

After several swipes with my claw, it felt like I had popped something. Suddenly, the wound I created expelled a dark-brown gas. *Is this what she was worried would happen? This gas is probably poisonous.* My eyes went wide before I slammed them shut. I held my breath as I grabbed the back of the toad again.

I slowly exhaled out through my nose, trying to make sure that nothing would sneak its way in and buy myself more time before my lungs begged for fresh air. My body rocked with the toad's rough movements.

There was almost no air left in my lungs when I cracked an eye open. Whatever sac produced the gas had stopped expelling the fumes. Now that the coast was clear, I opened both of my eyes and took a deep breath.

The toad was well past where Zane and Marigold were. They had put at least two arcs between them and the amphibian's path. I looked down at the toad and saw that its body was out of balance. One half was heavily bloated, possibly filled with more of that brown gas from earlier, while the other half was bleeding steadily and back to its original size.

I returned to digging for the toad's heart. I released my grip on its back and plunged my claws as deep as I could. It felt like I had stuck my hand into a pocket. I rummaged around in what I thought was its lung; my claws probably shredded everything in there, and the toad's movements noticeably slowed down.

The toad came to a stop. Its body shuddered, and the inflated half of its body deflated. As it did, more of the noxious fumes billowed out of its back. *Is that darker than before?* There was an uneasiness in my gut as I watched its pores open up enough to eject the gas. *I think it's time to get off this ride now.*

While holding my breath, I extracted my blood-covered hand and prepared to jump. The gas enveloped me before I could run. Panicking, I slammed my eyes shut and fell forward. I rolled off the creature and continued rolling, keeping my eyes shut. When my side hit something solid, I cautiously opened one eye, just like before. I didn't see any gas but noticed that a tree had stopped me. I got up on my hands and feet and looked for the toad.

It looked like I'd rolled an arc and a half away. However, the sight before me filled me with terror. The dark-brown cloud of gas was now almost black, and it didn't dissipate like one would expect gas should.

It must have been denser than the air because it didn't rise. Instead, it flowed like heavy syrup in every direction.

I scrambled away without standing up. Even in my retreat, I never looked away from the potentially deadly cloud, expecting the toad to jump out at any moment. I couldn't see it, and there wasn't any sound from it either.

I stood upright as I ducked behind a tree, remembering not to stay too close in case its tongue struck the trunk. The cloud had slowed its progress as it expanded, and I felt I had put sufficient distance between us. There was a nagging feeling in the back of my mind, but I dismissed it. *The toad won't surprise me again.*

Then I felt two arms grab my shoulders and try to pull me away. *No, my prey. Wait, is someone trying to kidnap me again? That's even worse!*

I growled as I pulled the arms off and pushed my limbs out. I easily overpowered my would-be kidnapper. Once I had leverage, I slipped down under their arms as soon as I was able. I then spun around and shoved the woman into the tree with one hand. *Woman?*

I looked at who I'd just attacked. The realization of the situation snapped my vision back to normal. Marigold fell to the ground with a mix of shock, horror, and pain on her face. *Why? Why did I just do that?* Tears filled my eyes as I backed away slowly.

Zane kneeled next to her. He put his head next to hers before he grabbed her waist.

"I'm sorry," I whispered.

Zane looked at the cloud and then back at me. "Then get over here and help me carry her away. We need to get further away!"

Guilt paralyzed me. I could only stare at Marigold as she struggled to gasp for air. "I'm so sorry."

"Later! Right now, we have to move." Zane kept shouting and pulling Marigold away from the still-expanding cloud.

I walked up to help him, sobbing. "I didn't mean to, I just..."

"Shut up! Now isn't the time." Spit flew from his mouth.

He's right; we need to go. The guilt didn't wane as I picked Marigold up by myself and moved her without Zane's help.

Marigold gasped for air. *Did I break her ribs? What if she doesn't make it? Will I be a murderer now?* Slowly, each breath she took pulled in more air than the last. I looked back and saw that there was plenty of distance between us and the toad. The thinning cloud of gas revealed that the toad wasn't moving anymore but lying on its side. *It has to be dead.* A feeling of joy tried to join my emotions, but sorrow and guilt shoved it out.

I stopped and carefully placed Marigold on the ground. Zane caught up to me with his limp and inspected Marigold carefully. She started coughing as she sat up. *She's alright.* My guilt lessened as I saw her condition improve.

"I'm sorry."

"What were you thinking?" Zane looked like he was ready to explode. "You could have killed her. She was just trying to get you away from the poison cloud."

"She came up behind me and I didn't think. I reacted because I thought someone was trying to kidnap me again." I sat down next to a tree.

"That's right, you didn't think." He stormed up to me. His face was bright pink and turning red with each word. "Who out here would kidnap you? And why did you jump on the toad in the first place? We told you to stay away. You didn't follow our orders, which you agreed to when you became our apprentice."

"I couldn't help it." Unable to face him, I stared at the ground. "I had to hunt and kill it."

"You can never help it, can you?" Zane dropped his volume, but I could feel all the judgment. "Once we return, we are through with you. Find someone else to work for. I never want to see your face again."

"Stop." Marigold's hoarse voice cracked. She was still collecting herself as I looked up. "I'm not that hurt. I'm partly to blame." She shifted her position so she could look at us. "I shouldn't have grabbed Lucia when she didn't react to me calling her name." She pointed a finger at Zane. "You're overreacting. I just had my breath pushed out of me. And I might have a bruise in the morning too, but nothing serious."

She's going to be okay.

"I didn't mean it, really. I panicked."

She held up a hand for me to stop. "I know. I heard you earlier." She closed her eyes and leaned back slightly. "But Zane is right. You disobeyed us. We told you to get back, and you did exactly the opposite. You jumped on the thing." Her voice was stern even though there was still a slight rasp to it. She opened her eyes and stared at me. "Yes, you brought it down, but you put yourself in a dangerous situation. Once we collect what's salvageable from the toad, we're going home. This will be your last and only time hunting with us." She had a look of regret on her face.

"Why?" The word was all I could get out as more tears streamed down my face.

"You don't have the patience for hunting," Marigold answered. "And your reckless behavior will get you hurt, or worse, and I don't want to have to ever explain to Nora why you didn't come home. I couldn't live with that on my conscience. There are far more dangerous animals out there than a giant toad. So until you can control yourself, I suggest you don't go hunting again."

My only response was to hug my legs to my chest and bury my face in my knees.

We rested while waiting for the poison cloud to clear completely. The tension coming from Zane was palpable as we cut the legs off the toad. According to Marigold, the gas fouled the rest of the meat.

Why do I keep messing everything up? Stupid instincts!

4

IT'S A WOLF-EAT-WOLF WORLD

I felt terrible about my blunder and ruining so much meat. As we walked back to town, I grew hungrier. It was getting close to lunchtime.

I frankly need a bath. Toad blood soaked the fur on my right arm up to the middle of my bicep. More blood splattered across my clothes, and with a light coating of dirt on everything, I cringed at how filthy I was.

But despite my lack of cleanliness, I felt relaxed. *I don't know why, but I no longer feel the nagging need to do something. Is it because of how I felt when I saw the toad dead, or is it the result of my impulsive actions?*

I didn't let myself carry the toad legs because I wanted to try them. *I have to show them I have some self-control.* The trappers carried the meat in large burlap sacks once they had made sure as much of the blood had been removed as possible. I moped behind them, trying to keep upwind of the meat and thinking of as many ways to redeem myself as I could.

I truly want to go hunting, but I don't know if it's a good idea for me to go by myself, especially if everything is as dangerous as or more dangerous than that toad.

Several unfamiliar scents disturbed my inner mental debate. *It smells like me. Not the toad-gore-covered me. It's more like when I've been running most of the day between each of the gates. Is that also a hint of blood too?* I turned around and saw something far behind us. A black wolf was staring at us. Every warning bell went off in my head.

"Um, guys, we have a problem," I said while never stopping or turning away from the wolf. "Wolf."

"What?" Marigold turned around just in time for me to walk into her.

"Why today, of all days?" Zane asked under his breath before he shouted, "Climb, quickly!"

I couldn't move as I watched the wolf slowly stalk towards us. Marigold must have noticed my inaction. She grabbed my shoulder and then pushed me towards Zane. "Help him. He can't climb well with his leg."

I climbed the tree. When I climbed a little higher than Zane had, I reached down and, grabbing his small backpack, heaved him up above me. He shouted something incoherent as he latched on to the tree.

I turned to look at the wolf to see how much time we had. It was running now, and it was getting bigger as it neared. Panic set in again. *That thing is huge! Uh, don't wolves hunt in packs? Where are the rest of them? Is climbing this tree going to be enough?*

Zane shouted something at me. Although I wasn't paying attention and didn't catch what he said, the pain in my ears snapped me back to reality. I returned to climbing and did the same thing as I did before—hoisted Zane higher to safety.

As I did, I could hear the wolf below me growling. I looked down and saw blood and drool around its mouth. It stared at me with its yellow, bloodshot eyes before it jumped.

I pushed off the tree to get away from its maw of teeth that looked like much larger versions of mine.

As I fell, I watched as the wolf snapped its jaws where I had been only a moment before. I contorted my body so that I would land on my feet. I hit the ground harder than I'd expected and tumbled onto my back, scrambling to my feet, not wanting to give the huge predator an opening.

The wolf was easily larger than a horse, with knotted and matted black fur. There were some scabs from wounds that had yet to finish healing. Vicious claws on both its front and hind legs dug effortlessly into the ground.

The wolf jumped again, attempting to get Zane, but it failed to reach him.

"Go. Run!" Marigold pointed in the direction we were going while hanging from her tree.

The wolf turned to Marigold after she shouted and walked over to her tree, seeming to forget I was even here. I looked at Marigold and saw she wasn't high enough. It could reach her if it jumped.

I ran up to the wolf before it could leap, grabbed its tail, and pulled with all my might. I dug my toe claws into the ground to give me as much traction as I could. When I heard a pop, the wolf yelped in pain, and I let go. *I think I just dislocated its tail. That sounded unbearably painful. No wonder I get agitated when people touch my tail.*

The wolf turned away from Marigold and towards me. It snarled and bared its teeth at me. *Time to go.*

"You idiot, run!" Zane shouted from his tree.

Not waiting for the wolf to make the first move, I bolted. I heard it take off after me. Every time it would get too close, I wove around a tree. It was faster in a straight line, but with its tail dislocated, I had better steering.

I hope this is the direction of the town. Otherwise I don't know how long I can keep running. Hearing the wolf's growls and barks behind me, I wouldn't let myself slow down.

I continued my tactic of weaving between trees every time I heard the wolf behind me surge forward, trying to catch me. *I'm glad this thing's animal mind hasn't figured it out yet.*

Unfortunately, the forest started thinning out. The distance between each tree grew, and each lifeline was farther than the last.

The wolf's breath was hot on my tail as he snapped at me one more time. I dove to the side, placing one of my last trees between it and me. I panted hard, and I could feel the fatigue in my legs. *How much farther until I make it to town? I can't outrun him like this. If it's chased me for this long, I doubt it's going to give up and walk away now. I can't take it on myself. Zane and Marigold are who knows how far back. I need the guards in town to save me.*

The wolf wouldn't let me think about a plan of action for long. I forced it to play "Ring Around the Rosie" with me to buy time to think and recover for a few moments. Time was a luxury that the wolf would not permit me to have.

The entire time, it kept snapping at me with jaws the size of my arms. Drool foamed around its gums as it tried to push past the tree to reach me. *Is that rabies? Wait, can I get rabies?* The wolf snapped again for me. *Now is not the time, Lucia.* I looked out to the field past the wolf.

I only have one last chance, and I really wish it hadn't come to this. Hopefully it will be enough. But if I do nothing, I'm dead. I dodged my way to the edge of the tree line and looked for Aquittemia. *This was not the area we entered through. This isn't familiar.* I eventually recognized a farmhouse we had seen in the distance on the way to the hunting grounds. It was much closer now, and I was on the other side of it. *I can't bring this thing to any innocent people, but I have to get away from it.*

Knowing I couldn't take forever to decide, I hoped the people weren't outside right now and took off towards the farmhouse. *When I see Aquittemia, I can correct my course.* I dropped to my hands and used them to run in conjunction with my legs. My arms were slightly longer for my body size when compared to a human, only by a couple of inches. When combined with the shape of my legs, it was enough that I could run on all fours.

There was only one problem: my mind struggled to move like that. It took my complete attention just to move my limbs in the correct order so I didn't trip on myself. I couldn't change direction well, but I was faster. In the open plains, with a colossal, rabid wolf trailing me, I needed speed more than mobility.

I could hear the wolf chasing me, but with all my concentration devoted to running, I couldn't tell if it was catching up or if I was finally faster. *It doesn't matter anyway. If I have the energy to gauge distances based on my hearing, I have the energy to run faster.*

29

When I ran past the farmhouse, I didn't see anyone outside, and I didn't hear any screaming. I kept running until I saw Aquittemia, and hope blossomed in my heart. *Or is that cardiac arrest?* My heart was beating as fast as it would physically allow. Every limb burned with pain and protested each command I gave it. My lungs were failing to keep up with the oxygen demand. But I pushed myself to keep going. *I'm not going to die now, not with safety so close.*

"Close" was a relative term. The wolf hadn't caught me yet, but I could still hear it behind me. I didn't dare look back. The closer I got to the city's stone walls, the more motivation I found to keep going. I saw the gate and adjusted slightly so I headed right for it. *That's the east gate, I think.* I could see that there were people lined up at the gate waiting to get in. *And I'm about to lead a giant wolf to an all-you-can-eat buffet. Please see the giant wolf chasing me, and let the people in and save me!*

I heard screams and horns as I neared the gate. Guards filed out while people were herded past the gate at an expedited rate. People left their wagons or carts and any animals attached to them. Thankfully, there weren't many. Several guards were lining up to intercept me, all armed with long spears. Others were doing their best to keep the pandemonium to a minimum.

My body protested more, and I could feel my arms and legs tearing. I was running on empty, and I had already spent the fumes.

Just one more step. I told myself that every time I took a step. *Just one more step. Just one more step. Just one more step.* Each step was harder than the last.

Just one more step. The soldiers that approached me were more heavily armored than regular guards.

Just one more step. The armored soldiers were getting closer to me. *Just one more step.* They leveled their weapons as they made a gap directly in my path.

Just one more step. Just one more... I reached for my saviors. My arms and legs exploded with pain as I collapsed. Agony flooded my brain as my face collided with the ground, and I performed my best tumbleweed impression. Everything spun as darkness threatened to swallow my vision and block my consciousness.

Just one...

I willed my limbs to move, but they wouldn't. Nothing responded to my command.

Just...

Darkness swallowed me up.

5

BEDSIDE MANNER

I snapped awake. I turned my head to examine my situation. *This is new. Almost every other time I've woken up after being unconscious, someone had tied me up. I'm okay if that never happens again.* It was my bedroom, and it looked like someone had cleaned everything and sorted my clothes away. *I guess this is the best place to wake up after passing out. Wait, what happened?* I tried to get up, but every muscle in my body erupted with pain, causing me to scream.

What happened to me? Why does moving hurt so much?

I heard someone running down the hall before they burst through my door. Molly came through, and she looked at me. "You're awake!"

She'd matured with the years, though she never grew tall. *I'm taller than she is, and I'm ten.* But her curves made sure you knew she was almost a grown woman. Her straight black hair touched her shoulders. She wore a simple, thick dress of her favorite color: white.

Molly walked to my bedside and put her hand on my forehead. Then she tapped the tip of my nose with a finger. I tried to flinch away, but I barely managed not to scream in pain.

"It looks like your fever has gone down." Her voice was her secret weapon. If her body could get a man's attention, her voice would ensnare him. It was so smooth, and it always sounded like she was having a good day. Even I had to admit that her singing was sublime.

"I had a fever?" I asked.

"You're lucky to be alive." Nora sounded a bit more upset than usual as she walked in. "I swear you're going to take more years off my life than any other child."

"I think I'm taking enough years off my own life." I turned my head to look at the ceiling.

"Don't." Her voice told me she was not amused. "But why were you screaming just now?"

"Everything hurts," I confessed. "I tried to get up, but it hurts to move. And now everything is throbbing with pain even while I'm not moving."

"That's because you tore most of the muscles in your arms and legs, you big dummy."

Zenny?

"What are you doing here, Zenny?" I didn't move, even though I wanted to.

"I'm here to check on a certain big dummy who can't control herself." Zenny's voice was full of life and cheerful now.

Her father had died in a logging accident, and her mother had died shortly after from some kind of sickness. Salien wouldn't give me the details. Even though Zenny's mother was treated, Zenny made it sound like she'd just given up on living. That left Zenny an orphan too. However, while Salien was treating her mother, they became the best of friends, and Salien adopted Zenny shortly afterward. The thing they bonded over the most was their infatuation with romantic tales. Nora said that it was one of the fastest adoptions she knew of. Salien had been raising Zenny as her daughter and was teaching her to be a doctor, just like her.

It'd been good for her. Watching the two interact always left me feeling a bit jealous. Salien devoted everything to Zenny, and every season she seemed just that much happier. Ever since her family died, Zenny had slowly traded in her depressing attitude for a lively and determined personality. Last year she gave me a nickname, something I never would have guessed she was capable of.

It's almost like a fairy tale with how quickly her life changed and improved. I guess as long as everyone is happy. Except for Zenny's father, who was a jerk. He can stay dead.

I sighed. *I'm in good hands.* "That would explain the pain. But what was that you said about a fever?"

Zenny had made her way to replace Molly and placed her hand on my forehead. "You had one. Mom said it was because you pushed yourself as hard as you did. How long did you run from the wolf? Does anything else hurt? How does your stomach feel? Is there any numbness in your toes?"

Why is she fussing over me so much?

"No, but I don't know how long that wolf chased me for. By the way, what happened to it? The last thing I remember is that I was still running from it and I hadn't reached the town gate yet." I looked into Zenny's calm blue eyes. Even with her barrage of questions, her face was still serene.

"That was two days ago," Nora interrupted. "The knights from Brian's Bedlam brought you here after they killed the wolf. I heard Zane and Marigold's side of the story. Now it's your turn."

"Well, what did they tell you?" I asked as I stared at the ceiling.

"Why don't you start at the beginning and tell us the whole story? I imagine yours will differ from theirs in some places." Nora's sweet voice told me I was not getting out of it.

"If you know the answer, then why bother asking?"

"Because I want to hear you say it." Nora sounded angry.

I tried.

I sighed as I began at the very beginning. Molly left because she had work to do. Nora and Zenny collected chairs and sat down to listen to my recounting of yesterday's events, or rather the events from two days ago. *It's not like I can do anything else.* I told them where we went and how boring it was while we waited for something to show up. I gave a brief version of the fight with the toad. That caused Nora to interrupt me, and she demanded all the details. With a groan, I didn't purposely omit anything else. I told them about the wolf and how it chased me.

After I finished my story, I had one question on my mind. "So, was that a dire wolf?"

Nora shook her head. "No, if it'd had large bone growths on its back and around its neck, that would have been a dire animal. Also, dire animals are far more intelligent." *So if it was, it would've killed and eaten me. Oversized intelligent animals... I'm thinking I should reconsider this hunting thing. I'm a lot further down the food chain than I thought.*

"Then was that a normal size for a wolf? Also, don't wolves hunt in packs?" *It might be time to start taking this education thing seriously. I don't know enough about this world.*

"Oh, so now you want to learn?" Nora asked in a mocking, surprised tone. "You think you know everything, and then you have one run-in with a wolf, and you decide maybe you should've taken the time to learn."

"Yes, Mom, you were right," I said sarcastically. "Happy now? But you know, you could try to make learning a little more fun."

"So it's my fault now?" Nora asked incredulously. "What's in those books is important. I told you that, and yet you refused to read them. You kept running around town or went out with Zane and Marigold to check on traps." She raised her voice, but not to the level that would hurt me.

"You know I have a problem sitting still!" I matched her tone.

"Stop it!" Zenny shouted louder than us. "Stop it." She lowered her volume once she got our attention. "Lucia, please stop arguing with your mom. She's only trying to help."

"You're taking her side?" I felt a little betrayed. *I thought we were best friends.* "She started it."

"But you're in the wrong this time." I could hear Zenny's voice start to waiver. "You told me anyone could be wrong. It didn't matter their age or station. She's trying to help you. Why do you need reading to be fun?"

I felt the need to bury myself in a hole. "I can't sit still. If I don't move around, I get anxious and my mind wanders. I can't focus on a book for more than a page or two." *I'm lashing out, and I know I shouldn't.* With a heavy sigh, I continued. "I have so much energy I can't deal with it. I constantly feel like a dam about to burst. Nothing I do works. If you want me to learn, it'll require me to move at the same time. Maybe make a game of it."

"You already take more of my attention than any of the other kids." Nora sounded tired. "Keeping up with you takes a lot out of me."

"Please don't just tell me to go to the classroom and read." I could feel my jaw tightening. "Please, teach me. Don't pawn it off on someone else."

Nora leaned forward and knelt next to my bed. "I need to take care of April now that she's sick. The others require my time as well." She sounded like she didn't want to say those words.

April was our newest addition. She'd joined us at the start of this last ice season. At seven years old, she was the quietest girl I'd ever met. It took her an entire season before she said a single word to me. Most of the time, she would run off. Her bright-red hair, her most note-worthy feature, didn't match her shy demeanor, but she cared for it almost as much as I cared for all of my fur. *I think I scare her more than anything else.* She hadn't told us why she was here, and Nora had been extra tight-lipped about it too. However, Nora told us that her aptitude was knives.

Zenny chimed in. "I'll do it."

The words I was about to say died on my tongue. Nora didn't say anything either.

"What?" My word ended the silence.

"I'll teach you," Zenny reiterated. "Nora, you give me the books you want her to learn, and I'll do my best to make it fun for her." Her voice chirped like she'd been planning this.

"Are you serious about this?" Nora asked, not attempting to hide her doubt.

I said, "Yeah, I know you're smart—smarter than someone your age should be—but are you sure you should be the one teaching me?"

"If it will keep you two from fighting, then yes." Her determina-tion was almost palpable. "Also, it feels like Lucia has been avoiding me lately. This way I get to spend more time with her."

It isn't because I don't want to spend time with you. I've just been literally running around town while you want to talk about the latest book you're reading. I kept those thoughts to myself.

"Also, I could learn something new. Like that one saying you used —it'll be like killing two birds with one stone." Zenny gave me a wide smile.

"I have to question the judgment of letting a twelve-year-old be in charge of a ten-year-old's education." Nora didn't sound impressed, and she let out a heavy sigh. "Nothing else has worked with you yet, so why not?"

Is she really going to let this happen?

"I haven't been that much of a problem child, have I?" I asked, more for myself than anything else.

"You have been, by far, the most difficult one I've had," Nora said without hesitation.

"I'm also the only beastkin you've had," I remarked with extra sass. My mind wandered to Zenny, and another thought bubbled out of my mouth. "I can't help but think I've been a bad influence on Zenny."

Nora broke into an instant laugh. "You know what? I think I feel a little better about Zenny being your teacher now." She continued laughing as she spoke. "Maybe she'll get through to you when nobody else will."

"I don't get it." Zenny's voice was full of confusion.

"Don't worry about it," I said sullenly. *I really need to put a filter on my mouth.*

"I'm sure Lucia will fill you in." I heard Nora pat Zenny somewhere on her body as she said that. "But back to the serious matter: what did Salien say about Lucia's recovery?"

"A week of bed rest and she should be able to stand, given her recovery rate." Zenny's voice lost all emotion.

A week? Not again. I groaned at the news.

"Oh, no," Nora quickly snapped at me. "You're to stay in that bed until Salien says so."

"But a week?" I whined.

"Yes." Nora stomped her foot.

"Once she can stand, she'll need to keep her movements heavily restricted. Mom says that at that stage, her muscles will still easily tear again. But she needs to move around slightly, otherwise she won't heal properly," Zenny continued, despite my protests against the prescribed treatment. "She'll be spending a lot of time over the next couple of weeks in that bed until she no longer feels pain while fully extending her limbs."

"Could you bring your mom with you when you come in two days?" Nora asked with honey-laced words.

"Of course, but she said that she wanted to stop by tomorrow to make sure the tonic was working for April." Zenny sounded confused.

"Tomorrow sounds fine. She'll be happy to know that April is doing better. She's breathing easier." Nora walked to the door.

"So, did you really outrun a wolf?" Zenny questioned me once Nora reached the door. "How? I know you're fast, but I don't believe you're that fast."

I blushed. "I can't outrun it on two legs."

I heard Nora's footsteps halt with a harder step than usual. "Care to repeat that?" I could feel Nora's gaze on me.

I guess the cat's out of the bag now. Nora isn't about to let this drop any time soon. "I kinda sort of ran on all fours to get away from the wolf." I wished the bed would swallow me whole.

"You never told me you could do that," Nora said. "But that would explain your arms."

"You never asked." My snarky reply got me nowhere. "I'm not very good at it. You've no idea how hard it is to coordinate moving like that. It's embarrassing, okay? So please keep it to yourself," I pleaded.

"As you wish," Nora replied just before continuing on her way.

"I won't tell a soul," Zenny said with way too much enthusiasm for my liking. "Since you're to stay in bed, and Mom said I could spend the day making sure you were doing well..." Her voice trailed off. It sounded like she was thinking. With a clap of her hands, she enlightened me with her epiphany. "I could read you my new favorite books."

It's going to be a long week. Unwilling to suffer physical pain, I prepared myself for the emotional onslaught I was about to receive.

6

THREE DAYS LATER

"Please tell me I can leave this bed," I begged Salien as she stood over me.

Last night I could move, but any physical exertion was painful. Nora threatened to strap me to my bed so I wouldn't get up. It was the only time I'd seen her yesterday. And I'd only seen her three times the two days before. She wasn't even delivering food to me. Melody was the one doing it. She was always walking past my door, never through it. *Zenny's been spending more time here. Her visits have helped with the emptiness I feel while I've been trapped in my bed.*

"The sun isn't up yet. How can you have so much energy this early?" Salien asked curtly. *I forgot, Salien's not a morning person.* "Besides, if you didn't have a history of ignoring my recommendations, I suspect Nora might have been more forgiving."

"Do you have any idea what it's like to sit here for three days listening to nothing but romantic stories from Zenny?" I gave the woman my most innocent look.

Zenny walked into the room. "What will it take for you to like my favorite stories?"

I facepalmed. *Of course you heard that.*

Zenny sounded heartbroken. "What's wrong with them? Isn't it wonderful that the girl gets the man of her dreams and he loves her back, then they live happily ever after?"

"Sure, they would be wonderful if they weren't so *boring*!" I groaned. *How many times do I have to tell her?* "Can we please stop talking about this? You can't convince me that your romantic novels are fun. You can like them all you want, but as for me, I want to do something, anything." I'd been itching to at least walk around all night while I couldn't sleep.

Salien continued to concentrate on checking all the muscles in my legs. I felt a small tingle of warmth from her fingertips. She was holding my left leg, the last limb she needed to inspect, meticulously going over every inch. There were moments when she would pull apart my fur, attempting to look at my skin. *Good luck with that. There's just more fur. I'd know because I've tried.*

I looked at Zenny's hands and saw her holding another book, one of the thickest I'd seen yet. It was bound in leather and had no labeling on the cover or spine, though it looked like it'd seen better days.

I haven't seen that book before. Please tell me it isn't another collection of romance stories.

"Zenny, you could have stayed in bed," I said to the girl, who barely kept her eyes open. "You know that, right?"

"I'm trying to help myself understand what you're going through by being awake whenever you are," Zenny said, only to stifle a yawn afterwards.

"You don't need to do that," Salien and I responded at the same time. I flopped backwards onto my bed.

Salien finished up her inspection, then stood up straight. Before I could jump out of the bed, she placed her hand on my forehead. I looked up at it, unable to understand the gesture.

"You know that I'm more than strong enough to move your hand, right?" I asked with a slight rumble in my voice. *She hasn't touched my ears, so she can have a warning first.*

"Go ahead and try." Salien's voice was annoyingly optimistic.

Doctor's orders. I grabbed her wrist and attempted to pull it away from my head. Pain shot through my arm; it felt like my muscles were about to pull apart again. I growled at Salien to hide the pain. She frowned slightly. I then used just the muscles in my fingers and squeezed hard. I felt some pain in my forearm, but it was manageable. However, Salien's face contorted with pain.

"Ow, ow, ow." She pulled her hand away from my head. I released it and sat up as she clutched her wrist.

Zenny dropped the book, and it landed on the ground with a hefty thud. After rushing to Salien's side, Zenny gave me a sad look. "Why did you do that?" She sounded more hurt than Salien.

"Because she told me to," I answered flatly. As I sat up, I felt some stiffness, but I didn't have any trouble moving.

"She said to move her hand, not break her arm," Zenny accused me.

"Relax, nothing's broken." I reined in my anger. "She didn't say *how* I had to move her hand."

Salien released her wrist and put a hand on Zenny's shoulder. "She's right. See, nothing's broken." She held up her arm for Zenny to examine.

Zenny took it carefully and felt around the area I'd grabbed.

"You're antsy and want to start moving around now, don't you?" She had a forced smile on her face.

"But?" *I can tell when you're about to give me bad news. Your lips curl more just before you talk.*

"On a scale of one to ten, how painful was it to move my arm on the first attempt?" Her face was now serious.

She knows? "Four," I lied. *I don't care about the pain anymore. I need to move, or I will go insane in this bed.*

Salien looked at me with disapproval.

Zenny blurted out, "She lied. It hurt her more than that."

How did she know? I looked at her and growled.

"You're going to stay in that bed for another day." Salien said that in the same manner that someone would sentence a prisoner to their execution.

My heart broke when she gave me her verdict. Slowly, my sadness turned to rage. *I'll show her that I can move around just fine.* Growling, I grabbed the edge of the bed. My ears were flat and pulled back as

41

I prepared to dash for the door. Before I could get up from the bed, Zenny tackled me. I grabbed Zenny's shoulders and froze.

"Don't do it," Zenny begged into my chest as she clutched me with everything she could muster. "Please don't do it."

"Why?" That was all I could get out as I stared at her face.

Her voice broke as she released her tears. "Because I don't want you to hurt yourself, you big dummy." *Alright, that nickname has gotten old.* "Why don't you listen to Mom and take care of yourself? All she's trying to do is make you feel better. She's just trying to help."

I guess I was about to do something stupid again, wasn't I? "I don't know." I flung my head back and stared at the ceiling. "Nobody seems to understand. I can't sit still. Do you think I run around so much and do anything to spend my energy because I enjoy it?"

"But you're always smiling. Aren't you having fun?" Salien asked with obvious skepticism.

"Okay, it is fun, but I originally started doing it because if I don't spend the energy welling up inside me, I'm afraid of what I'll do." I was getting anxious. "I'm getting really strong, and I'm afraid that if I lose control, someone will get hurt."

"But I've seen you. You don't want to hurt anyone. I don't believe you'll hurt anyone." Zenny slowed her crying.

"That's the thing. It feels like there's another part of me that loves to hurt things. I don't want to let it out." *It sounds like I have a split personality.*

"Have you ever felt like that?" Salien asked in her most serious tone.

I tilted my head towards her since Zenny was still holding me down to the bed and it would be too painful to move her. I expressed my confusion with an audible hum.

"Have you ever felt like a passenger in your own body? Have you heard another voice in your head, and you don't know where it came from?"

I lowered my head back down and thought about it. "No, I haven't. Why?"

"Since you had such a close run-in with a demon, it isn't impossible. But there may be some residual effects. Nora killed it, so as far as I understand, it can't do anything to you. Also based on your answers, it sounds like you're fine," Salien said with a smile. "That means that you've never truly lost control of yourself."

"Does that mean I'm this energetic because I want to be?" I asked with desperation in my voice.

"No, I imagine it has to do with the fact that you're a beastkin." Nora walked into the room. *Fantastic. Another person to cross-examine me.* "We just need to ask another beastkin when they come for the tournament." Her voice was terrifyingly optimistic.

"It hasn't been that bad these last three days, but I can feel the need to do something returning. And it's returning in full force. But what is this about a tournament?" I perked up at the possibility of meeting my first other beastkin.

"You can worry about that tomorrow," Salien said sternly. "Are you going to keep her in that bed, dear?" she asked her daughter.

"I am," Zenny said as proudly as she could.

"Alright, I'll leave you to it." I could hear Salien walking away. "She needs one more day of strict bed rest. Is it alright if Zenny stays to enforce that?"

"Of course," Nora said sweetly. "Now would you like breakfast?" I could hear them walking down the hall together.

"Please," Salien said. "But seeing her this mobile after only three days is unheard of. A week was optimistic for my original prognosis. That girl is full of surprises."

"And headaches," Nora added.

Go ahead, gossip about me. I'm kinda glad that I'm healing as fast as I am. My sanity would be gone if I had to wait a whole week.

"Do you want to get off of me now?" I asked as I tapped Zenny's head.

She turned to look at me with the most innocent, pleading eyes. "Do you promise to behave?"

"Do I have to?" My voice didn't hide my displeasure.

"Yes!" Zenny's grip tightened with her response.

"Fine," I huffed. Zenny smiled as she released me. She sat up next to me on the bed. I gingerly sat up and played the good girl and didn't leave the bed. "How did you know I was lying?"

"A woman's intuition." Her grin was as wide as her face would allow.

"You are as much a woman as me." I pointed to her budding bosom. "We're both just starting to grow." She looked at my chest and deflated slightly.

"That's not fair. You're two years younger than me, and we started at the same time." She had a playful pout on her face. "That, and you'll finish before me too."

How does she know? Did Mom tell her? Anyway, something else is bothering me. "Zenny, why are you here?"

"Do I need a reason to see my best friend?" Zenny looked at me with concern. *She's been friendly with all the kids that were here when I first arrived and the new ones since then too.*

"Why am I your best friend?" *I don't understand our relationship.* "How are we even friends? There are so many others you could spend your time with. So why me?"

"I don't understand. Why are you asking these questions?" Zenny looked hurt. "We spend all kinds of time together."

"Mostly when I hurt myself." I glared at her. "You have all kinds of friends now. You make friends with anyone you meet. What's so special about me? Besides the obvious physical differences."

Zenny dropped her head in sadness. "When my mother died, you were the only one who let me cry on your shoulder. You helped me through it. You didn't say anything. You were always there for me when I needed you."

"I could tell you'd heard enough platitudes, and I'm genuinely sorry you had to go through that." I shrugged my shoulders. "But I can tell you two things. One is that you know who your parents were. Two, you are in a vastly better condition now than when you were living with your parents. Seriously, I had never seen you smile before you started living with Salien."

"I guess you're right," Zenny said after she gave it some thought. "What I don't understand is what brought this conversation on."

"I just don't know how we can be friends when we're so different. We don't share any interests, and the only thing I can do is mess everything up." *I still need to apologize to Marigold and Zane.*

"I see how lonely you are."

Say what again?

Noticing that she'd caught my attention and that her words demanded an explanation, Zenny continued. "You don't have anyone else to call a friend. Your siblings don't really treat you all that well. They aren't mean to you because they fear you more than anything." I was about to protest, but before any words came out, she held up her hand to stop me. "Eleanah and Martin both regarded you as a little sister. One they needed to protect out of some sense of obligation."

I hung my head in defeat, and my mind turned dark. *She's right. I don't have any friends.* I glared at her and scowled. "So are you telling me you're only my friend out of pity?" I raised my voice and injected a slight rumble into it. The horror on Zenny's face did nothing to soothe my rage. "I'm right, aren't I?"

Tears rolled down her face. "No, that isn't it." Her voice was breaking. "Why—" She tried to continue, but I interrupted her.

"Leave me alone." I swiped a clawed hand at her, but pulled it back before it reached her. *No! I won't hurt her. It isn't safe for her to be around me.* "I don't want to see you again." *This is for your own good.* I turned away from her and curled up into a fetal position.

Zenny stumbled off the bed and ran out of my room, bawling.

My rage never abated. I looked for the closest thing I could take it out on. Another pillow suffered the wrath of my claws. There was a slight pain in my arms, but I didn't care. I continued until nothing was recognizable. As the shreds of fabric lay spread haphazardly around my bed, I finally came to my senses. *What have I done?* I cried just like Zenny had when she left my room. *I did something stupid because I didn't think!*

7

NOW ZENNY KNOWS

As I lay crying in my bed, I heard three sets of footsteps enter my room. I turned to tell whoever had entered to leave me alone, but I stopped the moment I saw Zenny standing behind Nora and Salien.

"I'm sorry!" I shouted as Zenny entered the room.

Tears continued flowing down the girl's face. She took a few steps forward to stand at the forefront. It looked like she was struggling to come up with what she wanted to say.

"Please forgive me," I whispered.

She held her hands together in front of her chest and shuffled towards me. When I looked into her eyes, I watched them constantly avoid looking at me for more than a moment. I'd never gotten angry with her before, let alone attacked her, until today.

I knew I had betrayed her kindness. *If she doesn't forgive me, I deserve it.*

She stood in front of me and looked me in the eye. There was a strange hardness to her stare.

"That's what friends do," she said before giving me a gentle hug. I gratefully returned it.

Nora and Salien remained silent as they stood by the door, staring at us. They gave one another a knowing glance and walked out.

"I'm sorry," I said again, this time with a little more control. "I don't know what came over me. Why would I push away my closest friend?"

"I know what happened." Zenny was still on the verge of crying again. "You don't want to hurt anybody. You're afraid that if you let someone get close to you, you'll hurt them." She broke the hug to look at me again. "You think that if you stay away from everyone, you won't hurt anyone. But you're wrong. You do hurt someone." She paused.

I stared at her, confused.

She poked my nose gently with a finger. "You."

My mind broke for a moment as everything came to a halt. Finally, my consciousness reset itself and a single thought ran through my head first. *How did we switch roles?*

"Who are you, and what have you done with my friend Zenny?" I stared at her, completely dumbfounded.

She giggled. "I've been where you are. I know what you're thinking." She released me and sat on the edge of the bed with her legs crossed next to me. "You helped me realize that I have value and showed me that things change."

"But I don't understand what that has to do with me." My mind wasn't keeping up with her. *Where is she going with this?*

"Even though you think you've done so many things wrong, you've done some good things too." She grabbed my hands and leaned closer to me. "You helped with the demon by finding Nora. You helped us find out there was something wrong with April. Your ears could hear that she had fluid in her lungs." She was pleading with me with everything she had. "When my mother was sick, you introduced Salien to us. You saved Marigold's life the other day. You're capable of doing good, no matter how angry you get."

"My actions summoned the demon in the end." *Was it a mistake to tell Zenny all of my secrets except one?* "April's coughing sounded weird to me. When you placed your ear on her back and had her breathe deeply, you heard it too. Salien is the only doctor that I know.

I know she isn't the only one in town, but the only other one I knew is dead. Okay, maybe I saved Marigold's life, but I nearly lost mine."

Even with me trying to downplay all my accolades, I felt much better. *I really am thinking like her. Things have just been so hard for me recently that I've forgotten what's important.*

Zenny was about to protest, but I didn't give her the chance. "I see what you're trying to tell me, and I get it. Thank you. I've been so focused on everything I've done wrong that I forgot that there are other things I've done." I gave her a grateful hug. She returned the sentiment.

My eyes fell on the book she left on the floor near the door when she arrived for the first time. "By the way, what's that book for?" I ended the hug and pointed to the book on the floor.

"Oh, that." Zenny hopped off the bed and retrieved it. As she returned to her spot on my bed, she opened the book to a page she had earmarked. "Your mom gave it to me because she said you might be interested in some parts of it. Is she talking about the sections about beastkin?"

"So this is the book that holds information about me." I grabbed the book from Zenny's hands. "Or more about what I am." I looked at the top of the page the book was opened to.

I was so eager to learn about myself that I almost missed Nora walking in the door carrying two plates of food. *Eggs, ugh.* I saw the contents of the breakfast plate and didn't bother hiding my disapproval. She handed a plate to Zenny and a plate to me.

"Yes, that's the book I found that had the most information about beastkin. I'll give the others to Zenny so she can teach you, but this will get you started." She smiled at us. "I see you've calmed down and settled whatever that was earlier."

"Yeah, we're good." I smiled at Zenny. "I'm just acting like a hormonal teenager." A thought exploded into my mind. *I am a hormonal teenager!*

"A what?" both Zenny and Nora reacted to my proclamation.

"Um, nothing. Don't worry about it." I tried to shrink into the corner of my bed.

"Oh, no you don't." Zenny glared at me. "You know something, and you don't want to tell me. We're friends. You can tell me."

Nora looked back and forth between me and Zenny. "Really? It's Zenny."

"What do I get for spilling my secrets?" I crossed my arms and pouted. "It's not fair that I tell you my last darkest secret and get nothing in return."

"You've been keeping secrets from me?" Zenny nearly jumped to her feet.

"Just one, mostly because I don't think you would believe me even if I told you."

"Do you want to get out of this bed?" Zenny's eyes lit up with terrifying greed.

Maybe I shouldn't have mentioned anything. Me and my big mouth.

"No, Salien said you were to stay in that bed for another day. You're not going to get up." Nora interrupted our little haggling session with a stomp of her foot. "I'm being lenient and letting her sit up and move around. I know you're itching to move, but please listen to Salien," she pleaded at the end.

"If you don't tell me, I'll read to you a story about a desert princess falling in love with a homeless orphan thief." Zenny had a look of desperation creeping on her face.

"Let me guess, he finds a magic lamp that grants wishes, and they lived happily ever after?" *I've heard that story before. More proof that there were other reincarnated people. I wonder what else they're responsible for. Have some of them introduced advanced sciences? How many have there been, anyway?* "Also, there are two more stories that follow that one. They have a series of short stories about all the same characters."

"What? That's crazy talk. How can a lamp grant wishes?" Zenny's voice rose. "No, there's a whole bunch of political maneuvering with the advisor and assassination attempts. But the other stuff is correct. How did you know?"

So there were some changes to the story. Not like they needed to worry about copyright protection.

"Fine, I guess this is as good a time as any. Mom, could you help me explain this?" I looked at Nora and she nodded. "Alright, time to pull off the band-aid," I whispered to myself. "This isn't my first life."

"Huh?" Zenny gazed at me.

Does she think I'm lying? I rubbed the back of my head as I worked through all the different ways I could convince her. "I know it sounds impossible..."

"That's because it is impossible," Zenny interrupted me. "Do you think that everything that happened before you lost your memories is a whole different life?" Then her face lit up. "You got your memories back?"

I dropped my arms in defeat. "No, that's just a cover I've been using so I don't have to explain this to everyone. Mostly because this is the reaction I expected."

"I know what she's saying should be impossible, but I believe her," Nora said as she put a hand on Zenny's shoulder. "I've met another one just like her."

Zenny looked around, panicked. *It's time to try a slower approach.* I attempted to change Zenny's train of thought. "You've noticed that I do things very differently than someone my age usually does, right?"

"Yeah, but I thought that was because you were just really smart." Zenny calmed down somewhat.

"As much as I shouldn't put myself down, I'm not that smart. Have you noticed that my mom hasn't taught me numbers?" I poked Nora in the arm to get her attention. "This might require a demonstration. Could you get a pen, paper, and ink, please?"

Nora nodded and left quickly.

"I thought she already taught you like she did your letters." Zenny was still in shock.

I held up a finger as I corrected her. "She taught me how to write the numbers of this world. But she never needed to teach me how to add, subtract, multiply, divide, or do any algebra."

"Algebra?" Zenny got distracted by the word.

"See, something else you don't know about. Something I know from before." I tried to urge her to understand.

"I don't know how that proves you have had another life."

I threw down the metaphorical gauntlet. "Alright then, what will it take for you to believe me?"

"I don't know." Zenny pondered for a moment. Just as Nora entered my room carrying the supplies I'd requested, Zenny had an epiphany and pointed a finger at me. "If you're from another world, how did you get here?"

"This isn't my original body. That one is dead. If what I've been told is correct, a tornado ripped me apart." I shuddered and grimaced. "This is the body they sent my soul to inhabit. I'm guessing the girl's soul which originally inhabited this body has moved on, as this body was killed by orcs. I believe when my soul entered this body, it was revived. Also, this was apparently the wrong body. I don't know *how* I was sent here, just that I was."

Zenny just stared at me, her mouth agape and motionless.

"That's more than you told me," Nora said, not hiding her disappointment.

"You didn't ask," I responded sheepishly. I waved my hand in front of Zenny's face and saw no recognition in her eyes. "She might need some time to process everything." I sat back, grabbed my plate of eggs, and took a few bites of the tasteless sustenance. Nora crossed her arms and watched silently.

I had almost finished eating my breakfast—*which I wish had grown up to be a chicken before I ate it*—before Zenny showed signs of life again. She looked at me. "If you're right—I'm not saying that I believe you yet—what does that mean?"

"Nothing really. I was sent here to defend the world against the demon king, but I was released from that duty." With food in my stomach, I was a little more relaxed. "So I can just live a life like everyone else."

"Wait, the demon king is here?" Zenny looked around in a panic.

"No, there seem to be some people trying to bring him to this world, and it's believed that they'll succeed eventually. And I was supposed to kill him once he arrived and banish him back for some arbitrary amount of time. But that's someone else's responsibility now, I assume."

"How do you know this?" Zenny kept derailing the conversation.

"The being that sent me here told me most of it. Other parts, I don't know. It's just me guessing. But does that mean you believe me now?" I wasn't enjoying this little runaround. *This is exactly why I haven't told her.*

"Kind of," Zenny said. Her eyes didn't look like they were focused on anything, but she still picked up her plate of eggs and bread with jam.

"It looks like you two are going to have fun today," Nora said as she placed the book on my desk next to my toy unicorn. "I'll leave this here for you when you're ready. If you need anything, call for me." Then Nora stood over me with an intimidating look. "Don't you dare leave that bed."

I nodded quickly. *She can still intimidate me. I'm stronger than she is, but I guess there's more to it.*

We spent the day going over the information in the book about beastkin. Nora had covered most of the information with me, but left out a few details. Apparently, I would smell enthralling to men whenever I went into heat. The thing about two kids was spot on.

I wonder if that means I had a sibling. It doesn't matter; they were likely killed when the village was sacked.

There was an entire section on the mating habits of beastkin that left both Zenny and me blushing with how much detail it went into. I learned, however, that a few types of beastkin were viewed as nobler than the rest. Lions and wolves for the carnivores, bears for the omnivores, and rhinoceros for the herbivores. Also, my silver fur was the rarest color a wolf could have.

I'm the most exotic version of a highly-sought-after subspecies. What's going to happen when I meet another beastkin for the first time?

8

THE THING

I strolled down the hall towards yet another dissatisfying breakfast of eggs in the dining room. That was, until I heard a door opening and closing behind me.

"What are you doing out and about?" I heard Nora call out.

I slumped forward. "I've been really good. Look, I can move around just fine now." To demonstrate, I held my arms out and spun around. "And before you ask, yes. I did my stretches just like Salien showed me last night before she took Zenny home."

Nora crossed her arms and tapped her foot. "You did?"

"Twice, actually." I extended my arm with two fingers raised. "Once when I first woke up, and again before I headed for breakfast. I've been up for a while now." After crossing my arms, I continued. "I've behaved myself and stayed in my room and I haven't done anything to hurt myself," I recited with an attitude, not bothering to look Nora in the eye.

"The urge to run around is getting bad again, isn't it?" Nora asked.

"It was bad yesterday, but I played nice." I stomped my foot. "Can I please run around town now?" I pranced in place.

"I have something better planned," Nora said as she placed her hand on my shoulder and gently turned me around to face the other direction. "I figured it was about time we got you started on your basic training."

"My what?" I stopped and grabbed her arm, halting her movements and forcing her to face me. "Why now?"

"Your basic training." Nora tried to get me to go to the dining room again, but I swatted her arm away. With a sigh, Nora continued, "Most of your siblings before you went through it. It'll give you a leg up on the requirements for joining a knight company. If you still want to do that, that is. Also, hopefully it will pull double duty and tire you out too."

Right, more stuff to do with my growing debt. I doubt it will tire me out, but we'll see. This was eventually going to come up, wasn't it?

"At least I hope it does," she whispered.

"I still do," I said as I skipped towards the dining room. "Finally!" *I don't care if my shout woke anyone up. It's time to get up anyway.*

Breakfast was just the five of us: Nora, Molly, April, May, and I. *How are there only girls living here now?* Nora left the division of chores to us. After I poked a bunch of holes in everyone's clothes with my claws, the other girls didn't want me doing the laundry again. *It was all an accident; I promise. Now that I think about it, I'm not in charge of washing anything because of my fur. I still wash the dishes once in a while, because when it's my turn, Melody brings a few extra towels for me to dry off with.*

Since April and I hadn't been able to do any chores for the last few days, May and Molly made sure we got the jobs we despised. I had to wash the bathtubs while April cleaned the floors. April had recovered enough from her pneumonia to move around. Melody made sure I would have plenty of extra towels to dry off with.

After we divided the chores and ate our breakfast, we each set out to begin our day. May followed me, humming and skipping. May had joined us a little more than three years ago. Actually, her full name was Maitibella, but everyone called her May—everyone except Nora. Like me, she was ten. But as a beastkin—something I just learned—I developed physically sooner than elves like her. She was slightly pudgy because she sat around all day sewing and she detested physical activity. May was wearing another one of the flashy dresses that she made. It looked odd. The style was an exact copy of a dress we saw some aristocrats wearing, but instead of being made of fine silk, it was made of the cheapest tan wool available. She could make anything she wanted with her sewing aptitude.

I guess when you love to do what your aptitude is, have at it. She's going to be in for a shock when she has to spend her time in the military.

She bounced to a stop. I never understood why she bounced every time she took a step. All it did was cause her curly brown hair to bob up and down.

"So, have you started shedding yet?" Her chirpy voice was unmistakable.

May loved making pillows and stuffing them with the fur that I shed. I shed twice a year, once in the middle of the water season and once at the end of the wind season, changing coats to fit the time of year better. *Not that it helps much during the fire season.*

"No. Now leave me alone." I clenched my jaw but didn't growl. *You were the one who made sure I had to wash the bathtubs. Now you want to play nice? I don't think so.*

"Why are you always in a bad mood?" She jumped out in front of me and landed with her hands on her hips.

Is she serious? "Just, no." I grabbed her shoulders and moved her with no effort on my end.

I was nowhere near one hundred percent; I felt half as strong as I usually did, but it was more than enough to move someone six inches shorter than me.

"That's not fair. I thought you weren't supposed to do any lifting." She huffed in an agitated tone.

"I'm not allowed to do any *heavy* lifting." I glared at her. A thought bubbled to the surface of my brain, and it almost flew out of my mouth. *No, don't say it. Be nice. Control myself. Don't say it.* I shut my eyes and concentrated on holding back the horrible sentence. *Waterfalls. Waterfalls.* Once I had my tongue in check, I remembered I had a request for her. "I need another pillow."

"Didn't you get one yesterday?" she asked.

"I did," I said without hesitating. "I need another one."

"Are you going to give me your shed fur?" she asked impolitely.

"When I start shedding later, I'll be sure to let you know. It will be a few more weeks." I attempted to wave her off. *I want to get my chores done so I can figure out what this basic training is about.*

"I might be gone by then." She sounded a little regretful.

I nearly lost a step, but my tail saved my balance. "Don't tell me." I turned to look at her and saw her staring at the ground while blushing. "Come on, really?" She nodded.

I shouted something incomprehensible. *How did someone like her get adopted?*

Nora walked towards us. "I take it you told her?" Nora asked as she looked at May.

"You were right. She didn't take the news well," May said. She looked at me and then slowly backed away from me to stand behind Nora.

"What are you doing?" I growled at May.

Her back went stiff as she jumped a bit. "Nothing," she squeaked.

I growled louder.

"Lucia!" Nora's shout got my attention. "Waterfalls." She pointed down the hall.

I silently stormed off to the bathroom. To keep from getting angrier, I blocked out what Nora had said to May. *Why is it bothering me so much that she got adopted? Or do I have too much energy again?*

Once I entered the bathroom, I saw a large stack of towels. There was an urge to do something. I didn't know exactly what it was, but it was getting harder to suppress. I started throwing the towels around the room.

"I hate this!" My tantrum of towel-tossing didn't end. "Why can't I stop? I hate having all this energy and I have no idea what it all means. What's wrong with me?"

The push in the back of my mind didn't stop. It wanted more. Even after all the towels lay strewn about the room, I couldn't calm down. I couldn't focus enough to visualize a waterfall, and controlling myself was getting harder. I looked down at a towel, and one thought ran through my head: kill.

I tore the towel apart.

I continued without thinking. One by one, my claws shredded every towel until there wasn't a piece large enough to grab. I'd just gotten my heart rate to rise enough for me to increase my breathing when Nora walked in.

Not again. This is going to get added to my tab, isn't it?

She surveyed the third cotton calamity of the week. She looked at me without emotion. "Are you done?" I nodded sheepishly. "Clean this up." She turned on her heels and walked out.

Tearing apart the towels had calmed me down enough to think more clearly. *Since I made this mess, I have to clean it up. I wonder how much this is going to cost me.*

While I picked up all the shredded towels and placed them in a pile, I had plenty of time to reflect on why I did it. *The only thing that stood out was the urge to kill. It was so strong. I felt like I couldn't ignore it. It's never been so clear about what I'm being pushed to do. Am I really just a murderous monster at heart? Do my instincts want me to kill everything? Why? That doesn't make sense.*

I cleaned the bathtubs. When I filled the tubs, I kept the water level as low as possible. The entire time, I tried to solve the mystery surrounding my urges. Every thought pattern I followed ended in the same way. *There's something I'm not thinking of.*

Once I was done, I dried myself with the largest scraps of the shredded towels. Somehow, I was dry enough to not drip water everywhere I went. I gathered the pile of towels from earlier and carried them to the bathroom.

Just as I walked to the bathroom door, I heard someone walking to the front door of the orphanage. Two people, actually. I tried to focus on them. *One set of footsteps was much heavier than the other.* It had become a little game of mine trying to learn what I could from footsteps as they passed by. *It will be a neat parlor trick when I'm good enough.* Then they knocked on the front door.

I sat quietly and let Nora answer it. When I heard steps arriving from the courtyard, based on how fast they were walking, I thought they might be hers. I put my ear next to the bathroom door so I could listen in more easily.

"Hello, Allen." Nora sounded a little disappointed to see him. But she changed her tone quickly. "Who is this?" She sounded like she was talking to a child.

This brings back memories. Allen, the captain of the Brilliant Crusade, saved me from orcs and brought me to this orphanage. Wait, is there another new kid?

I burst out of the bathroom door and threw the towels on the ground to my left. Now unburdened, I went to greet the newcomer.

"Can we come in?" I heard Allen ask politely.

"Please." Nora ushered the two in.

Allen wasn't wearing any armor; instead, he was in normal, light-brown clothes. While simple, they looked clean and well-maintained. He was holding the hand of a small boy. If you had told me that this boy was Molly's younger brother, I would have believed you. With light-brown skin and black hair, he stood at the entrance and stared at me, brown eyes opened wide. He looked about the same size I was when I first arrived, if not shorter. *So he's probably four, maybe five.*

I noticed Allen watching me. I gave him a simple nod; he wasn't who I was interested in.

"Ah, I see Lucia is already ready to meet you," Nora said as she rejoined us after closing the front door. She gave me a hard stare.

I know, play nice. I gave her a look, saying I knew what she meant.

She eased her glare before returning her attention to the small boy. Something told me she was going to keep a close eye on me. "Go on, say hi." Her voice was as sweet as she could make it.

"Hi, I'm Lucia. What's your name?" I squatted in front of the boy and put on my nicest, closed-lipped smile. *Don't show him my teeth. They always run when they see the teeth,* I reminded myself.

"I'm August!" the boy nearly yelled as his body quivered. His eyes never stopped watching me with a frightening infatuation.

"What?" I asked flatly. *Why do I live with people named after months now?*

"Lucia!" Nora's voice was judgmental.

"Sorry, I, uh... I'll tell you later." That was the universal sign that something had reminded me of my previous life.

"You have such big, fluffy ears." August reached out to touch my ears.

I leaned back to avoid him. I caught myself with my hands and quickly backpedaled to increase the distance between us.

Both Nora and Allen reacted as well. Nora grabbed the boy's arm and drew it away, while Allen pulled the boy away from me.

"No, don't do that," Nora said as she held the boy.

"Why?" He reached a hand towards me again.

"Because I said so," I said it with a little more hostility than I intended. I scrambled to my feet. "Listen, I have rules. Don't touch my ears; don't touch my tail; and most importantly, don't make me angry."

"Lucia!" Nora snapped at me.

What? Was I not supposed to tell him not to do any of that?

"You have big, pretty eyes," August said without ever taking his eyes off me.

A strange feeling emanated from my chest. It was both alien and familiar, but I didn't know when or where I had felt something like this before. I blushed. *No one has ever said I'm pretty before. People said my hair and fur were beautiful, but this feels different.*

Nora giggled. I shot her a glare, daring her to say one word. Allen looked at the two of us, confused.

Nora noticed his bewilderment. "Someone likes compliments."

Allen shrugged his shoulders.

I guess that's the best I'm going to get. Wait a moment, ears, then eyes. That reminds me of something. I might as well finish this out.

I smiled at the boy, showing him all of my very sharp teeth.

"What's wrong with your teeth?" August flinched.

Way to ruin it, kid. Why is it always the teeth with people? I might as well give him the answers anyway. That still sounds like fun.

"My ears are big so I can hear you better. My eyes are big so I can see you better. And my teeth are perfectly fine, thank you very much." I growled at him for thinking there was something wrong with my wonderfully perfect teeth.

August jumped at my outburst. Nora grabbed the child and gave me a look of disappointment.

"What?" I returned her look with a pout.

She closed her eyes. "Go upstairs with Allen and calm down."

I'm going to hear about this later, aren't I? I shouldn't push my luck anymore. I did what I was told and headed for the training room.

"Allen, please stay until I get back from registering August." She grabbed the boy's hand and started for the door. "And please keep her from doing anything irresponsible."

"Yes, ma'am," Allen said as he saluted Nora and followed me.

9

ONE INCREDIBLE CHILD

"You seem agitated today," Allen said as he closed the door behind him. "What's wrong?"

"May's getting adopted; the new kid thinks I'm a freak; I'm getting these uncontrollable urges again; I can't go hunting with Zane and Marigold because I can't control the aforementioned urges; and finally, I'm still not completely healed." I stopped and turned to face Allen. "Are those sufficient reasons for you?"

Allen stopped in his tracks and stared at me wide-eyed.

I turned and headed to grab a wooden stick so I could start hitting something.

"A few questions, if I may." Allen followed behind me. "Why does May getting adopted upset you? Shouldn't you be happy for her?" He stopped in the middle of the room.

"Why doesn't someone want to adopt me?" I could feel the desire to cry building.

"I'm going to be blunt with you. People adopt for reasons that are less than charitable." Allen's voice dropped lower than usual. "Most of the time, they're looking for an heir to their wealth because they don't have a child of their own. Others are looking for someone to keep their shop open when they get too old and to have someone who can care for them."

"Salien adopted Zenny because she really cares about her." I grabbed a wooden sword, still holding the tears back.

"I'm not saying adoptions like that don't happen, but they're rare." Allen lowered himself to look me in the eye. "But know that Nora is going to care for you just like a real mother would. I should know." He had a smile on his face as he changed his tone.

"You were raised here?" I blurted out.

"I was. Nora had just taken ownership of the orphanage when I was delivered by my parents. There was a massive drought that year, and my parents lost almost all of their crops. They didn't have enough to feed me. It didn't help that they were already struggling for a few years before that. They believed that in order for me to have a decent life, I needed to be given a chance by parents who could provide for me. It was the hardest decision they ever made. The worst part is that it was the right decision."

I could see the sadness in his eyes, and I started crying for him. "What happened to them?"

"They received a loan from some people. When they failed to pay it back, their debtors took the farm as compensation. They starved to death shortly afterwards." Allen balled his fists as he told me the story.

Loan sharks stole his family's farm and left them to die homeless and alone. That's an awful way to go. And there was nothing he could do to help them. And with how he sounded, I don't think he's gotten over it yet.

"I'm sorry," I said as I lowered my head. "I shouldn't have asked."

"You have nothing to apologize for." Allen was back to smiling again. "You neither brought up the topic nor caused the events. Now, what are these urges you were talking about?" He'd changed the subject almost too quickly for my liking.

The scene in the bathroom with the towels played in my head again. It was too much for me to handle. I dropped to the ground and cried. "I have moments when I want to do nothing but tear something or someone to pieces. I'm sure you saw the pile of shredded towels. Originally, I didn't want to tear them apart, but I felt like I needed to kill something. I've never felt that before. It's like my instincts are trying to force me to kill."

"But you said you were getting them again. That means they went away." Allen sat down next to me.

Did you miss the part where I said they wanted me to kill? "They stopped for a few days, but I was stuck in bed, recovering." My tears flowed harder the more I talked.

"Recovering from what?" Allen wrapped an arm around me.

"While running away from a wolf, I tore all the muscles in my arms and legs." *I have become a fountain of confessions.* Part of me wanted to stop this conversation, but another part wouldn't stop until I spilled everything.

"You outran a wolf?" Allen asked. "But how did you hurt your arms?"

"If I use my arms and legs and run on all fours, I'm a bit faster." I dropped the piece of wood in my hands and hugged my legs to my chest.

"I don't think you understand the incredible nature of what you are capable of." Allen sounded proud of me. "I've never seen anything outrun a wolf. Your physical aptitude had much to do with that feat, but don't discredit your determination to keep running. I imagine everyone else would have given up and died. But you didn't; you survived. You're still growing. You'll do some amazing things. I'm sure of it." Allen started scratching my back in between my shoulder blades.

"I don't want to do amazing things." I shook my head. "I just want to be normal."

"Then let's make that happen for you." He was full of positivity as he let up on his hug. "Stop crying and look at me." He gently took my chin and turned my head.

I looked at him through the tears as I tried to turn them off. They slowed, but I was still breathing sharply.

"Alright, now what does Lucia want to do? What would be normal for you?"

"I don't know," I whimpered. "Spend all my time hunting, maybe? Hunting that frog was kinda fun. It's something that I can do that lets me kill and run around. But I have to join the military to pay my debt."

"So now we know what your goal is. Next, we'll look at where you are." *This is sounding like a motivational speech.* "If you have to join the military, why can't you hunt at the same time?"

"Won't being in the military take up all of my time?" My vision was clearing as I was slowly calming down.

"Of course not. Do you think the guards stand around all day? No, most of them have families they go home to every night. And you can have more time for yourself if you join a knight company." Allen's smile was almost infectious. "If you join a company, especially a large one, you get to choose your missions, and your downtime will be your own. Yes, you will have obligations, but those are always negotiable." He gave me a playful wink.

"What company would ever want a beastkin who does nothing but destroy everything around her?" My mood plummeted again.

"We'll make them want you." Allen's grin changed to one that was much more mischievous. He caught my attention. "There's a tournament being held at the end of the water season. All the knight prospects are going to participate. If you win, many companies will be clamoring to get you to commit to them. They'll offer you almost anything."

One problem, sir. "I don't know how to fight." I bluntly presented the largest hurdle.

His mischievous grin never left his face. "*That* we can easily remedy."

"Stop leading me on and tell me everything." I sounded like a mess. I wanted to sound angry, but with the crying fit I'd had earlier, it just sounded pathetic.

"I've been receiving many requests from parents wanting me to teach their children or to find someone else to teach them. I've been turning them down. But for you, I'll find someone to teach you as a favor to Nora." Allen had turned his smile back to a warm, fatherly one. "Besides, if I'm correct, you're about the age where she wants to discuss your basic training, am I right?"

"Yeah, it's probably what she wants to talk about once she gets

August registered. But you said that I can hunt while I'm a knight. Are other knight companies okay with that?" My mood was getting more under control.

"Yes, there are many cases where things like that happen. Some companies seek people who have talents outside of fighting. I hired two people because one was a talented blacksmith and the other was one of the best chefs I've ever met." *I know you're trying to cheer me up. Congratulations, it's working; keep it up.* "Knowing how to hunt and track in the woods is an invaluable skill."

"Why do people like that join a knight company?" I asked, wiping my face with my arm.

"It would surprise you what people will do for lower taxes," Allen said with a laugh. "You're going to serve long enough to be completely exempt from taxes, right?"

"How long is that?" *No taxes? Perhaps it would be worthwhile to serve in a knight's company. I guess no matter what world you're in, nobody likes taxes.*

"Seven years, if you're in a company." Allen's nonchalant tone made it sound like seven years wasn't much. "Nine if you're in the general military."

"Why doesn't everyone join a company then? It sounds like that's the way to go."

"Because we have the more dangerous missions, and the requirements are far more strict." Allen became serious. "Not everyone is brave enough to lay their life on the line as a knight should. Also, we need the best so we can ensure everyone makes it home."

"So how does winning a tournament help make me a knight?" I asked. "What is this tournament thing anyways? I don't remember hearing anything about one before."

"It's a tournament that's held only when the king's firstborn turns seventeen. There's a whole festival that goes with it." Allen turned his head and stared into the distance as if he was lost in a memory. He gave a quick shake of his head. "But anyway, if you show everyone what you're capable of, you'll be surprised at what people will overlook."

Is that a touch of regret in his eyes?

"So being a beastkin won't be a problem?" I looked up at him.

"There might be a few who'll have a problem with it." Allen turned his head away from me. "But I imagine that there will be some beastkin that will have a problem with you because you weren't raised in The Wild Kingdom. This world is full of individuals who have their own side of the story. You have a story just like them. There may have been things that have happened to them that have caused them to see others with an unpleasant view."

I pouted. "That doesn't make me feel any better, you know."

"That doesn't excuse them from their actions," Allen immediately responded. "You remember Avollea, don't you?" *How could I not remember?* I nodded with a scowl on my face. "Eventually, I got her side of the story." *Oh, this had better be good.* "Her sister was visiting The Wild Kingdom as a trader. A feral beastkin attacked her caravan, and she died in the attack. They caught the beastkin who killed her and cured it of its feral condition. It was free to live out the rest of its life. Avollea has despised beastkin since."

"That doesn't excuse her treatment of me." I stood up and picked up the practice weapon off the floor. *I need to hit something.* "How is killing me going to make her feel better about her sister? It won't bring her back. I wasn't even alive when it happened. So why bother taking it out on me?"

I started carving a notch into the handle. *I hate having to carve a notch every time I want to use one of these swords. But if I don't, it will fly out of my hands, and I don't want to accidentally hit Allen.*

"You're right, it doesn't. She should never have acted like that." Allen stood up and watched my hands with a slight fascination. "But she's loyal to a fault. I gave her the orders I did for your safety. Once I gave her the orders, I knew she would have given her life to save yours."

I highly doubt that. But, if that's what you want to believe. I shrugged as I finished carving out the notch for my finger. I think Allen noticed I didn't want to keep talking about Avollea because he changed the subject once again.

"So about these bouts of destructiveness. Do you want to fill me in?"

And we're back to the next topic of my checklist of problems. "I don't want to destroy something. It's just that I have so much energy that I don't know what to do with it. It's so frustrating, and it makes me take my frustrations out on something." *Like how I'm feeling right now.* I suppressed a growl. "I'm very good at breaking things. It comes with the territory of being ridiculously strong for my age and size."

"As I understand it, you are stronger than most adults." *Is it me, or does he sound jealous?* Allen continued on as if he had never said anything at all. "So nothing you tried so far has worked? You said that it was starting again earlier. It sounds like something worked. Do you have any idea what caused it to go away in the first place?"

"I've been trying to figure it out, but every time I try, I get frustrated." I took the wooden sword and struck the headless dummy. "At one point, I thought it went away because I hurt myself, but I don't believe that anymore."

I struck the practice dummy repeatedly. It stood there unmoving, as if it were simply mocking my efforts.

"Stop that." Allen walked up behind me and tried to grab my wrist. "What kind of form is that?"

"The one that tires me out. I don't know anything about swinging a weapon." I flattened my ears as I stared at him.

"I guess we have our work cut out for us, don't we?" Allen had a playful smile on his face. "You're using only your arms in your swing. It's horribly inefficient." He turned me towards the dummy. "Plant your feet like this." He moved my feet slightly apart. "Now when you swing your weapon, use your hips to turn at the same time, and time your swing so that you contact your target while your arms are completely extended." He grabbed the wooden sword in my hand and pointed at a spot about three-quarters up the length of the blade. "This is where you want to hit, and you want to make sure that the blade is aligned properly so it doesn't deflect once you strike." He took a few steps back and waved his hands towards the dummy. "Now give it a go."

I attempted to follow his instructions and took my swing. I felt off balance, but my strike collided nonetheless. The crack that resulted nearly sent me to my knees. Splinters of wood flew out from the contact. A piece of the sword flew out past me, but not in Allen's direction. My hands tingled as they shook. I dropped the broken piece of wood and rubbed my hands together to ease the pain.

"Maybe I'll stick to using my claws." I stared at the dummy that wasn't standing anymore.

I'm still not at my best. What will happen once I become an adult? Am I going to be as strong as that demon? I turned to look at Allen.

He stared at me with both fear and admiration. "I don't think you're going to have trouble with the tournament."

10

WHAT'S NORMAL?

"That's a lot of damage," Allen said with an approving tone. "While most people would say that was a spectacular hit, there are still a lot of things you need to work on."

"I'm only doing this because I'm trying to tire myself out," I said as I continued rubbing my hands together, attempting to soothe the jarring feel of the impact. "I don't like holding weapons. It feels wrong."

"A shame. I'm curious to see what kind of damage you could inflict with a mace," Allen said cheerfully. He held out his hand. "Let me see your hands."

I held out my hands for him. Allen carefully grabbed one and massaged my palm below the pad. While he kept massaging, he prodded my fingertips, rubbed a finger on my pads, then on my fur, and ended by testing the sharpness of my claws.

"That feels much better," I said as I noticed the feeling return to my hand. "But be careful of those. They're really sharp."

Allen switched which hand he was massaging. "An unarmed combat style might suit you. We'll need to find someone to teach you. Although with these hands, there's nothing unarmed about you."

I chuckled. "That may not be necessary." Allen raised an eyebrow.

"I mean, up to this point, everything has been pretty instinctual." I admired my claws. "And these babies did a real number on a giant toad."

"When did you kill a giant toad?" Allen asked with skepticism filling his voice.

"Just before I needed to outrun an enormous wolf," I answered in a playful tone. "I was hunting with Zane and Marigold."

Allen released my hand and put his finger to his chin as he stared at the floor. I was getting worried that he wasn't saying anything. *What is he thinking about?*

Without warning, he sprang into action. "Were you having those urges before you killed the toad? How many days has it been since?"

Allen's stare startled me. "Yeah. The only reason I took it down was that I couldn't help myself and had this need to hunt it." I paused at the word "need." *Is that the right word? It feels like the right word.* "But it's been six days since then. It's been getting bad since yesterday though." The look on Allen's face told me what he was thinking. "Oh, no. You don't think that I need to kill something every few days, do you?" *I don't want to be a mindless killing machine.*

"Maybe not *kill*, but do something that makes you feel like you accomplished something. Have there been other times when you didn't have your urges?"

I didn't feel anything like this before the demon attacked. But I killed those two who tried to sacrifice me to the demon. However, it's only gotten worse in the last couple of years. About the time when I spend almost every waking moment trying to tire myself out. But after each time, I recovered even faster than the last time. "Each time it's gone away was when I tired myself out to the point I nearly passed out."

"So we just need to keep you busy." Allen straightened his posture. "Any ideas on how you want to go about that?"

"I want to go out hunting again," I said as I curled my tail around my waist.

"I sense a *but* coming," Allen said.

"Marigold and Zane said that until I can control myself, I can't go with them." The memory of what I did to Marigold flashed in my mind. "I kinda didn't do what they told me to do."

"I can believe that," Allen said as he started pacing.

As he was thinking, I heard the front door open and three sets of footsteps walk into the building. It sounded like one set of footsteps was heading towards us. I could still feel an excess of energy that needed to be spent.

This swinging around a wooden sword isn't helping much right now. Maybe a run will help me clear my mind. My limbs were feeling a bit painful, so I started stretching as prescribed by Salien. While I was in the middle of doing my hamstrings, Zenny walked through the door to the gym. She was carrying an old, heavy, leather-bound book. *Of course she has a book.*

Her smile was obvious as she watched me do my stretching. "Have you been avoiding heavy lifting and other strenuous actions?" she asked in a sweet voice.

I sighed. "Yes, and just so you know, this is the third time today I'm doing my stretches. See, I can behave."

"Are you my relief?" Allen asked Zenny. She stared at him, confused, and he said, "I suspect you're here to watch over her to make sure she follows her orders. Is that right?"

"Uh, maybe?"

Allen's militaristic verbiage is probably throwing Zenny off.

Allen turned to me. "I'm going to talk with Nora for a bit before I go. Think about what I said. If you want normal, figure out what that is and make it happen." He smiled at me before he walked down the stairwell.

Zenny still had a bewildered look on her face. "Who was he?" She pointed with her thumb towards the stairwell.

"That was Allen from the Brilliant Crusade. He saved me from the orcs and then again from one of his knights," I said nonchalantly as I continued stretching the rest of my legs.

"Oh." She turned back towards the door for a moment. She then shook off her confusion. "Are you ready to learn about bugs today?"

Her cheery tone frightened me. "Uh." In a vain attempt to find an escape, I looked around the room. "Can I go for a run first?"

"Are you going to run as fast as you can?" Zenny tried to put on a serious and intimidating look. It didn't work. "You can go for a jog.

Keep it slow. And don't you dare hurt yourself again! If you feel even the slightest pain, I want you to stop immediately and come straight back here. Got it?" She puffed her cheeks out.

I giggled at her display. "You know, that doesn't work on me. Maybe if our heights were switched it would. But since I'm four inches taller than you, you just look cute." I stretched my arms.

Zenny pouted in defeat. "You big dummy, how did you get so tall anyway? All you do is eat meat. I was told that if I didn't eat my vegetables, I would stay short."

"I only eat meat because that's what my biology requires," I said with a smile.

"But you enjoy it so much. Watching you eat is terrifying," Zenny said with a shudder.

"What can I say other than it tastes so good?" I shrugged with a blissful look on my face. "And there are many factors that determine how tall you will be. How tall were your parents?" I straightened my expression back to normal.

"Dad was seventy-three inches tall. My mother was sixty-six inches tall," she answered, although she looked at me skeptically. "What do you mean, many factors?"

Oops, I did it again. "It's more complicated than that. But all foods have these things called nutrients. While I'm fuzzy on the details, just know that as a human, your body has all kinds of needs, and those needs can be fulfilled with different foods. If you do, it won't hurt your chances." I gave her a friendly smile and a thumbs-up.

Zenny squinted at me. "Is this one of those things you know from your other life?"

"Yes," I answered sheepishly.

Her personality shifted wildly. "Please tell me I don't have to eat broccoli." She sounded desperate. "How can anyone find that despicable green abomination tasty?"

I blinked at her in surprise. She was clutching the book for dear life. "No one said you have to eat broccoli. You could just find other green vegetables to replace it." I held out my hands towards her. "But you really shouldn't take dietary advice from me. I have a very simple diet." *Good, now my stretches are done.*

"If they're so good for you, why do they have to taste so bad?" Zenny said as she looked at the floor. *That's one perk of being a carnivore beastkin: easy meal planning.* "But it seems like you'll have to wait for the lesson after lunch." She perked up and headed for the stairs.

"I've been meaning to ask about that," I said to halt her. "You eat here often. Who's paying for your food?" *That's been bugging me for a while now.*

"Mom does. If I'm going to spend the day here, she pays Nora a few coins for both watching over me and feeding me," she answered in a cheery voice.

"Doesn't that get expensive?" I blurted.

"Mom says it isn't a problem." Zenny just shrugged and proceeded down the stairs.

If she says it isn't a problem, it isn't. Case closed. Now about that run. I followed Zenny down the stairs and saw Allen leave through the front door out of the corner of my eye.

Nora was standing and waiting for us in the classroom. "So, Allen talked to you about being a knight?" Her tone was hard to comprehend. It was a mixture of worry, anger, happiness, and approval all rolled into one.

I stared at her, confused. "Yes." I drew out my answer, trying to think of where the conversation could go to prepare myself. I failed.

"You know what that means, right?" Her eyes were appraising me.

"Didn't you want me to do basic training?" I quipped back. "Wasn't that so that I had a head start to become a knight?"

"A head start, yes, but I want to be certain you understand what joining a knight company means before you just jump into it. Because the fantasy you may be picturing is far from the truth, I assure you." Nora had a stern look on her face. "Did Allen also talk you into participating in the tournament?"

"He may have mentioned how it would be beneficial for me to participate," I answered.

Nora pinched the bridge of her nose. "Did he talk about the prize money?"

"There's prize money?" My tail started wagging. "No, he didn't say anything about that."

"Zenny, dear, could you give us a few moments to talk alone?" Suddenly, her voice was sweeter than honey. *All anyone wants to do is talk. Nobody wants to run around town or exercise with me.*

Zenny had a worried look on her face. "Okay," she responded meekly. She headed down the hall to the dining room.

Nora ushered me into the classroom.

I'm not going on that run now, am I? I sighed. When I walked into the room, disappointed, I looked at the first chair I arrived at. *I can't sit down right now.* I started pacing from one side of the room to the other.

"You can't sit still right now, can you?" Nora asked rhetorically. "It's fine. Do what you need to do. I don't have a problem with you wanting to be a knight to serve your time. I want to know what you think being a knight is like." Nora took a seat in a chair at one of the four desks.

"Allen told me that I'll have more freedom and more time for myself." I continued pacing. "And how much money are we talking about for this tournament?"

"The prize money is only for whoever wins. And it would be enough to feed you for two years even with your ridiculous appetite. As for the other stuff, he's correct. But you have to earn it." Nora's tone was harsh. "Most companies give rewards after you complete the missions you've been assigned."

"'Most companies?' What was the one you were in like?" *You sold yourself out on that one, Mom.*

"That was a unique company," Nora said. "Midas liked to call us an adventuring party more than a knight company. Midas formed it specifically to hunt down the demon king, should someone have summoned him. You are very unlikely to find another one like that."

"Tell me what kinds of missions I'll receive. It sounds to me like the missions I'd have to do will determine if it's worth even trying." *She has a point. I should stop just rushing into things and think. I know I should plan and think about what I'm going to do. But for some reason, I either forget the plan or get distracted.*

Nora lifted her pointer finger and began counting, raising a finger for each item she listed. "Guard missions are the most common. The next is border patrol. Then you have dire animal exterminations. Finally, you have peacekeeping. Though these are the four most common tasks given to knights, during times of war you may be required to attack another kingdom, rescue prisoners, or work with other companies." She lowered her hand back into her lap.

"I could do that," I said confidently.

"I believe you can too," Nora gently replied.

"So, what's the problem?" I asked, worried about where this would go.

"The tournament." Nora's voice was icy. *I don't get it.* "You have quite the temper." *I still don't follow.* "How will you react when someone hits you? Can you even admit you lost? What's stopping you from killing anyone else?"

Her trio of questions hit me hard. As I took another step, I stumbled. *I do react violently to unwanted physical contact.* I looked at my claws and admired their sharpness. *When those two kidnapped me, I killed them quite easily. And I was only five at the time. I'm stronger, taller, and I'm sure my claws are both sharper and more durable, although that's hard to prove.* I scoured my memories for all the times I'd lost anything more than an argument. There weren't many, and they almost always ended with me sulking for a day or two. *I'm not that proud, am I?*

I looked at Nora. "What do you suggest?" My voice was meek. But suddenly, a thought ran to the front of my mind. My attitude changed immediately with the thought. "If you even think about the necklace again, I will do the same thing as last time. I will rip it apart now that I'm strong enough."

"I would never do that again," Nora immediately answered. "No, we must do something about your control. This is something beyond me. This requires professional help." Her tone was slightly uplifting.

A chill ran down my spine. "I don't like the sound of that. Where are you going to take me?" I started backing toward the door, away from Nora.

"You aren't going anywhere. She's coming here," Nora said cheerfully. "Don't worry, you'll be in good hands. Immianthe taught many members of the royal family proper etiquette. She's dealt with her share of difficult children."

"I don't see how that will help me," I said as I reached the door and placed my hand on it. I was ready to make a run for it.

Suddenly, the door opened from behind me. I jumped away into a tumble roll and ended up on my feet. I turned to see who was behind me.

Zenny stood at the door with a baffled look. I relaxed, knowing I had overreacted. "Lunch is almost ready. Melody wanted me to get you two," Zenny said as she analyzed the room.

"Immianthe has a reputation, and a price to match that reputation. Unfortunately, it's going to increase your debt," Nora said apologetically. "If anyone can handle you, it'll be her. Zenny will still teach you everything else, though." That brought a smile to Zenny's face. "Immianthe is just to teach you how to control that temper of yours." She stood up. "But enough of that. Let's go have some lunch. Then you can go do whatever it was you were going to do before I stopped you. I know how much you love lamb."

My mouth watered. I didn't wait for anyone as I ran past Zenny and straight for the dining room.

11

A GIRLS' NIGHT OUT

L amb may not be as good as bacon, but it's a very close second.

After enjoying my lightly cooked lamb sausages, Zenny and I left the orphanage. Zenny had decided not to let me go on a run before teaching me about bugs. Instead, we headed to the gate and then to one of the nearby farms. A nice old lady permitted us to snoop around looking for insects for as long as we liked. Zenny had decided that to get me to learn about bugs, I should catch some.

Armed with a book carried in a simple backpack and an extra layer of clothes, Zenny followed me to the fields. We spent the entire afternoon catching bugs and looking over her enormous book. Many of the bugs shared names and shapes with ones I was familiar with. They were just bigger. *From what I've seen so far, almost all animals are larger in this world. Except for the birds, they've all been the same size. That might have more to do with the physics of flying, though.*

We spent so much time having fun—and boy, was I having fun—that the sun had set before we knew it. It didn't bother me much since I could see well enough by moonlight.

Zenny wrapped her cloak tightly around herself. "I think we should go home soon."

"Is it still that cold at night?" I asked.

"Yes, and I'm also getting tired. I don't have the energy you do or the fur to keep me warm. Even with that fur, how are you not cold? You're wearing clothes others wear during the fire season." Zenny pouted.

"I don't know. Maybe my body just runs hotter than yours," I said with a shrug. "You know, during the fire season, I can't stand it when it gets too hot." *There's no air conditioning, and I can't get cool enough.*

"Maybe you're some kind of wolf that lives in mountains," Zenny said with a smile.

I paused for a moment. "I can believe that. Silver fur, comfortable in cold climates, and an aversion to heat." I looked at Zenny, and we giggled together. "Alright, enough talking about my sub-sub-species. Let's get you home."

I led Zenny back to the town gate. We waited in line behind a small group of people standing in the lamplight talking to the guard. They all wore matching black cloaks. Listening in on their conversation was too easy for me.

"I've never seen you lot before. How can you say you were here last week?" The guard's gruff voice carried through the air. *I'm sure Zenny can hear him just fine.*

A calm and lighthearted voice answered the guard. "You're right, we're not from here, but we don't plan on staying. We were here last week as we passed through. We're looking to do the same, but it's too late to travel, and we're tired from being on the road all day. All we wish to do is spend the night, and we'll be on our way."

"My job is to keep suspicious people out of town. And you're all suspicious in my book." The guard pointed at the group of five cloaked figures.

"And what's so suspicious about us?" *It looks like there's one guy doing all the talking.* "We're simple travelers looking to stay the night."

"The way you're dressed." *Now this guard is just profiling.*

With a sigh and a drop of his shoulders, the man brought a hand to his face. "What would it take for you to stop considering us suspicious?" It sounded like the man was losing his patience. *I'm losing mine. Zenny needs to get home.*

"You can start by removing those hoods." The guard grabbed his sword on his hip and stood up straight.

There was little movement from the group until the one who had done all the talking, who I believed was the leader, brought his hands to his hood and flicked it back. Shortly after, all the others followed suit. I never saw their faces, but they each had dark-brown hair, all in different styles. The leader had straight hair that went down under his cloak. There was one with wavy hair that again went under the cloak. In fact, all of them had hair long enough to be tucked back into their cloaks, whether they had a ponytail, curly hair, or a braid. *Are they all one family of brothers and sisters?*

There was another detail that caught my attention: they were all elves.

"Is this good enough?" the man said politely.

"A good start." The guard stared at each of their faces. *Is he trying to memorize them?* "Now, where did you say you were staying?"

"We didn't say, but where's the closest inn? We can stay there." The man was getting snippier.

"Eleven streets down, turn south and follow it until you see a sign that reads 'The Passive Pasture.' They have rooms most nights." The guard didn't let go of his weapon. He simply pointed with a nod of his head. "Go, but know that we'll keep an eye on you."

Without a word, they all returned their hoods to the top of their heads and headed into the city.

Zenny and I walked up to the guard. "Please tell me we aren't going to get the same treatment," I said in an annoyed tone.

"Nah, I know who you are," he said with a smile. "I believe everyone knows about the Silver Breeze by now."

"The what now?" *I have a nickname?* I blinked in shock, trying to determine if this was a good thing or not.

The guard continued smiling. "The Silver Breeze. Your running through the streets appears to be a silver blur, and everyone feels a breeze as you pass." I relaxed. "But what are two kids like you doing out this late at night?"

"We let the day get away from us," Zenny replied. "*Someone* was having so much fun, it was hard to stop her." She smiled as she pointed a thumb at me.

"Hey, I'm not the only one to blame." I gave her a playful, very light shove. "It isn't like anything distracted me."

The guard laughed. "Alright, you two. Go straight home. Your parents are likely worried about you." *He's a nice man. I like him.*

I stood up straight with my hands at my sides. "Yes, sir!" I grabbed Zenny's wrist and pulled her behind me into the town.

We walked down the streets. People were scarce, and there were few windows lit, giving almost no light for Zenny to navigate by. Combined with the heavy cloud cover, I imagined almost everyone would be blind. She pulled my arm to slow me down, and I walked at a pace she felt comfortable with. Zenny gave me directions when I told her where we were. Everything was quiet when we turned down a completely black alley.

"Are you sure this is wise?" I asked Zenny, who had my arm in a death grip. "It's really dark, and I'm getting this feeling that we're being watched."

"It's the fastest way to the orphanage," Zenny said. Her voice shook as her eyes darted around.

"Why are we going to my home first when you can't see where you're going, but I can?" I asked for the third time since we'd entered the town.

"I thought I would have enough light to get back home. Also, you still have a horrible sense of direction," she teased to lighten the mood. "How was I supposed to know that it would get cloudy?"

"Fine, but you're staying with me tonight." I made sure she kept moving. "We'll explain everything in the morning. I'm sure we can figure out a way to make sure your mom knows where you are."

I heard something moving behind us. I turned and looked to see someone following us down the alley. There was a little bell ringing in my head.

"What is it?" Zenny was concerned about why we'd stopped.

"Shh," I hushed Zenny. I moved her behind me to keep her out of the way. *This isn't an often-traveled alley. There's no way this is a coincidence.*

"So you heard me coming. Good," a nasally voice sounded from the person down the alley. "Here I was thinking the claims of a beast-kin's hearing were nothing more than exaggerated lies."

I growled.

"What do you want?" Zenny asked, sounding terrified.

"Quiet. He can't be up to any good following us in a dark, uninhabited alley during the dead of night," I said as I pushed Zenny even farther back and tried to backpedal away from the shadowy figure.

"Very astute of you." He started clapping. "I'm here to kill you."

That was quite direct.

"Why?" Zenny shouted.

Yes, make noise.

"Because a certain beastkin messed up our plans five years ago, and I'm here to make sure our plans aren't interrupted again." I heard something that sounded like a weapon being drawn from its sheath. "Since you're the only beastkin in this entire city, I think I have the right target."

"Even if you could kill me, you realize that would bring Nora's wrath down on you and your superiors," I said, stalling for time as I gave Zenny another nudge. This time, I stopped moving.

"Oh, we have something special saved for her. But it's a shame that one of your friends is involved in this. Loose ends and all that." He chuckled.

You will not touch Zenny!

I exploded. Red flooded my vision, somehow improving it. He was an elf and had a lazy stance with his feet together, approaching us as if we weren't a danger to him. He twirled a dagger in his right hand.

I burst towards him in a full sprint. I saw his shock as I positioned the claws of my right hand to impale him in the gut. He stared at me as my claws embedded themselves in his intestines.

The elf howled in pain and went to stab me with his dagger. I grabbed his wrist with my left hand. Growling, I brought his arm to my mouth and bit down hard. The guy screamed louder. He grabbed my hair and tried to pull me off his arm. I bit down even harder, and I heard bones cracking in my jaws.

I turned and shoved him against a wall and continued to bite down even more as he kept pulling on my hair. Suddenly, my head was moving away from his arm. He threw me into the wall on the other side of the alley.

He pulled me off? But as I looked, I saw a hole in his arm the size of my mouth. As I rolled the meat around in my mouth, I tasted something sweet. The man clutched his new hole as I absentmindedly chewed the elf meat. *It's pretty good.* I continued chewing and swallowed, spitting out a little sliver of bone.

"Did you just eat a piece of me?" His voice rose to a much higher pitch.

So?

I growled as I charged him again. He tried to get away from me, but I kept up with his movements and grabbed his shoulder. I slammed him into the wall. He changed the dagger to his other hand and wildly swung out at me, and I dodged.

The man regained some small measure of his composure as he kept the dagger between him and me. I made it look like I was about to lunge for him but stopped short of leaving the ground when the elf swiped his dagger back and forth. He started walking backwards out of the alley, but slipped on the blood pouring from his wrist.

I grabbed his leg and swung him around like a rag doll. He hit each wall with a satisfying thud and a cry of pain. I kept swinging him from wall to wall until I heard the distinct sound of metal scraping along the cobblestone ground.

I pulled him towards me and grabbed his left shoulder with my right hand. I hoisted him up and threw him against the wall again. He screamed when I dug my claws into his shoulder. It was music to my ears.

"What kind of monster are you?" His voice was weakening.

I responded with a snarl and then lowered his neck to my mouth and bit a huge chunk out of it. I tore away from it and dropped the dying elf to the ground like a sack of potatoes. Again, I ate the meat in my mouth. I enjoyed the sweet taste.

He placed his hands on the hole in his throat. His words turned to gurgles as he slowly drowned in his own blood.

I swallowed the meat. "I'm not a monster, I'm a beastkin," I said with a growl.

He tasted pretty good. Maybe another bite for the road. I shook my head. *No, I need to get Zenny home.*

My vision returned to normal as I turned to Zenny. "Let's go before someone finds this."

When I started walking past Zenny, I found my balance was off. My tail wasn't moving the way I wanted it to. I leaned against the wall as my vision started spinning.

"A little help here," I said. Unable to walk by myself, I held out a hand for Zenny. *Hopefully she can follow the sound of my voice.*

Zenny ran up to me, but she stopped to look at the mangled mess of a man. "Is he dead?" She sounded terrified.

I turned and looked at the elf. With so much blood pooling around his body, it would be more impressive if he wasn't dead. "Yeah, but I'm not feeling so good. Something about him..." My vision swayed, and I groaned. *There's something familiar about his ponytail. I can't quite put my finger on it. Ugh, something isn't right with me.*

Zenny wrapped one of my arms around her shoulders. Wordlessly, she led me out of the alley and down the street towards the orphanage. The farther we went, the more lanterns were lit in the street.

A guard patrolling the streets ran up to us and stopped us. The guardswoman panicked when she saw my blood-covered face. "What happened?"

"We were walking down an alley and a guy walked in behind us and said he was going to kill us, but Lucia killed him instead." Zenny spilled everything in one breath.

"Hey, Zenny, I feel funny." My world swayed even more, and I felt way too relaxed. I felt as if my limbs had lost all their bones and feeling.

"Where is this man? How could you have killed him?" the guard interrogated us. "Why is there all that blood around your mouth? Did you bite him?"

"Maybe," I said slowly before giggling.

"I know it may not look like it, but Lucia is very strong—stronger than any adult I know," Zenny said.

"Alright. Where are you going?" the guard asked as she looked behind us. "Where's the man's body?"

"Home!" I shouted, and tried to lift my arms up before giggling again.

"We're headed to Nora's orphanage. And the body is down in that alley there." Zenny pointed down to the alley. "Seventeen streets down."

"Oddly specific," she muttered. "I'll come find you after I confirm that he's dead. Go straight there, don't stop for anything. Your friend isn't looking good right now." The woman stood up and headed for the alley Zenny had mentioned. "Take care of her; something isn't right."

Maybe there isn't something right with your face.

Zenny carried me as my limbs became increasingly difficult to use. *I feel like a princess being carried home.* We arrived at the front door of the orphanage. Zenny didn't bother with knocking; she just opened the door and walked in, dragging me along with her.

As we entered, the door to Nora's room opened. Nora stood staring at our disheveled state. "Who did this?"

12

I'M NOT A MONSTER

"Who did this?" Nora repeated.

"You should see the other guy," I said before falling into another fit of giggles.

Nora's expression changed to confusion. Her shoulders slumped as her jaw descended.

Zenny didn't bother stopping; she just carried me in. "Can I have some help? She isn't as light as she looks." Her voice strained as she walked me into the building.

"Hey," I whined. "I'm not fat; it's all muscle. It's not my fault, my tail's in la-la land." I tried to put my foot down, and it just slid around on the wood. "Would you look at that? My leg went to la-la land too."

Nora snapped out of her confusion and helped Zenny by lifting my other arm over her shoulders. My vision tilted because Nora was taller than me while Zenny was shorter.

"Everything's crooked now." I giggled. "Did you know I'm called the Silver Breeze? Why does my tongue feel tingly?" I felt Nora vibrate as she stifled a laugh. I saw the bathroom door heading my way. "Why am I going to the bathroom? I don't need to go yet. Oh, I have blood on me. That's right."

The two carried me into the bathroom, where they stripped me and placed me in a tub as Nora filled it with water.

She turned to Zenny. "What's wrong with her? She never talks this much."

"Why are you so worried? I feel a little funny, and everything isn't working," I chirped at Nora. "It feels like all my limbs are asleep. But I feel so very relaxed right now. I think I'm getting tired too." I let out a yawn.

The two twisted their heads to watch me.

"Have you ever seen her yawn before?" Zenny asked without taking her eyes off me.

"No. You?" Nora whispered. She waved her hand, and the water stopped filling the tub.

"No." Zenny looked worried. "Maybe I should start at the beginning."

Nora grabbed the soap and a sponge, then nodded for Zenny to continue as she started cleaning me. "We lost track of time, mostly because someone was having too much fun."

"Yay!" I cheered as I heard a reference to me. I splashed the water around as I tried to lift my arms up.

Zenny gave me a quick glance before continuing. I saw her mouth move, but it didn't sound like she was saying words, just weird noises. I wanted to move and say something was weird, but my body didn't respond. My eyelids started closing by themselves. *No, stay open. I want to hear the story.* Despite my protest, my eyes closed, and I fell asleep.

I felt like I was floating in a bunch of fluffy clouds. I looked around and noticed that there was nothing else around me. *When did everything get so bright? What am I doing in the clouds? Wait, is this a dream?* I couldn't feel my body, but my body felt the clouds. They felt like cotton balls with a little moisture on them. I moved my arms and legs through the clouds and watched as the moisture swirled around my limbs. *If this is a dream, it's cozy, and I like it.*

My happy thoughts were interrupted as the clouds turned dark. It was slow at first, but they became darker shades of gray. As the clouds shifted to darker colors, they started swirling around me. Then the feeling of the soft dew turned into itchy thorns and shocked me. The sparks touched me but didn't hurt me. I stopped thinking and just watched the dream play out.

The clouds above me parted to reveal a large metal cage, and lightning in the clouds struck it. Even though there was plenty of lightning, there was no sound of thunder.

I couldn't take my eyes off the metal bars as they hovered above me. There was no bottom to it, and the bars were easily as thick as my head. I tried to run, but the cage dropped and my head hit the bars. I looked around for an opening, but didn't find one. *Something wants me trapped.*

I grabbed the bars and tried to bend or move them. No matter how hard I tried, they wouldn't budge. After I stopped and looked around, I noticed my prison was a lot smaller than it used to be. *I need to get out of here!*

I tried to free myself again, but the more I tried, the more the cage shrank. Even after I stopped, it kept shrinking until there was no room for me to move. Lightning struck the metal, but it didn't cause me any pain.

"Please, let me out!" *I don't know who can hear me, but I have to try something.*

The clouds above me parted to reveal a pair of massive blue eyes watching me from the darkness.

"Please, let me out!" I reached a hand out through the bars. "Let me out!"

I screamed and shut my eyes as the bars crushed my arm. Another scream joined mine.

I opened my eyes and found that I was sitting up in my bed.

"Lucia? What's wrong?" I heard a panicked cry. I turned and saw Zenny holding her forearm. There was blood seeping from between her fingers.

All of my senses flooded back to me, and my mind caught up with all of them. My heart was racing, my breathing was ragged, and I could hear the distinct sound of rain pelting the roof.

"I had a terrible nightmare," I said, feeling unsure of myself. *It was a dream, right? It felt so real.* Then I recognized the smell of blood.

My vision snapped to Zenny. "You're bleeding. What happened?" I reached for her arm.

"You were screaming and thrashing around. I tried to wake you, but you scratched me." Zenny grabbed the shirt she was wearing from last night and pressed it against the wound. "It's not that deep. I'll be fine."

"I'm so sorry. I didn't mean it." When I looked at my claws, I found proof of my action. "Here, let me help." I held my hands out.

Zenny placed her arm in between my hands. "I know you didn't mean to. What was that dream you were having? Do you normally get nightmares that cause you to scream?"

I started wrapping a shirt around Zenny's arm like a makeshift bandage. "No. That was a first." I shook my head. "What are you doing here in the first place? We have a spare room for you to use."

"Nora told me to sleep in here. We thought someone needed to keep an eye on you." Zenny's concern was obvious. "Are you okay? How are you feeling?"

I sat still as I ran through my mental checklist. *Head, ears, face, neck, shoulders, arms, hands, legs, tail, and feet. All good. Wait, something feels off.* "I feel good." My voice was even more hesitant. I looked at Zenny, confused, and watched her face shift to confusion too. "Actually, too good. Something's different."

I vaulted over Zenny and off the bed. My landing was perfect. I moved around, trying to find what was out of place.

"What's different? You look the same to me. At least you're clean after falling asleep in the bathtub." Zenny took a seat on the edge of my bed.

"Have you ever had one of those mornings where you wake up and feel like everything is going to go perfectly?" I struggled to describe how I felt. Zenny shook her head. "It feels like that. I..." As I kept moving, I noticed something wasn't there, and a light bulb went off in my head. "It's gone!"

Zenny jumped onto the bed. "What's gone?" She put her hands on my shoulders.

"All the soreness and stiffness in my arms and legs." I wagged my tail. I smiled at her and started giggling. "My head is clear too. This is fantastic!" I grabbed Zenny and gave her a big hug. I lifted her and started to twirl and skip around the room, giggling the whole time.

"That's great, but could you not squeeze so hard?" Zenny said through labored breaths.

I stopped immediately and blushed. *Oops.* I gently set Zenny back down on the ground and released her. My tail never stopped wagging.

Zenny hugged me back. "I'm glad you're okay. You really had Nora worried when you passed out. Once we learned you were just sleeping, we cleaned you up as best we could and put you to bed. You were sleeping so soundly that nothing we could do would wake you." She released the hug.

"Yeah, the last thing I remember was you carrying me home, then that nightmare, and then..." I looked out the window and saw that the sun still hadn't risen. "How long have I been asleep?"

"There's still some time before breakfast. Why?" Zenny shrugged. A rumble in my stomach answered that question, and Zenny giggled. "I guess some things don't change, do they? Come on, let's get ready for breakfast."

"I just wish what I got for breakfast would change," I said wistfully.

We brushed our hair and my fur before changing into fresh clothes. Zenny had to borrow a shirt, and we needed to get a bandage for her arm. I opened the door to my room and jumped when I saw someone standing in the doorway.

Wide-eyed and mystified, August stared at me. *How long has he been standing there?*

Zenny ran to the door in front of me and put her hand on my shoulder. "Relax, he was probably just walking by to get breakfast." Her voice was full of worry and concern. "He doesn't sleep much like you since he has the recovery aptitude too."

"I'm fine," I said. "I'm not angry." After I eased Zenny out of the doorway, I proceeded to the classroom for a bandage. "Go to the bathroom and start washing your arm. I'll be there in a moment."

So, August has the recovery aptitude too. That's interesting. Maybe Salien might use him as a test subject too. Volunteer! A testing volunteer. He's bound to hurt himself eventually, right?

It was quick and easy to clean Zenny's arm and wrap a bandage around it. Zenny then headed home so Salien wouldn't worry about her anymore. The sun was almost up, so she should be safe.

It's time for breakfast. I felt like skipping, so I skipped lightly down the hall towards the kitchen. *It was a rough start to the day, but we patched that up. I'm in a good mood. Today's going to be a good day.*

I entered the kitchen and saw Melody diligently at work. August was watching her.

"Morning," I said as I passed her by, still skipping. Out of the corner of my eye, I saw Melody's jaw flapping soundlessly.

I sat at the dining table. While waiting for everyone else, I swayed back and forth while humming a nonsensical tune. I closed my eyes and focused on the rain. The sound was rhythmic and relaxing. The consistent, constant splashes of the droplets colliding with the roof and exterior walls were easy to lose myself in. In the midst of the rain, I heard footsteps approaching.

I opened my eyes and looked towards the kitchen. Everyone was standing there looking at me, awestruck.

"What?" I asked innocently.

Nora snapped to attention first. "Who are you, and what have you done with Lucia?"

"I'm just in a good mood. I'm allowed to have good days, right?" *What's gotten into them?*

Molly spoke up. "There are good days, and then there's..." She waved her arms in non-symmetrical circular motions towards me. "This."

"Are you sure you're okay?" Nora asked.

"I'm fine. In fact, I'm better than fine." I flexed my arms. "Whatever was in that elf I ate did wonders."

Nora exploded. "You did what?" She didn't contain her volume.

I covered my ears. Everyone else had backed off and covered their ears too.

"All of you out!" Nora pointed to the bedrooms before she stormed over to me. Everyone scrambled out of the kitchen. She stood over me, intimidating me more than any other time before. "You had best begin explaining."

"I ate a few pieces of the elf that attacked us last night." My voice was barely audible as I made myself as small as I could. I grabbed my tail and held it close.

Nora sighed as she set a finger to each of her temples and rubbed them. She then pulled the chair out next to me and sat down, taking a deep breath in and slowly exhaling. "Alright, how about we start from the beginning?" She calmed down, and I didn't feel as frightened anymore.

I continued to hold my tail and spoke quietly. "We stayed out too late because we lost track of time. We got to the gate, and some strange people were trying to get in. They were a group of elves. After the guard let them in, he was nice to us. While we were on our way here, it got really dark and I was the only one of us who could see, and we turned down an alley and some guy followed us. He said that I had messed things up for them and that he was going to kill me because of it. I mentioned you, but he said that they had something planned for you. Then he said that he was going to kill Zenny because she was a witness. When he did that, I just couldn't stop myself. I had to protect her." I fidgeted with the fur on my tail because I thought I knew what was coming next from Nora.

I was wrong.

Nora hugged me. "I understand. It must have been scary to be cornered like that." She held me close and rubbed the top of my head to calm me down. It worked. I could feel my anxiety melting away. "What happened after that?"

I took a deep breath and released my tail. "I killed him," I said flatly.

Nora didn't react. I slumped my shoulders as I continued. "During the fight, I bit him twice, and each time I removed chunks of flesh. I ate them like I would eat dinner. Before you ask, I don't know why. I just did it without thinking. Like it was natural. If I'm being honest, I didn't think about anything in the fight, like I just knew what I needed to do."

"Did he hurt you?" she asked. I shook my head. "Did he hurt Zenny?" Again, I shook my head. "Did he have a weapon?" I nodded. "Was there anything about him that seemed odd to you?"

"He had a ponytail like one of the elves who had entered the town just before we did. I thought that was odd. Why would someone come to town to kill me?" *Why didn't Zenny ask about him? Maybe she doesn't want to think about it.*

Nora scowled for a moment before shaking her head like she needed to snap out of something. "That's something someone else has to look into. I'll take care of that. But I want to know what went through your mind after you killed him." Her voice was almost cold. *She isn't worried about the fact that I just ate pieces of another person?*

"Nothing," I answered as best I could. "I felt nothing. I told Zenny we needed to get home. But shortly after, I started feeling funny. It was like everything was slowly becoming numb. Zenny had to help me back here."

Should I have felt anything? Is there something wrong with me that I would eagerly kill a man? Why do I feel no remorse over my actions? I ate a person! I started crying.

Nora hugged me closer. "It's okay. Everything will be okay." She did her best to console me. "There's nothing wrong with defending yourself or those close to you." My tears were now flowing in a steady stream. "You're feeling remorse. This is normal. It shows you're a good person."

"But I'm not!" I shouted. "He called me a monster, and I think he's right!"

"No, we are not having this discussion again. You're not a monster. You are Lucia." Nora was stern. "Why do you keep believing strangers when they call you such horrible things?"

The tears were flowing down my face, soaking Nora's dress. "Because I did a monstrous thing; I killed someone. Killing is wrong. But I don't feel bad about killing him. Not only that, I ate some of him. He tasted good. I want to eat more of him!"

"Shh. It's okay." She was back to hugging me.

I don't know how long we stayed like that, but eventually my tears slowed down. As they did, Nora lifted my chin so I looked her in the eye.

"Feel better?"

I nodded. *Why do I feel better after crying?* I sniffled as I wiped my face with my arm.

Nora leaned back and wiped the tears from my face. "Now, how many people have you killed?"

"Three." My voice was still weak and on the verge of breaking. "On two separate occasions."

"And both times you killed someone, they called you a monster. Is that correct?" I nodded. "But I want you to tell me why you killed them." Her voice was soft, and the smile on her face put me at ease.

"The two who kidnapped me were going to sacrifice me, and the other guy wanted to kill me and Zenny." A light bulb went off in my head. *It was self-preservation both times.*

Nora smiled, and I knew that was what she wanted me to realize.

"I'm not a monster." *Stupid hormonal teenager body. I need to stop and think.*

Nora's smile grew even wider. "Now don't forget it."

"What about me eating parts of him?" *That's the part that bothers me the most.*

"How about we chalk that one up to being a carnivore?" Her voice was calm and sweet. "Honestly, I have no idea if there's anything saying you can't. You didn't start eating him after you killed him, right?"

"No, but I wanted to," I begrudgingly admitted.

"And what matters is that you didn't. I believe you have a good conscience. Because you were so bothered about not feeling anything when you killed someone, that means you understand the value of life." Her voice calmed me down. "I will admit, there are times when killing seems like the only option. Just make sure it's not murder. Do you understand the difference?"

"Yeah. What I don't understand is how I can jump to the conclusion that I need to kill so quickly and easily." I stared at the floor.

"Because you never do anything half-heartedly," Nora said with a smile. "In all the time I've known you, if you ever decide to do something, you give it everything you have." There was an uncomfortable pause. "I guess that might be why you get so frustrated easily." It sounded like she was unsure of what she was saying.

"I guess I don't understand." I looked at her, hoping she would clarify.

"When you try your hardest and it doesn't end up being what you hoped for, you get angry at yourself. You don't take failure well. And you're too hard on yourself when you don't succeed. It isn't all bad to have that kind of attitude. When you fail, you attack the problem until you succeed, and that kind of determination is admirable. But it has its pitfalls too. It can be self-destructive. You've got to be careful not to be consumed by your drive. You just need to find a balance between the two. There's only one person who is going to know what that is for you." She paused. "You." Nora touched the tip of my nose before scratching my head between my ears.

My stomach growled and broke the mood. The two of us started giggling. "I guess someone is ready for breakfast." Nora's smile returned. "That's enough serious talking before food. How about we go get the others?" Nora released me from our embrace, stood up, and headed for the kitchen.

I nodded, but my eyes landed on the wet spot on Nora's dress. "Sorry about that." I pointed to the location where I had deposited my tears.

She turned to me and smiled. "You should never apologize for expressing your emotions to me. It's unhealthy to keep them crammed inside of you." I thought I saw a tear forming in her eye. "If you ever need an ear to listen to you, a shoulder to cry on, or a hand to hold you, I will be there for you."

Why do I feel like I don't want to be adopted by anyone else right now?

13

COMBAT INSTRUCTOR

Is he almost here yet?

There were too many people walking around the training facility for me to focus. I paced back and forth, impatiently waiting for Allen to return with the man who was supposed to train me. It had taken him five days to find someone he believed would be suitable.

He said he would be back soon, yet here I am, still waiting. I'm getting so antsy that I might just tear apart one of the punching bags.

I'd been doing well with controlling my urges since that guy ambushed Zenny and me. Until today. When Allen knocked on the door and took me to his company's training room, it felt like a godsend.

The Brilliant Crusade training room was far superior to the one I used at the orphanage. Hanging from the ceiling were several punching bags filled with sand. Unlike the wooden training dummy in the orphanage, several metal training dummies stood lined up in a neat row. There was a small water dispenser installed, too. It reminded me of the water coolers you would see in office buildings on Earth, but it was made of copper, not plastic, and it didn't have a cover over the water. There was a spout on the bottom and a drain in the floor below it.

The thing that surprised me the most was the section that looked like a weightlifting room. There were benches with metal bars suspended above them, and instead of round metal weights, they used large chains attached to the bars.

Who taught these people about weightlifting? Another reincarnated person? Did other reincarnators bring something from their previous lives with them? How am I going to leave my mark?

My admiration of the facilities could only entertain me for so long before I wanted to use some of them. *But I promised Allen that I wouldn't touch anything until he got back.*

"Now, don't be alarmed, but Lucia is a beastkin." I heard Allen talking. *He didn't tell them beforehand? How did he get them to agree to this in the first place?* "She has a bit of a history of violent outbursts, so please go easy on her."

"I will," an extremely deep voice replied. "I'm curious to meet this beastkin."

I watched as two humans turned the corner and walked into the room. Allen's fatherly face was comforting to see. However, my heart plummeted as I saw the mountain of a man walking beside him. I looked around for exits but found that the only one was behind the hulking individual.

He's huge! I've never seen anybody that large before.

He was head and shoulders taller than Allen, who was already taller than the average of what I'd seen. His skin was dark brown, and he had no hair on the top of his head, but he had a neatly trimmed full beard of black hair on his chin. I watched as he studied me, and it looked like his muscles had muscles.

If he were the strongest man in this city, I would believe it.

Allen looked concerned. "It's okay, Lucia. This is Simyn, the one I told you was going to train you." He talked slowly while raising and lowering his tone repeatedly, trying to calm me down.

I kept backing away from the two until my back was against a wall. The man, Simyn, terrified me.

He looked apologetic as he spoke. "I understand you're fright-

THE BIG BAD WOLF

ened. I'm here as a favor to Captain Allen." He put on a smile. "I'm not going to hurt you. In fact, I dislike violence."

I shook my head. "That isn't helping."

"Then what would?" he asked as gently as his deep voice would allow.

I froze. Ideas flew through my head, but I couldn't focus on any one of them. "Could you sit down?" I blurted out.

To his credit, Simyn simply nodded and sat down with his legs crossed.

"Does this put you at ease?" Allen asked as he inched closer to me. "Do you want me to get Nora? Would that help?"

I shook my head. "No, I can do this," I said, more to myself than as a reply to Allen's questions. "Just give me a moment." I closed my eyes and took several deep breaths. I also tried focusing on a waterfall in my mind—anything to get control of my emotions.

Why is this guy scaring me so much? I know he's huge, but the frog was larger than he is, and I jumped on that thing without hesitation.

Allen and Simyn patiently waited for me to calm down. It took me a while, but I eventually did it. I felt guilty about my demand for him to sit down, so I moved off the wall and sat down on the ground myself. I couldn't sit cross-legged like him—it was extremely uncomfortable for my feet—so I sat down with my legs together and to my right. I patted my skirt down nervously.

"Are you feeling better?" Allen asked softly.

"Yeah. I don't know why he scares me so much." I lowered my head. *This is embarrassing.*

"I'm sorry, but I've never seen a beastkin before." Simyn did his best to sound friendly. "But I'll do whatever you need to keep me from frightening you in the future."

"It isn't something you did; it was just the sight of you," I clarified for him. He looked surprised when I said that. "A giant toad didn't frighten me as much as you did. But I have this feeling that if I were to attack you, it would be bad for me. With all those muscles, you might be stronger than me."

"Allen told me you have the physical aptitude." Simyn leaned forward. "That's why he asked me to train you. I also have the physical aptitude."

I shook my head frantically. *He has all those muscles and the physical aptitude? And my instincts pick up on something like that? No wonder they're telling me to stay away from him. If they can tell me that, what else can they tell me?*

A knowing look showed on Simyn's face as he looked at me. "While I can carry a stone slab twice my size, I'm not fast enough to outrun a wolf. Actually, a child can be faster than me." Simyn's laugh boomed around the room. I tucked my tail around and scurried back until he stopped laughing.

Simyn bowed his head. "Apologies."

I settled back down. "No, it's my fault. Loud noises tend to..." The apologetic look on Simyn's face grew. I felt guilty that he felt bad about laughing. "Sorry. I don't want to sound rude, but your voice is loud. And in a room like this, it makes it louder. Laugh all you want. But maybe tone it back a little?"

I'm a terrible person. That was rude. But it felt like I needed to explain myself. I folded my ears forward and lowered my head.

"You have nothing to apologize for. If something makes you uncomfortable, tell me. I won't be offended." He turned to Allen. "So, what did you want me to teach her?"

"She wants to learn how to fight." Allen turned to me. "But I'll let her explain what she wants. I know not to put words in a woman's mouth," he said with a smirk.

"How polite of you." My voice was full of sarcasm. I flicked my tail back and forth. "I don't like holding weapons, mostly because my hands aren't designed for them. Besides, I'm quite partial to using my claws to tear things apart." I held up a hand and extended my claws as I grinned.

Simyn flinched as I flexed my claws, but his face shifted from fear to seriousness. "I will not teach you how to kill." His voice hardened and deepened.

"I want to be a hunter, so I'll kill animals," I said as I waved my hand. "Don't worry. I don't want to kill people unless I have to. I need to learn how to fight so I can compete in the tournament and become a knight."

Simyn arched an eyebrow. "Why do you want to be a knight? What do your parents say?"

"I have to join the military because I'm an orphan, and I might as well have as much control as I can get." *Control is something I dearly want to have.* "Also if I can win, the prize money will go a long way to reducing my debt to the kingdom."

Simyn's shoulders slumped. "I'm sorry, I didn't know."

I waved my hand nonchalantly. "It's fine. I don't remember them anyway."

He looked like I'd just eaten his pet.

Allen stood up. "It looks like you've gotten comfortable with Simyn here, so I'll leave you two and get back to work. I haven't retired yet." He laughed. *Dude, read the room.* "If she ever gets too worked up or frustrated, just say, 'Waterfalls.' It's a code word." He walked out of the training room.

"How can you be so cruel to your parents' memories?" Simyn never moved. It looked like he didn't acknowledge Allen's leaving.

"While my village was raided by orcs, I was hit in the head, and everything before that moment is gone." I pulled my ears back and flicked my tail. "Besides, Nora is more my mother than they were."

"But they were your parents. You just can't forget about them," he pleaded.

"It wasn't my choice!" I stood up. "I have amnesia. Orcs captured me and brought me here. And now I'm forced to do things I don't want to do, like joining the army." I growled at the man.

Simyn stayed seated as he asked, "Why are you yelling and getting angry?"

"Because when I get agitated, I can't stop myself." I stomped my foot down. It still didn't make a noise, making me even more agitated.

"Alright, I'll drop the conversation." Simyn, still seated on the ground, motioned with his hands for me to calm down. "Can we go back to the calm conversation we were having earlier?"

"It's too late for that!"

I marched over to one of the punching bags hanging from the ceiling. With a growl, I jumped on it and tore into it savagely. After shredding much of the container holding the sand, I dropped to the ground and pulled on the poor bag, making the metal groan as I pulled as hard as I could. Without warning, it dropped from the ceiling as the nails holding it fell and danced on the floor. Sand spilled everywhere. I took what was left of the punching bag, threw it on the ground, and continued to rip it to shreds.

With the punching bag thoroughly shredded, I stood up and looked at Simyn.

Allen was also standing in the doorway. "Is everything okay?"

Simyn stared at me wide-eyed. "What was that word? Waterfalls," he said almost absentmindedly.

"I'm fine now, Allen." I moved closer and got out of the sandy mess I had made to sit down once more. "Again, you're a little late," I said calmly.

"Alright." Allen watched me as he left.

"What is 'waterfalls' supposed to mean?" Simyn was still confused, but he never shifted from his spot.

"There are times I get worked up and I don't realize it. This time I was aware of it and could take care of it myself. It's my code word that I give to people to say when I need to calm down." I relaxed even further.

"And that?" He pointed to the destroyed punching bag and the sandy mess.

"Is the best way for me to calm down quickly," I said flatly. I sighed. *He probably still doesn't get it. I might as well give him the tutorial.* "I'm what is known as a carnivore beastkin. So I have a predisposition to violent outbursts. And I can only eat meat."

"Are all beastkin like that?"

If he keeps making that face, it's going to stay that way. "No idea, really," I said with a shrug. "Honestly, I know far too little about myself. I do know that the way you can tell that a beastkin is a carnivore is by the teeth." I smiled and gave him a full look at my sharp teeth.

"Are those real?" He stared at them, fascinated.

"Are your muscles real?" I quipped back.

A moment of realization washed over Simyn's face as he broke into laughter. His laugh was still deep and terrifying. It sounded like something a villain from a story would have used as he gloated about his triumph over the hero. But this time, he did as he said he would and held back a bit.

"I guess I deserved that one," he said as he continued laughing. I laughed nervously. "Again, I apologize for my ignorance." He was smiling at me.

"You aren't the first, nor will you be the last." *It's upsetting how true that is.*

"So, do you want to get started today? Or do you want to keep talking?" he asked politely.

"I need the exercise, so can we start?"

"As you wish." Simyn finally stood up. "Your earlier display made me believe you really are a hunter. It reminds me of how animals hunt, or at least how it was described to me. However, that will never work against a trained warrior." He signaled with his hand for me to follow him. I complied. "You have the physical aptitude, which, while rare, isn't unique. Also, just because you're stronger doesn't mean that you will win automatically. Your opponent can defeat you through skill and speed."

"Then there's magic," I interrupted.

"Yes, magic is capable of far more than you can believe," he continued patiently.

"I live with Nora. I've seen a lot of magic. Trust me, I'm well aware of what it can do. But she keeps refusing to teach me any." I let out another slight growl.

Simyn looked at me, dumbfounded. "You okay?" I nodded. "Anyway, let's start with the basics and go from there." He waved at one of the still-functioning punching bags. "Let's see a punch."

I looked at my hand and then at Simyn. "That isn't going to happen." I held up a hand and demonstrated that if I made a fist to punch, I would stab myself four times.

"Oh!" He looked flustered. "This is going to be a lot more complicated than I thought." He looked at my legs and looked even more confused.

"This isn't going to work, is it?" I lowered my ears as my shoulders and tail dropped. "I guess being a beastkin is so different from being a human that I can't learn to fight from you."

"I wouldn't say that." He sounded like he was lost in thought. "How about we just figure out how strong you are and get you the exercise you want? I'll try to think of something over the next few days."

What do I have to lose? I shrugged my shoulders and followed his lead.

14

SO VERY VERY FRIGHTENING

"What happened to you?" May's head bobbed as she analyzed me from head to toe.

It just had to start raining on my way back. I stood in the entryway, dripping water. *There wasn't a cloud in the sky this morning, so I didn't take a cloak when I left to follow Allen. This is so annoying.*

"Shut up and go get me some towels," I said sharply. "I'm going to need a lot."

"Having all that fur must be a pain," she said as she headed down the hall.

"Go!" I pointed to the hallway. *Aren't you moving out soon?*

"Eek!" she squeaked as she scurried away.

I heard the distinct sound of thunder. It was still a long way off, but I knew what it meant. *Another night of locking myself in my room.*

Instead of May returning with towels, April walked around the corner holding a few. Her bright-red hair brushed her shoulders. I have seen her green eyes a few times, but most of the time she kept them aimed towards the ground like they were now. She stopped short of me and held the towels in her outstretched arms.

"Thank you," I said as I grabbed the towels from her.

She hummed in acknowledgment. She fidgeted with her nails as she stood nearby.

We don't see each other much outside of the dinner table. "What's wrong?" I asked as I covered my head with a towel.

"Have you ever eaten a human?" Her voice was quiet and full of concern.

"Is that still bothering you?" She nodded slightly. "You don't have to worry. I'm not in the habit of eating people. Unless they were made of bacon, which they're not. I don't willingly eat people. Besides, while elves taste sweet, the last human I bit tasted like dirt."

April shot up in fear and ran away.

That is not how you make friends, Lucia! Why did I tell her that humans taste like dirt? What possessed me to say that? Can people be made of bacon? Wait, are there pig or boar beastkin? Would they taste like bacon? Horrified at my thoughts, I hit the side of my head with the palm of my hand.

After hitting myself a few times, I got very dizzy. *I shouldn't hit myself so hard. I guess I can dish out the hurt but receive it just as easily. Maybe if I get something to eat, I'll stop saying stupid stuff.*

My stomach continued to insist on being filled.

"I know. I'm late for lunch." I hunched over and glared at my stomach. *This is your fault, you know.*

I hurried to dry myself off so I could run to my room and get out of these wet clothes. I almost slipped as I turned the corner. Desperate to silence my ever-insistent stomach, I forgot to dry the bottom of my feet. My wet pads slid across the wood floors. I didn't want to listen to Nora scold me for gouging the floors with my claws again, so I ran to my room a little slower.

I quickly changed into some dry clothes. Now that I was no longer dripping wet and the towels were thoroughly soaked, I threw them to the side with my wet clothes and promised myself that I would come back and take care of them later. *I hope there's food still available.*

As I ran down the hall, I could hear May humming to herself in her room, April muttering something incoherent to herself, August practicing his writing, and Molly's room was quiet. As much as I wanted to apologize to April for saying something stupid, I had a feeling that barging into her room would upset her. I didn't even want to know what would happen if my stomach growled while we were talking. I simply added it to my mental to-do list after she hopefully calmed down and I had something to eat.

Molly's absence of sound could only mean that she was outside in her garden in the middle of this rain. But then I heard a scream from the kitchen.

That sounded a lot like Molly. I opened the kitchen door and saw Nora and Melody huddled around Molly. Molly squirmed on a chair as Melody held her in place and Nora poked something in Molly's hand.

I cleared my throat. "Am I interrupting something?" I asked.

"Someone stabbed themselves with felonweed again." Nora dropped Molly's hand. "I'm sorry, but it's embedded in your skin. I can't grab it with the pincers." Mom placed the pincers on the kitchen counter. Pincers were basically tweezers, but wider.

"But it hurts. It can't stay in," Molly complained.

"Then get it out yourself, or we have to cut it out," Nora said coldly as she placed the pincers in Molly's other hand.

Melody released Molly and turned to me. "You're late for lunch, you know." Melody sounded slightly upset with me.

"I'm very aware." I said, as my stomach expressed its displeasure shortly after.

"It hurts. I can't do it." Molly tossed the pincers to the ground.

Your shouting won't help. "If felonweed is so dangerous, why do you grow it?"

Molly pouted. "Because they make great soaps."

"Then grow up, it's just a little pain," I mocked. "If you grow it, you should know how to handle it."

She glared at me. "I remember the time you stepped on a piece of glass. You came home and cried about it the whole day."

I couldn't hold back a growl. "That's because I walked the whole way back from the noble manor district after I pulled the piece out myself!"

"Girls, stop it!" Nora stood in between us.

"If you're so good with the pincers, you get it out!" She held the pincers out towards me.

"Knock it off! Stop, Molly!" Nora's voice rose as she again tried to end our bickering.

I gave an evil grin. "Fine."

Nora's magic pushed against me, and I glared at her as she said, "You will do nothing. Go to your room." She pointed towards my room.

Melody stepped up to Nora, then grabbed her arm and lowered it before whispering to her, "How about you let Lucia try? Molly wants the thorn out, and Lucia might be able to help."

"Can't you see she's angry? She might hurt Molly," Nora whispered in response, not letting her gaze move from me.

"She won't, trust me on this." Melody gave me a wink.

Molly looked around, confused. She likely couldn't hear them. *But I have no problem hearing them.*

I could feel the magic barrier drop as Nora said, "Fine, but I'll be watching." There was nothing sweet in her voice.

"It hurt going in. It's going to hurt coming out," I said with a huff.

"I don't care anymore. Just get it out!" Molly shouted as she extended her arm.

I walked up to her and grabbed her hand with the thorn in it.

"By the way, I didn't use the pincers," I said while grinning.

I watched as all the color drained from her face. She tried to pull away from me, but holding her arm still was effortless. The offending barb sat embedded in her thumb. The black spot was easily distinguishable from her now-red skin.

I guess that's why she is so insistent on having it removed. With one hand I immobilized her thumb, and with the other I moved a clawed fingertip to the thorn.

"What are you doing?" Molly started thrashing around. I held her tighter, but I was careful not to squeeze hard enough to break anything. Once I had made a small incision next to the thorn, I pulled the skin on both sides apart, making the splinter accessible. Since both my hands were occupied, I leaned forward with my face.

Molly's thrashing reached a whole new level. "No! Stop her! Don't let her eat my hand!"

I growled and flicked my ears at the screaming from the hysterical girl. *Now you're asking for it.*

I could feel the thorn with my teeth and bit down on it gently enough to not break it but hard enough to grip it. Molly kept struggling, and her finger pushed towards my teeth, making me push down on the barb slightly and causing her to scream even louder. After shrugging off the pain her screaming inflicted on my ears, I pulled on the thorn. It was halfway out before it slipped from my grip. Without thinking, I bit down on it again and finished removing it. I tasted the blood in my mouth as I released her hand. *Hmm, tangy.* I walked over to the sink and spat the splinter out. The barb was completely black and curled almost into a semicircle shape.

"You're welcome," I said with a growl. I then turned to the two adults. *No more pleasantries.* "I'm hungry. I need food."

Molly stared at her hand, seeing the small incision I had made and the absence of a certain thorn.

Melody was the first to recover. She grabbed a small roll of cloth and handed it to Molly. "Tell her 'thank you' and go bandage that up."

Nora looked at me in disbelief and pointed at my face. "You have a little blood on your chin." She reached for a towel, and as she turned back to face me, I stuck my tongue out to lick up the blood.

After licking up the blood, I grinned at Molly. "Mm, tangy." Molly reached a new level of terror. She ran out of that room faster than I had ever seen her run before. "What? No 'thank you?'" I called out to her before laughing.

"What is wrong with you?" Nora pinched my cheek, and I stopped laughing immediately. "Why would you say that to her? What has gotten into you recently?"

"It was a joke." Something about Nora always gave her the power to scare me. "I'm sorry."

"It was in poor taste." Nora released my cheek and wiped my face with the towel.

I thought the joke was about good tastes. I don't know how, but I kept that thought to myself.

"Do you have any idea what you've just done? That's all your sisters have been concerned about the last few days. They're truly frightened of you eating them now." Nora's voice was sorrowful. "Then you pull something like this." She was now on one knee in front of me. "Please tell me you don't want to eat any of them."

"I don't. It was just a joke." *Nora's really worried, isn't she?* I dropped my head and let my ears and tail droop. "I'm sorry."

"Just don't do it again, please," Nora pleaded in a soft tone. I nodded. "Alright, I guess I have to go explain this to your sisters." For a moment, Nora looked exhausted as she stood up. "I believe there's some lunch saved for you. Do you mind, Melody?"

She looks tired. Is she having trouble sleeping too? I haven't caused that much trouble lately, right?

Melody smiled. "Of course not. Go, I'll take care of Lucia."

Nora gave me a look of disapproval and walked off, shaking her head.

After Nora left, Melody walked over to me and placed a hand on my shoulder. "Go have a seat at the table, and I'll bring some food out to you." She gave me a kind smile.

"Could you not cook it today?" I asked optimistically.

"Unfortunately it's already cooked." Her voice was apologetic.

I shrugged my shoulders and headed for the dinner table. *I figured I could at least ask.*

I sat in my usual seat and waited for Melody to bring me lunch. The thunder got closer while the rain came down harder. *I'm going to have to eat really quickly.* It wasn't long before Melody arrived, carrying a plate with half of an entire hog leg on it. I salivated as I watched the delivery. Melody placed the plate in front of me and a fork beside it.

I wagged my tail. "Thank you, but, um, do you mind?" I asked hesitantly. *Is there a tactful way to ask if it's alright to just use my hands?*

"Go ahead and eat." She sat in the chair next to me. "I'm here to keep you company and, if you're willing, to have some conversation."

That's good enough. I picked up the leg with both hands and tore into it savagely with my teeth.

I was so fully devoted to eating the meat provided that I almost didn't hear Melody stand up from her chair. She headed to the kitchen without saying a word. Not concerning myself with her actions, I went back to the blissful moment of devouring my lunch. Melody had cooked the wild hog leg, but she'd left the center near the bone cooked to medium. She returned with a towel and held it in her hands as she watched me eat with a smile on her face.

I savored the flavor, but never slowed down as I ate it. After I had eaten all of it, I let out a loud burp.

With a contented smile, I turned to Melody. "My compliments to the cook."

Melody's face was a cross between amused and disappointed. "That's not very ladylike, you know." *I don't care.* She took the towel and tried wiping some stray juices from my chin. "Are you finished?"

I pushed the towel away. "Nope, time for dessert," I said as I snapped the bone in half.

I took a half, put it in my mouth, tilted my head back, snapped the other end off, then sucked the marrow out. *I don't know why or how bone marrow tastes like a sweet and savory jello, but I don't care.* After finishing the first half, I did the same with the second piece. I let out a satisfied sigh as I placed the bones on the plate.

Melody resumed her previous task of cleaning my face. I let out another burp, but this one was much smaller than the first.

"I'm glad you enjoyed it. But you really shouldn't eat like that." She was sweet, but I could tell she didn't think too highly of my belches. I took the towel from her to clean the fur on my hands. She sat in her chair patiently. "Did you really remove a piece of glass from your foot with your teeth?"

"Yeah, I'm pretty flexible. Afterward, I limped all the way home. It really did hurt, and I may have complained a bit once I got home." I finished cleaning my hands and gave my face one last wipe. "Since you asked a question of me, may I ask a question of you?" I placed the towel on the table.

"Go ahead." Melody grabbed the towel.

"Why did you talk Mom into letting me take the thorn out of

Molly's thumb?"

Melody visibly relaxed. "Oh, that. I feel we need to trust you more if you're going to trust us. You're growing up, and we can't keep making your decisions for you. Not that it's been going well as is. But there are a couple of other reasons I knew things were going to be fine." I blinked a few times. "First, you've never seriously hurt anyone lately." *Does she know that I've killed three people?* "Second, honestly, Molly has been too whiny recently, and I used you to give Molly her comeuppance." She smiled apologetically.

"It was kinda fun to see her running scared like that." I giggled before letting out another burp.

Melody shook her head. "We really need to keep you away from anyone who can summon a demon."

I flicked my ears to the side. "Why?"

"First it was a sin of wrath. The next time it could be a sin of gluttony." The woman gave me a wry smile.

"What do you mean?" I could hear the rain coming down even harder than before.

Melody grimaced. "I might know a thing or two about summoning. Anna often asked me questions about it and used me as her study partner. And demons, specifically sins, are attracted to those who are susceptible to their sin."

"I'm not that gluttonous, am I?" I looked at the plate with the broken bones. "I mean, I eat a lot, but that's because I'm still growing."

Melody snorted. "I've never seen anyone eat as much as you. I've seen people three times your size eat less than half of what you put away easily. There's a clear difference between growing girls and"—she pointed to me—"whatever this is."

The sound of thunder crashed in the distance. If I had to guess, it was somewhere just outside of town or in the nearby forest. The sharp crack caused me to flinch and cover my ears reflexively.

"Are you okay?" Melody placed a hand on me.

I slipped out from under her hand and got out of the chair. "I'm fine. It's just..." I paused, trying to figure out what I wanted to say. "It's thundering outside, and I need to be alone."

I took off running for my room while covering my ears. As I ran down the hall, August left his room and turned to look at me. He stood in the center of the hall, and I didn't want to stop. I jumped over him and cleared his height with room to spare. Nora walked out of August's room just in time to see me jumping over him.

"Wow!" August said. *Fantastic. Now he'll be even more fascinated with me. Since Mom said he's five, it probably doesn't take much to impress him.*

I didn't bother to see what he and Nora did after I landed. I dove into my room and slammed the door shut. Another sharp crack of thunder sounded. My heart nearly skipped a beat as my ears flattened themselves.

I really hate thunderstorms. They're so loud. And they remind me too much of the amulet. I had that stupid shock collar around my neck for two years until I was strong enough to literally break it apart with my bare hands. That of course showed me how much magic there was in that little thing. My ears bled while I was blinded for a few days. And ever since, thunderstorms have scared me far more than they used to.

I knew I shouldn't be scared of thunderstorms, but since I'd destroyed that necklace, I hadn't been the same during one. The sound of the amulet activating had sounded similar to real thunder, but it felt flatter and duller compared to the real thing.

I grabbed a couple of shirts before running to my bed. After I rolled the shirts up, I placed them on my ears and covered my head with my pillow before wrapping myself in my blanket. I prepared my anxious heart for another fear-filled afternoon.

I'm messed up. Here I am, hiding in my bed like a scared little girl again. Thunderstorms had always been a problem for me since I'd come to this world. The lightning was never the problem, just the thunder. My sensitive hearing made every crack and boom a painful experience.

The sounds of thunder increased in frequency and intensity as I curled up in my makeshift defense against the sonorous assault of sharp cracks and the rolling rumble of thunder. Every crack made me flinch and try to curl up even tighter. I stayed in that position throughout the night. Everyone knew enough to leave me alone.

15

DANCING WITH DANGER

I sat in the middle of a round platform with Simyn standing at the edge. Sweat beaded on his brow.

"Have you calmed down?" His voice still sounded as deep as ever.

I cracked an eye open and glared at the mountain of a man. "Some, but not enough. This isn't working. Every time we start, there's this urge demanding that I kill you." I dug my claws into the ground. "And every time you hit me, it makes things worse."

Simyn crossed his arms. Even though his hands were wrapped in layers of cloth to cushion the blows I received, my instincts just kept wanting to lash out. We tried covering my hands like his, but all that did was overheat me, and my claws would tear them apart far too quickly.

"I appreciate your restraint. But if we have to stop so frequently, you'll never learn anything. And I promised to get you ready for the tournament." The man hummed for a moment. "Though if getting hit makes you lose control, then all we have to do is train you not to get hit."

"How is that going to help me win a fight?" I stood up. "Isn't a fight over when one side can't fight? Shouldn't I be more concerned about how to finish a fight as quickly as possible so I don't get hit?"

"There is more than one path to victory." Allen stood up from his chair in the corner. "Yes, winning a fight as quickly as possible is one way, but if you have many foes, you need to know how to defend yourself because if each enemy inflicts a wound, each enemy will be that much harder to face than the last."

"And that's why I should sneak up on my prey," I said.

Allen shook his head. "In the tournament, you won't have that luxury."

"And that's hunting. This is fighting. They're very different." Simyn unfolded his arms as he stepped towards me. "Besides, if you get angry, you'll make mistakes in a fight. And mistakes can cost you your life. So we'll start by teaching you how to fight defensively."

I rolled my eyes. I did ask for someone to teach me. They were at least giving me some exercise, too. "Fine. What do I need to do?"

"Let's start with dodging," he said. "I'll throw some punches, and you try to dodge them. Keep your eyes on me and be ready to move at any moment."

I nodded and got into a defensive stance while flexing my claws. Simyn began to throw punches, slowly at first but gradually increasing in speed. They were easy to dodge, and I moved out of their way.

Then Simyn grunted and started moving towards me, and he stepped into his punches.

Simyn's next punch came for my head, but I managed to duck underneath it. I wanted to follow up with a quick swipe of my claws, but I remembered that this was about dodging.

"Good dodge," he said. "I can see you're itching to attack. Don't be too eager. Your priority should be to avoid getting hit. Don't overexaggerate your movements, either. Dodge only as far as you need to."

Simyn threw a series of punches. I dodged and weaved with impressive speed as he started throwing his punches faster.

Simyn was stronger than me, but I was faster. And my tail gave me far more control over my balance, so I used my superior agility to my advantage. I twisted and flowed around each of his attacks. There was a point where I started hugging his strikes as close as I could. As we kept going, he started adding kicks.

I don't know how he did it, but his body kept moving. Every limb danced in a never-ending flow that wouldn't let me catch my breath. Soon, his attacks were getting closer to hitting me. I could feel the wind brush against my fur as his blows missed me by inches.

Simyn threw a feint, and when I leaned back to dodge it, he followed up with a sweeping kick that caught my feet. I tumbled to the ground but rolled away from him and sprang up as he followed up with another kick. This time, I reached to grab his leg, but he pulled it back before I could wrap my arms around it.

"Not bad," Simyn said. He was breathing heavily as sweat glistened over his exposed muscles. "Better than I was expecting. You learn quite quickly."

Simyn continued to catch his breath, and then Allen stepped forward with a quarterstaff in hand. "Let's get some complexity into the mix," he said. "Lucia, I want you to focus on dodging my attacks. You won't always fight unarmed opponents. In fact, it's very unlikely you will fight any unarmed opponent."

I remembered when the two guys kidnapped me—one had used a sword, and the other hit me with a club. The swordsman likely didn't know what he was doing with it other than keeping the sharp end towards me. Allen knew what he was doing. This was going to be much harder.

I nodded, eyeing the staff warily. Simyn moved to the side to observe. His eyes locked on to me as I got into a defensive stance.

Allen took a few steps back, then lunged forward, swinging the staff in a wide arc. I ducked under to avoid it, but the end clipped my tail as it passed. I winced in pain and suppressed the urge to charge and rip the weapon from his hands. When he swung it around again, I took a step back to avoid the hit.

Then the knight captain opened the floodgates. The staff swirled around, and attack after attack came for me. Each swing was faster and more forceful than the last, and I found myself struggling to keep up. I knew Allen was a skilled fighter, but this was crazy. His movements were precise, deliberate, and minimalistic. I had even less time to keep up compared to when Simyn was attacking.

But as I desperately dodged, I remembered what Simyn said about keeping my movements as minimal as possible. It helped. I didn't feel rushed, and I started noticing a pattern to Allen's attacks.

When I started anticipating his strikes, everything became so easy. He spun his staff around again. I leaned forward, and the weapon flew over me. When I straightened, I hopped up, knowing that he would follow up with a trip attempt on my ankles.

The staff collided with my stomach. I immediately folded over the weapon as the wind flew out of my lungs. My knees buckled and I fell to the ground, clutching my gut.

"Easy there." Allen's voice cut through the haze of pain. "Slow, deep breaths." I could feel his hands on my shoulders as I heard the sound of the wooden staff being dropped. "Focus on breathing in."

I continued to try. But it was like my body wanted to exhale while there was nothing in my lungs. Eventually, I got my breathing started again.

"Are you okay?" Simyn asked. "That looked like it hurt."

"It did hurt." My voice was barely louder than a whisper since breathing was my focus.

"You got complacent," Allen added. "I could see that you were anticipating my movements before I made them. Don't do that. Wait for your opponent to commit to their attack before you dodge or block."

"Right." I lay down on the ground. "Can I just stay here for a while?"

"I think we've made quite a bit of progress today." Simyn rubbed my shoulder. "We can call it a day. Go home when you feel better."

Allen sat down next to me. "I'll stay here with you until you're ready to go."

I glared at him. "That really hurt. Why did you hit me so hard?"

He smiled. "Would you have learned your lesson if I just told you or gave you a light tap?" I groaned. "Sometimes pain is an effective teacher." He placed his hand on my shoulder. "But trust me, I wouldn't do anything to hurt you too badly. You have an unbelievable level of talent. What we need to do is figure out how to hone it and focus it."

"So you're saying there's a chance I could win the tournament?" I gave him the puppy-dog-eye look.

He laughed. "I would be more shocked if you didn't win it."

INTERLUDE: SHE'S NOT ALONE

Relegation. Another fate The Voice wanted to avoid. That meant The Judge would undo all The Voice's efforts to get to where it was now. The Voice enjoyed its dream job. Seeing all the different entities of the multiverse and giving them new lives was always thrilling.

But if it was relegated. Then it would have to start over again. The thought of going through thousands of iterations over as many worlds in as many universes, with no two being the same, nearly broke the entity. Being subjected to the same fate it imposed upon others, again, didn't sit will with The Voice. It went through the trials once. The Voice doubted that if it had to go through them again, it would succeed. Even if by some miracle it did, The Judge's decision would almost certainly be enough to deny it a chance to return to its original post.

Two bodies of light hovered in a large cylindrical room made of a single piece of white marble with swirls of tan and gray mixed. The swirls of color continued to move, as if they were liquids dancing on the marble. A violet sphere of light shone, but its brightness flickered constantly in the presence of the large pillar of orange light.

"I have a plan if they fail." The Voice watched the infinite pillar of orange light for a reaction. Anything to escape the fate that would befall it should the worst come to pass.

There was no visible reaction from the pillar. The Judge remained passively unbiased. "Then submit it for review. If I deem it sufficient to deal with your first major infraction, your sentence will be adjusted."

The Voice pulled at its consciousness until it found the plan it wished never to implement. Doing so would put it in debt to another. And while some of its colleagues were standoffish, others loved to mingle and make deals. One such entity offered to help The Voice with keeping its first major infraction from killing them. It was a terrible deal, but The Voice was desperate. No matter how far a being ascended, the fear of death was always in the back of their mind. So The Voice struck a deal with The Broker despite everyone warning it not to.

The Broker always came through with his side of the deal. However, he had a reputation for always taking more than he gave. Even if he took everything from The Voice—its world, its hope for future ascensions, and even if it had to work to pay off the debt— anything would be preferable to the vengeance sworn against it by its first major infraction.

That mistake had haunted The Voice since the one she sent that became her first major infraction had learned how to reach it. The mistake swore that he would do whatever was needed to get to The Voice, dismantling everything The Voice had created along the way. The vow wasn't the problem; it was that he could follow through with it, which The Voice feared. And once he'd dealt with The Voice, it didn't want to know what he had planned afterwards.

So The Voice sent the fragment of its consciousness to The Judge. It prayed that it would be enough. The Judge flickered brighter for a moment, a signal that it had received its plan.

Because The Judge didn't respond immediately, The Voice returned its focus to the two reincarnated souls it had sent. Watching the kids grow up was fun. A collection of fluffy white clouds stacked on one another held an image of a wolf girl running from a large black wolf until she collapsed, then some soldiers with long spears fought and killed the creature before they carried the child back through the city walls.

"You are watching the girl more than the boy." The Judge's voice broke the silence.

The sudden remark from the evaluator startled The Voice. "Oh. I hadn't noticed." It dimmed its light slightly. "She's much more interesting to watch. And since the old guy I sent before found the boy, things have been really boring. He's always being forced to read textbooks. No wonder he keeps sneaking in his favorite story books. I would be just as bored as he is." The Voice giggled nervously.

The Judge didn't express any emotion. "With the girl, I hope you realize that you have made yet another mistake with her. Although that is not an infraction, it is something that you should consider not doing in the future."

"What do you mean?" The Voice knew what The Judge was talking about. But it hoped that just this once, something would go its way if it ignored it.

"Do not play games with me." The Judge's voice sounded like the most powerful thunderstorm in existence. The orange light flashed, briefly blinding The Voice. "I am talking about how the girl is not alone in her body."

"There is a completely logical reason for that." The Voice tried to back away from the pillar of light as much as possible. A marble wall blocked any further movement. "As I sent the soul to Centari, the girl's original soul may have been just on its way out. And they may have touched, leaving a piece of her soul attached to his."

"It is too late to fix it now," The Judge said. "They are already fusing. At this point, separating them will do more damage than leaving them together. For now the soul you sent will be the dominant one since the wolf girl's original soul is just a fragment. Each soul will influence the other more and more, until there is no difference and you can't tell which one was which."

"The wolf girl is definitely more active and aggressive now than as a human," The Voice mused as it watched the beastkin child wrestle with a man three times her size. "That might be a good thing."

"Only if he doesn't lose his sanity." The Judge's attention seemed to shift away from The Voice. "So long as your mistakes of the past stay away and don't come here to disrupt our order, very little else matters."

The Voice hoped Lucia wouldn't find out what it had done. One immortal with limitless potential hunting it was more than enough to handle. The only saving grace was that Lucia wasn't an immortal with limitless potential yet.

16

CARROT

My mind raced with every worst-case scenario. *I'll be in front of hundreds. I know I've been practicing for this tournament all season, but I don't know if I'm prepared for the crowd. One mistake, one slip-up, one miscalculation, and my life is over. Training with Simyn and Allen has been fun and helped with my urges, but they haven't gone away entirely.*

Someone approached my door.

"You can come in, Mom." I didn't stop pacing.

Nora walked in. "You have to tell me how you always know it's me."

Someone's in a good mood.

"Trade secret." I stopped moving and pointed to my ears. I gave them a playful wiggle and smiled at Nora. *It's the way you stop before you knock. You always stop with three steps, then you put your feet together.* "I don't know about this." I dropped my playful mood to return to my panic attack.

"What's wrong? Is everything okay?" Nora walked up to me with a water wand in her hand. She closed the door behind her as she entered. "Do you want to sit down and tell me?"

"I would rather stand." *I just can't hold this anxious energy down.* But I took a deep breath before I continued. "I'm terrified."

"What's there to be scared of?" Nora kneeled next to me. "Isn't this what you've been practicing for?"

"It is, but there are going to be spectators." I scratched at the floor with my toe claws. "I think I have stage fright, and I don't know what to do."

"'Stage fright?'" Nora whispered to herself. "I haven't heard it called that before. Then again, I don't know much about stage performing." Her shoulders slumped a bit. "I'm sorry that I don't have any advice for you." Her voice softened. "You've been able to handle so much by yourself. If anyone can find their courage, it's you." Her smile was a small reassurance.

"I'm most worried about how everyone will treat me when they see me." My stomach felt heavy. "I'm so different from everyone else. Plus, I don't know if I can control myself every moment, especially if someone does something to make me mad. What if someone sees me get mad? What'll happen?" My heart rate increased.

"You are different." Nora grabbed my shoulders and forced me to look at her. I didn't fight her. "You are Lucia." Her voice was stern but still caring. "You are a wolf beastkin. That means there is a wolf that is a part of you. Don't smother it. If that means you eat raw meat and hunt with your claws and teeth, then so be it." Her head dropped slightly. "I owe you an apology."

I was confused. "You owe me an apology? For what?"

"It took me too long to realize that you really are always going to have that animalistic side of you. I've been trying to hold you to the same standard I've been holding everyone else to." Her apology sounded heartfelt. "If there's anything you need or feel you need to do, just let me know, and we'll do what we can. Okay?"

I stood dumbfounded. "Who are you, and what have you done with my mom?"

"I'm still here." She closed my mouth with a finger. "Just because Immianthe has been too busy to fit you into her schedule doesn't mean that my visits to her have been a waste of time." She smiled again. "A lot of the things we talked about were about how I could be better for you. She said that the parents of unruly children also need to be taught. The child isn't always to blame. We talked about trying a different approach with you. We just need to figure out the best carrot."

Carrot? Oh, right. "You're going to bribe me."

"Oh, no. That never works in the long run." Nora dismissed the idea with a wave of her hand. "No, we're going to focus on rewarding you more than punishing you."

I stared at her, annoyed. "Isn't that the same thing as bribery?"

"I didn't say punishments would go away." Her tone hardened for a moment, but her expression softened quickly. "And yes. We can promise rewards. A bribe happens before the task is complete." *Technicalities.* "You keep talking about how you want to hunt something." I nodded. "Maybe we don't have Zane and Marigold to take you. We can find you another chaperone. I might go with you, or I could ask Eleanah if she has time."

I remembered the talk I had with Zane and Marigold when I went to apologize to them. They apologized first. It was something I wasn't ready for. Originally, they didn't know how to say they were sorry after they found out that I was so injured from running from the wolf. They were happy to hear I'd survived when they went to tell Nora. They thought I was dead for sure. *For a while there, so did I.*

When I asked if I could go hunting with them again, they said no. It hurt, but the reason they gave felt almost understandable. They were trappers by trade and hunted to supplement their income. When they saw me stalk the toad and run from the wolf, they thought about it and decided that they didn't deserve to hunt with me. They thought they would only slow me down. *Wolves in this world are solitary hunters. But that's because in this region, they're an apex predator.*

As I finished reminiscing, my tail wagged vigorously. "Do you mean that?" *I've wanted so badly to go into the forest since talking with Zane and Marigold. Going out every once in a while with Zenny has been nice, but she can't keep up with me, so I have to go at her slow pace.*

Nora smiled. "Of course."

All my thoughts of anxiety were gone and replaced with happiness. "I'll hold you to that." I pointed a finger at her. "No more just telling me to go train with Allen and Simyn."

"Okay, okay." Her warm smile widened. "But first you have a tournament to attend. Have you finished packing? Do you have enough clothes? Extra underwear? Your brush?"

"Yes, Mom," I answered in a playfully exasperated tone.

She held out the wand she had brought with her and winked at me. "Just in case."

I took the stick and looked at her, confused once again. "Really?" My tone reflected my annoyance.

Nora looked offended. "It's a water wand." She sounded like that was the most obvious thing in the world. "If you need extra water to clean yourself or drink, it's yours to use for the time being."

I grabbed the wand. "Sorry. That makes sense."

Nora lightly scratched the top of my head. "Maybe if things go well, when we get back I can try to teach you something about magic."

I placed the wand in my wooden travel box. It was a simple crate that had a small latch with a ring to put a lock on, if I'd owned one. Neatly packed in it were my clothes, my hairbrush, a few of my left-over coins from when I was working, and now the wand.

"When I first arrived, you said that you weren't going to teach me magic. What changed?" I turned to face her, my tail wagging once more.

"What I said was, 'Just because I can use magic doesn't mean I'll teach you,' but I never said that you couldn't learn. But if anyone will teach you, it'll be me." Nora's grin widened. But her smile disappeared quickly. "Unfortunately, we don't know if you can learn magic yet."

"Don't ruin my happiness like that," I whined.

"It's part of the bad news. Some people can learn magic, others can't. Have you ever seen Molly use magic without a wand?" Nora grabbed my box and handed it to me. "Besides, you have something else you need to concentrate on." She held a finger up to my nose. "Remember, I said things needed to go well, but you don't have to win to do well."

"I'll try to keep that in mind," I responded. "But why do I have to go ahead of you? Why can't I go with you?"

"You need to arrive early to get fit for your gambeson." She placed a hand on my shoulder and led me out of my room. "Allen has agreed to take you with him. After all, it was his idea." *Something tells me that she didn't like that Allen has been pushing this whole tournament idea.*

Since May had left several weeks ago, I said my goodbyes to April, August, and Molly before walking out the door. Melody made sure I had my lunch for the trip and a little extra as a snack, just in case. *At least this morning she gave me a few strips of bacon with my eggs for breakfast.*

As we went to leave, Nora wrapped my rain cloak over my shoulders and tied it off. *It's better to have it and not need it than to need it and not have it.* Armed with a sack and a wooden box, I followed Nora to the north gate.

As we left the city, we walked up to a gathering of a dozen lightly armored individuals and their horses. Allen was talking to an elven woman with short blond hair. When he saw us approaching, he waved us over. The rest of the Brilliant Crusade were having trivial conversations that I wanted to ignore.

"Here comes our charge. You're going to treat her with respect," Allen said after he finished waving us down.

"What's so special about her?" I felt a tingle in the back of my neck as the woman's voice sounded familiar. She turned to see who he was waving down, and the world came crashing to a halt.

"You!" Avollea and I shouted simultaneously.

Even though I had grown a lot, we instantly recognized each other. She hadn't changed a bit though, physically speaking. I was almost as tall as she was, maybe an inch shorter.

"Oh, that's right. Lucia, you've met my niece already," Nora said cheerfully.

"This is what you want us to guard on the way to the tournament?" Avollea circled back to Allen. "You gave your recommendation away to *that*?" Avollea pointed in my direction without looking at me.

"Excuse me?" Nora and I exploded. My vision started turning red as the memories of the last time I met her came flooding back.

125

Allen stood up straighter. "Yes, she is. I told you to treat her with respect."

"I'm going nowhere with that racist." I pointed at Avollea.

"Avollea!" Nora's voice rose to a slightly painful level. I could see Avollea flinching too. "You will look at me this instant!" She stormed towards her niece.

I watched as Avollea slowly turned to face Nora. *That's it. You will get your well-deserved punishment.* I grinned as I stood back, ready to watch Avollea suffer.

Nora reached out and grabbed a hold of Avollea's long, pointed ear.

"Ah! What did I do?" Avollea shouted in pain. Her back arched as she reached up to grab Nora's wrist.

"You know full well what you did!" Nora's tone deepened. She forced Avollea to face her. "I know my sister raised you better than that. You will apologize to Lucia this instant!" Nora's tone intimidated me to the point of almost apologizing to her myself, though I didn't know what for.

Avollea grabbed Nora's wrist and easily removed the hand holding her ear. "I'm not that same confused little girl from all those years ago. I will not apologize to that beast."

I'm not doing this again! I placed my wooden box on the ground and my lunch on top of it, safe and clean. *You want an animal? Fine, you've got an animal.*

I growled and charged Avollea.

"She's our responsibility. We will—" Allen started, and then saw me running. "Lucia, don't!" He tried to move but wasn't fast enough. His words were enough to cause both Nora and Avollea to look at me just before I jumped off the ground to tackle Avollea.

My shoulder crashed into the bottom of her rib cage. I thought I heard a crack as my momentum carried us past Allen. As we collided with the ground, I was the first to orient myself as I sat on her stomach with a leg on each side of her. Avollea lay there in obvious pain and confusion.

"I've had enough of you!" My voice rumbled as I growled out the words. I reached for her neck, but before I could grasp it, she threw a punch, hitting the side of my head.

My world spun for a moment. I saw another punch aimed right at my face, but I caught her fist with my hand. Once her right hand stopped moving, she stared at it in disbelief. I looked at her and growled as I dug my claws into her skin. She screamed and she didn't stop, even when she rapidly and repeatedly punched me in the right side.

I growled and pressed down hard on her chest with the hand I was holding captive. Her punching stopped once I forced all the air from her lungs and prevented her from taking another breath through pure force.

Desperately gasping for air, Avollea grabbed my shirt and pulled me towards her. As our faces neared, I grinned as I prepared to bite her. The thrill of biting her was short-lived—everything turned upside down as she threw me over her head. I could feel my claws slice through the flesh of her right hand, scraping the bone as my momentum carried me away from her.

I tumbled to my hands and feet, then looked for my prey. Avollea had stood up. She cradled her wounded hand close to her chest, catching her breath as blood leaked from her injury.

I ran on all fours towards her. Without warning, the ground rose and collided with my chest, knocking me back even more.

I growled loudly as my prey kept getting farther away from me. My vision was completely red, and the pain quickly became irrelevant. Allen ran and grabbed Avollea. I ran towards them again, using all four limbs.

I'll kill you before you try to kill me. I let out a vicious growl.

Nora stepped up to block me. Her face was hard and showed no hesitation, though her voice betrayed her regret. "Don't do this."

"Stop this!" Allen shouted at Avollea.

"She started it," Avollea screeched.

"I'll kill her!" I continued my charge as I lost myself in my rage. There was nothing left of me as one thought ruled my actions: *I will kill her!*

17

A MOTHERLY PERSPECTIVE

Nora had never seen that look in the wolf girl's eyes before. It frightened her.

Lucia's charge was swift, but so was Nora's response. As the mother it was her duty to stop the girl. She willed the air around the beastkin to hold her still. She didn't want to hurt her, just stop her.

Lucia hung suspended, mid-stride, in the air. The primal growl that came from the wolf girl would have left many in a state of panic, but Nora stood resolute as a tear formed in her eye. Lucia flexed her muscles and fought the spell. Nora stumbled backwards as the spell shattered, and she suffered from the backlash.

As the wolf girl touched down on the ground again, she resumed her charge with the sole purpose of killing Avollea. Nora lifted her hand and punched forward with her fist towards Lucia. A hand, made from dirt, clay, and small rocks formed in front of Lucia's path and sought to grab her. The girl dropped into a slide under the hand's grasp.

Nora caught sight of some of the knights heading towards her charge. "Stay back!" The knights paused and looked at each other before turning back to Nora. "I don't want her to hurt any of you."

That seemed to be enough to get the knights to stand down.

Nora let the magic holding the hand together fade, and the hand crumbled back to the ground. She lifted her other arm, holding it perpendicular to the ground, summoning enough magic to create a narrow tidal wave of earth. Lucia couldn't stand up in time before the wave forced her away from Avollea. The sides of the wave closed in on the enraged girl, creating a dome of clay and stone, and the girl screamed as she pushed against the earthen wave, halting its momentum.

Nora wrapped her other hand around the wrist of her outstretched arm. She grunted as she focused on casting another spell, casting two spells at once draining more magic than if she had cast them separately. Her focus was more on the second spell , a spell she hadn't used in five years.

Lucia's screaming intensified as she clawed at the dirt barrier, digging her way through. Her arms were a flurry as the dirt piled up around her, but she never slowed down, and it didn't take her long to break through the dirt wave.

Once Lucia was through the wall, she started running on all fours. Nora collapsed to her knees as if she were a puppet that had had its strings cut. Her vision went blurry for a moment from the backlash. She knew her original spell wouldn't hold her charge for long. She simply wanted to buy time. Without getting up, she focused on Lucia and finished her holding spell.

The magic prevented the instructions from Lucia's brain from reaching her muscles. She tripped, and her face collided with the ground, hard. Like a tumbleweed, Lucia rolled head over heels several times before landing in an ungraceful heap.

Nora slowly stood up. The strain from how hard she was concentrating was obvious with how sweat poured down her skin. She approached Lucia, who lay paralyzed just an arc away.

Nora couldn't believe how hard Lucia had fought against her. The effort she put into her spell far surpassed the amount she had the last time she'd used it on the child. The closer Nora got to the girl, the easier it was to hold her. But with each passing moment, she could feel her resisting even harder.

Lucia stirred slowly. Nora was so shocked that her concentration shattered, and the backlash from the spell left a throbbing sensation in her bones.

Lucia stood and growled deeply as she narrowed her eyes on Nora. Blood dripped from her nose. Nora was glad she could finally get the berserking child to focus on her, but when she saw her daughter's eyes, her heart broke.

Tears fell down her face. "Lucia? Are you still there?" Nora asked.

The beastkin responded with a bloodthirsty growl. Her eyes didn't show the usual twinkle of playfulness; instead, their color had dulled slightly. Consumed by an unrelenting need for blood, the wolf girl sprinted towards her new adversary. Nora raised her arms in front of herself and, without changing her melancholic expression, clapped her hands together. She focused on the sound and used her magic to amplify it as much as she could with so little preparation.

Lucia's stride faltered as the sound overwhelmed her. She placed her hands on her ears reflexively as she stopped and lowered her head, and Nora watched her reaction with hope.

When Lucia raised her head to look at Nora again, there was a look of surprise and fear in her bright blue eyes. Nora's heart soared at the sign of Lucia's old self. But then the color dulled in her charge's eyes once again, and the pained expression shifted back to blind rage.

"Come back to us, Lucia. I know you can do it."

With newfound hope, Nora performed the same spell again, but when she clapped her hands, the girl didn't even flinch at the sound.

Nora tried to figure out why it didn't work, and she guessed Lucia couldn't hear anything anymore. However, the beastkin wouldn't give her any more time to think, as her target was almost within arm's reach.

Nora backpedaled and tried to call forth more earthen pillars to intercept Lucia, but the wolf girl crashed through the first one effortlessly, showering Nora with debris.

Claws outstretched, Lucia assaulted Nora, but the first two swipes fell short.

Nora hurriedly used her magic to launch the debris at Lucia, but her defense did nothing to dissuade the assault, and the girl slashed her claws across Nora's stomach, shredding through the fabric of the dress and leaving four horizontal red lines. Nora fell back, clutching the wound in pain.

Lucia intensified her attack, invigorated by the smell of fresh blood. She took a swipe at Nora's face and both slapped and clawed her. Nora collapsed to the ground, defenseless, her vision blurred. She knew better than to underestimate an opponent. But she wasn't fighting any opponent, it was Lucia, her charge, the beastkin child she was so fond of. The slap was a wake-up call; either she took her seriously, or she would die. Lucia wasn't in control anymore. Something else was.

The wolf girl stomped a foot on one of Nora's hands and buried her toe claws in her wrist. Nora let out a small cry of pain as her vision quickly returned to her, and she reached for the foot to pry it off. The girl growled as she raised a clawed hand.

Nora, afraid for the first time in many years, raised her free hand and conjured a small ball of fire, then launched it. The flame hit nothing because the child jumped back from her.

The wolf girl slowly circled around, watching Nora as she still lay on the ground. Then Nora remembered Lucia's phobia of fire. She slowly stood up but never took her eyes off the girl. What she was about to do would either work or drain the rest of her energy. If that happened, then Lucia would do something she would regret for the rest of her life. But it was her best chance to wake the girl up.

Nora started a fire in her hands as she cupped them into a bowl shape. The fire grew, and Lucia's eyes flickered with fear. Nora willed the fire to move towards the child, and she ran away from it. As the fire moved, it continued to grow and stretch out into a line, making a circle of flames around her and forcing her to stop and look for an exit. When she couldn't find one, she moved to the center and cowered.

"...nster." Nora heard a weak voice in the ring of fire and ran towards the beastkin child.

"Monster." This time, Nora could hear the word as Lucia spoke. Her voice was shaky and still weak. Nora released the ring of fire, and it evaporated into nothingness. Lucia lay huddled, face down, towards the ground in the fetal position.

"Not a monster." Lucia's claws dug into the ground. A smile filled Nora's face as tears flowed freely from her eyes.

Lucia leaned back and screamed out at the top of her lungs, "I am not a monster!"

Nora slid next to her and embraced her tightly. "That's right, you're not a monster," Nora said through tears of joy. She didn't know if Lucia could hear her, but she said the words nonetheless. "It's alright, I knew you would come back." Lucia cried as she returned the hug, and they cried until neither one had any tears left.

AVOLLEA RAISED her arms to defend herself. The wolf girl surprised her once, but she wasn't going to let herself die without a fight. A beastkin had killed her sister, and she wasn't going to share her fate.

Allen ran and grabbed her, pulling her farther away from Lucia. Avollea never lost her balance as she twirled before coming to a stop. Each breath she took was labored and full of pain as she stared at Allen with defiance.

"Stop this," Allen commanded Avollea.

"She started it," Avollea shouted. "Give me a weapon so I can defend myself and put this rabid animal down." Avollea moved towards her horse to get her sword.

Allen intercepted her, standing between her and her horse with his arm raised. "Nora will see to Lucia, and you will stand down. You will not murder that child."

"That animal wants to murder me." Avollea stared at Allen. "Am I supposed to allow that to happen? No, I'm going to defend myself." She resumed her march towards her horse. Once Avollea stood in front of Allen, he put his arm out to stop her.

"Do you want me to die at the hands of that creature?" she asked.

"If we were okay with her killing you, we wouldn't have intervened," Allen said bluntly. "No, we stopped her for her benefit, not yours." Allen's voice dropped to an annoyed tone. "After the way you treated her when you first met, how you reacted to her just now, and how you're continuing to act, I'm not surprised she has animosity towards you. I'm tired of your attitude as well."

Avollea took a step back in shock.

Allen locked his eyes on her as he bore down on her. "After I heard the story of your sister, I felt sorry for you. After the birth of your daughter, I thought you would have matured more. I gave you a second chance to redeem yourself, but you ruined that opportunity. Your actions are not befitting of a knight."

Avollea backpedaled from him, and her voice was much quieter than before. "Why do you defend it so? It's just a beastkin, and it wants to kill me."

"She's a child," Allen said glumly.

"We should put it down before it hurts someone."

"Your daughter is capable of everything she is!" Allen threw his arms out wide. His posture relaxed as he composed himself. "You should never judge someone based on what they *could* do. Do you see what you've done?" Allen pointed to the fight between Nora and Lucia. Lucia was lying motionless on the ground as Nora slowly approached her.

"Why doesn't she just kill her?" Avollea asked. "If she can't do it, I'll do it for her."

"Do you even hear yourself right now?" Allen grabbed Avollea's uninjured arm. "You're asking Nora to kill her own daughter. She views each child in her care as one of her own." Allen's voice became menacing. "Could you do it? Could you kill your daughter?"

Avollea shrieked in response. "No!"

"How would you feel if someone decided that your daughter needed to die because she was an elf? Because she could do horrible things?"

"They can't. I will raise her better than that." Tears formed in the corners of Avollea's eyes.

Allen extended an arm towards Nora. "Why can't Nora do the same? Imagine if someone killed your little Tamnila. How would you feel? That's how Nora would feel if you killed Lucia. Is that something you wish for her?"

Avollea dropped to her knees as her strength evaporated. She stared as Lucia ran from the fire Nora created, then fell into her inner turmoil caused by Allen's words.

Allen released Avollea's arm as she fell to her knees, broken.

Lucia leaned back and screamed out at the top of her lungs, "I am not a monster!"

Allen kneeled next to Avollea. "Did you hear that? She's just a child trying to find herself in this big world of ours. She's a person, just like you." Allen then stood up as Nora embraced the girl.

Avollea's neck went limp as she stared at nothing but the ground.

"Leave. Go home to your daughter and think about what you've done. I'll deal with your discharge later," Allen said as he turned his back on Avollea and walked towards the emotional pair.

18

TWO WOLVES

My actions were like a horror film playing out in my head. Each scene replayed itself as I felt like a passenger in my body. I felt every sensation and every emotion just as vividly as the moment I perceived them: the all-consuming need to kill Avollea; the helplessness of being unable to move; the satisfaction of injuring Nora; and the fear of the fire as it chased me. All of it flooded my mind. There had been one moment when I snapped out of it, but I was unprepared, and I lost control again. But once my fear overtook my rage, I could fight for control. My humanity won out in the end, and I cried out, determined never to let this happen again.

The tears flowed from my eyes until there were none left. I cried in Nora's arms as she cried over me. The only sound I could hear was a high-pitched ringing. My emotions slowly filtered themselves out until sadness was the only one that remained. I could feel my fatigue gradually catching up with me.

I tried to tell Nora how sorry I was, but I couldn't hear myself, so I don't know if what I said was what I wanted to say. But Nora brushed her fingers through the hair on the back of my head. Again, I couldn't hear anything, but I could feel Nora's jaw moving.

I leaned away from Nora so I could see her face, then shook my head to tell her I couldn't hear anything. She smiled, put her hand on top of my head, and scratched. My tail started wagging as I enjoyed the head scratches, but when I saw the claw marks on Nora's face, guilt overwhelmed me. I grabbed her hand and regretfully pulled it off my head.

I don't deserve any head pats.

Nora turned her head away from me after looking at me sadly. I followed her vision and saw Allen walking towards us.

His lips moved, but I couldn't guess what he said. Nora just gave me a quick glance and nodded. She pointed a finger towards me and then pointed up.

I think she is wondering if I can stand.

I released Nora and attempted to stand. An emptiness filled my heart the moment I let go. Reflexively, I wrapped my arms around Nora's torso until I saw the blood on her dress from the wound I'd inflicted. I flinched away and latched onto an arm. A hand patted me gently on the back.

Allen assisted Nora as she stood and pulled me up. I could stand, though my legs were weak. Allen held out a hand towards me, but I fervently shook my head as I squeezed Nora's arm tighter. She tensed up, and I looked to see why. Her expression looked like she was in pain as she tapped my arms.

I needed personal contact because I was feeling more alone than I had ever felt. Allen dropped his hand and said something to Nora, but she dismissively waved him away.

She helped me walk towards the town gate. *I guess we're going home. That's probably for the best.* As we left, I saw Avollea sitting on the ground with her head down, motionless. I felt nothing—no hate, anger, or satisfaction.

Our walk home was slow, and everyone stared at us. They were looking at me with sadness and pity. *How would they react if they knew I was to blame?* Eventually, we made it home, and Nora stopped just after we entered. I saw that one knight had followed us. *He has my stuff. I completely forgot about it. I guess I should thank him.*

Nora closed the front door, then lifted my chin so that I looked at her. She pointed towards the bathroom and gave me a questioning expression.

A bath? Sure, why not? I shrugged my shoulders. I didn't have the energy to feel much of anything anymore.

As we headed to the bathroom, Molly walked in from the courtyard. Her mouth moved as she looked at me inquisitively, and I watched as she kept talking. At some point, Molly just shrugged and walked around us while Nora led me to the bathroom. Even though an unending ringing filled my ears, I could have sworn that there was something else I could hear while Nora and Molly were talking. It was faint and impossible to identify, so I just chalked it up to my imagination.

Once in the bathroom, Nora and I worked together to strip, bathe, and clothe me. I wouldn't let go of her because I didn't want the empty feeling in my heart to overwhelm me again. She made no motion to deny me. Painfully, we straightened out my nose so it would heal correctly. Nora also cleaned and addressed her wounds, though I couldn't look at them. Every time I did, there was a pain in my heart that forced me to avert my gaze. The ringing lightened up as Nora was drying me off.

After I had put my nightgown on, Nora whispered, "Let's give you some time to lie down." She wasn't looking at me and was probably talking to herself since she likely believed I still couldn't hear anything.

"That might be—ow." The volume of my own voice hurt my ears. *Okay, new eardrums are sensitive.*

The shock on Nora's face was obvious as she knelt in front of me. "Your hearing is back?" Her volume wasn't much better.

"Ow." I flattened my ears as I desperately wrapped my arm over them to prevent the pain from getting worse. "Shh. Quiet please, but yes," I whispered.

Nora's eyes softened as she apologized in a whisper. "I'm sorry. Do you want to lie down? You've been quite lethargic."

"I might need that. Though I don't know if I can sleep." My voice wavered as I failed to look her in the eye.

"Do you want me to put you to sleep?" Nora gave me a warm smile.

"With magic? Sure." I continued holding Nora's hand. "But could you please not leave until I'm asleep?"

"Of course." Her genuine, full smile helped me feel a little better about the situation. "Come on, let's get you to bed."

We went to my room, and I saw my chest and lunch sack sitting next to my bed. I crawled into my bed, still holding Nora's hand. After she tucked me into my sheet, I looked at the bandage on her face. "I'm sorry, I—"

Nora placed a finger on my lips to silence me. "Shh. Go to sleep now. Come get me when you wake up." Her unwavering smile was the last thing I saw as she placed a finger on my forehead.

A tingling sensation emanated from where she touched me. I didn't fight the magic but gratefully accepted it, and my eyelids dropped like stones just before my consciousness slipped into a dream.

I was cognizant of the fact that I was dreaming because I found myself in the middle of a cave. Even with no light source, I could clearly see everything. I was curious to see where this dream was headed, so I walked forward, presumably farther into the cavern. The stone walls and floor looked real, but as I touched them, they had no texture.

I continued until I found myself in a spherical room, and in the center of the room was a large steel cage. I jumped at the sight of the creature inside of it. An enormous wolf, coated with the same silver fur as I had, thrashed around as much as it could. It bit and clawed at the bars with little effect, but it desperately attempted to escape its confinement that was barely larger than it was. I had heard no sounds until I entered the room. But once I did, growling, barking, and claws scraping against steel overwhelmed me for a moment.

I felt a unique connection between me and the caged wolf, but I feared what would happen if it got out. *Will it kill me or thank me?* I looked at the wolf closer and saw several outlines of ribs. The wolf was female, and its fur looked mangy.

"Poor girl, who would force a creature to die of starvation like this?" I asked, knowing that nobody was around to answer.

The wolf turned its head towards me as if it could hear and understand me. It growled and snapped at the bars in my direction. A recognizable fury filled the wolf's eyes as it futilely reached for me through the bars.

I took a half-step back in surprise, feeling conflicted. I wanted to run from the furious animal, but I couldn't take my eyes off it.

It feels so real that it's hard to remember that this is nothing more than a dream.

The wolf stopped reaching for me from its cage. I saw the expression in its eyes change. Its eyes shifted, becoming intelligent, though I don't know why I knew that.

The scenery shifted around me. I went from standing in a cave to standing in the middle of an open field. Wind blew through my hair, and the smell of the clean air relaxed me. However, just as I was enjoying those feelings, they went away as the dreamscape changed again.

The land changed into a lush forest full of flora and fauna. The joy of running through the woods gripped me. I soon savored the thrill of the hunt, chasing prey until I caught it.

Everything shifted back to the cave as I lost the feeling of those wonderful emotions. I noticed I felt all of them without moving an inch.

I collected myself and turned to the wolf. It glared at me.

"Was that you?" I whispered, worried that something else was in control of my dream. The wolf nodded. *This thing is sentient? What is it doing in my dream?* There was a more important question that needed answering. "Why are you angry with me? What did I do?"

My vision swam as I soon found myself in the same cave, but this time it was full of humans and elves. They were all holding makeshift weapons and torches. I saw the wolf cowering as they corralled it into the cage. The sharp points of spears and pitchforks stabbed at the wolf. She flinched each time, slowly backing into the cage. As she entered it, a beastkin walked out of the crowd, a mirror image of myself with the same silver fur. My imposter closed and locked the cage with the wolf inside.

I looked at my hands in shock.

What does this mean? I didn't do that, did I?

A low growl forced me to look up. I was standing next to the cage, where my double had locked it. My eyes were inches away from the wolf's face.

"Am I really the one who put you here?" The wolf nodded slightly. "Do you want to kill me?" She shook her head, then pawed at the door. "You just want out." She nodded.

"There's a story where I'm from." I felt an uncomfortable feeling in my gut as I continued to talk to the wolf. "A child goes up to an adult and tells him he feels like there is fighting going on within him. The adult tells the child that within everyone, there are two wolves fighting. One is dark, and the other is light. The child asks which wolf wins, and the adult tells the child it's the one you feed." I chuckled at the scene I found myself in. "You're the wolf inside me, aren't you?" The wolf didn't react. "I see that story in a new light now. There was more to the story, but I've forgotten it. I'm not even sure if what I remember is correct anymore, but the general gist is there, I think. All those times I lost control or got restless. That was you."

The wolf moved to lie down in the cage and gave me a knowing look.

"But I can't bring myself to trust you. You're just too wild. How many times have I hurt someone because you were too violent? How many times did I break something because of you?"

The wolf lay there, unmoving.

I turned and walked away from the cage. "Maybe it's time I starved you out. Then maybe I can control myself."

The wolf stood up and her growl followed me as everything dissolved around me and I felt myself waking up.

Wow, that was a weird dream.

I sat up in my bed. It was the middle of the night. My body was feeling better, although there was some stiffness in my muscles. The feeling of loneliness was gone. I reflected on my dream before I felt a familiar tug to go for a run and a rumble in my stomach. For the first time, I knew what the message was.

It's time to go hunting. I don't care that it's the middle of the night.

She won't shut up. Until I can figure out how to shut her up for good, I'll appease her just enough.

After hopping out of bed, I got dressed and, since I didn't want to wake anyone up, I went out my window into the courtyard. As I walked towards the street, each step felt lighter and easier than ever before.

19

WHO LET THE WOLF OUT?

I jumped the fence leading to the street. *A quick warm-up run to the forest north of town sounds like fun.* The streets were dimly lit as I jogged through them at a relaxing pace. It was easy to avoid the few guards patrolling. I didn't want to explain why I was running around in the middle of the night. It just sounded like a recipe for misunderstandings. I ran out the north gate, enjoying the feeling of the wind flowing through my hair.

"Hey, wait!" the guards called out as I rushed past them.

Don't worry, I'll be back to answer your questions. I'm hungry.

I raced straight for the woods, picking up the pace. A simple nudge urged me to lean forward and run on all fours. *It looks like someone's eager for a run.* Desperate to shut her up, I dropped to all fours, and it was much easier. It was like the wolf inside me took over and showed me how easy it really was. There was a rhythm to it. And now that I saw it, I felt stupid for not getting it sooner.

Okay, fine. That wasn't too bad. You aren't completely useless.

Once I arrived at the edge of the forest, I stopped. I admired the atmosphere. A sliver of the green moon remained while the other two moons, the yellow and red ones, were full and filled the night with light. The branches swayed with a gentle breeze. I could hear some insects buzzing in the distance.

I always enjoy how quiet things are at night. Nobody shouting or running around, no blacksmiths or carpenters hammering, and no stench from the city's sewage system.

I started into the forest, driven by another growl from my bottomless pit of a stomach. As I prowled the woods, I searched for any signs of wildlife. I found many tracks, but that didn't help because I would constantly lose track of what I was following. I was slowly getting frustrated.

Aren't forests supposed to be full of life? Where are all the animals?

In the middle of my mental rant, I heard the subtle noise of something breathing. I froze as I focused on locating the direction of the sound. It was some distance off.

I then considered the wind's direction and adjusted my approach to come from downwind of whatever was making the noise.

It's so quiet at night that it makes any sound that much easier to hear. I have to be extra careful.

I curbed my excitement as I picked my steps carefully, avoiding all the fallen twigs and small vegetation. My patience was rewarded when I found the source of the noise: a sleeping deer.

The deer in this world look like moose, but I think they're related, so it isn't too difficult to follow the logic.

The buck slept soundly with its head facing me, completely unaware of me.

I almost feel bad about killing an animal in its sleep. But I smirked to myself. *Oh well, survival of the fittest. I believe that's how it works in the wild. Unfortunately, everything is vulnerable while it sleeps. I'm just rewarded for being able to sneak up on it. Wait, why do I need to rationalize this to myself? I came out here to hunt, and now there's prey lying right in front of me. So what's the best way to do this?*

I suppressed the urge to jump on its back and start clawing and biting. *There is definitely a better way to do this.*

The deer was lying on its stomach with its legs curled underneath its body. *That neck looks like a juicy target. Go for the jugular? I don't know, its neck is pretty thick. The spine? Yeah, that will work.* I wagged my tail excitedly. With my plan ready, I crept soundlessly towards my soon-to-be victim. When I was within pouncing distance, one of its ears twitched. *Too late.*

The deer lazily opened its eyes as I left the ground, mouth open and claws extended. I landed on the right side of the deer's front shoulders. Because I didn't want to be introduced to its impressive horn display, I grabbed the base of the neck and dug in with my claws as I brought my mouth to where I believed its vertebrae should be.

The deer panicked and stood up with me dangling from its neck. I curled my legs under the deer's ribs. My bite met resistance from what I assumed to be bone. I bit even harder, attempting to sever the spinal cord, killing the deer quickly and easily.

The creature flailed around as the bones cracked and gradually gave way. I growled as the deer bellowed in pain and fear. It made another attempt to skewer me on its antlers as it jumped and turned. I pulled myself closer to it, but I could feel the back of the antlers almost collide with my ribs.

Snap! My jaws closed completely as the bone relented to me. The deer fell to the ground gracelessly. I flipped over the beast as it hit the dirt, carried by the momentum of the fall.

"Yuck, hairball." I giggled. I kneeled next to its throat. "Nothing personal, buddy, but a girl's gotta eat."

I opened his throat and lifted the back half up to drain the blood. Certain organs could ruin the meat, so I opened the deer up to remove them. I moved carefully even though I had practiced field dressing smaller animals that were caught in traps with Zane. With the offensive organs removed, I cracked the sternum and opened the chest cavity to help cool it down faster.

I looked at the heart. *You know what? I earned a quick snack before heading home.* I plucked it out and ate it like a human would eat an apple. The taste was decent, but the texture was divine. *It's like my version of bubble gum, except that I can't blow bubbles with it.*

After savoring the chewy texture of the heart, I grabbed the antlers and hoisted the carcass up on my shoulders, then happily trotted off towards where I thought the south was. *My sense of direc-*

tion has gotten better, but if I spend a little more time walking in this tranquil forest tonight, I won't complain.

I arrived at the gate before sunrise, but I could see the light on the horizon glowing orange. There stood a guard, staring at me like I had done something wrong.

"You returned." The guard walked up to me from just inside the gate. His voice was lower than most, while still being quieter than most.

Looking around exaggeratedly, I tried to see if someone else could be the target of the comment. "Yes, I live here. Of course I would come back. There was something I had to do." I adjusted the deer on my shoulders. *Even as strong as I may be, after carrying this guy for a while now, it's wearing on me. I may have underestimated its weight.*

"Did you kill that?" he asked. "How are you carrying it?"

"That's the Silver Breeze. She has the physical attribute. Didn't you pay attention to the briefing?" Another guard approached us and stopped next to the first one. He was a lot smaller than the other guy.

The large guard turned to his coworker. "They actually have something important to say in those briefings?" he asked with exaggerated surprise. "I sleep through them with my helmet on."

"You always do that. After all the work that's put into them, how could you just spit on our superiors' effort?" The shorter guard sounded honestly distressed.

"Even after all your brown-nosing, you're still just a simple guard."

I watched the two guards bicker between themselves. "Look, I'd love to listen to you bicker all night. However, this deer is heavy. I'd like to go home and set it down," I shouted.

Both guards flinched at my outburst.

"Yeah, you're free to go. Just don't stop until you get home. I'm sure Nora's worried about you," the smaller guard said without moving.

"Thank you." I walked past the pair. "As you were, gentlemen." *How famous am I? They had briefings about me? Why?*

"Just so you know, my time is coming someday." *Who are you trying to convince there, buddy—your friend or yourself?*

"Yeah, and the sun rises in the west." The mocking tone was the last thing I heard before I blocked them out, before I lost more of my intelligence.

I slowly made my way back to the orphanage because carrying the deer was getting really tiring. Unfortunately, once the orphanage was in sight, I saw Nora standing at the front door with her arms crossed. I knew I was going to get an earful.

She's upset. After yesterday's events and now that I snuck out of the orphanage, I guess I haven't been all that well behaved. I walked meekly up the steps but stopped short, bracing myself for whatever was to come.

The expected yelling didn't happen. Instead, I heard snickering. I looked up and saw Nora clutching her stomach as she laughed so hard that her breathing became labored and tears ran down her cheeks.

Okay, I may have been ready for a lot of things, but not this. I stared dumbfounded at my caretaker.

Once Nora had finished laughing, caught her breath, and wiped her tears, she smiled at me. "Of all the times you teenage girls sneak out, you're the first to bring something back. And a whole deer at that." Nora held back more laughter.

"So you're not mad?" I asked stupidly.

"I'm upset that you didn't tell me." She looked at me a little heartbroken. "We have food for you, or did you need to burn some energy?" Then her gaze changed. *What's she looking for?* "Your eyes, they're different. It's like they're brighter."

"I'll tell you about it later, but can I put this somewhere? It's getting heavy." I nodded my head at the deer carcass on my shoulders.

She opened the front door. "Bring it to the courtyard. Do you want to tell me why there's blood all over your face? Or am I right to assume you had a taste of your catch?"

I entered the orphanage, eager to put the deer down. *Once I set this thing down, I won't be able to pick it up for a while.*

I joyfully answered Nora's question. "I already ate the heart."

"Of course you did," Nora said under her breath. I could feel her eyes rolling as she closed the door behind her while she followed me.

"I'm guessing you're still hungry and want some breakfast." She moved past me to open the door to the courtyard.

"Yeah, I'm still hungry, just not starving like I was earlier." After I entered the courtyard, I headed over to a table that was set up. After putting my prize down, I turned to Nora. "I know you have questions. I have a few of my own, but can they wait until after I take a bath? All this dried blood is starting to itch."

"You are a bit of a mess right now," Nora said lightheartedly.

She extended an arm towards me, inviting me to walk beside her, and I walked silently next to her until we reached the bathroom. She filled a tub while I went to grab some clean clothes.

She greeted me at my bedroom door. "Go clean yourself up and then come get some breakfast. I'll wake everyone else up. There should be enough towels for you."

Today's going better than I could ever have hoped. I got some meat for a few days, and I didn't get in trouble for sneaking out.

With a bounce in my step, I nearly skipped to the bathroom. I quickly took my bath, even though it required more scrubbing than I expected, getting all the dried blood out of my fur. While I dried myself off, I stopped and stared at my breasts.

They're definitely growing. I don't know how I feel about that. I guess, being a woman, they come with the territory. This cements it for me. I can have kids. Do I want kids? Part of me is going to really want kids. That means I'll want to find a mate. I don't know if I can bring myself to have sex with a man. Do I find men attractive? I pondered for a moment. *Nope. Do I find women attractive? Again, no, but that may be because I'm still a little young. I have another two years until I start going into heat. Then, three years after that, I'll be a full-grown adult. It's kinda weird growing up so quickly.*

I snapped out of my mental rabbit hole. After drying, I put my clothes on. I dumped the bloodstained clothes on the floor inside my room as I grabbed my brush, then took care of my hair as I walked towards the dining room, my tail wagging behind me.

20

THE WOLF'S OUT OF THE BAG

The smell of cooked eggs informed me that everyone was likely waiting for me or that they had started without me. *This is my second breakfast, after all.* I walked into the dining room and the three other kids stopped eating to stare at me. They clearly all wanted to ask the same question, but for some reason, they didn't.

"I know what you all want to ask, but I don't want to talk about it." Each of the kids flinched slightly.

I looked at Nora's face and saw that it was no longer bandaged. She had a large bruise that was centered on her upper cheek and formed a perfect circle from her left eye to her nose, down to just below her lip, and reached halfway towards her long ears. There were three thin scabs from my claws that reached for her hair from the bruise. The guilt of my actions threatened to ruin my composure. I opened my mouth to apologize, but before any words came out, Nora shook her head to tell me not to say anything. *I guess we'll get it all out once breakfast is done and the other kids are busy elsewhere.*

I moved towards my seat and saw the infamous plate of eggs. *There's a perfectly good deer outside. Why do they insist on feeding me these stupid eggs?* I slammed my brush down on the table and then shoved the plate of eggs away from my seat towards the other kids. They didn't move an inch, other than following my movements with their eyes. I walked towards the courtyard door.

"Where are you going?" Nora tilted her head slightly.

"To get a proper breakfast," I said curtly.

I grabbed the door when Melody called out to me. "But there's a plate of eggs for you."

"No!" I threw open the door. "No more eggs." I infused my voice with a slight rumble.

Stomping my feet, I stormed outside and harvested a new, proper breakfast for myself from my morning hunt. I carried a whole tenderloin back to the dinner table. The look on everyone's faces was priceless.

"This is a proper breakfast." I held up the tenderloin triumphantly. Everyone stared at me in shock as I sat down.

"You aren't going to eat the whole thing, are you?" Melody whispered.

"Probably," I replied before I took my first juicy bite. A few drops of blood rolled down my chin. I leaned forward so that the blood would drip onto the table and not onto my clean clothes.

"Could you at least use a plate and fork?" The energy usually found in Nora's voice seemed to be gone.

The plate will be fine, but it's too late for the fork. I grabbed the plate of eggs that they expected me to eat earlier and, with a tap on Nora's plate, dumped the pile of eggs there. I placed the cleared plate under my meat and chin, ready to catch more drippings.

"You can split that amongst everyone but me. We wouldn't want it to go to waste now." I was in a sassy mood and let my impulses mostly run wild. I continued my crude carnivorous consumption.

Nora's face twisted and scrunched up. She silently stood up and walked to everyone else's plates, scraping a portion of extra eggs on them, never taking her eyes off of me as she walked around the table. As she sat down, everyone slowly returned to eating.

This has got to be the most awkward moment since we had to explain to August why he's a human and I'm a beastkin.

I peeked at August as he ate. He stared at me with the same fascination he always did. I ignored him and concentrated on my food. Everyone finished eating in silence.

"Melody, please take the other three and help them pack properly," Nora instructed while staring me down. I started wishing I could run away. The room felt warmer as I felt Nora's stare burn a hole through me. "Leave the dishes. They'll be taken care of in a moment."

Melody herded the three kids out of the dining room and then through the kitchen, quickly leaving me alone with Nora.

"Are you going to explain yourself?" I shivered in fear at the sound of Nora's mom voice.

"There's a perfectly good explanation." I held up my hands in surrender, and Nora waited for me to continue. "To begin with, I was a hypocrite." The shocked expression on Nora's face told me she didn't see that coming. "You were right. There's a wolf inside me." She looked like she was about to say something, but I lifted a finger to stop her. "Let me get it all out before you say anything."

I took a moment to recompose myself. "I've been dealing with my more animalistic tendencies. I was still clinging to trying to be a human that was just physically different. Trying to fit in. I know it looked like I had accepted what I am, but I merely cherry-picked what aspects I liked. My sharper senses and my tail, for example. But I never paid attention to my need to hunt something, and I fought the excessive amount of energy, hoping that I would just grow out of it." I dug my claws into the edge of the table. "I realize now that it won't work and that I shouldn't have tried. But there's something different about the wolf in me—something more. There's one thing it won't abide by and I have to agree with it." My voice dropped as I tried to explain what had happened yesterday. "All threats to me will be eliminated."

"Stop," Nora interrupted me. "We will not talk about yesterday."

"But I need to." My eyes started watering. "A part of me hated that you tried to stop me, but I also can't thank you enough for succeeding. I never wanted to hurt you, but I won't let anyone treat me like I'm less than a person." The water in my eyes turned into a fiery fury.

"I'm glad you're strong enough to stand up for yourself." Nora smiled slightly. "But she's my niece, and I wouldn't let you ruin your life by murdering her." I opened my mouth to protest, but Nora spoke up first. "I know you were caught up in the moment, but in that situation, the letter of the law would have labeled you a murderer the moment you killed her. If she'd had a weapon on her and drawn it, then you would have been able to claim self-defense. Racism, no matter how repulsive, is technically not a punishable crime in any kingdom." I could feel Nora's heart drop as she said that.

"I guess that never changes, does it?" I felt defeated. "Here I am in a whole other world, and racism developed here too."

"There was racism in your world too?" Nora perked up at my mentioning my previous life.

"Yeah, it was pretty bad too. There was an entire war fought because one race of people thought that the other race was a blight on the world." *I don't remember who fought who, but I remember a world war and something terrible that happened to a certain race of people during it. I'm forgetting more and more of my old life. Not that I could remember anything about myself to begin with. But I've been losing details of historical events and other facts. I guess if you don't use it, you lose it.*

Nora was speechless. She slowly gathered herself. "Did you have to live through it?" Her voice was quiet and sorrowful.

"No, that war was long since over before I learned about it." I waved off her worry as I shook my head.

Nora exhaled audibly as she lowered her head. "That's good to hear. A war like that sounds awful." I nodded in agreement. "But let's drop that topic and return to why you had such an attitude this morning after your bath." She sat back in her chair and folded her hands in front of herself on the table.

"Ah, that." I wrapped my tail around myself so I could fidget with my fur. "Part of what happened with accepting my wolfish side is that I now don't argue with her. When she says to do something or not, to eat something or not, I'll try to do it." I held my tail close as I continued. "I'll try to keep things on the mellower side."

"That was mellow?" Nora sounded unconvinced.

"When I saw the plate of eggs, I really wanted to throw them as far away from me as I could. I know you paid for the eggs, and we shouldn't waste money. You know how much I hate eating eggs.

There is an entire deer just outside, ready for me to eat." I raised my voice as I released my tail, stood up, and pointed to the door to the courtyard.

Nora didn't flinch. "Sit down." I sat. Her voice was even and cold. "I'm not saying that you shouldn't have had a piece of deer for breakfast. But when you dumped your eggs on my plate and spoke to me in the tone that you did, that's what is on trial here."

As I held my tail again, I tried to make myself smaller. "I was on a bit of a power trip. I'm sorry. This is still new to me." My voice was quiet and full of honesty.

Nora's face softened. "And for that, you're going to have all your meat cooked all the way until that deer is finished. Got it?" She made my punishment sound like she had forgiven me. "And no extra snacks until you show me you are in control."

"Yes, Mom." *That could have been worse.* Throughout our conversation, I could hear the other kids packing their things, but a distinct sound caught my attention. "By the way, someone's knocking at the front door," I said, returning to my more normal posture.

"I'll go see who it is." Nora stood up to leave. "In the meantime, clean the dishes since you're already packed." I watched as she walked out of the dining room.

I turned to stare at the dishes. *Ugh, fine.* I looked at my hands and saw there was more blood on them from the tenderloin. I instantly wanted to lick them clean. *Listen, there's a better way to get clean than licking oneself. Soap and water are so much faster and more effective.*

I then looked at the blood with a small desire to taste it again. *Alright, fine. I'm quite the glutton, aren't I? What was that saying again? Oh yeah, the fastest way to a girl's heart is through her stomach. Or was that a guy's heart? I think it works both ways, regardless.* My thoughts drifted as I licked the blood just enough to get a quick taste before gathering the plates.

I washed the dishes in the sink using a wand stored in the kitchen. The wand pulled water from the air into a liquid form. I remembered the few lessons I received on magic, and my minimal knowledge of the subject made me believe that magic followed some principles of physics. *I can't wait until I get to learn more about magic after the tournament.*

I stopped in the middle of scrubbing a plate. *Oh, no! The tournament! I was supposed to go yesterday with Allen, but I didn't. Does that mean I can't compete? Do I still want to go? Will Allen and Mom let me go? Will it be safe for me to go?*

I resumed washing the dishes. *Maybe I should still go. I shouldn't let what happened stop me from at least trying to see the plan through. Besides, Allen was nice enough to introduce Simyn to me.*

Simyn was a sweet guy, even if he was a bit on the awkward side. He had spent three years as a knight before he settled down with his wife, Lesslie. She wanted to smother me every time we met. I couldn't stand her anymore the last time we talked. She tried to put a bow on my tail because she thought it would look adorable.

I don't want to be treated like some fragile princess who can't do anything for herself. I want to kill animals for a living. That makes me sound like a serial killer. Maybe I should rephrase that to "hunting," not "killing." Yeah, that sounds much less like a serial killer.

I refocused on my surroundings and heard footsteps heading towards the kitchen. *Mom is probably coming with towels.* However, I noticed a second set of footsteps. They sounded familiar, and I curiously turned to see who was walking with Nora. I was initially surprised when Allen came into the kitchen. *He might be concerned about me after yesterday.* With an arm full of towels, Nora walked beside the knight captain.

"Are you almost done?" Nora asked with a sweet and relaxing voice.

"The utensils are done, but there are a few plates left. And the pan still needs to be washed." I stared at Allen as I replied.

"Well, finish up. We can talk while you work." I knew Nora was trying to encourage me with her happiest tone, but she didn't succeed.

I turned to the sink to resume my chore. I flicked my tail back and forth aggressively. "If you are here for an apology, don't bother. If you want to talk about it, don't bother either." I almost snapped a plate in two trying to hold back my aggression.

"I wasn't, and Nora made it clear when I asked to talk to you that you didn't want to talk about yesterday." Allen's voice trailed off at the end. "There's something different about you." His voice was soft, and he sounded unsure of himself.

I growled as I threatened him. "If you say I did something with my fur, I'll throw you out of this building faster than you can say 'I'm sorry.'"

"Alright, I won't. Your fur does look thinner, by the way. But I can't put my finger on it." Allen sounded like he was still thinking about it.

"Because it is thinner," I snapped back. "I finished shedding my ice coat two and a half weeks ago." I stopped washing the last plates, trying to calm down before I broke something.

"Lucia, do you need a moment to calm down?" Nora stepped between us, but kept her distance from me. I shook my head. "How about you tell her why you really came, Allen?"

"That would be a good start," I interrupted.

"Did you still want to participate in the tournament?" He sounded regretful about asking me. "I completely understand if you don't—"

"Yes." I didn't let him finish.

"Are you sure?" Nora asked me again.

I growled as I spun around towards Nora. "Yes!" I shouted as I flexed my claws and dripped water on the floor.

"Can you tell me why you still want to?" Allen asked.

"Because I'm done being scared of what I could do. When I'm seventeen, I have to join the army. It won't matter if I'm a cowardly, sheltered little girl or a grown woman who took control of her life." I relaxed my claws and returned to the dishes. "The world won't make room for me, so I'll carve out my life for myself."

"That sounds a little too bleak." Nora walked up to me and put her hand on my shoulder. "Why such an aggressive outlook on life?"

I turned my head slightly towards her and grinned. "Don't worry." I rinsed the last plate and grabbed the pan to wash. "We're taking the deer with us. I don't want to leave it behind to rot."

"When did you hunt a deer? And by yourself? How?" Allen interrupted us again with his annoying questions.

I replied in an exasperated tone. "Last night, I killed a deer by myself by biting down on the base of its neck until I bit through its spinal cord. Now, if you're done asking pointless questions, you can wait for us where we were to meet up yesterday." I watched Allen grimace as he moved to leave. "Also, I never want to see that elf again." My voice lowered as I growled the words.

Allen turned just before he left the kitchen. "You don't need to worry about Avollea ever again." *He wanted to apologize to me, didn't he?* He then left with his head downcast. "I just hope she can find peace in exile," he whispered.

I don't think he meant to say that out loud. But exile? Good. Keep her away from me.

21

WHY RIDE WHEN I CAN WALK?

I watched the scenery of rolling hills and grassland as I sat in a wagon with my travel chest and bag of food next to me. The other provisions the knights required for their stay at the tournament grounds surrounded me. I sat pouting in the wagon, being pulled by a single horse, as Jones, a knight from the Brilliant Crusade, drove onwards.

I was upset that I couldn't keep the deer that I hunted. The butcher, Hugue, wouldn't have been able to work on it until tomorrow, and then it would take another three or four days to cure. I tried to reason with Nora that we could chop it up and put it in chests with lots of ice. Apparently, I hadn't been the first to try that. Unless we constantly restocked the chest with ice, the meat could still spoil after a few days. So we sold it to Hugue for a few days' worth of cured meat.

Nobody looked my way or talked amongst themselves. Five knights on horseback trotted alongside the cart as my escort to the tournament grounds. Out of the five, only one knight was a woman. Allen had ordered these five knights to stay behind because he wanted to see if I still wished to participate in the tournament. The other twelve members of the Brilliant Crusade had headed to the tournament grounds yesterday to act as additional security.

I listened to the clopping of hooves, the creaking of the axles on the cart, the birds chirping, and the wind blowing through the fields. *I'm getting bored just sitting here.*

Unable to sit any longer, I jumped out of the cart. All the knights turned their attention to me. "Relax, I just want to walk for a bit."

Each of the knights relaxed one by one until Allen was the only one who didn't. "Do we need to go at a slower pace for you?" Allen asked.

"Can these horses outrun a wolf?" I didn't bother holding back my sarcasm.

Allen returned his attention to where he was going. "Just let us know if you get tired."

"Stop babying me," I huffed. "I'm not an idiot. Besides, I want to get tired." I started jogging faster than the horses.

The other knights were silent. Whether it was because Allen told them to leave me alone or because of my aggressive demeanor, I didn't care. I jogged in front of everyone so that I didn't have to smell the horses. The beasts were surprisingly calm around me, especially considering I'd already had three distinct moments where I wanted to eat one.

I can't just kill a horse someone's riding. Another reason I need to move around. How did anyone travel in the medieval ages? It's so boring. I really need something to do.

Once we finally made it out of the farmlands, the road shifted from cobblestone to packed dirt. We traveled until the sun was on its way down from its apex. I had been getting hungry and almost asked if we could stop to eat when we came upon some rolling hills.

Allen called out without warning, "Alright, let's stop for a short break and give the horses some time to recover. In the meantime, we can eat. We can rest on that hill over there." He pointed to a small hill just off the road.

I sprinted off to the spot as fast as I could while just using two legs. I reached the top of the hill and turned to face the knights I'd left behind. With a smug look, I watched them arrive.

"Did you need me to slow down so you can keep up?" I placed my hands on my hips.

Before handing out the orders, Allen gave me a disappointed look. After the cart had stopped, I jumped up and grabbed my food. I decided, since I was up here, to grab the knights' food and hand it down to them.

Allen walked up behind me after I jumped off, my sack of food in hand. "What's up with you? You made such a rude comment to me, then helped out without being asked to." He sounded curious and annoyed at the same time.

I crossed my arms as I turned to him. "I can be nice. Besides, rudeness is a matter of perspective. You were rude when you asked if you needed to slow down for me. I'm clearly faster than your horses." *I'm a bit of a showoff, I know. But I can do things now that nobody on Earth would ever believe.*

Allen lost his curiosity but stayed annoyed with me. "I was trying to be nice and look out for you."

I stomped my foot. "I'm not some fragile princess you need to coddle, and I don't need people treating me like a kid." I stormed away from Allen towards a rock where I could sit and eat my lunch.

"But you are a kid," Jones said quietly as I walked away.

I turned to him and growled as I curled my lips, baring my fangs. He flinched backwards, and I left him with his warning. Allen sighed as I continued to a stone that was separated from everyone and large enough to sit on.

I'm ten years old. I have seven more years of this. Why is it more frustrating now than it was before? Why am I so on edge today? Am I just hungry? My stomach growled. *I guess I get snippy when I'm hungry.* I opened the bag Melody had prepared for me. *Oh yes, a liver! Awesome! And sausages too.* I giggled as I admired my lunch.

When I'd first started helping Zane and Marigold with checking traps, I caught a badger. They allowed me to take it home. As I watched Zane remove all the organs for me, I snatched the heart without thinking. He'd simply watched me eat it in just a few bites. After that, I tried almost every organ just to see how they compared.

Melody was very much against me eating organ meat. But when I told her what parts I liked, she came around slowly.

Hearts and livers were the best, while kidneys and intestines were okay. Although intestines need to be thoroughly cleaned before they were stuffed to make sausages to have my attention. Stomachs, brains, and lungs were repulsive. Stomachs tasted like vomit, brains tasted like nothing with a crumbly, grainy texture, and lungs tasted similar to cartilage, but with the added flavor of some kind of slime that reminded me of phlegm and tasted like it too. I ate the regular meat of animals most of the time. But since I had an appetite and a half, I usually ate a snack in the afternoon. I always ate my organs away from the prying eyes of the other kids so I didn't disgust them. Turns out nobody wanted to buy the hearts of slaughtered animals, so I could get them cheap from Hugue because he was going to throw them out anyway.

But I refuse to eat a tongue. There is something wrong with eating something else's taste buds.

I ate my food in solitude. As much as I wanted to eat all of it now, I exercised some restraint and set aside a few sausages for later. *I don't know how long we'll be traveling today, so I'd best save myself a snack, just in case.*

Everyone else finished their food while having light conversations that didn't interest me even slightly. After the horses had a bit to drink to finish their rest, we set off on the road again. With food in my belly, I was much more relaxed. I resumed walking out in front, to Allen's displeasure.

I need to know a bit more about this tournament and festival thing. I moved to walk alongside Allen's horse. *And I probably should apologize for my attitude earlier. He didn't do anything wrong. He was just looking out for me, like he always does.*

I got Allen's attention by poking his leg. "Sorry about earlier." Allen didn't say anything as he raised his eyebrows. "I was bored, hungry, and just in a bad mood. I shouldn't have taken it out on you. So, sorry."

Allen gave me an apologetic look. "I know traveling isn't much fun. But we need to keep aware of our surroundings." He leaned forward in his saddle. "While I don't expect anything to happen, we still need to be careful. We'll make it to the tournament grounds before nightfall so you can sleep in a bed tonight." He turned his head to look forward again.

I did a quick check of the area with my ears and heard nothing unusual. "So why is this tournament being held, anyway? You said you would give me more of the details later. Is now a good time?"

"The king's son has come of age. Since he wishes to serve as a knight, they're holding a tournament to showcase his martial prowess to the entire kingdom," Allen said, while glancing at me periodically. "If he'd decided that he didn't want to be a knight, there'd have been a grand ball instead."

"But what's this festival about?"

"Nothing really. It's a big excuse to bring lots of traders to one location. Sometimes people just want to celebrate. Any reason to get drunk and away from work." There was an undertone of displeasure in Allen's voice.

"What if his firstborn was a daughter?" *How sexist is this country?*

"Same thing," Allen said without pausing.

I was a little taken aback, but I thought about it for a moment. *I guess since the army doesn't care if I'm a woman, why should it change for the ruling government's family?* "So how does this tournament thing work? And is there anything I need to know about this festival?"

"The festival is mostly people gathering, bringing their wares, cooking different foods, or celebrating while the tournament is in between matches. That's why the majority of knight companies are sent: to provide general peacekeeping. Mostly we'll be keeping drunks from hurting themselves or others." The lament in Allen's voice was thick.

"You don't sound too enthusiastic." There was a woodland area up ahead that I noticed we were walking towards. "Are you sure we're going to make it to the grounds today?"

"We should make it there just before nightfall. The coliseum will be visible once we exit this small stretch of forest."

He's trying too hard to sound happy.

"So Simyn taught me how to fight, but how will the fights go? Are there any rules I need to know about?" I eyed the forest cautiously. *Something doesn't feel right.*

"The first half of the tournament is all about the knight candidates. That's what your concern should be. The second half is for those who are already knights to compete in various challenges, such as who's the strongest, the fastest, the best archer, horse racing, and so on." Allen turned to look at me. "The most important rule is: do not kill your opponent." The harshness in his voice was unnecessary.

"Obviously," I said sarcastically.

Allen ignored me as he continued. "You'll fight in an arena. To win, you can force your opponent to yield, push them out of the arena, or knock them unconscious. The only magic that's banned is fire." *I wonder why that is. Too many severe injuries?* "The first day is the preliminary round where they will split everyone into groups of four and you just have to be the last one standing. You'll only fight once each day, so don't worry about tiring yourself out. Just watch for any injuries, as they may make future fights more difficult. After the preliminary matches are done, the main tournament starts. At that point, the fights will be one-on-one. They will continue until a victor emerges. Any questions?"

"How well do I have to do to win any money?" I asked.

Allen gave me an apologetic look. "Did Nora tell you about that?" I nodded. "The only position that wins any money is first place. For the part you will be competing in, if you can beat everyone, including the prince himself, you'll win the prize money, which will be immediately taken against your debt, reducing your years of required service."

As I expected. Looks like I really need to win this whole thing.

"Any more questions?"

We'd arrived at the edge of the forest, and my instincts were screaming at me not to go in there. I stopped short, much to the surprise of everyone.

"Not about the tournament, but do we have to go through there?" I pointed to the forest.

Everyone stopped, just as I did. "What's wrong? This is the shortest route. If you need to, you can sit in the cart again." Allen sounded genuinely worried about me.

"You know how I said that my instincts often warn me of things? Well, I just can't bring myself to go into that forest right now." I hadn't been this scared since I met the demon.

"We're here to make sure you stay safe. How about you climb back into the cart and let us know if you hear anything? I'm not sure if your instincts take us into account." Allen attempted to brighten the mood with a lighthearted tone.

"My instincts haven't been wrong yet. Can we go around?" I took a step back from the forest.

"That'll take us too long. We didn't bring anything for camping overnight," Jones said with a smile. "Trust us. We'll keep you safe."

Allen pointed to each of the other knights. "Reyner is the best archer in the entire company. Jayne, Barney, and Quinn are the most senior members behind me. Jones, despite his age, is very capable with a sword." Allen dismounted and walked up to me. "I promised Nora I would see you there safely. I extend that promise to you." Allen grabbed my hand gingerly.

"It isn't that I don't trust you. I'm just scared." I allowed Allen to lead me by the hand to the cart again. "There's something wrong here."

"It's okay to be scared. If something happens and I tell you to run, will you do it?" Allen's face was hard.

"What about you?" I asked. "You have a family."

"And I'm a trained knight. I'll be okay." Allen stared into my eyes intently. "Now, will you run if I tell you to?"

"Yes." My body quivered. *I don't like this, but I can trust Allen. He takes his job seriously. Maybe my instincts are wrong. There's a first time for everything, right?* I slowly climbed into the cart and crouched in a corner, then hugged my tail tightly.

Allen got back on his horse just as everyone started moving again.

22

DIRE STRAITS

The uncomfortable fear never went away or lessened. Allen and the other knights promised they would move through the woods as fast as they could with the cart. Before, the roads were clear and heavily packed with dirt. This forest, on the other hand, had a smaller path with random roots poking out of the ground. Fallen branches needed to be moved so the cart didn't have to run them over. Each knight took turns running ahead to remove any obstructions. I would've taken a turn to help if I wasn't scared stiff and huddled in the cart like a child.

I don't know how long we traveled through the woods, because once my adrenaline got going, everything slowed down. It's like my mind got faster, and I could process information more quickly. It makes it much easier not to trip over or run into anything when I run as fast as I can.

As I lay curled up in the cart, an awful smell assaulted my nose. A wave of nausea came over me, and it took everything I had not to vomit.

"What is that smell? It's awful!" I plugged my nose as carefully as I could with my fingers. "It smells like something died."

"I smell something, but nothing that I would say is that bad yet," I heard Jones say as he turned his head back towards me.

"It looks like there's something ahead," Allen called out. "Quinn, go check it out."

I peered over the edge of the cart to see what was going on. Quinn was the easiest to distinguish from everyone else. While all the knights wore what they called their traveling leathers, Quinn had one accessory that nobody else had—a red scarf wrapped loosely around his neck.

Quinn dismounted and carefully walk ahead of us as we stopped, his hand on his sword on his hip. I saw his goal: a large brown mass that looked hairy. He walked three-quarters of the way to the mysterious object before relaxing and turning back.

"That's the source of the smell Lucia mentioned," Quinn said. His smile was creepy because of how he always showed all of his teeth. "It's a dead bear. It looks like it started rotting."

"Well, it looks like your nose is spot-on," Jones joked as he leaned back slightly.

"Thanks, but could we get past this smell? It's making me sick." My nasally voice was slightly comical to hear, but the stench killed my mood.

"Alright, let's go." Allen's tone put an end to our conversation.

We resumed our advance, but when we came across the bear corpse, a thought went through my head. *Was I acting scared because I was going into the bear's territory? How did I know?* I bolted up and jumped off the cart, surprising everyone.

I walked over to the bear to see if I could identify how it had died. I kept the corpse downwind of me so I didn't have to smell it as much. As I stood next to it, I felt tiny. This bear was easily the size of the cart plus the horse. *I thought the wolf was huge, but this bear could have probably handled it.*

"What are you doing, Lucia?" Allen called out to me.

"This might be why I didn't want to go this way," I called back without looking away from the body.

The back, which was visible from the path, was untouched. I walked around the corpse and looked at its face. There was some blood around its mouth and claws. The eyes were gone, likely eaten by scavengers.

"This thing has been dead for a few days, I think." I looked around and saw dozens of flies buzzing around. "But what killed it?"

"Something killed a bear?" Quinn shouted in disbelief.

"If you'd looked at the other side, you would have seen the gaping hole in its stomach and the crushed rib cage." I attempted to chastise Quinn's quality of reconnaissance. "Animals of that size don't just fall down and die like that." I walked away from the corpse. My fear returned in full force. "I don't want to see what did this."

"That's something we can all agree on. Let's move quickly," Allen said, with a touch of worry in his voice.

I didn't hop back in the cart. Instead, the air in the forest felt even heavier. The need to get out of the woods was worse. I started out ahead of everyone else and cleared the path as needed. I moved faster than the knights could with their cart, and I had no wish to wait for them.

I'll stop for them at the edge of the woods. I worked diligently until I saw daylight past some trees. Ecstatic, I moved even faster.

I made it out of the small forest and relaxed. I paced slowly as I waited for the knights to catch up. Allen and Reyner were halfway between me and the cart. *Probably to keep a closer eye on me.*

"Do you feel better now that you're out of the woods?" Allen asked as he approached me.

"Yeah, I feel better," I said. It no longer felt like something was trying to smother me.

"See, I told you there was nothing to worry about."

"I don't see it that way," I said. Allen's face contorted with confusion. "If that bear had been alive when we ran into it, that would have been a much different experience. Also, whatever killed that bear is still out there. Are we just going to leave it?" I pointed to the trees as the cart exited the woods.

"Until we know what it is, we won't do anything," Allen stated matter-of-factly.

"Well, I'm glad that we made it through with nothing bad happening." I heard a rhythmic pounding, although it was still faint. I looked back at the forest and saw something moving. "Um, guys, I may have spoken too soon." I pointed a finger back at the distant object. "It looks like something is heading this way."

Allen snapped his attention to where I was pointing. "Reyner, you and Jones grab your bows, stand on the cart, and prepare to fire. Shields and spears for the rest, Barney. Lucia, get on the cart or get ready to run. For the rest of you, Barney and I will be the vanguard. Jayne and Quinn, cover us."

They passed weapons out as I jumped onto the cart behind Jones and Reyner. All the knights dismounted and guided their horses in front of the cart, and the four knights on the ground armed themselves with a steel-tipped spear and a round steel shield that covered them from the middle of their thigh to their shoulder.

The mysterious object grew in proportion to the sound of the pounding. *It almost sounds like hooves.* I squinted to focus as much as I could on it.

"It looks like a boar, I think," I said hesitantly.

Allen turned towards me as he stood next to Barney. "Are you sure?"

"It doesn't look right, though." The shape moved really fast and was getting way too large to be a boar. "Rhinos aren't supposed to be in this area. It isn't running like a wolf because I can hear it." The creature finally came into focus enough that I could identify it. "No, it is a boar, but why does it have six tusks?" I watched the color drain from each of the knights' faces. "What?"

"Are there white spots along the spine and rib cage?" Allen asked quickly.

"Yeah, why?" I felt a sense of dread watching the battle-hardened warrior's eyes go wide.

"Lucia, run!" Allen shouted. "We'll buy you enough time."

"Why? What about you? Isn't it just a boar?" *They know something I don't.*

"No, that's a dire boar!" Allen pointed into the distance with his spear. It looked like there was something in that direction, but nothing discernible. "We'll be fine. Just go in that direction."

A dire animal? Is that what killed the bear? It followed us while staying downwind of me. Zenny's book was right; dire animals are more intelligent.

I couldn't move a muscle as I watched the boar advance. With each step, the thunderous hooves became louder and louder. I was torn between running for my life and the desire to kill this creature that thought it could come after me.

Allen shouted, but his voice was drowned out by the charging dire animal. The boar lowered its head as it closed in on the two knights out front. Two arrows sailed towards the creature's face. One arrow struck just above the right eye and the other hit the bridge of its nose, but both bounced off. The boar headed right for me, ignoring the six knights.

A small cloud of dust exploded each time the boar's hoof struck the ground. I threw my pride away and ran away from the cart. I immediately dropped to all fours when I hit the ground. Based on how loud the boar's steps were getting, it was catching up to me. *I can't do the same thing I did with the wolf. That almost killed me.* I made a perfect ninety-degree turn towards the woods. *Maybe I can outmaneuver it like the wolf. A bull-in-a-China-shop sort of thing.*

I heard the boar try to change directions like I did, but it sounded sloppy and slow, like it slid to a stop to make the turn to keep chasing me. There was a brief break in the beast's running, enough for me to hear Allen shout, "This way, Lucia!" I turned to look and saw the four knights with spears lined up like goal posts.

I made another hard turn towards the knights as two more arrows flew past me. The grunts coming from the boar urged me to keep running, and I pushed myself harder to keep that murderous beast away from me. As I ran between the knights, I dared to look back.

I shouldn't have looked.

The beast focused on me as it charged along the same path I was running, and it was far closer to me than I would have liked. I could see its dilated pupils as they followed me.

The knights simultaneously stabbed it with two spears on each side. It looked like one knight aimed for the neck while the other aimed just past the rib cage.

I heard a grunt, followed by a lower, indescribable sound. I changed to just running on my legs as I stood up before I turned to see how the knights were doing. The knights each struck the boar and retracted their spears with speed and precision. While the beast was now bleeding, it looked more angry than hurt. I watched as the boar lowered its head and attempted to gore Jayne and Quinn while spinning around. Quinn got his shield up to block the attack, but the force of the blow still knocked him onto his back. Jayne's backpedaling was fast enough to get her out of reach.

I stopped. I didn't know if I should help them or do as Allen said and run. *I can't leave them to handle that thing on their own. But what do I do? Lucia, calm down. Remember your training. This is a real fight. Step one: should I fight? I don't want Allen and the others to die for me, so yes, I will fight. Step two: what is my win condition? Chase it away or kill it. What should I do? Let's just try to chase it away and go from there.*

While I gathered my resolve to fight, Allen barely dodged a kick from the boar's hind legs. A hoof collided with Barney's shield, leaving a large dent and launching him backwards before he landed on the ground with a painful grunt.

Jayne moved to cover Quinn as he tried to get back to his feet. Two more arrows flew towards the boar, but this time, they struck its side. I watched as they landed on the ground on the other side of the boar. Jones and Reyner dropped their bows and each picked up a spear and shield before charging out of the cart.

I charged the dire animal in order to save Allen now that the boar had wheeled around to attack him with its tusks. Allen attempted to create any distance he could, but the boar kept charging him. He dove to the side as the beast attempted to run him over.

Okay, the danger zones are directly in front of and behind the creature.

The boar skidded to a stop as it turned its attention back to me. *This is a bad idea, but I have to do something.* I moved to the left to avoid the boar's charge. It made a last moment's effort to reach me with its tusks, but I was much faster. I dug my claws into the ground and reversed my direction instantly as the boar passed by. I darted to its side, readying my claws to strike.

I aimed at its ribs, hoping I could get between them and puncture a lung, but when my claws tried to dig into the hide, I found much more resistance than I was expecting. *This creature's hide is tougher than anything else I've tried to cut in this world.* My claws left a visible wound, but I missed my target and hit its ribs. I could see that the spears had been leaving wounds too, but my claws had left the largest one yet.

The boar threw its shoulder into me as we continued running. I stumbled away a short distance before regaining my balance and charging back in before it changed directions again. Quinn and Jayne lined up in our path, prepared to strike when we got within reach.

I jumped on top of the boar and latched down with all of my claws to get out of the way of Jayne's attack. *I really hope I don't regret this.* The creature turned its head to look at me. *I think I have its undivided attention. Can I use that? Maybe Allen and his knights can get coordinated and focus on killing it safely.* The little white spots on its spine looked like they were coming out of its skin, like spines, but they were too short and blunt to worry about.

My ride drifted along its path towards Quinn. *No, you stupid pig. Pay attention to me!* I climbed the boar's back towards its head, one claw at a time. Climbing an unwilling mount while it was running was way more difficult than I'd imagined, even with the added benefit of my claws being able to make everything a handhold.

Quinn dove out of our way as Jayne struck at the boar's face. A tusk deflected her blow. *I need to slow this thing down.* I got to where the shoulder blades and the base of the neck meet. Holding on with everything I had, I used the last weapon available to me, my teeth, to bite down on the spine.

I worked my teeth through the tough hide, and when I reached the bone, I felt I would never crack it as I'd done to the deer. I moved to the right, next to the spine. *Maybe if I dig down beside it, I can slide a claw in between the vertebrae. That should work, right?* I spat out the hair and hide from my first bite before going in for a second.

The second bite forced a reaction from the boar. It stopped running and bucked wildly, like a horse. I hit my face on its back as I tore away another chunk of its hide. Spots peppered my vision as I recovered from being dazed, and I poured all of my energy into hanging on.

It continued turning, kicking, and jumping. I don't know how long I spent pushing and pulling myself, reacting to its movements, but, eventually, the boar started getting tired and its erratic movements slowed slightly.

The dire beast stopped jumping around, and the world started rolling. Except it wasn't the world, but the boar. It was attempting to crush me. Panicking, I released all my claws and pushed away with everything I had. My landing wasn't graceful as I hit the grass and rolled to a stop. I turned to look at the creature and saw that all six knights were standing between me and the beast, spears and shields raised. The boar let out a loud snort as it eyed me.

It didn't charge again. Instead, it slowly walked towards the forest while still keeping its eyes trained on me. The knights slowly rotated around me so that they were always between me and the beast. As the boar finally turned its head away and moved farther into the woods, the knights finally relaxed.

Allen knelt down next to me as I lay on the ground, exhausted and panting heavily. "Are you alright?" he asked worriedly, looking me over.

"Yeah." I needed to catch my breath. "I'm just tired."

"You are either very brave or incredibly stupid, jumping on a dire animal like that," Jayne chided me as she extended her hand to me. "Can you get up?"

Allen also extended his hand to me. "What were you thinking? I told you to run away. It could have killed you."

"That thing could have killed you too." I grabbed their hands. The two knights pulled me to shaky feet. I put my hands on my knees to steady myself. "I don't want anyone to die for my benefit. What would I say to your family, to your kids? 'Sorry, your father died so I could run away.'" I glared at Allen, still trying to calm down. "Besides, that thing had it out for me. It ignored you guys. If I had run away, it would have chased me all the way to the tournament grounds. I don't know if I would have made it. I don't want another incident like the wolf."

"That was odd," Jones said as he collected everyone's spears. "Why did it go after her so fervently?"

"My best guess is that it saw her as an invader of its territory," Reyner joined in. "I imagine it killed the bear we came across earlier too."

"But how did it know?" I asked. "Did I leave a scent for it to follow?"

"Possible," Reyner said with a shrug. "Though I want to know why it gave up."

"I think it thought Lucia was more effort than she was worth," Jayne said with a smile.

"I guess I'll go back to the cart. I got what I wanted—to be tired out." I slowly made my way to the wagon.

Jayne lifted my right arm and pulled it over her shoulder. "Here, let me give you a hand."

"Thanks." I turned to give Allen a hateful glare. "And the next time I say we go around, we go around."

A guilty look appeared on Allen's face as he looked at the ground. "Noted."

23

A FRIENDLY FACE

I can already tell that this won't be as much fun for me as it will be for everyone else.

I stared at the small village before me. A sprawling expanse of tents and stalls full of people bustling to get everything closed up for the night threatened to swallow up the humble village. On the other side of the settlement was a massive wooden structure that I believed was the stadium, or coliseum, where the tournament would be. Other than the small buildings that possibly held the residents of the small town, there was one more building that stood out—a mansion surrounded by stone walls. Everything from the outer walls to the roof of the mansion looked meticulously maintained. The walls were made of brick and mortar, and I saw stained-glass windows.

I turned to Allen. "Who lives there?" I pointed to the extravagant dwelling.

"That would be the keepers," Allen responded without turning away from the giant coliseum.

Keepers. I remember that lesson. They were the equivalent of governors or barons. They were responsible for the safety and general peacekeeping in the area. Most often, they were one of the larger knight companies that made a deal with the king. Keepers didn't collect taxes because, apparently, a representative of the crown made a trip to a village like this once a season to collect the taxes.

I saw a few other carts and wagons headed towards the village from other directions. "I have a question." Allen turned his attention to me. "Where does everyone sleep?" I asked while waving my arm towards the crowds of people.

"Most people will sleep in the tents they brought. The inns in the town rent out rooms for people too. There's a large stable on the other side of the keepers' base. Everyone's horses and other animals will be cared for there." Allen pointed past the second-largest building, the mansion. "That's where all the knight companies will be staying. You'll be staying in a room provided to you on the tournament grounds." He then pointed to the large wooden coliseum.

"So where will Mom, April, August, and Molly stay?" I asked.

"You can ask them once they arrive tomorrow." Allen smiled at me. "But right now, you need to get your gambeson fitted for the tournament."

Oh, right, that's the whole reason I had to come early. "Where do I do that?"

"I'll take you," Jayne answered.

We stopped in front of the colossal wooden structure. "Jones will take care of your chest. Hop off and follow me." Jayne dismounted her horse and handed the reins to Reyner.

I jumped off the cart and caught up with her so I could walk right behind her. She took me to a small armory where a guy was waiting for us. Being measured was something I was accustomed to since half my clothes needed tailoring. The gambeson was altered quickly since the only thing they had to do was cut a slit for my tail and give me a belt. Jayne also taught me how to wrap my breasts. Even though they hadn't grown to the point of being a distraction yet, Jayne said that I might as well get used to it now. She also suggested that I wear the gambeson for the rest of the day to acclimate myself to moving around in it. We then asked around for directions to where I would be staying.

The directions we received led us to a wooden door with a small copper plate with my name engraved on it.

"It looks like this is your room." Jayne waved at the door like it was a prize that I'd won.

"Does that mean I can take this stupid thing off now?" I grumbled.

"I know a gambeson isn't the most comfortable of clothes to wear," Jayne said sympathetically, "but it will protect you from a surprising amount of damage. And compared to most armor, it's the easiest to wear."

"Uncomfortable? You think I'm just uncomfortable?" I raised my voice with each word. "Sitting on my leg until it's asleep is uncomfortable. This is unbearable. It feels like I'm in a heatwave in the middle of the fire season!" I tugged at the cloth armor.

"It isn't that bad, is it?" Jayne asked. "I find they're the most comfortable armor you can wear."

"Says a person who wears extra layers of clothes during the ice season," I pouted.

"You don't?" She sounded surprised.

"No! What do you think this fur is for?" I suppressed the urge to growl at the woman.

"I guess you have a point," Jayne said as she looked to be lost in thought. "You can take it off if you need to. There's no reason to pass out from overheating. It's late, though. You'll want to get some sleep. But I still think you should do some exercises in it. Maybe do some practice swings while wearing it tomorrow. You need to familiarize yourself with the feel of it so it isn't distracting when you fight in the tournament in two days."

"Okay," I grumbled. I looked up at Jayne, who looked understanding of my plight. "What do I need to do tomorrow?"

"Whatever you want." Jayne was back to her cheerful self. "Do you want to look at the stalls? Go ahead. If you just want to hide in your room, you do you. We wanted to give you a couple of days to explore the festival so you can have fun and relax."

"Alright, I'll think about it. Good night." I opened the door to my room and waved to Jayne. The sun had gone down as we entered this building, so most likely everyone else was asleep.

"Good night." Jayne started walking down the hall but stopped and turned back towards me. "Oh, did you want Captain Allen to show you where you need to be for the start of the tournament?"

"Um, you know what? You've been really nice. Could you do it?"

Jayne smiled and nodded.

I giggled as I closed the door.

I heard a slight laugh from the other side. "Alright, get some sleep. I'll get you first thing in the morning before the start of the tournament. Try to enjoy yourself tomorrow." Jayne's voice trailed off as she left.

I turned to inspect my temporary accommodations. One bed, one window with shutters, one bucket, and my travel chest sitting at the foot of the bed, with one nearly empty sack neatly folded on top of the chest. Though calling the mattress lying on the ground a "bed" was generous. The bucket in the corner carried an implication that I found revolting. The room was tiny, barely larger than the mattress. *And now I sleep in a closet.*

I quickly changed into my nightclothes and climbed onto the mattress. The few remaining sausages from my trip didn't last long. The bed was lumpy and wouldn't hold its shape for long. *What is this thing filled with? Cotton balls?* There was also no blanket or pillow. *If I had known that I needed to bring my own, I would have. I guess I'll have to get some tomorrow.* I took the gambeson and folded it into a pillow. *Would you look at that? This thing* can *be comfortable.* I smiled at my thoughts as I relaxed before drifting off to sleep.

I was faced with a familiar view, and it was just as unfriendly the last time I was here. A large wolf with silver fur stared at me from her cage, her blue eyes locked on me.

Her cage was a little larger than last time. It looked like she had at least enough room to turn around. *Is it me, or is the cave smaller too?*

"What do you want?" I glared back at her.

Everything shifted around me until I wasn't looking at a caged wolf anymore but instead at a forest. The same forest the dire boar had come from.

"I figured that was you warning me about the dire boar."

I found myself back in the cave with my inner wolf. There was a strange feeling coming from her. It was like she was hurt, but not physically—emotionally. Her inability to speak made these conversations harder. Especially since she communicated with feelings.

She lay down in her cage, and I could feel what she wanted to get across to me. She was afraid of dying. More importantly, she was afraid of me getting her killed.

"What are you going to do about it?" I pointed at the bars. "You're stuck in that cage. And I don't need you to survive."

A heavy growl came from the wolf before she turned her head and chomped down on her front left leg. There was a shooting pain in my left arm. I grabbed it and looked down reflexively. Blood poured from a horrible bite wound. My fur soaked up some of the blood, and I tried to cover the wound, but more blood slipped through my fingers.

The wolf wore a smug look.

"You've got to be kidding." I looked back and forth between the wolf and the bite on my arm. "That isn't right. Does this mean if you die, I die?"

The wolf didn't answer. Instead she started licking the wound on her leg. As she cleaned it, her wound closed up. Eventually, there was no proof of her biting herself other than the blood that had dropped to the ground.

My arm was still happily bleeding.

I decided to see if it went both ways. I took my claws and raked them across the back of my right forearm. And just as the bite mark appeared on my arm, four red lines appeared on her front right leg.

The overwhelming feeling of anger exuded from the wolf. I could feel the impression of a puppy playing with a campfire and getting burned.

"We're stuck with each other," I said. "If I die, you die. If you die, I die. So much for starving you out."

The wolf licked the wound on her right front leg until it was gone. Then she looked at me and I could feel that she wanted me to go closer to her.

Hesitantly, I inched forward until I was standing next to the bars. Then her message changed to a mother wolf cleaning her pup's wounds after it got hurt.

I lifted my arms to look at them. Blood still dripped to the ground, but it wasn't as bad as it was before. Before I could react, she licked my arm, and her massive tongue engulfed it for a moment.

I flinched backwards, and my inner wolf looked annoyed. But there was a tingle in my arm, and as I looked at it, it wasn't bleeding anymore.

"You want me to trust you," I absentmindedly said. "I guess. If we're stuck in this situation together, we shouldn't be trying to kill each other. There's enough out in the world as it is trying to do that."

I walked back up to the wolf and let her finish licking my arms, and the wounds healed.

"But I still can't trust you around people yet. When we're alone, you aren't so bad." I turned to leave. "You need to let me handle people."

I turned my head back one more time. There was a smile on the wolf's face. And her cage grew while the cave shrank.

"Huh." Everything dissolved around me.

I woke up as the sun came up and went through my morning routine. *I wish I had some more answers about my inner wolf. Do all beastkin have one?*

After I got dressed, not wearing the annoyingly hot gambeson, I decided I should take care of my purchases before things got too busy. *It sounds like I'm not the only one awake right now.* I could hear all kinds of movement going on outside of my tiny closet-sized room. *Maybe I can beat them all out since it doesn't sound like anyone's walking down the hall yet.* I grabbed my coin pouch and filled it, then tied the string around my neck so that I knew where it was at all times. *Nobody's tried to pickpocket me, but I'm not about to allow that now.*

I opened the door to my room and walked out into the hallway. I heard someone coming up behind me. "What are you doing in Lucia's room?" a cheery, sing-song voice called to me.

"What? Are you asking me what I'm doing in my own room?" I asked incredulously. I turned to see the idiot who'd made such a wild accusation.

A human girl who was about an inch taller than me stood in front of me in brightly colored clothes. She wore a bright-green collared shirt with a leather vest with yellow embroidery of vines on it over her top. Her long green skirt flowed down to her ankles and had more yellow embroidery along the bottom, although it was of flowers, not vines. The same rugged brown leather boots adorned her feet. She was thin enough to make me question her health, and she had her golden-blond hair pulled back into a long ponytail that stretched to the small of her back. Her hazel eyes stared at me with wonder and innocence.

"You're Lucia?" She sounded confused as she tilted her head.

"Yes." I folded my arms in front of me. My tail flicked behind me. "Is that a problem?"

"No, it's just that you're a-a beastkin." Her cheeks flushed red as she stumbled with the words.

"And?" I drew out my one word, almost hoping that she would say something that would warrant me slamming her face through a wall.

"If you're here, that means you're participating in the tournament," she said, more to herself than to me, but I nodded in confirmation nonetheless. "I know there was talk about some beastkin ambassadors that were here to watch. But how did they get permission to allow someone to participate?"

"I'm from Aquittemia." I narrowed my eyes, as it looked like she wasn't hearing me. She seemed to be in her own little world.

"But what are you doing here?"

So she did hear me. "I'm going to be a knight." My tone got harsher as my patience quickly dried up.

"You shouldn't be a knight." She sounded almost desperate.

Oh, here it is. "And why is that?" My voice dripped with the promise of violence if I heard a certain four words.

Without skipping a beat, her eyes exploded, and she balled her fists as she stomped her foot. "You could get hurt."

My world lurched forward as everything came to a screeching halt. I stared blankly at the lunatic in front of me. "What?" *I don't want to believe that I heard what I heard.*

"If you get hurt, it could ruin your cuteness." Her voice rose as she went from an angry stance to holding her head up as she gave me a dreamy-eyed stare.

"Oh, no." I took a few steps backwards, away from her. *It's the return of Molly, the younger years.*

She noticed me backing up. "Did I say something wrong?" Concern filled her voice, and I could see a slight quiver in her eyes.

I continued to distance myself. "You're insane. If I can't be a knight because of my looks, then neither can you."

Her eyes lit up. "You really think I'm that cute?"

I stopped and stared at her. "Well, you're a bit on the thin side, but I would say you're more beautiful than cute."

She visibly shivered with the half-hearted compliment. "You mean that?" She leaned forward as she eagerly awaited my response.

I looked around and saw nobody was in the hall with us. "I don't have a reason to lie to you. Your face is really pretty. When you smile, it's kinda enchanting."

"Your fur is so shiny. Is it soft?" She took a step forward and reached her arm out.

I lifted my hand, ready to stop her. "Care to give me your name? You know mine, and I'm not into letting complete strangers touch me."

"Oh! I'm so sorry. My apologies." She looked mortified but did a quick curtsy. "My name is Evalana." Her smile returned to her face as she held a hand out to shake.

I grabbed her hand and gave her a handshake. I squeezed hard enough to hint at my strength.

"Oh, you're stronger than you look." Her surprise was enjoyable to watch.

"How strong do I look?" I asked with genuine curiosity.

"It's really hard to see anything under your fur." She looked at me with the same look I would judge steaks with. "But why do you want to be a knight? I know you said you were from Aquittemia, but since when did beastkin leave The Wild Kingdom?"

"I'm an orphan. So, since I have to join the military eventually, I'm going to be a knight."

She gave me quite a sad look. "How can you be an orphan? Didn't your parents love you?"

"It wasn't by choice. They're dead, and I don't have any memories of them. They died when I was four," I responded dismissively.

"That's so sad." She approached me with her arms open, and I ducked under her attempt at a hug and spun around her faster than she could react. "What? Don't you want a hug from a friend?" She turned to me with tears welling up in her eyes.

I gave her a suspicious stare. "When did we become friends?"

"Can we not be friends?" She dropped her arms.

I sighed in defeat. *I believe I've seen this play out once before.* "Why do you want to be my friend?"

"I want to be everyone's friend, and you're so cute. What's wrong with making friends with everyone?" She eyed me with a desperate plea.

People started exiting their rooms. Everyone was female on this floor. Several of the other girls gave us strange looks, but most ignored us. *I guess they separated the floors by gender.*

I leaned closer to Evalana. "If we're going to continue this conversation, can we do it elsewhere? Preferably a place with food involved." I recognized the rumble in my stomach.

Evalana lit up like a beacon as she jumped. "I know the perfect place. You're going to love the food they make." She grabbed my wrist and attempted to pull me along.

I pulled her back towards me. She looked at me, perplexed, as if I had betrayed her. "I can walk on my own. I'll follow you." After removing her hand from my wrist, I waved for her to lead the way.

The look of betrayal never left her eyes as she turned to lead me down two flights of stairs and out of the building. There wasn't much movement last night, but this morning everything was in full swing. I cringed at the sound of people yelling and talking over each other.

Yeah, large crowds and I don't get along. My new tour guide led me to the heart of the festival. *This had better be the best meat ever.*

Evalana suddenly stopped and pointed in the direction that I'd come from last night. "I wonder what they're doing."

She pointed to a large gathering of soldiers in armor I wasn't familiar with. They all wore cloth armor with some kind of rectangular plates underneath. They also carried a long metal spear with three points and a sword on their hip.

I shrugged. "They may be going to deal with the dire boar." *Hopefully if they kill it, they'll bring it back so I can taste it.*

"How do you know there's a dire boar in the area?"

"Because I had a run-in with it yesterday," I said nonchalantly.

"You survived an attack from a dire?" She looked at me in a way that left me believing this girl would worship me if I told her I'd survived a demon attack. *I barely survived and was bedridden for days, but I survived nonetheless.*

"There were six knights from the Brilliant Crusade with me." *I need to downplay my involvement. This lady is nuts. But she promised food.* "They chased it away. I think they're going to finish the job today."

"Poor thing," Evalana whispered.

Who's she talking about, me or the boar?

"You promised me food. Can we go get it now?" I extended my arm in the direction we were heading before our distraction.

"Oh, right!" Her perky demeanor returned as she skipped towards our destination. "You're going to love it. It's the best food I've ever eaten, and I've tried lots of different kinds of food."

I'll be the judge of that.

24

CULTURE SHOCK

"What is this?" I asked as I held a stick of skewered vegetables. They looked like they were marinated in spices and oil. The vendor that Evalana bought them from kept them warm on a metal grate over a low-burning fire alongside others that he was still cooking.

Evalana pointed to the first square of orange matter on the stick. "This is called a yam. This is a potato. That's a radish. And my favorite, jicama." She moved her finger down as she named each piece.

"It's not meat." I approached the vendor with the vegetable skewers. "Do you have any meat?" I was as polite as I could be, but I sounded desperate.

"Sorry, kid, but this is all I have," the cook responded with a scratchy voice.

"Why do you want meat? You didn't even try it." Evalana sounded sad.

I shoved the stick into her hand and stormed off. We were in the middle of a growing crowd, and hearing all the conversations going on around me was evaporating my patience.

She jogged to keep up with me. "Hey, where are you going?"

"To get some breakfast," I said with a slight rumble in my voice.

I pushed and shoved my way through the people. Everyone was too preoccupied with what they were doing to notice me. I didn't knock anyone to the ground, but several times I surprised people enough to earn a few dirty looks.

I don't care. I'm hungry and on a mission.

I headed to one of the nearby fields of crops with my tour guide in tow. She ate her skewer as well as the one she had given me.

"Where are you going? I thought you said you were getting breakfast." Evalana was short of breath as she attempted to keep up with me. "The merchants are that way."

I stopped and faced her. "How much do you know about beastkin?" I asked, perhaps with a bit more hostility than I intended.

She froze and eyed me cautiously. "Not much."

I gave her a full view of my teeth. She jumped back at the sight of them as I said, "You see these? This means that I can only eat meat," I growled. "There are three kinds of beastkin: carnivores, herbivores, and omnivores. I'm a carnivore. I eat meat." *Besides, I needed to get out of the crowd. All those people around me talking and shouting—I can't stand it. I need to find something to eat.*

"But what are you doing out here?" she asked.

"One of the biggest problems farmers have is rabbits eating their crops. It was something I set a lot of traps for when I worked for a pair of trappers." I waved my arms around to show we were now on farmland.

"What does that have to do with your breakfast?" I stared at the girl, who still sounded genuinely confused, then turned away from her, shaking my head.

I then saw a sign of my quarry: a shallow hole in the ground. I stopped talking and crept up to the hole. *If she can't understand what I'm trying to tell her, I think it's time I gave her a demonstration.* I heard Evalana stomping behind me, and once she moved close to the rabbit's burrow, a plump, tawny-colored hare bolted from it and sprinted away. I ran after it and caught the little morsel easily, plucking it off the ground with one hand and watching it squirm in my grip. It kicked at my fingers with its hind legs as I turned around.

183

"Isn't she a cute little bunny?" Evalana's voice squeaked as her eyes glittered.

I took a clawed finger and severed the rabbit's head as it futilely struggled against me. *It was a cute little bunny. Now it's going to be a tasty bunny.*

I looked up to see Evalana cover her mouth and nose with her hands. "Why did you do that?"

"Because I'm going to eat it." *I thought I'd made it quite clear what I was doing out here.* "What did you think I meant when I said I was a carnivore?" I turned the hare upside down so that the blood would drain out of its neck.

"But she was still alive!" I watched as her face turned greener the closer I walked to her. "She looks pregnant too."

I held up the rabbit to see if I could verify her claims. "Are you sure she was pregnant? I guess I can check." After flipping the bunny on its back, I split it open with a careful incision of my claw. *I need to remove a few organs and skin it anyway.*

I looked at all the organs and found the womb. "I guess you were right. She was pregnant." I removed the organs I found offensive, including the womb, and dropped them to the ground. *I can't bring myself to eat unborn rabbit children. That's a little too far for me.*

Evalana turned her head and vomited all of her grilled vegetables. She continued to dry heave, holding back her hair as she dropped to her knees. I stared at her, worried. Eventually, she stopped. Tears flowed from her eyes, and the look of despair on her face was still kind of cute. She failed to speak, only guttural sounds escaping her lips.

I walked around so that the smell of her vomit wouldn't ruin my appetite as I ripped the skin off the rabbit. Once the skin was gone, I cut off a front leg and placed it in my mouth, bone and all. Evalana stared at me, mouth agape. Ignoring her, I sliced a claw down along the side of the spine. Once that piece was cut off, I finished separating the meat and bone in my mouth, then swallowed the meat and spat the bones out.

Some women tie cherry stems into a knot inside their mouths. I debone rabbits. After popping the heart into my mouth, I coupled it with the loin and belly flab.

I watched my tour guide's reaction to me eating with a bit of amusement. "I don't know what your problem is, but I didn't have that kind of reaction when you ate your vegetables in front of me."

Evalana's mouth opened and closed soundlessly as her face turned a bright shade of pink. Slowly, words did eventually leave her mouth. "I, it, but..." She sputtered before deciding on a sentence. "How can you just eat her?"

I found her reaction comical, and I decided I wanted to see how far I could take this. "That's easy. Like this." I punctuated my point by cutting off the other foreleg and eating that too. Watching Evalana's eyes grow with each bite made me deeply satisfied.

"What's wrong with you?"

I narrowed my eyes as I flattened my ears. *That's rude! Oh well, I'll play along.*

I listed everything off as cheerfully as I could. "I have a short temper, I constantly break things, I hurt people even when I don't want to, I have a short attention span, and I have horrible mood swings." *That covers everything, I believe.*

Evalana's face twisted somewhere between unhinged rage and stupefied. I tried very hard to suppress a laugh. I noticed I was wagging my tail now. *No, keep it together. At least for a little longer.*

"How can you just eat a living creature?" she whispered.

"Don't worry, I killed it before I started eating it." I smiled mischievously.

"Nope. I can't do this." Evalana threw her arms in the air as she moved to leave, but turned back around after taking a few steps. "How can you be so cruel?"

Alright, the game's over. "It's just a rabbit." I held up the carcass for emphasis. "There are literally thousands more." I gestured around and waved at the horizon. "What's so cruel? I killed it quickly and I'm eating it. It isn't like I hunted it for sport. Don't you eat meat too?"

"I don't! I could never eat something that was once alive. Besides, why did you have to kill her? She was pregnant. Shouldn't the babies have had a chance at life?" Her voice rose as she spoke.

I looked at her like she was crazy. "To do what? They're rabbits! If I went to the owner of this farm and told them that I had just killed a pregnant rabbit, they would thank me and, possibly, give me money." *That's a good idea. I should try that.*

"But it was just being peaceful. It wasn't hurting anyone." She stopped yelling and sounded heartbroken.

I stood straight up in surprise at her statement. "So you want to claim that, do you?" She nodded her head. "Fine, but what about that dire boar I told you about? Remember that? Do you want to know what I did to get it to chase me down and try to kill me?"

She was about to talk, but I didn't let her.

"Nothing!" *I hurt my ears a bit with that one.* "In the wild, it's eat or be eaten. Would you have the same reaction if an actual wolf caught and ate this bunny instead of me?" I eyed her, daring her to say yes. She made no response or movement. "How can you be so naïve to think that you can tell me what I can and can't eat? Did I say anything to you when you ate your food?" I marched towards her, and Evalana flinched with each step I took. "I will not have you look down on me while you sit on your ivory pedestal! I am half wolf, and yes, I can be a bit of an animal at times. If that's a problem for you, then you can just leave me alone." I poked a bloody claw at her face with each word.

After I finished my rant and saw the terrified look on her face, I headed back to my temporary lodging. I took out my frustrations on my breakfast by tearing off one of the hind legs and eating it. As I took a few steps, I heard something behind me. I flicked an ear back; it sounded like Evalana was shuffling her feet as she walked.

"Sorry," Evalana said in a barely audible voice.

I swallowed my food. "What was that?" I asked while turning slightly to look back at her.

"I'm sorry." Evalana stared at the ground as she clasped her hands together nervously. "My parents keep saying that I'm naïve, too. I don't want to be." She inched closer to me but never raised her head to look at me.

I sighed. "I guess I may have gone a little overboard with my rant, but I meant everything I said." I ripped off the last leg, pulled the last of the organs out, and threw the remainder of the bones on the ground. "If you want to stop being naïve, think about the situation from the other person's point of view."

"How do I do that?" She finally lifted her head, and I saw the tears streaming down her cheeks.

"The first thing you need to do is accept that there are those who believe differently than you." I held up the last of my breakfast. "I told you I'm a carnivore and can only eat meat. But you believe it's wrong to eat meat, so am I supposed to not eat anything?"

"How is that possible? Why can you only eat meat?" She still looked confused.

"Because that's the type of beastkin I am. There are other beastkin who can't eat meat and can only eat vegetables." I tossed the kidneys in my mouth and savored the juicy burst as I popped them. "And if they're anything like me, they love raw vegetables." I gave her a wink.

"I guess it isn't that bad. You did do it for food." She wiped the tears from her face. "But why did you come out here? Couldn't you have gotten something at one of the stalls?"

"That would have cost me money, something I don't have a lot of. This was free." I shoved the last leg into my mouth.

"Why don't you have money? Can't you ask your parents for some?"

Fantastic. She's a rich kid. That explains a few things.

I stopped eating for a moment. "I'm an orphan, remember?" I tried to finish eating quickly.

"Oh, yeah. I forgot about that. Sorry." Her tone darkened a bit. "If you needed money, I could have given you some." She brightened right back up. "Wait, my brother said that orphans are given money from the kingdom. Could you just ask for more money?"

"You don't know how money works, do you?" I asked as soon as I finished eating.

"I ask my mom and dad for money, they give it to me, and I buy things with it." She sounded proud of herself. If my hands weren't covered in blood, I would have facepalmed.

"Where do your mom and dad get the money they give you?" *I'm getting tired of her naïve ignorance.*

"I don't know." She put a finger to her chin. "I've never asked."

"But money has always been there when you asked for it?" She nodded her head. *I really want to tear or break something apart now.*

"Alright, basic economics. I get money from the kingdom and spend it on food. Whoever I buy the food from then takes the money and buys the things they need. They then give money to the kingdom when they pay their taxes. Then the kingdom gives a small amount to me in return for required military service. Then the cycle repeats. Understand?"

"Wow, when you explain it like that, it's much simpler than when Daddy tried to teach me." Her voice was chipper and back to its normal perpetual excitement. "So, what's that part you said about military service?"

"Since I'm an orphan, I don't have anybody who can pay for my food and housing. I'm too young to be taken seriously as a worker. There's a building called an orphanage where kids who have lost their parents or kids whose parents don't want them or can't afford to take care of them go. My opinions on the matter aside, the kingdom feeds us, clothes us, and gives us a place to sleep. But the kingdom doesn't do it out of the goodness of their hearts. No, they want us to pay them back, but they at least give us a method to do so. Also, if I serve long enough, I never have to pay taxes. So I guess it could be fine." I tried to sound happy at the end, but the smile I put on was obviously fake.

"So is that why you want to be a knight, because it pays better?" She walked up next to me, carefully avoiding any blood and hare remnants.

"It is a benefit, but the main reason is that I want more freedom to do what I want and not stand around. I don't sit still well." I cracked a smile. "But now that you know a lot about me, tell me about yourself. Other than that you're from a rich family and a vegetarian."

"How do you know my family?" She looked at me, worried.

I rolled my eyes. "I'm not even going to answer that. What does your family do?"

"My mom teaches me magic, and my dad is someone very important." She looked into the distance, distracted for an instant, but she returned her gaze to me almost instantly. "I'm thirteen and my aptitude is earth magic."

She's thirteen and doesn't understand economics? She's doomed if she doesn't find someone to fix that. Wait, that's me, isn't it? Why does this feel like a page out of one of Zenny's storybooks?

"Mine's physical." *Let's not mention recovery, since that's the less obvious one.*

"You would make a great knight then." She clapped her hands together. "Um, are you going to clean yourself of all that blood?" She pointed to my claws.

I looked at my hands and saw that they were still very bloody, and the blood was drying. I licked at it. *It's going to take a while to get back to my room and grab the wand.*

She tried to pull my hand away from my face. "What are you doing?"

"I don't have any water to wash my hands, so I'll use what I can. Unless you have some water on hand."

Wordlessly, Evalana knelt down and pulled up some soil from the grass. The dirt floated up to her hands, then broke apart into a cloud of dust until it was a light-brown swirling mist.

"Hold out your hands and stay still," Evalana said.

I followed her instructions as she guided the dirt cloud between her hands until it engulfed my hands. It was an odd sensation: there was a tingling that I started believing was the feeling of magic, as well as the sensation of my hands being constantly compressed and released by pressure. I stood still for a few moments until the dust cloud moved from around my hands to just above them, where it was then forced back together into a ball that Evalana let drop to the ground.

"There we go, all better," she said cheerfully, trying to hide her shortness of breath.

I inspected my hands and claws. *They're clean?* "Wow, that's a pretty neat trick," I said absentmindedly. "Thanks."

LET THE GAMES BEGIN

"What are you going to do now?" Evalana asked me in an almost regretful voice.

"Probably go find a stall that has a few of the things I need." I started walking towards the throng of people amongst the tents, carts, and stalls. "I didn't know that I needed to bring more stuff, including a pillow."

"You don't have any specific needs for your pillow, do you?" she asked, unable to look at me as she walked beside me.

"No. Outside of my obvious wardrobe adjustments, my diet is the only thing that is extremely specific," I said as I waved my hand lazily. "But I like full and fluffy pillows since I sleep on my side." I stopped for a half-moment before continuing. "Oh, and if you notice me getting aggressive to the point you feel frightened, just say 'waterfalls,' alright?"

"'Waterfalls?' What does that have to do with anything?"

"It's my code word to calm down," I explained. "You remember how I said that I get angry easily? Well, I wasn't kidding. I have a very short temper." I glared at her.

"You did say something about that, didn't you?" She looked up at the sky as she went through her memories.

"I only told you that because I think you're going to keep following me. Am I wrong?" I leaned back and continued to glare.

"Is that okay? I'm sorry for how I acted earlier. Can you forgive me?" Evalana sounded remorseful.

"Yeah, I can forgive you," I said.

Evalana stopped and exploded with happiness, and I wheeled around to face her and lifted a finger to prevent her from gushing whatever words she wanted to say until I was done.

"I will be eating meat, and there are likely other things that I will disagree with you about. If that's too much for you, you'd best walk away now." I tried to impress upon her the seriousness of what I'd said earlier.

She deflated slightly but still held on to her smile. "I understand. Friends?" She held up her arms to invite me in for a hug.

"Don't touch my ears or tail," I said as I welcomed her hug. She gave me a quick squeeze. "So if you're going to follow me around, do you want to show me where to get some things I need?" I gave her a slight smile as we parted.

"We're going to do much more than that." She had a wide grin on her face. "There's more than just stalls to buy stuff. There are people who set up games of skill for prizes, and you're going to show off your physical aptitude and get us some cool stuff." She marched to what I thought was a giant marketplace, but it turned out to be more of the carnival.

"Shopping first," I said as I walked up beside her.

After finding what I needed, I took the stuff to my room. On our way back, there was a new table set up with a line and a crowd gathered around it. Evalana urged me to follow her to see what the commotion was about.

"I think now might be a good time to remind you that I'm not good with crowds," I said as I looked at the people.

"What's wrong? You're cute. Yes, you look different from everyone else because you're a beastkin, but you shouldn't worry about that."

"That isn't the problem, mostly. You see these ears?" I pointed a finger at them as I asked my rhetorical question. "They're very good at hearing everything. Loud noises can hurt, and I can hear every conversation going on around me. It's not as much fun as you'd think it would be." I flattened my ears to help reduce the sounds of the crowd that we strolled towards.

"Hmm, that does sound unfortunate. But I imagine they're great for when you go hunting." I could tell she was forcing herself to sound happy while she grimaced as she talked.

I watched a person throw a disk-shaped bundle of straw. Another person was lined up at the table with a crossbow and fired at the airborne bale, missing as the bolt sailed low. "If I tell you we need to leave, just go with it, okay?"

"Okay." Evalana looked at the table. "It looks like an archery contest." She pointed to the table. "I want to try, don't you?"

I held up my clawed hand. "Does it look like I can shoot a bow? Also, my fingers are too short to shoot a crossbow comfortably. But I'll go with you for moral support."

We stood in line and waited until we were at the front of the table with a bow, some arrows, a crossbow with a winch, and some bolts.

"So, do you little girls want to give it a shot?" an elf dressed in colorful silk clothing greeted us with overplayed charm. His boots were sturdy leather with signs of heavy wear, but his pants were a pristine bright blue. He wore a shirt that was a darker blue than his pants, and a black silk vest finished his outfit. He was slightly overweight and shorter than me, and his head was round and held two brown eyes; if you looked at them, you knew he was scheming something. The dark-brown hair on top of his head was thinning, but he covered the balding spot with long hair from the side that he combed over.

"What are the rules and the prize?" I asked as I crossed my arms, putting up a front of confidence.

I could feel stares narrowing in on me. There were some whispered conversations and other conversations that weren't so secretive going on in the gathered crowd. *Focus. I need to ignore them and concentrate on the task at hand.* I flattened my ears as much as possible.

"A fair question from a fair beastkin." The pudgy elf gave a fake smile. "The rules are simple. It costs three coins to participate, and you continue until you miss a shot. There are three levels, each one further than the last. And to show you that there's no favoritism, each level is indicated out there with a marked rock."

He pointed to three rocks in the field, each with a different number of white spots on its face. The closest one had one white spot. It was at least three arcs away. The next closest rock had two white spots on its face while being twice as far away. The farthest rock had three white spots, and it was easily twice as far away as the second rock was.

"Stanley here will throw the target when I give him the signal. All you have to do is stand behind the table and hit the target while it's in the air. Simple, right?" The host raised his arms out to a burly man without a shirt and heavy brown pants. Sweat shimmered off his muscled torso.

I felt something stirring in the back of my mind. *He looks nice and strong.* When I realized that this was in fact my thought and that I was wagging my tail as I admired his muscles, I shook my head to remove the absurd notion. *He isn't that attractive.*

I nudged Evalana. "How far is that?" I whispered as I pointed to the farthest stone.

"The first is four arcs, then it's eight, and the last one is sixteen," Evalana whispered back.

Sixteen arcs and a moving target? That's a tough shot.

"What are the prizes?" Evalana asked in a polite tone.

"If you can hit the first target, I will return one coin to you. If you can hit the target a second time, I will refund the rest of your money and add a coin as a reward." He put his hands on his hips. "And if by some miracle you can hit the target at the final distance, you can win one of these wonderful cloaks." The elf drew our attention to a tent that held three different cloaks. Each one looked to be made of silk, with yellow embroidery on the edges and yellow braided strings for ties. One was a brilliant blue with snowflakes embroidered into it. A glistening green cloak with ivy twisting and turning as it decorated the edges was positioned on a stand next to the blue one, and the final cloak was made of radiant red silk with outlines of bird wings running along the edge.

"They are magical and will never get dirty, no matter what you put them through." Evalana and I snapped our attention back to him. He smiled mischievously. "But as you can see, nobody has been able to hit the final target. Three coins, and you can take your shot. Who knows, you might be one of the lucky ones."

Evalana pulled out six coins and slapped them on the table with an unnecessary amount of force. I looked at her, confused. *Did she forget how to count?*

She looked at me and bounced with excitement. "You have to try; you would look so cute with one of those on you."

"I can't shoot," I complained.

"Well, figure something out. You have to at least try," she said as she grabbed the crossbow.

The elf came to the table and swiped the coins in a single motion. He stepped back, away from Evalana and her line of sight. Once she had the crossbow loaded and was looking down at the sights, the game master held a hand up to his mouth.

"Throw!"

I was prepared for the shout, so it wasn't as bad as it could have been. Stanley heaved the target into the air about an arc over his head, much higher than I was expecting. Evalana lined up her shot and fired the crossbow, barely flinching from the recoil. Her shot flew harmlessly to the left of the target.

"Oh, what terrible luck, but that's your shot, missy. You're up next, young lady." The pudgy elf pointed at me.

Evalana placed the crossbow down softly, her face dark. "Sorry, I'm not a very good archer." She stepped back from the table.

"You paid for two shots. Try again." I motioned for her to return to the table.

"I'm sorry, but she missed. She doesn't get a second chance. She's paid for your attempt, so you might as well take it." *I don't like the tone of his voice.* "Or are you too scared to give it a simple shot?"

Something snapped when I heard him call me cowardly. My blood boiled as I glared at him, studying him. *Wait, carnival games are rarely based on skill. There's always a trick that stacks the odds in the vendor's favor. What is his trick?*

"Fine," I said with a slight growl.

My growl caught everyone's attention, and suddenly, all the conversations stopped. I grabbed the crossbow, and, without grabbing the winch, I pulled the string back to reset the weapon. *Wait, that was too easy.* I looked at the elf again, and I could see him starting to sweat.

"How did you just do that?" He trembled as he stood there.

"I'm stronger than I look." I grinned.

"Wow, you really *are* strong." Evalana's eyes grew wide with amazement.

Allen had tried to give me the basics of ranged weaponry. I was strong enough to pull most crossbow strings back with my hands, even though it took a great deal of effort; I just needed to be careful and not cut them with my claws. Simyn showed me he could do the same thing, but he needed gloves so the cord didn't hurt his hands as much. But when I tried to shoot the weapon, I could never hold on to it quite right. If I had one that was specially made for my hands, I might be able to use one. But the one I held right now was poorly made, and I believed that the strength of the arms was far weaker than what should be expected on a weapon like this.

So that's how he does it. Nobody can hit the last target because the bolt or arrow can't make the distance. I guessed the bow would have a similar story if I tried to pull it back, but I wasn't going to. Allen had had me try to shoot a bow three times. I cut the string three times. We agreed I should never try again.

Without taking my eyes off the elf, I put the crossbow down. He started to shake and sweat even more. *He knows that I know. Now, how do I beat him at his own game?*

An idea hit me. I turned to Evalana. "Give me a rock."

I felt the ground shake as everyone's jaws collectively hit the dirt.

"What? Why?" Evalana collected herself and pulled a rock from the ground with her magic. It was about the size of a baseball, maybe a bit smaller. *Perfect.*

"No, you can't do that." The elf flailed his arms around. "That's against the rules."

I gave him a toothy grin. "And what rule would that be?" He

stopped instantly. "You said that all we needed to do was hit the target. You never said what we needed to hit the target with." He sputtered as he searched for a way out. "Or are you too afraid of a little girl with a rock?"

All the color drained from the man's face. I tossed the rock lightly in the air to judge its weight.

The sweat on his brow was a waterfall at this point. He turned his head, placed his hands around his mouth, and shouted, "Throw!"

I panicked and turned to see the target airborne. I focused and threw the rock sidearm, watching as it hit the dead center of the target and causing it to move backwards as it returned to the ground. I could feel every single eye of the crowd glued to me.

"I need another rock. If you could, make it the same size and shape as the last one you gave me." I held out a hand to Evalana, who was awestruck at my display. Without taking her eyes off me, she slowly collected another rock and shaped it so that it was perfectly round like the last one.

I've always had a knack for throwing things. I don't know why, but I can just feel the throw and what I have to do to hit my target. The first few times were difficult, as my balance was a little off. Learning to throw with a tail and while on my toes was challenging. I wonder if I was a baseball player in my last life because of how naturally good I am at throwing stuff.

I gave a sidelong glance at the elf. "My coin?"

I pointed to the table and watched as he begrudgingly pulled a single coin from his leather pouch. He placed it gingerly on the edge of the table.

"Throw!" I shouted as soon as his hand left the table. I turned to see Stanley shrug as he chucked the target into the sky while standing next to the second stone. I knew how high it was going to go and threw the stone hard, aiming for the apex of the target's trajectory. The rock whistled as it flew through the air until it embedded itself into the straw bundle.

Got it!

I held in my excitement. The target, again, landed away from Stanley, who looked even more flabbergasted than everyone else and stared in total silence as I embarrassed the swindler.

I turned to Evalana, who was busying herself with getting me more ammunition. I then pointed to the single coin on the table as I turned to look at the elf. The look of terror on his face left me elated.

"Be careful about who you taunt, little man." I lowered my voice to intimidate the idiot. He fumbled with the coins as he tried to grab them and place them on the table as fast as he could.

Once I had a stone in my hand, I turned and shouted as loudly as I could, "Throw!"

Stanley threw the target one more time, this time at the third stone. Adrenaline coursed through my body as I wound up my arm. I aimed low because I knew that travel time was my enemy. I put my whole body into it, throwing harder than I ever had before. As I released the stone, I almost lost my balance and nearly dislocated my shoulder from the force I used.

Ouch, that hurt.

The rock sailed through the air as it seemed to defy gravity and air resistance. The target was now slowly returning to the earth. I watched in anticipation. I'd aimed the rock correctly, but I hoped it would arrive at the right time.

Time slowed as the wrapped straw attempted to reunite itself with the ground. My rock was slowly beginning its downward trajectory. *It has the distance, but does it have the speed?* My thoughts shifted to doubt. Inch by inch, gravity pulled the target to the ground, quickly increasing the rate at which it fell. Once the target was almost at eye level with Stanley, panic crept up on me. But then I saw it and smiled.

The stone struck the top half of the target, causing it to spin. The target continued downward, but now it looked like a coin that had been flipped. It bounced as it hit the ground and flipped a few more times before finally settling.

"Yes!" I threw an arm up and celebrated. There was no holding back the laughter as I reveled in my victory. I turned to the elf, who was lying on the ground.

I think he fainted.

I grabbed the coins from the table and placed them in Evalana's hand while she just stared at the target at the other end of the range, speechless. I walked to the tent to claim my prize and put my hands on my hips as I examined the cloaks.

Now, what color would look best on me?

26

SAFETY BLANKET

I studied my three choices. *The green looks alright, and since I spend a lot of time in the woods, it would blend in.* I held my arm against the green cloak. *I don't like the way it looks next to my fur.* I turned my attention from it to the red cloak.

Me wearing a red-hooded cloak. That's ironic. I felt the texture and compared how it looked to my fur. *It looks better than the green, that's for sure. But I'm not the defenseless little girl who needs to be saved. That just leaves you.*

I walked up to my last option and held it as I examined the embroidery closely. *Like real snowflakes, each of these snowflakes is unique. The amount of work that went into this must have been incredible.* I smiled in amusement. *I think I like the way the blue looks against my fur. And it matches my eyes.*

I removed it from the stand and draped it over my shoulders. I tied the cords, securing the cloak in place. *This feels nice. Silk is much better than wool and cotton.* I enjoyed the feel of it against my fur as I returned to Evalana, who was looking at me with approval.

She smiled as I approached and gave me a thumbs-up. "It looks good on you. See, I told you. You look so cute."

I grabbed the sides of the cloak and fluttered them. "I like it too."

I could hear Stanley running towards us. The elven game master was still lying on the ground. I smirked at the sight.

Serves you right.

I then turned to see the throng of people staring at me, still in shock. *Why are they all staring at me?*

My heart quickened its pace as I eyed everyone nervously. We stood looking at each other. The air grew heavier the longer the silence continued.

Without warning, the crowd erupted into cheers and applause. Their sudden movement and shouts hurt. A few people started jogging towards me.

They're going to surround me, question me, and never leave me alone. I've got to get out of here.

I sprinted away from the people and back into the tent that housed the other two cloaks. I looked around frantically for another exit, but I couldn't find one.

Fine, I'll make one.

I cut a vertical line through the backside of the tent with my claws and jumped out. As I exited the tent through my impromptu door, I looked around and saw more people around me. A portion of the people in the crowd at the game saw me and continued to cheer for me, but their volume hurt my ears.

No! Leave me alone.

I looked around frantically to get away from the noise and saw a small opening between a pair of tents that some people had walked out of. They looked at me with shock as I sprinted to the small opening.

As I dove between the two tents, I turned and saw that the people had followed me. This time, they had a look of curiosity. I turned around and continued into a stall full of rugs. All the rugs possessed beautiful and intricate patterns in various colors and sizes.

A conservatively dressed human woman looked at me with disbelief.

"Who is she? Is she your helper?" someone called from the table as they looked at the rugs on display.

"No. Who are you, little girl? What are you doing back there?"

Her scratchy voice didn't help my nerves. "Leave me alone." I jumped on to the table displaying the handcrafted rugs.

"No, get down from there!" The woman pointed a finger at me.

I got off the table by jumping from it over the crowd of people to another cart filled with bright-green bananas. I stood on the edge of it, carefully trying to maintain my balance. I glanced down and saw another row of people looking at me while pointing.

There were some shouts, but I didn't bother listening to what they said. I jumped over the crowd once more and ran to the side of a tent to cut my way through again. The heavy scent of grass assaulted my nose. From the floor to the ceiling of the structure, someone had stored piles of plants in neat columns. It looked very similar to wheat grains, except that it was green and covered in very fine hairs.

This is the plant, haze! Mom will kill me if she sees me anywhere near this stuff.

I looked at the light at the entrance of the tent and navigated through there to the exit.

"Hey! You aren't supposed to be back there." I was approached by a tall, scrawny man wearing an olive-green shirt and brown pants. He reached for me, but I easily stayed out of his grasp, his movements like those of someone stuck in thick syrup.

I continued to run through crowds, tents, games, stalls, and even a couple of performances. Each moment raised my heart rate as people looked at me and pointed. Shouts surrounded me, causing my ears to hurt even more. I desperately looked for a way out, but I didn't know where I was or where I wanted to go. I threw all rational thoughts out of my mind as I chose my directions haphazardly, attempting to find a place without people, but things only got worse for me because people started chasing me.

I don't know what they want, and I don't want to know. Leave me alone. Where's my room? Mom, where are you?

I continued running and jumping around, but the people following me were trying to cut me off and surround me. I eventually found an exit from the maze of tents, carts, tables, and people.

In the distance, I saw a cart next to the entrance of the arena, and I spotted a beacon of hope beside it.

Zenny! I don't know why she's here, but I need her help. The shouting continued to follow me as I raced to my closest friend.

Zenny turned her head in my direction a moment before I tackled her. "Lucia?" Zenny had a confused look on her face right before I tackled her. "Oof."

I clutched my friend close as I whispered in her ear, "Help me."

"It's okay. What's wrong?" She held me close as she whispered back.

"Too many people," I said in a shaky voice.

"Alright, come with me," Zenny said with a caring tone. She stood up and urged me to follow her. "We'll get you somewhere quiet."

I complied and followed her into the building.

When we entered, Salien greeted me with a surprised look. "Lucia? What happened?" Her voice was gentle, as always. She immediately moved to inspect me.

Zenny stopped her. "Lucia just needs to calm down. She's having another panic attack. She's been around too many people again."

"I'm sorry. You shouldn't have to do this for me. I need to get over this myself, but I just can't." My voice caught in my throat as tears formed in my eyes.

"Shh. It's okay. I'm happy to help." Zenny opened a door to a room full of beds lined up with folding wooden screens stationed between each one. "Come on, we'll be alone here until you calm down." We sat down on the bed closest to the door.

"You can stay here with Lucia until she's feeling better," Salien said as she closed the door.

I held Zenny tightly but made sure I didn't squeeze too hard. I broke down in tears.

Zenny sat quietly, holding me softly as I unloaded my emotional turmoil onto her shoulder. Slowly, the tears stopped, and I felt my heart slow down. I could hear footsteps heading to the door.

"No, leave her alone. She needs to calm down. She'll come out when she's ready. You will wait until then." I heard Salien talking and walking this way.

She's not alone.

"Then we'll wait here," a calm, feminine voice responded.

"If you wait too long, she'll escape again." There was a third voice. It was familiar, but it sounded like they were in a panic.

"There are no other exits in that room. You have my word." Salien's tone shifted to a much darker one.

"Listen, we'll get this all sorted out soon enough." The calm voice sounded like they were talking to the familiar voice.

The three sets of footsteps settled just outside the door. *This won't be good. I guess I caused a bit of a scene. Now I'm in trouble with no legal guidance.*

"Are you feeling better?" Zenny asked as she continued to hold me close.

"Yeah. Thanks." After I released Zenny from my hold, I wiped my tears on my arm. "I wish I was half as good a friend to you as you are to me."

"I'm sure you'll have your chance to make it up to me," Zenny said with a gentle smile.

"So what are you two doing here?"

My friend's smile grew disproportionately large. "Nora asked us to come with you so that you had even more friendly faces."

I glared at her. *You're still not telling me everything.*

She laughed nervously. "Okay, Mom says we need the money. Apparently this is supposed to pay really well." She dropped her shoulders for a moment before putting on a genuine smile. "But since Mom is such a good doctor, they invited her personally."

I guess that's fair. Except the part where you said I need friendly faces. Ah, who am I kidding? I couldn't be happier that she's here. Especially at this moment.

I gave my friend a slight smile as I heard the shuffling of footsteps just outside the door. "I guess I should see what the commotion is about." Zenny and I stood up to leave. "Apparently somebody wants to talk to me."

Zenny furrowed her eyebrows. "How do you know? Oh, that's right." I gave her a wry smile. "Your ears are..."

"A double-edged sword," I interrupted.

"I was going to say really useful," Zenny said with a pout.

She isn't wrong. But my statement still stands.

I opened the door to see Salien standing between me and two figures. One was the short, heavy-set elf from whom I'd won the cloak. The other was a taller elf woman who looked like a knight. Her pristine breastplate armor nearly glowed in the dim light of the windowless room. She had round metal pauldrons with chain mail from her shoulders to her wrists. Heavy leather gloves covered her hands, and a white quilted gambeson skirt flowed down to her shins, where metal plated boots covered her feet. A short sword sat quietly sheathed on her right hip.

"Ah, the little thief shows herself at last." The elven game master pointed a thick finger in my direction.

"Thief?" Salien, Zenny, and I shouted simultaneously.

"This gentleman here is claiming that this beastkin has stolen one of his prizes. The blue cloak that she's wearing." The knight pointed towards the other elf, then to me.

"No, I didn't. I won it fair and square." I glared at the elf.

"I didn't give it to you. You just took it." The elf raised his voice at me.

"You fainted. So I left you on the ground and claimed my prize." I pointed my finger at him as I took a few steps towards him.

"Waterfalls." Zenny grabbed my arm and tried to pull me back.

Everyone except Salien turned to Zenny.

"You want me to calm down as this lying little cheat is accusing me of something I didn't do?" I jabbed a claw towards the shorter elf.

"You need to calm down before you do or say something wrong," Zenny pleaded with me.

"I'm sorry, little girl. Since she is being officially charged with a crime, she has to come with me for questioning." The woman moved between me and my accuser. "Are you going to cooperate with me?"

I pulled my arm away from Zenny. "Where are we going?" I crossed my arms and flicked my tail.

"The oracle stone," the knight answered calmly.

"Fine," I said, not holding back a growl.

"Am I going to get my cloak back now?" The elf's voice grated on my ears.

"Since you've had nothing but an attitude with me, no." The

knight rounded on the game host, raising her voice at him. "You will come with us. If she's guilty, then you will get your precious cloak back."

"But, but, but—" the pudgy elf sputtered.

"No buts!" The sight before me reminded me of a mother scolding her child, and the man lowered his eyes as he hunched over in defeat.

"Alright, let's go," the knight said, returning to her normal, smooth voice, but I could tell her frustration remained.

I need a second opinion. Oh right, Zenny has the memorization aptitude. She's read all the laws. She'd make the best lawyer. "Can Zenny come?"

"Will she be a distraction?" The elf narrowed her eyes at me while she stood in the doorway.

"She's much better behaved than me," I quipped. "Besides, she might know the laws better than you."

"Right." The knight glared at me as she turned around. "There's nothing keeping her from coming with us." She started down the hall.

We followed her out of the room.

"Aren't you going to restrain her?" the elf asked. "What if she runs away again?"

I'm going to hurt this man if he says another word. I growled at him.

"Do I need to restrain you?" the elven woman asked as she looked at me. I shook my head. She then turned her attention to the whiny little bug next to her. "I will bind and gag you if you say another word. So unless I ask you a question, keep that mouth closed. Got it?" The woman poked the top of the man's head as she put her face inches from his, and the man's eyes went wide as he nodded. She straightened her breastplate.

Salien nudged her daughter towards me. "Go, take care of Lucia. I'll get everything set up, and you can bring her back for lunch."

"We'll be back soon." Zenny waved to her mother.

When we exited the building, I saw a girl in green clothes running our way. *Evalana?*

The knight continued to lead us to the grand building, where Allen told me all the other knights were staying.

Evalana soon caught up to us. She was winded, and I thought I could hear a whistle in her breathing. "What's going on?" Evalana inhaled roughly between each word as she struggled to stay upright.

The elven knight turned to see who was asking. "Who are you?" she asked as she placed a hand on her short sword.

27

COURT SUMMONS

"Evalana? What are you doing?" I asked the exhausted girl.

"Shouldn't I be asking you the same thing?" Evalana asked as she caught her breath. "I need to tell you that the knights are looking for you. That elf you won the cloak from is accusing you of stealing it." Her voice rose with each word.

I cleared my throat and pointed to the knight on my right. "You're a little late."

Evalana turned to the knight and blushed at the sight. "Oh," she mumbled.

"What do you have to do with Lucia?" Zenny asked Evalana with a look of disbelief.

"Who are you?" Evalana used Zenny's tone.

"Enough." I flinched at the knight's volume. "Listen, we are going to deal with..." She looked at the short elf and blinked a few times. "You know, I don't actually know your name."

"Paeris Brown Opal," the pudgy little elf answered with a bored look on his face.

I shook my head to dispel the pain from our escort's shout. "I'm Lucia. This is Zenny, and that's Evalana." I pointed to each person

when I said their name. "The only name we're missing now is yours."
My tone carried with it all the intended sass.

Everyone turned to look at the elven woman.

"Captain Aenwyn Glimmerstance." She bowed slightly. "Now
that everyone has made their introductions, can we return to the business at hand?" She waved in the direction we had been heading before
Evalana stopped us. "Paeris has charged Lucia with stealing his prop-
erty. You can have your chat after we settle everything."

"I'm coming too," Evalana blurted out.

"This is a trial, young lady, not a play date." Aenwyn lowered her
voice. "We already have one tagalong, and I would like to get this mess
sorted before lunch."

"But I saw the whole thing," Evalana said as she puffed out her
chest when she stepped up to the knight.

"A witness?" An amused look crept onto Aenwyn's face. "Well,
that changes everything. Please follow us this way." The knight gave a
glance at Paeris. I looked too and saw the elf dripping in sweat.

That's right, little piggy, panic.

"Maybe we could come to some kind of agreement." Paeris's voice
shook as he fidgeted with his fingernails. "We don't need to use the
oracle stone. If she would just give back the cloak, we could just forget
this ever happened."

"Or you could just drop the charges and run away with your tail
between your legs," I taunted. "I like this cloak, and I won it fairly."

"No, you cheated!" Paeris pointed his stubby finger at me again.
Everyone stared at him. Panicking, he put his hands over his mouth.

"Please, continue," I said with a wide smile.

Aenwyn crossed her arms as she glared at the short, balding liar.
"Yes, what really happened?" She tapped her foot as she put her hands
on her hips.

Evalana started talking before anyone else. "Lucia and I played his
game after he told us the rules. He said that if we could hit the target
three times, we would win one of the cloaks. I missed my shot, but
Lucia threw rocks and hit the target three times. After she hit the
target the last time, he fainted, and she picked her prize." She took a

deep breath. "But when the crowd began cheering and congratulating her, she took off running, and I've been trying to catch up with you. Why did you run? And how are you that fast?"

"Did you really use rocks?" Aenwyn looked at me, studying me.

"You were supposed to use the bow or crossbow on the table," Paeris blurted out.

I flexed my claws as my tail flicked back and forth behind me. "You mean use the obviously insufficient equipment you provided? That crossbow was terrible. You thought I couldn't hit the target, so you agreed to it anyway. It isn't my fault that I proved you wrong."

"Lucia, calm down. Waterfalls," Zenny whispered in my ear.

I closed my eyes and took a deep breath.

"Nobody can throw a rock like that! You had to have cheated." Paeris's shouts broke my concentration.

"How far was it?" Aenwyn looked down at Paeris.

"Sixteen arcs," Paeris said as he put his hands on his hips. "You see? She had to have cheated. Maybe she used her friend's magic."

I snapped my eyes open and stared at Paeris. I growled as I bared my fangs at him.

Zenny walked in front of me and put her hands on my shoulders. "Waterfalls. I'll handle this. Just concentrate on calming down," Zenny whispered to me. "She has the physical aptitude, so she's much stronger than she appears," she said as she turned to face Aenwyn without taking her hands off my shoulders. "Please, she needs to calm down."

"What happens if she doesn't calm down?" Evalana asked.

"I will hunt down a little piggy and make him squeal." My voice rumbled with a growl. *I wonder if all elves taste sweet.*

"You heard her. She's going to hurt me. Restrain her." Paeris pointed at me and waved his other arm around.

"Stop shouting," Zenny barked in a low tone. "Please. She hunts things all the time. It's what she wants to do, be a hunter."

Aenwyn started laughing.

Snapping out of my intense stare-down with Paeris, I watched the elven knight's bizarre actions.

Once Aenwyn stopped laughing, she wiped away a tear from her eye. "I believe she said she was going to hunt a pig. Are you calling yourself a pig?" She looked at Paeris, grinning from ear to ear.

Paeris's eyes popped out of his head as his mouth gaped open. "I-I-I..." He spurted sounds more than words. He shuffled his feet and looked at the ground. "I wish to drop the charges." He moved to turn and run.

"Oh, no you don't. Halt." Aenwyn's voice stopped Paeris mid-stride. He slowly turned his head back to us with an undeniable look of fear on his face. "I'm not done with you." A shiver ran down my spine from her tone even though she hadn't directed it at me.

"But I dropped the charges." Paeris's voice rose in pitch. He held out his hands as he ducked his head into his shoulders.

"Yes, you did." Aenwyn walked up to Paeris and put a hand on the back of his neck. "But now there are charges against you." She leaned in close to the whimpering man. "You falsely accused a citizen of this kingdom." She turned to me quickly. "You are a citizen of this kingdom, right? I remember there being some kind of rumor going on about a beastkin living in Aquittemia for the last few years. Are you that beastkin?"

I raised an eyebrow. "I am."

Aenwyn returned her attention to Paeris. "So, as I was saying, for disturbing the peace, false accusations, and annoying me, you are going to settle these charges." Her voice was deceptively upbeat. Paeris swallowed hard as his knees started shaking. "Don't move." She put a finger an inch from Paeris's nose, and the color drained from his face as he slumped to his knees. "Ugh." Aenwyn let go of Paeris, leaving his body a lump on the ground, and flicked her hand like she needed to wipe something disgusting off.

"Am I free to go?" My tail still flicked behind me in a jerky motion.

"Just one moment." Aenwyn reached into her belt pouch and pulled out some coins. She walked over to me and presented me with ten coins. I looked at her, confused. "For the inconvenience."

I looked at Zenny and Evalana, still confused. Evalana looked as unsure as me, but Zenny nodded and motioned to Aenwyn's hand.

"Thank you," I said as I tentatively grabbed the coins.

"You're welcome. Now that we've finished with that business, do you really have the physical aptitude?" Again, Aenwyn gave me an appraising look.

I rolled my eyes and held out my hand. When she took it, I squeezed as hard as I could. She cried out in pain and surprise.

Once I released her, she gently cradled her injured hand. "Yeah, you sure do."

"Why does that keep surprising people?" I placed the coins in the pouch that hung around my neck.

"You know that the physical aptitude is rare, right?" Evalana inched backwards from me as she brought her arms to her chest.

I gave her a glare to shut her up.

"As I said, I'm a captain. More specifically, captain of The Maidens." Aenwyn straightened up. "I'm quite tempted to extend you an invitation to join The Maidens right now. That is, if you want to become a knight. Where do you live?"

"I live at the orphanage in Aquittemia." I crossed my arms as I eyed her up and down. *She wants something. Nobody wants me.*

"Oh, I'm so sorry." Aenwyn covered her mouth as her eyes welled up with tears. "Don't worry, we'll take good care of you when you join us in a couple of years."

"Seven," I muttered.

"Huh?" Aenwyn said.

"Seven years. I'm ten." I scraped my toe claws through the dirt. *Seven long years. Two years after I'm done growing up, too.*

"But you look like you're fifteen. Maybe a little underdeveloped, but that may be because you won't grow that big." Aenwyn's words gushed from her mouth as Paeris moaned as he showed signs of life. Aenwyn gave him a quick glance. "Well, I'm sure you will grow up to be a really tall, beautiful woman. I'll take care of this fool. If you want to speak with me, just look for any woman with this symbol on her breastplate and ask to talk to me." She pointed to the crown wrapped around a sunflower etched into her armor. "By the way, that blue is a lovely color on you. It matches your eyes."

I smiled as the three of us watched as Aenwyn carried Paeris away towards the large mansion.

"You never told me you were ten years old," Evalana interrupted the silence with a whiny tone. "You're almost as tall as me. I know I'm small in the chest because my mom is."

"It's because I'm a beastkin." My shoulders dropped now that Paeris was out of my sight. "Also, you never asked."

I smelled something acrid. *Did he pee in his pants?* I took a few deep sniffs. *He did. Gross!* I walked away from where Paeris had fainted. The two other girls followed me.

"What's wrong?" Zenny asked me as she placed a hand on my arm.

"That pig of a man wet himself when he fainted, and I can still smell it." I kept marching away from the spot until we were close to the door we'd exited through earlier.

Zenny relaxed as she let go of my arm. "So, Evalana, who are you to Lucia?" Zenny asked the girl.

"Oh, I'm staying in the room next to hers," Evalana chirped. "We're friends. But who are you? You act like you know what she's going to do before she does it."

"I've been her best friend for five years." Zenny smiled at me. "Is she really your friend?"

I shrugged my shoulders. "I guess so. She's been friendly enough once we sorted out our dietary differences."

I watched both girls look at me with wide eyes.

I can understand Evalana's reaction, but why is Zenny acting the same? Zenny jumped up and gave me the biggest hug she could muster. Evalana followed her example.

"Um, what's this?" I held out my arms as I looked at the two girls holding me.

"I'm so happy for you," Zenny said as she squeezed me. "You made a friend."

"You said I was your friend," Evalana said shortly after Zenny.

"I guess that is an improvement for me, isn't it?" I lowered my voice as I talked more to myself.

"Now that you have another friend, you can make all the friends you want." Zenny released me from her hug and looked up at me.

"How about I work with the ones I have now?" I said with a smile. I collected my friends for another group hug, and a warm feeling rose from my heart.

2 8

EXTRA RULES

S pending the rest of the day with Zenny was fun. We invited
Evalana to join us for some lunch, but she said she needed to
see her parents. Salien didn't get everything set up before lunch
like she wanted, so after we ate, I helped her and Zenny finish, and a
couple of other assistants joined us. I still had to fulfill my promise to
Jayne and exercise with my gambeson on, so I put it on and ran
around the entire village and festival grounds several times until I felt
tired. And I hated every moment of it.

I closed the door to my room to get away from the stares of the
other girls in the hall. *The feeling of Zenny and Evalana hugging me
felt so much better than their stares. I guess having friends isn't too bad.
I've been going it alone for this long. Now that I've made peace with the
wolf inside me, I need to make peace with everyone around me.*

After stripping off the awful gambeson, I threw it on my bed as I
changed my clothes. *I know Zenny's always been my friend and treated
me like one. But each time I went to her for help, it had always been
when I couldn't handle my problems by myself. The same has been true
with Mom. I should try to let them help me.*

The other girls had already settled in for the night. Evalana gave
me a quick "good night" before settling down in her room.

I just hope I don't hurt them in the end. I think I need to learn how to tell them how to help me, but I'm still lost trying to figure out how to help myself. Over the years, I've forgotten what it feels like to have friends. Even if they don't understand everything about what I'm going through, that doesn't mean I should just block myself off from everyone.

I stuck my head out the window. The moons were still climbing as they dodged the few clouds in the sky. A light breeze carried the scent of the festival. Despite the unpleasant odor, the stillness of the night was calming. *Zenny was right; I'm my own worst enemy. Maybe I should try to open up more. Who knows? Maybe one day I'll meet someone who knows what it's like to be such an outcast. That elf knight lady was really nice to me. Even though she was there to arrest me.*

I looked at the azure cloak, neatly folded on top of my travel chest, and grabbed my brush to start brushing my fur. *Everything worked out in the end. And she said she wanted to extend an invitation to join her company. Maybe I have a chance. Maybe I can be a knight. If I do well in the tournament, I can ask her. The tournament starts tomorrow. Right, tomorrow.*

I sat on the lumpy attempt at a mattress. *Tomorrow is the big day. The big day where I'll stand in an arena and fight with who knows how many people watching. I had another episode today after playing the game. I did just fine during the game, but as soon as I noticed the crowd and they started cheering, I freaked out.*

I placed my hands on my head. *How am I going to survive tomorrow? I know I talked a big game when I decided to do this, but it's a whole other thing to actually go through with it.*

I curled my tail around my waist as I brushed it. *I need to sleep, but I just can't. I've already run four laps around the whole festival, and I'm tired, but I just can't relax.*

I looked at my gambeson. Sighing, I folded it into a pillow again since nobody sold a decently priced pillow. I lay my head down and huddled in my new blanket. Eventually, I fell into a dreamless sleep.

I heard my door open. I shot out of my bed, throwing off my blanket. *An intruder!* With my claws at the ready, I stood in a low three-point stance as I scanned the room.

Jayne stood in the doorway with her arms raised defensively. "Sorry," she said as she backpedaled out of my room. "I knocked, but you didn't answer."

Seeing a friendly face, I relaxed. *She's not an enemy. I knew she was coming in the morning. Wait, if she's here, that means it's morning.* I looked at the shutters and saw that the sun hadn't risen over the horizon, but the light foretold its eventual arrival. "Sorry." I turned to Jayne. "I didn't sleep well last night, and I'm a bit on edge." My heart was racing. "Okay, a lot on edge."

Jayne relaxed as she entered. "Are you nervous about today? Don't worry, you'll do fine."

"I'm not worried about how I'll do." I motioned for Jayne to close the door. "I'm more worried about what I will do and how people will react to me." My head dropped, along with my ears and tail, as I sat down on the bed.

"Do you want to quit now, before you even try?" Jayne kneeled next to me. "Why are you doing this, then? If you didn't want to do it, why even come? If you don't want to answer me, at least answer it for yourself." She placed a hand on my shoulder.

"I want to prove to myself that I can do this, but I'm scared." Tears welled in my eyes. "I'm so scared that I'll lose control again, scared that I'll kill someone, scared that I can't be saved this time."

"I can't even begin to understand what you're feeling right now," Jayne whispered to me. "But sometimes the wisest decision is to run away."

I fought back the tears as I wiped my face with the back of my hand. "If I run away now, what's to stop me from running away the next time? Or the time after that?" I looked at Jayne. "I have to take a stand, but it's terrifying me to do it."

"Deciding to do the things we know we should do will never be a simple decision. It's always easier to do nothing. Deciding to act even though you have every reason not to, that takes the greatest amount of courage." Jayne smiled gently. "Remember, courage isn't the absence of fear, it's the will to overcome it."

"I've heard that before," I said as I stood up. "It still doesn't make it any easier."

"Yeah, I know." Jayne glanced at the ground.

There was something in the air. I took a few experimental sniffs. "What smells so good?"

"I figured you might want some breakfast." Jayne stood up and reached behind her back and presented a small sack.

My stomach growled as I snatched it. I ripped it open with a claw and saw a few small pieces of jerky. "Is this it?" I looked at Jayne, hoping there was more.

"You're welcome, by the way. If you don't want it, then give it back." She reached for it, but I pulled it away from her and growled. *Mine!* "What's up with you? Shouldn't that be more than enough?"

"Sorry, I shouldn't have growled at you." I looked at the ground, trying to hide my flushed cheeks. "Thank you for thinking about me. But I can easily eat three times this amount. I mean, just yesterday I ate an entire rabbit for breakfast. Organs and all."

"How? How can you eat so much and still be so thin?" Jayne sounded exasperated. "I wish I was a dozen years younger and could eat like that. Even when I was your age, I still couldn't eat that much. Where do you put it all?" She laughed.

"I run around a lot." I placed the jerky on my bed and moved to my chest to dig out some clothes to wear and my gambeson. "You don't mind, do you?" I held up the clothes I picked out to Jayne.

"Don't worry about me." Jayne waved her hand as she turned to look out the window. "Did you do as I suggested yesterday?"

You just had to remember.

"Yes," I said in a grumpy tone. "It wasn't any better. With the sun down, it was a little cooler, but it was still awful. Don't tell me I have to wear it the entire day?" I progressively shifted to a whiny tone.

"No, just any time you're in the arena," Jayne said in her usual upbeat voice.

I finished changing. "Good, because I hate it." I glared at the offending garment. I scooped up the jerky and gnawed on it. "If I'm not mistaken, this is deer jerky." I admired the next piece of meat before I devoured it.

Jayne turned and looked at me, perplexed. "Can you tell the difference?"

"Oh, yeah," I said as I swallowed the next piece. "You could say

I'm quite the connoisseur of meat." I smiled as I popped the next piece into my mouth and savored the gamy, sour taste.

"A what now?" Jayne's face contorted further, putting her confusion on display.

I shrugged my shoulders. *I guess that word isn't used in this world.* "It means I know what every kind of meat tastes like and can tell the difference." I grabbed my gambeson and prepared to follow Jayne. "If it walks on land or flies in the sky, I know what it tastes like."

Jayne gave me a sidelong gaze. *Oh, no. Please don't ask if I know what people taste like. I* will *lie.* She just mercifully walked by and opened the door.

I popped the last piece of jerky into my mouth and made a show of chewing on it.

"Since your breakfast is done, let's get you where you need to go. I know Allen wants to talk to you before the opening ceremony." She waved her arm out to the empty hallway. I could hear other people moving around their rooms and a few unpleasant sounds coming from the person across the hall from me.

I looked at the nameplate on the door where it sounded like someone was constipated. *Diana* was engraved on it. *I really hope the smell is gone by the time I get back.* On my way out, I grabbed my brush because my fur was sticking up in several spots, then followed Jayne down the hall and to a small room near the hospital wing where Zenny and Salien were staying.

Allen sat at a square table across from Nora, which was barren except for a large clay cup sitting on the edge closest to the door. Crates of varying sizes lined the walls. Allen looked to be still trying to wake up, while Nora smiled at me as if she had been awake all night.

"Thirsty?" Nora motioned to the cup.

"Yes, thank you." I threw the gambeson on the nearest crate and placed my brush on the table as I picked up the cup and drank the water. "Ahh. I needed that." As I put the cup back down, I wiped the small drops of water from my lips. *I guess I hadn't realized how dehydrated I was.*

"Feel better?" Nora asked as she continued to smile at me.

"How did you know I was thirsty?" I picked my brush back up and resumed taming my fur.

"Your nose looked dry. Here, let me help you with your hair." She waved her hand to invite me over. "How did you sleep last night? Are you ready for the big day? How do you feel?" Her tone became increasingly more upbeat with each question.

I walked over to Nora and handed her my brush as I turned my back to her. "Honestly, I didn't sleep that well." My tone darkened the mood. "I'm still terrified about today. It feels like there's something in my stomach, something heavy." I felt Nora place a hand on top of my head and begin scratching, and my body melted as she did. *I guess this calms me down.* I wagged my tail as I pushed my head into her hand more.

"Oof." Nora stopped scratching my head.

I turned to see what had happened, and I saw Nora clutching her stomach. "Your tail has some kick to it." She giggled through her grimace.

"I'm sorry, I just..." I began pleading, but Nora put a finger on my lips.

"Shh, it's okay. I know." She smiled as she again placed her hand on my head and scratched right behind my left ear.

I bit back a moan as I wagged my tail enthusiastically.

Without warning, she removed her hand. *Why did you stop?* I stared at Nora, longing for her to return to the head scratches.

"You want more?" Nora looked at me mischievously, and I nodded. "Then be a good girl."

Give me more head scratches. "I will be the best girl you have ever seen," I blurted out. *Now I sound like an addict.*

"Do you promise?" Nora said, holding her hand over my head.

"I promise!" I shouted.

"Does that mean you're going to wear your gambeson?" Allen asked.

I deflated. "Don't worry, I'll wear it, but only while I'm in the arena." I stared at the ground, fidgeting with my claws.

"What's wrong with it? Doesn't it fit? They should have fixed that yesterday." It was easy to hear Allen's concern in his voice.

"No, it fits fine." I continued picking at my claws.

"She says it's uncomfortable." Jayne revealed my secret.

"It's not uncomfortable. It's borderline torture," I whined, and Allen stared at me. "It's too hot. I can't wear it for long periods of time."

"I never thought about that. Do you sweat that much?" Allen continued to look at me curiously.

"I don't sweat." I crossed my arms as I pouted. "While I share some human anatomy, sweating is one thing I don't do." *Technically, I sweat through my pads, but that does almost nothing to help cool me down.* "To cool down, I have to pant like a wolf." I gave Nora a side-long look. She was just sitting and watching me with a smile.

"I'll try to remember that," Allen said as his cheeks turned red and he looked away from me. He cleared his throat after an awkward silence. "Anyway, I wanted to talk to you about your special circumstances."

I snapped my attention to Allen. "I have special circumstances?" My tail flicked back and forth as I lowered my ears.

"After your display yesterday, running through the festival, other knights from Aquittemia thought it was required that we give the rest of the knights here the same briefing they received," Allen said unenthusiastically.

I narrowed my eyes at Allen. "What did you tell them about me?" My voice was low as I growled.

Allen gave me a look of concern. "Only what I believed to be relevant for everyone's safety."

"Elaborate." I let out a more threatening growl.

Allen watched me closely. "Anytime you feel anything is too much for you, just shout your code word, 'Waterfalls.' Everyone is also being told that if you say the word to them, they need to leave you alone. Coincidentally, if you say that during a match, they will understand it as you surrendering."

"Salien's informed of everything and has set up an extra room for you to use whenever you need to," Nora whispered in my ear.

"I don't get angry on purpose, you know." I stopped growling, but I still flicked my tail back and forth.

"We know. But there are many more people that have never dealt with you. We're trying to give you options to get away should you need to," Nora said.

"Fine." I stormed to my gambeson that was still sitting on the crate and picked it up. "When does this whole thing start?"

"The opening ceremony will begin shortly, and then the matches will be determined by drawing lots," Jayne said as she stood next to me.

So I'm being treated as a threat to public safety. They talk about all these things to do when I'm angry, like it's supposed to put me at ease. All it does is rile me up.

I left the room behind Jayne and slammed the door shut. *Just in case they don't already know that I'm irritated.*

Before we headed to where all the participants were gathering, Jayne made sure I knew where the hospital wing was. *I won't remember this. If I have to leave, I'll find the nearest exit and run to the woods or fields. At least then it will be quiet.*

After walking the corridors some more, Jayne led me to an underground armory. Different swords, spears, maces, bows, and other weapons of every variety were displayed on racks. Everything was made of either lusterless metal or orange-colored wood, and each weapon was blunt. The arrows and bolts intended for the bows and crossbows had ball-shaped tips. Across the room was a doorway where I could hear voices.

Jayne waved her arm, presenting the room to me.

"Go ahead, pick your weapon of choice," she said happily. "And you should put your gambeson on now. It can't be much longer until things get started. It looks like we're the last to arrive."

I looked around at the collection of weapons more closely. Everything was made to be as blunt as possible. I couldn't cut myself on a single blade no matter how hard I tried.

"It's a good thing I don't need to pick a weapon then, isn't it?" I said as I reluctantly opened the gambeson up.

"You don't use a weapon?" Jayne didn't hide her surprise.

I held up my hand and flexed my claws. "That's what these are for."

"Just remember, no killing," Jayne said.

"I'm destructive, not murderous." I pulled the gambeson over and adjusted it so my tail was comfortable.

"Is that any better?" Jayne said as she tied the strings at the back of my neck.

"I think so." I walked to the doorway and towards the voices. "But what do I know? I'm just a kid." I could tell Jayne wanted to say something, but she decided that she was better off following me silently.

29

A GENTLE NUDGE

Thirty-one teenagers stood in a long, wide hallway that ended in a doorway to the outside. My heart raced as every conversation flooded my ears. A few kids in the back noticed me and stopped talking to stare at me. I kept my distance from everyone as I constantly glanced back towards the armory, making sure my escape route was clear. Jayne stood next to me patiently.

Evalana caught sight of me and attempted to wave me over from the crowd, but I shook my head. She must have noticed my apprehension because she walked towards me. A pair of girls who looked to be about her age glanced at each other as they watched her walk away from them.

I locked eyes with her and shook my head. *I don't think I can handle meeting new people right now. It's taking everything in me not to run away.* Before she could reach me, a horde of trumpets started playing outside.

A booming voice filled the hall, silencing everyone. "Alright, quiet down!"

A human man walked into the hall from the large doorway. He was in plate-mail armor with a red sleeveless surcoat. The surcoat had many intricate designs of purple thread, all of which I couldn't discern. Everyone stopped talking to look at the man.

"Listen up. We're beginning now. When you hear your name, please come forward and follow the instructions I give you." His deep voice carried through the wooden hall.

At least everyone else stopped talking.

I could hear another voice from outside competing with the music and the growing cheers of the spectators. "Ladies and gentlemen, welcome. I will be your master of ceremonies for this part of the tournament."

One by one, everyone in the room was called forward and directed outside. Each time someone exited the hall, the crowd erupted in cheers. I didn't bother learning any names, and Evalana was called early, so she didn't get the chance to talk to me. My heart climbed higher in my throat with each person called. I couldn't stand still anymore, but I knew if I moved, I would run out the door. Standing in this hallway that was full of people, dressed in my gambeson, didn't help me. It wasn't long before I was getting too hot, and after about half the people were called, I started panting heavily. That earned me even more stares. Then the whispering started.

I imagine they're talking about me. There were too many conversations to discern anything. *They don't know what it's like to have a fur coat and wear this cloth armor that most people would wear during the ice season.*

I ignored them as much as I could so I could focus on keeping my panic to a minimum. Jayne went and retrieved a waterskin for me to drink out of.

Everyone else was called out of the hall, leaving me standing alone with Jayne behind me.

The man finally called my name. "Lucia."

I trudged up to him. *I can do this. I can do this. I can do this.* As I stood in front of him, I felt the roar of the crowd was too much for me to handle.

"Are you alright? You don't look so good." The man's hard, unshaven face looked down at me.

"No, but I'm going to do it anyway," I said, more to myself than to the guy. *I can do this.*

"Just go and stand at the end of the line on the right side. Next to James." He pointed in the direction where the last kid stood.

I can do this. I reached the threshold of the arena.

The crowd was cheering at the instigation of the announcer, and I froze. *I can't do this. What was I thinking? This is too much.*

"Please welcome our final contestant, Lucia!" the announcer shouted.

I could see the announcer. He wore a purple robe with gold trim. His bald head made it easy to see that he was an elf. He stood tall with a wiry arm outstretched towards me. I couldn't move. I locked every muscle in my body tight, and my mind was a whirlwind.

The announcer saw me standing perfectly still. A frown showed on his face for a moment before he put a smile back on. "Everyone give it up for Lucia!" He struck the same pose.

I have to do this. But I can't. It's too hard.

As I stood panicking, a small fire grew in my stomach. I felt a nudge on my back. I stepped forward reflexively. The crowd was silenced. I turned to see who had pushed me. Nobody was behind me, but I could feel a familiar feeling.

Was that you? I asked my inner wolf. *It had to have been.* Suddenly, an immense feeling of pride overwhelmed my fear. *I'm a wolf. I shouldn't fear food.* My feelings returned to what they were with the echo of pride still present, and I strode forward. *I'm still scared to death, but now it seems that the other part of me wants me to go through with this. But what was that thought about food?*

After I arrived at the spot where the man instructed me to stand, I noticed the crowd remained completely silent, and my heart pounded against my chest with increasing urgency. I stood next to some boy who was apparently named James. I clenched my fists and tried my best not to look at the people around me. The elven commentator had a smile on his face as I stared at him.

"Lucia joins us from Aquittemia. She is an orphan under the care of the national hero Nora Stormleaf." I watched as the well-dressed announcer addressed the audience. "For those who are wondering, yes, she is the beastkin that's rumored to have won an archery game by throwing a rock nearly twenty arcs."

The crowd stayed silent.

"Actually, it was only sixteen," I said as I turned my gaze to the ground at my feet.

There was a moment of silence from the announcer. I could feel everyone's eyes on me.

"Only sixteen arcs?" The master of ceremonies' voice pierced the silence throughout the arena. I looked up to see everyone staring at me. A switch flipped in my brain. I looked around for an exit, completely forgetting about the one I'd come in by. A small doorway was visible to my right. I sprinted towards the doorway.

I can't! Tears pooled in my eyes before they ran down my cheeks. The crowd exploded with noise that I couldn't handle. I ran straight into the doorway and into a small hallway with stairs going down.

Nora stood at the bottom.

I tackled her. She caught me, and we hit the ground. I shook as I grabbed onto her.

"Not so tight, please. I need to breathe." Nora barely got the words out.

I'd had enough of the horrible gambeson. I cut the strings on the back and pulled it over my head, then threw it away from me with a cry. Tears flowed down my face as I returned to clutching Nora. "I can't do it. I'm a failure," I said through my sobbing.

"Shh. Calm down." Nora grabbed ahold of me. She rubbed my back with one hand as she placed her other hand on the back of my head. "It's just the two of us. There's nobody else around. Nobody will hurt you. Shh." Nora sat up against the wall with me still attached.

"I can't do it." I buried my face farther into Nora's torso. "I'm a scared little girl who can't do it!" My wailing continued.

"Shh. Just let it out. You're safe." Nora rocked back and forth and held me as I broke down in her arms.

I don't know how long we stayed like that, but at one point, Nora put her hands on my ears to cover them. In the background I heard some muffled talking, but in my hysterical state, I didn't bother paying attention. Eventually, I found my emotional footing again, only to find a whole new level of depression.

"I'm sorry." I felt drained after releasing Nora. "This was a waste of time. Even though I talked big, I needed a shove from my inner wolf just to step out, only to chicken out in the end."

"What you did was a tremendous step for you." Nora held me even closer as she placed her hand on my head, just behind my right ear. "Focus on the fact that you said you would do this, and you did. That's worthy of praise." She started scratching behind my ear, but I moved my head away.

"But it's too much for me. It's too hard." I couldn't look her in the face.

"If it's hard, then the reward will be worth so much more once you succeed." Nora wiped the tears from my eyes. "Whether you believe it or not, what you did was extremely brave. You stood there in spite of your fear. Yes, you ran, but you fought your fear head-on. If you've done it once, you can do it again. Take as many attempts as you need, because I know one day you'll conquer it." She continued to wipe the rest of my face with the sleeve of her blue dress. "Remember, you're the wolf who said that she would carve her life out no matter what. Aren't you also the wolf who took on the challenge of a rigged game and won despite the odds against you? When that merchant accused you of stealing, did you back down? No, you stood your ground and defended yourself."

"How do you know about that?" My head snapped towards Nora.

"I met Captain Aenwyn." Nora smiled at me and gave me a wink. "She's taken quite a liking to you."

"But that was just one person." I pointed towards the arena. "There are hundreds out there."

"That's correct." Nora stared at me with a look of determination. "But what's the difference between fighting one opponent and fighting many? You've never backed down from a fight before. More often, you go looking for fights." Her face softened. "You keep saying you can't do it. But look at what you've done when you say you can't do it. Yesterday, you stood in front of a crowd and won a game that wasn't winnable. Today, you walked out in front of a crowded stadium and declared your accomplishment." She put her face inches from mine. "Imagine what you'll do tomorrow with even more courage than today."

"You're right." I finished wiping my face on my arm as I tried to collect my composure. "I should focus on what I accomplished instead of regretting that I missed the goal." Relaxing, I placed my head on her chest. "I'll take my head scratches now."

Nora giggled. "Alright, but you have a match coming up. Do you think you can do it? Or are you done?" Nora scratched right in the sweet spot behind my ears, and my heart rate dropped as I enjoyed the wonderful feeling.

"If I go, will you give me more head scratches?" I looked up at her, full of hope.

"If that's what you want, I can give you some after." Nora giggled again.

"Oh, and I want some of the bacon from the dire boar if they bring it back. Its heart too." I wagged my tail. "You know what? I'll just take all the organs. Nobody else wants them anyway. Except the brain, stomach, bladder, and lungs. Even I don't like those."

Nora gave me a look of shock. "Aren't you being a little greedy?" Her face shifted to thoughtfulness. "I'll make a deal with you. If you compete in every match that you're supposed to, at the end of the tournament I'll make sure you get some meat from the dire boar. That doesn't mean you need to win. If you lose this first match, it's okay. You'll still get the meat." Nora placed a finger on my nose. "But that doesn't mean you can forfeit right away. I want to see you try. I'm not worried if you try and lose."

I pulled out a trick I hadn't used for a while now. I looked up at her with a slight pout and quivered my eyes. "Promise?"

Nora gave me a knowing glare. *It didn't work.* "You don't need to do that to me. I promise. Now, is there anything you want before your first match?"

"Something to drink," I said as I got up to retrieve my gambeson.

30

ROUND 1, DOGPILE

Do it for the head scratches, I reminded myself when I came back out.

This was the last match before the lunch break. Since I wasn't present during the drawing of who fought in which order, they gave me the final remaining number. I stood in a corner on the square, raised platform known as the field.

To my left was the guy I'd stood next to during the opening ceremony, James. He was easily the tallest and largest competitor in this match, standing at over seventy inches tall. His golden hair was cut short, and his face was soft enough to likely earn him many looks from other girls. He wore a gray gambeson, and he held his longsword in both hands.

On my right was another boy, and I think I'd heard his name was Anno, or something like that. He was just a couple of inches taller than me. His boyish face was kind of cute to look at, especially when it was topped with his orange hair that flowed in waves to his shoulders. Everyone could see his pointy ears sticking straight up through his hair. His gambeson was green, and he held a mace in his left hand and a small round shield in his right.

Straight ahead, I saw the other girl in the match. The announcer said her name was Lestrana. She looked similar to Anno, with slightly pointed ears that weren't as long as Anno's. Her ears were on display since she had her green hair tied back in a ponytail that barely reached the base of her neck, and her bangs were a straight line an inch above her eyebrows. If she stood up straight, she would be the same height as me if you didn't include my ears. She wore a brown gambeson and held a bow in her hands. A quiver of arrows hung on a belt behind her, ready to be drawn by her right hand.

I stood watching them in my black gambeson, wishing I could rip the thing off. The three of them exchanged a wordless look and nodded to each other before staring at me.

I don't like where this is going.

I was barely holding myself together as the announcer spurred the crowd on. Nora had told me that he was also the judge. So, if he said the fight was over, it was over, usually because someone landed what would normally be a lethal blow.

Allen didn't mention that part when he explained the rules to me.

"Ready? Begin." The announcer's voice filled the arena.

The half-elf girl drew back an arrow and shot at me. I tilted my head to the side to avoid the projectile.

Did she just aim for my eye? I looked at the two boys and saw them charging right at me. *Do you want to gang up on me?* My vision tinted red as I prepared to charge in response. *You've picked the wrong prey.* As my vision finished shifting completely to red, the roar of the crowd lessened, and I charged straight for Anno.

Anno stuttered to a stop just before I reached him. He attempted to hit me with his mace, but I grabbed his wrist and dug my claws in. He screamed in agony and thrust his shield at my face. My vision blurred for a moment as I recoiled from it hitting my cheek. I grabbed the edge of his shield as I released a vicious growl, then pushed his shield towards his other arm.

A sickening snap sounded as the shield collided with Anno's arm and broke it, forcing the bones to protrude through the skin. Anno screamed, staring at the exposed bone as blood poured from the wound. I kicked his right foot before I turned and pulled him by his shield. He tripped, and I turned his arm around as I forced him to the ground.

An arrow slammed into my right shoulder. The rounded tip sent a shock of pain through me as it bounced off me and hit the ground.

I glared at Lestrana as she reached for another arrow. *You're next!*

I twisted and pulled at Anno's shield. Each scream from his bones breaking and joints dislocating filled me with indescribable joy. I stood over the elven boy triumphantly, his shield in my hands. His arm, from his elbow to his hand, had a few new places it could bend. I placed a foot on Anno and kicked him behind me. I heard him scream in agony as he tumbled out of the arena.

I looked at James and saw him standing still. His eyes were wide open, and his sword was angled towards the ground. Lestrana wasn't any more composed.

Are you scared now? Good, you should be.

Lestrana's courage broke as she realized that my gaze settling on her meant that she was my next target. *You shot at me twice. It's my turn.*

I sprinted towards her. She had enough presence of mind to shoot the arrow that she had nocked, but it was a trivial effort to block the shot with my borrowed shield. Once the arrow bounced off, I threw the shield like a frisbee at the half-elf. It was never designed to be thrown like that, and so it flew towards Lestrana but took a sharp dive towards the ground. It still struck her left knee.

The shrill shriek of pain that escaped her lips filled my chest with pride while also hurting my ears. She dropped her bow as she clutched her knee and fell to the ground.

I kept running towards her, and the fear on her face enticed me more.

Lestrana rolled over and tried to crawl away to the edge of the arena. She managed only a short distance before I grabbed her back and pulled her close to me.

"Where do you think you're going?" I asked with a low growl. "You aren't getting away from me that easily." I smiled as I savored the sounds of her whimpering.

"I yield!" she screamed. I flinched at her volume. Holding her closer, I growled even louder. "I yield." She broke down into a sobbing mess.

No killing! I reminded myself. *I can cause all the pain I want, but I can't kill them.* Hearing the words that put an end to my fun, I "gently" threw her face to the ground in frustration. She went silent as I stood and turned my attention to my last opponent.

James was running at me with his sword held high. I picked up the shield and threw it at him, just as I had done to Lestrana, but he was much better prepared and jumped to the side as I released it. Seeing how he kept his sword above his head, I smiled. I took a few steps towards him, but before I could get close, he moved his sword over his shoulder and pulled it across his body diagonally. I stopped short of getting hit by his attack and felt a slight breeze. Even though there was no edge on the sword, I could imagine that any contact with it would hurt a lot.

I attempted to step into his reach now that his sword had passed, but I was foiled as he pulled his blade back and held it up while pointing it directly at my heart. I growled.

We watched each other, waiting for the other to make the first move. I lunged forward as a feint, hoping he would overextend. He kept his sword movement short as he cut horizontally in the direction I was leaning.

Make a mistake, you idiot.

I attempted another lunge, but this time I intentionally stepped into his reach. James swung his sword horizontally again, and I ducked under the attack and reversed directions as fast as I could.

He released his sword with his left hand and brought it back to hit me with the back of his hand.

Finally! I opened my mouth as I prepared to catch his fist with my teeth.

I bit down on James's hand, and he yelled in pain. He tried to bring his sword back to drive the pommel down into my face. I stood up and tried to move out of the way of his attack, but he still drove the pommel into my collarbone. I bit down on his hand even harder. His bones cracked and blood seeped through the leather gloves. I tasted it and felt a tingle in the back of my mind.

Mm, tangy.

James looked to bring the sword's edge to my throat, but I released his hand from my mouth before I pushed both his arms up. Then I brought my knee to his groin. He howled and dropped to his knees. I kicked him in the chest and forced his back to the ground.

I stomped on his forearm that held the sword and drove my toe claws down. He hollered in pain as he reached to remove my foot. I grabbed his other hand and pulled him up. His cries hurt, so I pulled harder, hoping he would shut up eventually.

James looked desperately at me as two distinct pops came from his shoulders. His wailing reached a new level of pain in my ears. I stared at him as I released a loud growl.

His neck is nice and vulnerable. That will shut him up. I licked my lips. *Just one bite, just a taste.*

"James can't continue. Lucia wins." A penetrating voice pulled my attention. The announcer had stepped onto the field and was walking towards us. "Release him."

I looked down at James and saw he had fainted.

But just one bite. I again stared at his exposed neck. *No! Don't eat anyone.* I slammed my eyes shut. *Calm down. It's over. I can get food elsewhere.*

I slowly released James and extracted my toe claws from his arm before taking a step away from him. My vision gradually filled with colors other than red. There was no crowd cheering, just whispers.

"It's always the quiet one you need to look out for. Am I right?" the announcer addressed the crowd as he raised his arms. He then turned to me. "That was quite a performance from our shyest competitor." He held his hand out to me. "Anything you would like to say to the crowd?"

I looked at the crowd staring at me. *They're criticizing me, judging me, and talking about me.* My heart pounded in my chest as I looked for Nora. *I can't see her. I was about to kill him. Do they know I wanted to eat him? What would they do if I had taken a bite and eaten it?* I continued to look around and saw everyone murmuring to each other.

"Waterfalls!" I shouted before sprinting towards the exit.

I ran through the halls, shoving anyone in my way into the walls. I left a trail of claw marks at each turn I took. My world was a blur as I ran through the exit of the tournament grounds. I noticed the village's structures and looked around for fields to hide in, then ran through someone's crops as I found a massive willow tree in the distance.

After reaching the shade under the tree, I finally stopped running and tore off my gambeson. As I placed a hand on my chest, I could feel my heart painfully pounding against my ribs. I knelt down, exhausted, then dropped to the ground and sat at the base of the tree. Tilting my head back, I tried to open my airways as much as possible.

Why did I want to kill them so badly? I hope I didn't kill the half-elf girl. What's her name? She yielded, and yet I still threw her face into the ground. I had more control this time. But what about next time? Can I stop myself? Maybe I should stop.

My stomach growled, breaking me out of my introspection. *Is it because I'm hungry? I know I get a bit aggressive when I want food.* My breathing slowed, but my frustration grew. *Why can't I figure this out? What's the secret? Can I talk to the wolf inside me? Can she give me answers? I really should try to learn how to communicate with her outside of my dreams. Hopefully it's possible. But first, I really should get some lunch before my stomach eats its way out of me.*

I was preparing myself to get up when I heard someone walking through the field in my direction.

I peeked around the tree trunk and saw a lone human with gray hair walking towards me. His hair was short and slicked back, like oil held it in place. He wore purple silk clothes, and yet he wore a black cloak over them. As he got closer, I could see a few scars on his face, along with plenty of wrinkles.

My instincts aren't warning me, but I don't like this. He's heading out here for me. There's no other reason he should be walking towards me like this.

I crouched down and attempted to slip away.

"No, stop. I just want to talk." His voice was clear, yet emotionless.

31

IT'S A TRAP

"Please. I just want to talk." The man put his hands out.

How did he know I was moving? Fine, I guess I'll talk. "What do you want?" I responded while I stayed crouched.

"There's nothing to fear, Lucia. My name is Sadim." He pointed to the tree I was just sitting under. "I don't share your youth, and you ran quite a distance. May I sit down? My old bones aren't what they used to be." He put on a smile as he looked right at me.

How does he know where I am? I stared at the old geezer as I stood up. "Fine, but you're going to tell me how you know who I am." I injected my voice with a slight rumble as I eyed his every movement. "And how did you see me?"

"While your white fur is beautiful, it doesn't help you hide in this environment. Maybe if this was the ice season, it would be a different story." The old man took a few steps towards the tree where there was a protruding root that would serve as a good seat.

"Silver." I deepened my growl. "My fur is silver."

He stopped his stride to place his hands on his chest and give me a slight bow. "My apologies. It seems my eyes are starting to fail me too."

Not failing you enough, it seems.

I watched him slowly walk towards his destination with my claws extended and leaning forward in a half-crouched stance, ready to attack him should he try anything.

Sadim sat down and let out a sigh of relief.

"Now that you've sat down, you can tell me what you want from me." I held up my extended claws. "But if I don't like your answers, there will be a price to pay. We're far enough out that there's nobody around to hear you scream." I grinned in a way to display all of my wonderfully sharp fangs.

His face scrunched into a scowl. "Nora warned me you could be aggressive, and after your performance today, I believe it. But threatening someone my age is not only impolite, but also completely pointless."

"To say I don't trust strangers would be an understatement. Most people who knew who I was before they met me have wanted to kill me. So excuse my lack of trust." I rolled my eyes. "Besides, I'm not in a good mood. I'm hungry, and I'm cranky when I'm hungry."

"Do you want something to eat?" he asked nonchalantly. *Is he not scared of me?* "After I rest up a bit, do you want to go to some place with food? My treat."

I retracted my claws and lowered them to my sides. "Only if you answer my original question. What do you want with me? And what's your relationship with my mom?"

"That's fair," he said as he stayed seated comfortably on the roots. "I knew Nora before she owned the orphanage. We were in the same knight company together. And I said all I want to do is talk."

My instincts have been silent from the moment this guy showed up. But I really don't like his attitude.

"I didn't run that far." I crossed my arms and looked in the festival's direction.

The town and surrounding buildings were visible, but were much smaller than their actual size. *I guess I'm further out than I thought I was. Whatever. I can't let him think that I didn't go this far on purpose.* I snapped my head back to Sadim as he started laughing.

"Oh, to be young again. How I envy your energy." Sadim clutched his stomach as he continued laughing, a full, heartfelt laugh that was almost contagious. He continued until it felt awkward for me to stand there watching him. Sadim collected himself and wiped the tears from his eyes.

"What's so funny?" I asked now that I was sure he could answer me.

"Are you always so energetic?" His voice returned to its flat tone.

"You don't know the half of it," I said under my breath. "Have you rested enough? I'm getting hungry enough to eat an entire horse." The sound in my stomach told me it agreed.

"I believe I'm ready. Would you help me back?" He placed a hand on his knee and extended the other.

"No, you got yourself here. You can get yourself back," I answered him while my tail whipped back and forth. *I still don't trust him.*

"Nora really needs to do something about your lack of manners." His disapproving look was back.

Yeah, yeah. She's said the same thing.

He lifted himself up, using his hands to straighten his legs. I thought I heard a crack and a groan from him.

"Remember, any funny business, and I'm gone," I said as I backed up to keep an arc between the two of us.

"What happened to you to foster such trust issues?" He looked at me curiously.

I growled in response. *What part of "I don't trust you" did you not get? Why on Centarti would I tell you my life's story?*

"Food. Now." I lowered my ears and glared at him. *If you promise food, you had better deliver.* A memory floated through my head. "And it had better be meat," I added quickly.

Sadim gave me a confused look as he flinched. "Whatever you want," he said wearily.

He walked ahead of me as I kept a comfortable one-arc distance. I collected my gambeson and wore it as I followed him.

Even if it's this uncomfortable, wearing armor to a potential ambush is probably a better choice.

He limped, and I noticed he favored his right leg. It looked like the range of motion in his knee was limited, as if he was wearing a brace. The closer we got to the edge of the village, the more I was reminded of why I disliked being in towns. The smell of sweat and human waste filled my nose. It wasn't as bad as it was in Aquittemia, but it was enough to bother me.

I shortened my following distance so Sadim wouldn't think I'd run off. I tightened my muscles, readying myself to either tear him apart or run away.

He stopped in front of one of the largest buildings in the small town. It was a wooden building, three stories tall, and well maintained. A pair of large bay windows flanked the entrance. A sign was nailed over the heavy, worn double doors, branded with the words *Amberhost's Ruby Lodgings* on the wooden sign.

So is Amberhost the name of the owner or the town? I never thought to ask what this village was called.

Through the windows, I saw several round wooden tables with matching chairs. People sat around them eating, talking, and drinking. I thought I saw two girls having an arm-wrestling match too. We entered a restaurant.

Why does it have to stink so badly?

On one side of the room, a myriad of people sat on stools, drinking and leaning against the bar, harassing the female elven bartender for more of their preferred drink. Two human girls, probably ten years old or so, walked between tables, collecting empty and used dishes and wiping down tables with rags. An elven boy, who looked to be fourteen, carried out a large platter of food from a doorway towards a table where seven men and women sat dressed in simple clothes. All of them had a mug in their hands, boisterously laughing and talking. I counted more empty tables than filled ones, but those that had anyone sitting at them never had fewer than four people around them.

I stood still, my senses flooding my brain with information at a rate I wasn't prepared to handle. All the conversations around the tables and at the bar were so loud that it was impossible to tell who was talking and what they were saying. I was getting a headache from the volume of everything going on around me, and the assault of smells made me dizzy. It was a mix of body odor, cooked spices, beef, alcohol, fruits, and burning wood.

This isn't going to end well.

"Good day, sir." The boy with the serving tray circled back to us after he dropped off his load. "The usual in your room?" He was full of energy and carried a smile on his still-childish face.

"Yes, but could you bring something for Lucia here too?" Sadim motioned to me. "Just add it to my bill."

"Of course, sir." The server turned to address me. "And what would you like, ma'am?"

Miss, ma'am—yeah, not my thing.

"Call me Lucia, and I'll take whatever meat you haven't cooked yet. Just put it on a plate," I said, with my ears flattened. I kept my breathing light, trying not to breathe in the stench as much as I could help it.

"We'll cook that right away for you, Miss Lucia," he said in a cheerful tone.

"I didn't say you could cook it," I growled, grabbing the attention of almost everyone in the restaurant.

"You want it raw?" The boy's cheerful demeanor dissipated, and in its place I could see fear and worry.

"Yes." I lowered my voice threateningly.

The elven boy swallowed visibly. "Yes, ma'am."

I growled at him again, and he scurried off to the kitchen with a whimper. *He called me "ma'am" again.*

"Come on, my room is upstairs on the third floor," Sadim said in an exhausted tone.

We walked towards the stairs through the crowd of people I had silenced with my growling. Many people gave me a curious look, and I responded with a threatening glare. I wanted to growl at them more.

I shouldn't add too much more to the beastkin stereotype. I'm hungry. All these people are being too loud, and they reek. I think I understand why beastkin have the reputation they do. Humans don't understand what it's like to have senses much sharper than theirs.

Watching Sadim walk up two flights of stairs was painfully annoying. He had to take each step one at a time, and each one was a great deal of effort for him. *Getting old must stink.* I was tempted to aid him up the stairs, but that meant I would've had to touch him and put

239

myself in a dangerous position. I waited until he'd reached the next landing before I followed him up. We kept up this pattern until we reached the third floor.

The third floor presented itself as a hallway that held two other hallways on either side of it. Sadim walked in front of me down the one on the right, pulled a key from a pocket, and unlocked the first door on the right. He opened it and waved for me to follow him. I eventually did, after I prepared myself for the possibility that I might have to kill him.

Sadim's room was simple and, more importantly, didn't stink. Also, the voices of the rowdy patrons on the first floor couldn't reach me up here. A bed sat in the corner, raised off the floor by four posts. The taut sheets on it were pristine. A chest sat at the foot of the bed, unassuming yet locked with a padlock. Two tables sat in the room, both with candles sitting on their surfaces. Books in neat stacks covered the table beside the unlit candle in the far corner of the room; the other table had just a single candle on a raised candlestick adorning it. A single chair sat next to the table with the books, whereas the other table had two. Each chair was wooden, full-back, and had a fluffy blue cushion. The meager light fought its way into the room through the closed shutters covering the only window.

Sadim walked to the table with the single candle, pulled out a wand from the sleeve of his shirt, and flicked his wrist. A small orange flame danced an inch from the tip of the wand. I hesitated at the sight of the fire and watched the old man light the candle before waving the wand around back and forth, snuffing out the flame on the end. The candle provided more light than I was expecting, but I didn't have trouble seeing in the dark.

"There, now we can see each other properly," Sadim said. *I'm beginning to forget how weak a human's senses are.* "Please have a seat." He waved his arm towards the mostly empty table.

I stared at the chair. *There isn't a place for my tail. Ugh.* I pulled the chair out and sat on the edge to give my tail as much room as I could. I then glared at the man who sat across from me and crossed my arms. "Are you going to talk or not?"

"I think it's best if we wait until the food arrives," Sadim said.

I tapped my toe claws impatiently as we sat in silence waiting for the food we ordered, and I tugged at my gambeson. *This thing is too hot.* I pulled the armor off and tossed it by the door.

Thankfully, there was a knock at the door after a brief wait. "Come in," Sadim called to the person.

A girl who I'd seen wiping down tables downstairs earlier walked into the room. Her chestnut hair was in a braid that rested on her left shoulder, and her amber eyes darted towards me then away nervously. She took slow, measured steps, staying out of arm's reach.

In her hands was a tray with two wooden plates and a clay mug. One plate had a small pile of random-length strips of meat, and the other had a sandwich. I looked at the sandwich with surprise. There were lettuce pieces, tomato slices, strips of meat, and a pale yellow substance oozing from inside it. I took a few sniffs and smelled a familiar, wonderful smell. *Is that bacon?* I stared at the plate, expecting mine would hold a similar treasure.

"Thank you, Ecin," Sadim said with a grateful voice as the girl placed the sandwich and the mug in front of him. She grabbed the plate of meat and placed it in front of me while stretching her arm so she could stay as far away from me as possible.

"I won't bite unless you give me a reason to." I looked at my unceremoniously stacked meat and didn't see any bacon. "Why does he get bacon and I don't? And is this it?" I glared at the girl. She squeaked and hid behind her serving tray.

"I'm sorry." She trembled as she answered.

I sighed. "I'm sorry. Just bring me lots of water and a plate of bacon, please." *I shouldn't take it out on her. She's just doing her job. And I didn't ask for bacon in the first place.*

"Yes, ma'am." Her stammering worsened. She darted out of the room, still hiding behind her serving tray.

I placed a hand on my forehead. "I'm not that scary, am I?" I stared at the plate in front of me.

"You've been trying to look intimidating from the moment I met you," Sadim said nonchalantly. *So he noticed. But he didn't react. Why?* "Most people would be terrified by the display you've been giving me."

"I could tell she would have wet herself if I growled at her." I felt guilty. But then I smelled the bacon again. "Besides, what are you eating?"

"I call it the BLT—a bacon, lettuce, and tomato sandwich. It's my last guilty pleasure. Don't tell my daughter I got this." He gave me a wink. "I'm supposed to watch what I eat. Having too many of these isn't good for my heart."

"And the yellowish stuff?" I watched him closely. *Something doesn't feel quite right, even more so than before.*

"Mayonnaise spread. You take mustard seeds that you pulverize into dust and mix them with water, vinegar, and a little salt. Then mix that with egg yolks from a chicken egg. That's the yellow part only. And while whisking, you slowly add oil to it, and eventually, you have mayonnaise." He smiled as he described mayo to me.

How does he know about mayo? Wait, did he know Midas and learn it from him? I stared at him, confused.

"You want to try some?" He held up his sandwich towards me.

"I can't." I waved his sandwich away. "If it isn't meat, I just throw it up."

"I know you're a carnivore. Who else would order a plate of raw meat?" He took a bite of his sandwich. *So he is aware of what I am. Why did he bother asking, just to be polite?*

As he spoke about my plate of raw meat, I picked up a piece and noticed that it had almost as much fat as meat. *They couldn't give me any quality meat?* I ate the undesirable trimmings anyway. *I like the fat, it tastes great. But I really want something to sink my teeth into.* After I had eaten a few strips, there was another knock at the door, and the other girl came in.

She was likely the first girl's sister because they shared facial features, hair, and eye color, but she'd styled her hair into a simple bun. They might have even been twins, given their shared appearance. She placed two large clay cups of water next to my plate and another plate with a slab of bacon the size of my head.

I drooled at the sight of the bacon. As I wagged my tail, it kept slamming into the back of the chair. *Best restaurant ever!* I ditched the meat scraps, scooped up the bacon, and dug my teeth in greedily.

"Thank you. Here, take these and share them with the other two. For having to put up with her unique disposition." Sadim gave the girl a handful of coins.

I didn't pay too much attention because I was rocking from side to side, savoring my delicious meal. *I love bacon. I love bacon.* As I ate, I chanted those three words to myself. After I finished the slab, I grabbed a mug and drank the whole thing. *I knew I was thirsty, but wow.* I grabbed the second mug and drained it just as quickly as the first. My stomach was full, and it felt like I could use a nap to digest it all. *I love bacon.* I sat with a mile-wide grin on my face as I placed a hand on my belly.

"I take it you're in a better mood? I have to admit, I didn't think you could eat the entire thing." Sadim had been watching me with a look of awe once he'd finished his sandwich.

I let out a loud belch. I could feel the food in my stomach settle in better. "Don't judge me. I'm still a growing girl." I narrowed my eyes. "You wanted to talk after the food, so can we stop stalling and get to the business at hand?" I sat back up.

"You're an impatient one, aren't you?" Sadim didn't show any emotion. "You're aware of the rules of the tournament, right?" I nodded. "I'm giving you your official warning. What you did today could be seen as malicious and done with the intent to kill." His voice dropped into a hard and deep tone as he warned me.

"They'll live. If they hadn't teamed up on me, I wouldn't have gotten so angry." I puffed out my cheeks and crossed my arms. "Besides, what did I do that was so wrong?"

"The condition you left Anno's arm in, attacking Lestrana after she yielded, and continually injuring James after he'd fallen unconscious," he stated flatly.

"Lestrana shot at my eye first!" I slammed my hand on the table hard enough to crack it.

"Regardless, any more incidents like this and you'll be expelled from the tournament and charged accordingly," Sadim said without flinching. "That means you'll be charged with attempted murder and sentenced to death. This is serious."

"Fine. I'll try to control myself." I stared at him with my ears pulled back. *They weren't hurt that bad. I've suffered far worse than them.* "But they should consider themselves lucky. Almost everyone else that has wanted to hurt me has ended up dead."

"Then maybe you should withdraw. Your temperament isn't welcome in this tournament." Sadim crossed his arms. "Being a knight isn't just about fighting prowess. It's about restraint too."

Of course he can figure it out. Why else would an orphan join this tournament? "I won't withdraw." I pouted. "And I'll behave. I won't hurt people too badly anymore."

"Good." Sadim looked like he was about to continue when I heard the door open behind me.

I snapped my attention to those who entered without knocking. Two beings I had yet to see in this life walked in.

First came a tall man, taller than anyone I had ever seen so far, with short black hair, small round ears on top of his head, yellow eyes, and black fur covering him. The claws that tipped his fingers and toes looked like they would compete with mine in sharpness. *If I had to guess, he's a panther beastkin.* He moved without making a sound.

Behind him, an even taller woman walked in. She was thin and lanky, with very few curves to speak of. Her most prominent features were two long, oval-shaped ears on top of her head. A mix of dark- and light-brown hair and fur covered her. She had claws too, but they were small and didn't look that sharp either. *Is she a rabbit or a hare beastkin?*

Their faces were very different from each other. The man's face was angular and looked menacing, while the woman's gentle, round face with brown eyes looked pretty. They both wore bright-green vests with skirts that flowed from their hips to their knees in the same color. I saw that they each also wore a silver band, about three inches wide, on their right wrists.

I knew it. He wanted me cornered and lulled into a false sense of security. Well, it worked. But he's going to find that I'm the wrong kind of prey to corner.

32

OOPS

My instincts screamed at me to fight the panther beastkin. I growled as I stood up and grabbed the table. With one swift movement, I swung it around at the panther beastkin.

His smug look turned to shock as he saw the table heading straight for him.

I'm not as defenseless as you thought.

The table struck him and forced him into the wall. A satisfying crack resounded as the table splintered into several pieces, and he fell to the ground in an unconscious heap. The sudden movement snuffed out the meager flame of the candle as it crashed to the floor. The plates and mugs from our lunch went flying too, but that was none of my concern.

"Stop." Sadim stood up and held his hands out towards me.

"Lamso." The hare beastkin dove to check on her companion.

I grabbed the chair from behind me and threw it at Sadim. He put up his arms to protect his face. The chair collided with him and he fell backwards into the seat he was just in. His extra momentum caused him to tip over and fall to the ground, landing on his back. He groaned in pain.

I need to get out of here. My focus landed on the window shutters. *I think I can do that.*

I dashed to the window and slammed my hand into them, expecting resistance, but they opened so forcefully that they flew away from their hinges, sending the wooden shutters falling away from the building.

I guess they weren't blocked. Whatever, it's time to go.

I jumped onto the windowsill and saw that the female beastkin was still clearing chunks of the broken table off of the male beastkin. Sadim was groaning, clutching his sides.

I grabbed the side of the building, dug my claws into the wood, and began climbing down, using my claws on my hands and feet to turn everything into a proper handhold. *Mom will be livid if she sees me like this. I haven't told her I can climb a building.*

I made it to the second level with no problems.

"Lucia, what are you doing?" a familiar voice called out to me.

I just had to think about it, didn't I? I turned to see Nora staring at me with panic in her eyes.

I put on a smile. "Nothing." I tried to sound as innocent as possible. From the scowl on Nora's face, I could tell she didn't find it amusing.

"Come down here right now." She used her mom voice.

I scurried down quickly and jumped the last bit. I walked towards her, my tail tucked between my legs and my ears low.

Her hands were on her hips as she looked down at me. "Now, are you going to tell me what's really going on?"

"I'm running away from Sadim and the two beastkin with him because I don't know what they had planned, but I didn't want to find out," I rambled off in one breath.

A fear I had seen only once before filled Nora's face. "What have you done?" She ran off to the front door of the building I'd just evacuated.

I stood still, confused. *I'm missing some key details, aren't I? What does she mean? What did I do? I just tried to run for my life. They were after my life, right?* I followed her, worried that I had done something very wrong. *Wait, didn't someone say something about some special beastkin visiting? I should follow her to find out what's going on. It should be fine with Mom around, right?*

Nora had entered the building before me, but I wasn't far behind her. I could catch her easily, but I played it safe and stayed behind her. Once I entered the building, the two serving girls glanced at me with bewildered looks. One even started pointing to the ceiling and back to the door, obviously trying to figure out how I'd gotten where I was.

All the patrons watched Nora run through the restaurant, then they turned their heads to watch me do the same. I didn't disappoint them and followed Nora up the stairs to the third floor again. Nora took a moment to think about where she needed to go and headed to the right hallway.

The door was still wide open, with one beastkin treating the other. She had him cleared of the wood and had moved him farther into the room, where she had him sitting upright as she attempted to wake him. Nora stood just inside the doorway, surveying the state of the room. I stopped behind her, ready to move if needed.

"Lamso, wake up," the hare beastkin begged. Her voice was soft despite her frantic emotions.

"Midas, you idiot. What did I tell you? I told you not to surprise her." Nora marched towards Sadim, stomping her feet. Her voice left a tingle in my ears. "I said you needed to be open and honest with her."

I stood confused. *Midas? Sadim was the only other person in that room with the two beastkin.*

"Your paranoia-driven antics will one day get you killed. You're lucky they didn't kill you today. Are you that lost in your scheming?" She waved her hand, and I watched the old man she called Midas float off the ground and gently land on the bed.

He still groaned before rolling over. "I think you might be right," he said in a strained voice.

So his real name is Midas, that two-faced liar. He just reversed the letters in his name. I growled as I made the connection.

"It's our fault." The hare beastkin turned her head towards Nora but wouldn't look her in the face. "We walked in unannounced. I told Lamso we should knock first, but he believed it wasn't necessary." Her voice was quiet as she spoke slowly, like she was trying to find each word before saying it.

Now that I had taken some time to look at her more closely, I could see her mouth didn't have human teeth, which meant she was an herbivore. I then turned my attention to the unconscious panther beastkin and saw human teeth.

Nora turned her attention to the two beastkin. She waved her hand again. This time, a small splash of water materialized and connected with the unconscious beastkin. His eyes slowly fluttered, and he groaned with a low rumble as he grabbed the back of his head.

"What happened?" His voice was quite low, and it almost had a perpetual growl to it.

"The wolfkin pup hit you with a table and knocked you out," the hare beastkin said as she wiped the other's face.

"Where's that pup?" He pushed aside his companion.

"You will leave," Nora said flatly. The panther beastkin stopped in his tracks. "If you want to talk to Lucia, you will go through me." Nora stepped up to him, her voice still carrying a tingling sensation with it. "I'm her guardian. Not this man." She pointed to Midas lying on the bed.

After hearing the word "guardian," I felt a tearing in my heart— not a literal one, but an emotional one. *She said she was my guardian. That's right, she isn't really my mother. My parents are dead. I've been playing this game for so long that I forgot I was playing it.*

The two beastkin left without a word, but the panther beastkin gave Nora an angry stare.

"And now for you." Nora returned her focus to the elderly man groaning in his bed. "I'm willing to give you the chance to explain yourself." She marched over to Midas and stared down at him, her hands on her hips.

"After all of your warnings, I thought it would have been better to disassociate myself from her." His voice was weak.

My voice was low as I spoke. "I wanted to meet you. If you had said your name was Midas from the beginning, I would have been much nicer."

"Why does knowing my name change your attitude towards me? Shouldn't you treat all strangers the same?" Midas stared at the ceiling. I could tell every breath hurt him.

"Sadim was a complete stranger. Strangers have tried to kill and sacrifice me. Midas was someone I wanted to meet. A friend to Nora." I crossed my arms as I moved to sit on the only still-standing chair.

"Why did you want to meet me?" Midas's voice carried a tangible level of curiosity.

"To talk." I gave my best impression of his voice.

Midas released a gentle laugh that provoked another painful groan.

"It's not so much fun when people do it to you now, is it?"

My snarky attitude earned me a glare from Nora. "Haven't you done enough harm already?" Nora asked. I resumed my pouting. "She's like you. A reincarnator."

"Hey, why did you just tell him that?" I stood up.

"There's two?" Midas turned his head towards me. "Why didn't you tell me about her sooner?"

Two?

"Because I wanted to make sure she was raised right. Not to be a paranoid schemer." Nora gave him a harsher look than she gave me. "Besides, did you just say there's a second one? Does that mean you found the other one?"

"Yes, he's my apprentice." Midas stared at me with a scrutinizing gaze. "He's safe, away from here."

"What do you mean, 'safe and away from here?'" My eyes grew in proportion to my worry. "Aren't we safe with all these knights here?"

"We believe that there are cultists organizing something big here. We've let them get away with it because we want to catch as many of them as possible. But we can't pick them out of the crowd. Somehow, they're blending in perfectly. Also, we have no clue what their final objective is. I have a hunch they want to try to create a blood anchor again, but I don't know how." Midas relaxed as he closed his eyes and looked like he was going to take a nap. "How am I going to explain the bruises to my daughter? Tellma is going to be upset with me."

"As she should be." Nora poked Midas's sternum. He placed a hand on the spot where she'd poked in a wordless complaint. "Maybe next time you'll listen to me and not do anything stupid, like scare Lucia. Now, stay in that bed and get some rest." Nora extended a hand to me. "Come on, let's get something to eat."

I stood up. "I already ate."

"She isn't kidding." Midas's tone carried with it the slightest hint of mirth.

"Nobody asked you," I growled as I grabbed my gambeson from next to the door.

"I would like to talk to you more after the tournament, Lucia," the old man called out to me.

"Maybe if you can ask me like a regular person, I'll think about it." *My instincts don't care about him, but I can't stand him.*

Nora and I left the inn, receiving more stares from the people on the main floor. We walked to a large rock at the edge of the village. I sat on the ground with my back to it, and Nora sat next to me. I placed my gambeson behind me against the rock to act as a cushion.

"Do you want to talk about it?" Nora leaned her head on mine.

Not really. "Why did he tell us all that stuff about cultists and the blood anchor?" I asked while leaning into her shoulder. "Are these the same cultists from five years ago that tried to sacrifice me? The same guy who tried to kill Zenny and me in the alley?"

"I think so. He was warning us." I could hear the sorrow in her voice.

"Then why doesn't he warn everyone?"

"The only thing that would do is cause mass hysteria. I don't like his plan to allow them to get away with so much. But I can't do anything." Nora wrapped an arm around my shoulders.

"But why us?"

"He wasn't so much warning us as he was warning *me*." Nora's voice still sounded regretful. "This way, I'm prepared to protect you and the others."

I guess that's one problem figured out. On to the next one.

"Won't the beastkin ambassadors have something to say about what I just did?" I hugged my knees to my chest.

"Most likely." Nora's flat tone didn't make me feel better. "But they still have to go through me. I'll make sure next time you'll be ready to handle them." She removed her head from mine, and before I could protest, she placed a hand on top of my head and scratched. "I believe these are overdue."

I melted at her touch. I remembered the words Midas had spoken to me before the beastkin surprised me. "Are you mad at me?"

"For what?" Nora sounded surprised.

"For attacking the ambassadors, attacking Midas, and for hurting the other kids during my match as much as I did." I rested my head on my knees.

"The first two things we worked out. What you did during your match, on the other hand..." She suddenly stopped scratching my head. Immediately, a pang of loss and despair filled my heart. "Why did you hurt that boy with the shield so much?" Her tone was dark and full of concern.

"I couldn't get it off easily. I wanted it to defend myself from the girl's arrows. Then all I did was shove him out of the arena." I closed my eyes and flattened my ears, ready for my lecture.

"Is that it?" She placed her hand back on my head and continued scratching. "Then there's nothing to worry about."

"But what about Midas telling me that if I do something like that again, I'll be charged with a crime and ejected from the tournament?" I blurted out as I turned to look at Nora.

"One of the kids is likely an heir to some wealthy family. He was probably just playing politics." Nora smiled at me as she patted me on the top of my head. "But you should try to have a little more restraint in the future."

"I'm sorry. I keep messing everything up." After a pause, I reflected on the many things I'd done recently. "I take that back. The only thing I can do is hurt people. Why can't I do anything useful?"

Nora stopped scratching behind my ears. "Because finding what you want to do with the rest of your life isn't easy. I was a knight for

251

many years before taking over the orphanage. You're challenging everything I've done up to this point."

Nora placed her hand in her lap as she stared into the distance, focusing on nothing. "For the many years that I was a knight, I felt like you. The only thing I could use magic for was to cause harm. I was really good at it too. One of the best, even. I met Midas and fell in love. A love he never reciprocated, but he was the only one I've ever felt such feelings for. It awakened a desire in me for a family. I couldn't watch any more of my friends die. So I gave up on being a knight, and now I'm trying to give every kid who walks into the orphanage a family experience they're deprived of." Her eyes shimmered as tears clung to them.

"Except that it's not," I said before I could phrase it tactfully.

The tears in her eyes rolled down her cheeks. "What? Why? How?" The look of betrayal in her eyes left me feeling as much pain as she did.

I stared at the ground. *How do I say this without hurting her more?* I took a deep breath as I prepared to struggle through what I wanted to say. "You're our guardian. You say you want us to see you as a mother, but that's nothing more than a lie. How can you treat every single one of us with the same passion as a genuine mother when, as soon as we're gone, you have other children you're trying to treat the same way? How can you keep doing that while also letting us go once we grow up? You're living this lie as much as we are. It's your job to feed us, teach us, and put a roof over our heads."

Tears trickled down my cheeks, and my throat choked up, but I pushed on, spilling every emotion I had. "Once we leave, you have to reset and move on to the next child. And you can't make us be siblings and get along. Molly hates me and is terrified of everything I could do. April is so withdrawn that it feels like she wants nothing to do with us. May made us feel inferior because she got adopted while we weren't. I've never been able to get along with anyone else other than Zenny. I'm trying to learn how to be friends with Evalana, but we're still working on it. Even Eleanah, Martin, and Anna saw me as someone they were obligated to look after because they thought it was the right thing to do, not because they liked me."

There was a long pause. Although we were sitting right next to each other, it felt like there was a never-ending expanse dividing us, an unbridgeable gap that separated us emotionally.

Nora spoke first. "It hurts to hear you say that." She grabbed the front of her shirt and bunched it up. Her breath shuddered as her bottom lip quivered. "I didn't know you felt that way."

"Then don't worry about it. As soon as a knight company takes me, I'll be out of your hair. I'll see if I can join when I'm fifteen, if not sooner. You tried, but I don't belong here." I stood up, grabbed my gambeson, and walked to my room. My footsteps felt heavy as I left Nora alone, crying.

After returning to my closet-sized room, I breathed a heavy sigh as I closed the door behind me. I crawled into my bed, using my gambeson as a pillow again. I stared at the same thing that I felt: nothing. My mind had shut off, but I couldn't drift to sleep. The light in my window slowly shifted as the sun retreated behind the horizon. I listened as some people returned to their rooms and a few other girls said their salutations before retiring.

A knock at my door brought me back to the conscious world.

"Leave me alone," I said.

"But I brought a snack that Melody said you might like." It sounded like August.

"I don't care. I'm not hungry." I rolled over to stare at the wall.

"Melody said that it's a spitfire's heart." August opened the door and walked in. There was a pungent sulfurous smell, and it caused me to turn and see what he was holding.

"What happened?" August said as he stood with a bag in his hand, looking at me. "Who hurt my sister?"

"I'm not your sister." I stared at August. "Nora isn't our mother, either."

"What do you mean?" Worry filled his voice.

"Nora's our guardian. That means this is nothing more than a job for her." I looked at the small boy. "She's just impressing her dreams and desires onto you. You need to figure out what you want. Just put the heart on my travel chest and leave me alone."

August did as I asked and walked to the doorway. He stopped and turned to me, a few tears resting on his cheeks. "I always thought you were the coolest sister ever." He closed the door and ran down the hall before I could say a word.

I slammed my face into my improvised pillow and screamed. *I'm an idiot!* It took everything I had to hold back the desire to tear my bed and gambeson to shreds. At some point, I drifted off to sleep, no longer able to stay awake.

33

A FIGHT WITH A FRIEND

I woke up early. It was still dark outside, but I wasn't tired anymore. A familiar tugging from my instincts informed me it was time to go for a hunt.

I could use the distraction. But will I finish before my next match? I guess it can wait until I'm finished with my fight today. Unless I'm fighting last, then I'll go and hunt for something. But what about breakfast?

My attention fell on the bag August had brought. A knot developed in my stomach.

I shouldn't have said those things to him. I let my emotions run away from me again.

I picked up the sack. *August said it had a spitfire heart inside. Wasn't that the lizard that lives underground with the dwarves? Yeah, they don't actually spit fire. They have two glands in their cheeks that spray an oil that, when it comes in contact with air, will catch fire.*

I opened the bag and pulled out the heart. It was the size of my fist and purple. I bit into it and experienced a new sensation in this world —the heart was spicy. My eyes watered instantly as I chewed. *This is fantastic.* I polished it off quickly, then cleaned myself up.

I brushed my fur until the sun came up. After I changed into clean clothes, I grabbed my gambeson and headed for the arena before everyone else.

When I arrived, I saw a huge board nailed to the wall in the large hallway leading to the arena that wasn't there yesterday. There was a single-elimination tournament bracket posted on it. Seeing eight names lined up in all the beginning bracket slots, I looked for mine. I was second from the top, and my opponent was Evalana.

Oh no. She's my first opponent after the preliminary rounds. I hope she won't have any bad feelings after the match. I hope I don't hurt her too badly. When I heard people walking into the armory, I put on my gambeson and found a distant corner to stand in.

Half a dozen kids entered the hall and stood around talking about random things. Evalana entered and walked up to the board first thing. She found her name and jumped while shrieking excitedly, then looked around the room and found me.

I guess I'm going to have to talk to her eventually, aren't I? I put on a brave face once she got closer.

"Morning, Lucia," Evalana said as she skipped until she was right in front of me. She was practically vibrating.

"Hi," I replied half-heartedly.

"What happened to you? I couldn't find you anywhere after my match. Did you even watch me? Because I watched you and you were so cool." Her eyes looked like they were ready to pop out of their sockets. She held her arms close to her chest as she bounced up and down on her toes.

"I had a rough day yesterday." I turned and stared at a wall.

"Oh, what happened?" She leaned her head into my vision.

"I don't want to talk about it," I said as I turned away from her again. My heart still sat in my gut from what I'd said to August last night.

"You can tell me. We're friends, remember? Maybe talking about it will make you feel better." She placed her hands gently on my shoulders.

"It's private," I growled.

Evalana jumped backwards from me. I turned towards her and saw that she looked betrayed. "But I thought we were friends."

Right, I did say that.

I sighed as I relaxed. "I know. Sorry. Being a friend is something I'm not very good at. And just because we're friends doesn't mean I'll tell you all of my secrets. Some of them I want to stay buried." My voice reflected my gloomy mood. "I only met you two days ago."

Evalana looked at me, but her eyes looked like she was looking past me. Her eyes lit up as she raised her arm and held up a finger, making me jump slightly. "I got it," she said. "I'm scared of heights. My favorite color is orange. And one time, my older brother convinced me to eat yellow snow. Don't do that, by the way. It was awful." We both shuddered at the same time at the mention of yellow snow.

I stared at the girl. "What was that?"

"I thought since we've only just met that we don't know much about each other. So, I told you a few things about myself. Now it's your turn." She held out her hand, inviting me to respond to her.

She might be naïve, but she is making an honest effort to be friendly. I should try to open up more. I've got to start somewhere.

I put on a smile. "I'm afraid of fire. My favorite color is red because that's how I like my meat. One time, I climbed to the roof of the orphanage to hide from Nora after I destroyed half the tables in the classroom."

"Did she find you?" Evalana leaned forward and stared at me with her eyes wide open.

"No." I giggled. "She shouted my name while looking for me for a long time. Unfortunately, I had to come down. I wasn't going to sleep up there."

"What did she do?" Evalana stared at me, transfixed by my story.

"I got into a lot of trouble." I laughed again. "My punishment was that I had to transcribe the monthly expenses of the orphanage for the tax collector."

"That doesn't sound too bad." She sounded almost disappointed.

"It is when you have hands like mine. I hate writing, and I have to be extra careful not to get any ink in my fur." I held my hand up in demonstration. "Do you have any idea how hard it is to get ink out of fur?" Evalana shook her head. "Very." I smiled.

"See, we're better friends now." Evalana held out her arms towards me. Her bubbly mood was almost infectious.

"I guess you're right," I mused. "Thanks." *Now I have to ask.* "Did you really eat yellow snow?"

Evalana blushed, but as she opened her mouth to talk, the announcer guy entered the hall. Everyone stopped talking and stared at him as he walked to the archway leading to the arena.

He turned, and with a single word, he silenced everyone. "Listen!" I flinched at the volume. *People need to stop being so loud.* "We are about to begin. The matches are ordered as you see them on the board from top to bottom. That means Lucia and Evalana, you're our first match. Please wait here until you're called out." He turned and walked out to a waiting crowd.

"We're first. Are you excited?" Evalana could barely keep her excitement contained. "Take it easy on me, would you?"

How do I feel about this?

"I wouldn't say I'm excited. I'm more glad to get this over so I can take this stupid coat off." I tugged at the collar of my gambeson, trying to let as much heat escape as I could. "Sorry, I'm not allowed to take it easy on you. But I promise I'll do everything I can not to hurt you." *Who am I promising that to, me or her?*

"You won't hurt me. I trust you."

That makes one person. I looked to the ground, unable to face her positivity.

"Your first entrant into today's tournament is none other than our earthen princess, Evalana," the announcer said, breaking the awkward silence that had developed.

Evalana gave me a smile, a wink, and a thumbs-up as she headed to the exit.

I watched her leave, knowing that my name was up next. *Ignore the crowd. Try to ignore the crowd.* My nerves were ramping up. I knew what was out there and I had to face it: my fear. *Focus on Evalana. I was doing well until she left.*

"Her opponent is the one, the only, Lucia!"

The call woke me from my internal struggle, and I swallowed the knot in my throat as I slowly marched out, hanging onto the meager threads of my courage. I stepped into the sunlight and closed my eyes briefly to let them adjust to the brightness.

The roar of the crowd erupted the moment I stepped into their view.

Ignore them. Focus on one thing.

Evalana was already standing in the field when I looked at it. I walked towards her, not taking my eyes off of her as I stepped onto the field in the opposite corner of where she stood.

"Today we are starting off with a real showstopper, folks." The announcer's voice was too loud to ignore. "Evalana is the contestant with the fastest victory in the entire preliminary round. Lucia was the fastest of all the martial competitors. Yes, folks, she was faster than the prince himself. Who would have thought that the quiet shell we saw first thing yesterday would hold such a ferocious beast?"

I flinched at that, and a fire lit in my heart after hearing his words. I stared at the announcer with contempt. *I'm not a beast, you bald freak!*

"She won with the most convincing victory, with a truly savage display of her feral nature. What will she do to this poor little girl?"

Nothing compared to what I'm about to do to you if you keep talking. I could feel my vision wanting to shift to red as I imagined the look on his face as I ripped his arms off and shoved them down his throat.

"Begin!" The elf stepped off the field before turning to watch us. I growled when I saw the smirk on his face.

I heard the ground move under me. Snapping out of my blood-thirsty daydream, I looked down and saw the dirt moving, pushing me out of the field. I jumped towards the center of the arena.

So that's how she won her match so quickly. She probably dumped them all out of the arena just as the bout started.

"Aw." Evalana crossed her arms and puffed out her cheeks.

"I said I wouldn't go easy on you." I charged towards her.

Evalana returned to a normal posture before she waved a hand from her right to her left in a slapping motion. A low rumble came from my left, and a pillar of stone drove straight for me. I saw it too late, and it collided with my ribs, nearly breaking them.

Who's taking it easy?

The pillar continued to drive me towards the edge. I went to push off the pillar, but suddenly a pair of stone tendrils grew from it and wrapped themselves around me. I looked at Evalana and saw her smiling.

Okay, since you want to play that way.

I grabbed the tendrils from where they grew and found that they had hardened. I growled as I twisted my hands to break them. *Every time I disrupt Nora's magic, there's always a moment when she's in pain. So Evalana should have the same reaction.*

With a dull crack, the tendrils holding me to the pillar shattered. I brought my knee to the bottom of the pillar and kicked myself to the ground, landing on all fours. Adrenaline flowed through my body as everything slowed.

Evalana stumbled for a moment, a look of shock on her face.

You aren't used to that happening, are you?

I pushed off the ground and sprinted towards her. She lifted several chunks of rock out of the arena and threw them at me in one motion. I sidestepped them all except one, which I grabbed. I spun my body around as I went to throw it back at her, aiming for her shoulder because I didn't want to hurt her too badly. But I needed to slow her down.

With a panicked look and a wave of her hand, she erected a stone pillar to block the incoming projectile.

She's lost sight of me. Time to move! I dropped to all fours and angled myself to strike from her left side.

Evalana lifted the barrier out of the ground and flattened it, turning the pillar into a disk.

Oh, I didn't see that coming.

I skidded to a stop, using my claws for added traction.

Evalana, face strained, waved her arms towards me. The giant stone disk sailed through the air at me.

Up, down, left, right, or catch it? The disk was twice my size. *Yeah, I'm not going to catch that thing. It's too wide to go around. Up we go.* I ran towards the disk and jumped on it before it collided with me.

That was a mistake.

As soon as I landed, I dug my claws in for stability. My vision blurred as I spun with the disk. *Why didn't I notice it was spinning?*

The world spun faster. It didn't take long before my stomach released its contents. The spitfire meat burned as much coming out as it did going down.

Someone get me off this crazy thing!

I heard a scream from Evalana, and the disk plummeted to the ground. The spinning stopped, but my vision continued to turn without the aid of the disk.

I stumbled off. My arms and legs were moving in every direction except the one that I wanted them to. I fell to the ground, closing my eyes, hoping this dizziness would soon pass.

I don't feel so good.

I felt another push from my stomach. I raised myself to my elbows and knees before my nausea forced me to heave even more acid from my belly, the burning sensation in my mouth and throat tempting me to call it quits.

Once I finished my retching, I heard a similar sound from somewhere nearby. I opened my eyes and saw Evalana on her knees, holding back her ponytail with one hand while supporting herself with the other as she vomited up her breakfast.

I guess she doesn't handle vomiting well, does she? We might as well end this now.

I attempted to get to my feet. I managed, barely. My tail behaved and held me upright. I took a small step towards her, then another, and another. Each step was easier than the last as the dizziness faded.

I finally stood over Evalana and reached out to grab her so I could place her outside the field.

She turned to look at me after she finished spewing the last remnants of her stomach. Pain and fear filled her eyes.

Sorry that things turned out like this, but it's time to be done.

I reached for her, but she fell into the ground. I stood and watched, bewildered, as the dirt swallowed her up.

What did I just see?

There was a low rumble from below me. I tried to follow the sound with my ears, but I couldn't focus enough. The rumbling continued until, on the far side of the field where I'd started the fight, Evalana rose out of the ground. I blinked several times as I watched her stand up.

She turned to me with renewed determination.

Round two?

Evalana's expression unnerved me.

Is she taking this seriously now? What was that stuff from before? How could Allen possibly believe I stand a chance against someone this powerful? Is this normal?

I jogged towards her, waiting for her first move. She didn't disappoint me as she raised her arms and a tidal wave of stone spread out around her. I leaned forward as I picked up the pace to a run and prepared to jump over the spell. The stone wave grew at an alarming rate.

I think I might have trouble getting over this one.

Before the wave could grow any taller, I put everything I could into my jump. The earth towered over me, but I could see the crest getting closer. *Yes, I can reach it. Wait, no.* I slowly descended back to the ground, and I still hadn't cleared it. I reached out a hand and dug my claws into the stone. After catching myself near the top of the wave as it continued on its path towards the edge of the arena, I heaved myself up with one arm and vaulted over.

Sliding down the backside of the wave, I saw Evalana swirl her hands in front of her and pull them to her chest. The swell I was sliding down shifted and turned to follow me. I kicked off of it towards the ground, believing I could outrun it easily. I hit the ground with my hands first, and, without letting my legs touch down, I pulled myself towards her and shifted to running on all fours.

Evalana startled as she saw me charging straight towards her, and the ground swallowed her up again.

I could hear the wave behind me crumble. I skidded to a stop to look behind me as it collapsed and left a pile of rubble.

Where did she go this time? As I focused on my ears, the shouting crowd became impossible to ignore. *I can't focus like this.* I thought back to my first match. *Wait, all of my senses sharpen when my vision turns red. But I also lose control when that happens. Can I focus like that without losing control? I don't want to hurt her; I promised.*

I focused on my feelings. *Every time I slipped into that state, I wasn't just angry; someone threatened me or someone close to me.* I searched for that feeling, and I found it. A shiver ran down my spine, and I closed my eyes. The sounds of the crowd became muffled as I opened my eyes. Everything in my vision was tinted red, except for the announcer. *I would love to tear him apart, but now isn't the time.* After scanning the field, I saw the ground open up on the far side. I sprinted towards it without hesitation.

Everything blurred as I ran, everything except for Evalana. Her rising out of the ground was crystal clear, everything from the stitching in her orange gambeson to the sweat on her forehead and the look of horror in her eyes as I closed in. She shrieked and allowed the ground to protect her again.

I dug my claws in and stopped. Listening carefully, I could hear the low rumble below my feet. Following the sound, I ran above it. An opening appeared, and inside was Evalana, looking up at me.

I reached in and grabbed her before the hole closed up again, hoisting her up by her gambeson. She screamed the entire time I held on to her. I wanted to slam her head-first into the ground. *No. She's my friend. I promised.* I fought against my urges.

"Don't hurt me. I yield," Evalana said while on the verge of tears as I held her a few inches off the ground. "Waterfalls," she said between deep breaths.

I shook my head, trying to shake the red from my vision. *It worked; I controlled it.* A heavy sigh of relief escaped my lips, and I set her down softly.

"Would you look at that, folks? We have a winner." The announcer stepped onto the field. "I told you it would be a showstopper, and boy, was it. Give it up for Lucia." He waved his arms up and down, urging the crowd to get louder and louder.

I looked at Evalana and could see she was exhausted. "Let's go. Can you walk?"

Evalana hesitated.

I'll take that as a no. I scooped her up into my arms.

"Ah." Evalana wrapped her arms around my neck for stability. "What are you doing?"

"I want out of here, but I can't just leave you. I'll take you to Salien to make sure everything's alright." My friend clung to me while I carried her in my arms and sprinted to the exit.

"How can you keep going?" Her breathing was still heavy.

"And there she goes. No winner's interview this time either," the announcer said lightheartedly. "I don't think she likes me very much." There were many laughs from the crowd.

I stopped at the archway to the main entrance hall. I turned my head to glare at the guy and bared my fangs as I growled. *If you ever give me a reason to kill you, I will.*

"Why are you so angry?" Evalana asked.

"Later," I said as I carried her towards the hospital wing.

34

BIRD BRAIN

I carried Evalana into the medical facilities. There were five kids lying or sitting on beds. Brown privacy curtains hid two more of them. Three of them looked familiar. *Oh, it's Lestrana, Anno, and James. I hope they aren't too mad.*

"There she is!" A shrieking voice caused me to flinch. Lestrana, with bandages on her face, stood up and marched towards me. "This is all your fault." She pointed a finger at me. "What did you do to this one? Why are you delivering her here yourself?"

I placed Evalana on the ground gently. *Yeah, she's angry. But she started it.* I opened my mouth to defend myself, but Evalana spoke first.

"It's just magic fatigue," Evalana said, sounding winded. "I'll be fine after some rest."

Magic fatigue? Is that different from regular fatigue? I really need to learn more about magic.

"So you didn't hurt her, but you disfigured me?" Lestrana winced as she spoke. "Are you racist against half-elves?"

"No, no, no, no." Zenny came running out from behind one of the privacy curtains, her arms raised towards us. "Stop, don't make her mad."

"Evalana and I are friends," I said, holding back a growl. "I don't know you, and you tried to shoot out my eye. You're lucky all I did was slam your face into the ground." I extended my claws, ready to tear her apart.

"Lucia, please don't. Calm down." Zenny placed a hand on my chest as she turned to Lestrana. "She isn't racist. She just has a short temper. If you get to know her, she can be quite friendly."

"Why would I get to know such an uncivilized beast?" Lestrana folded her arms.

My vision flooded with red. I shoved Zenny onto a nearby empty bed. I lunged for Lestrana, grabbed her chest, and threw her against the wall. *You want an uncivilized beast? I'll show you a beast.* I pinned her to the wall with my claws around her neck. She froze, her eyes and mouth wide open. I readied my free claws to rip out her heart, but I felt a tug on my arm.

Zenny held on to me. "Please don't. Don't hurt her. Waterfalls." Zenny's cheeks sparkled with tears.

"She called me a beast." My voice rumbled. "She has to pay."

"You're not a beast. But if you do that, you'll prove her right." Zenny tugged at my arm harder.

"Why do you want to hurt people? Don't you want to be friends?" Evalana limped towards me.

They're right. I growled as I threw Lestrana onto a bed. *Why do they have to be right?*

"But it's her fault for calling me a beast. Who will punish her for that?" I stormed to the door to leave.

My blood boiled as I stared at the door. It stood before me, ignorant of my seething need for violence. Unafraid and perpetually stoic, the door did its job and remained a barrier to the hallway.

I kicked it.

It flew off its hinges and crashed into the other side of the hallway.

Why is it still in one piece?

I grabbed the door off the ground and swung it at the wall. A piece cracked off it, and a sizable chunk went flying from the wall. Unsatisfied, I continued slamming the door against the wall until it was nothing more than splinters.

Breathing heavily, I turned to see everyone watching my display. "What are you all looking at?" *Say something, I dare you.*

Zenny stepped up. "Come with me." She held out her hand to me.

I grabbed it and followed her down the hall, Evalana trailing us.

We walked down a passage I hadn't been down yet. Zenny led me down to a room with a door locked with a padlock. *Why the lock?* She pulled out a key from a pouch on her belt, unlocked the door, and opened it. She then handed me the lock and key and waved for me to follow her inside.

I entered a room full of toy stuffed animals. "What is this?" I glared at Zenny. I could smell grass and something else. *Whatever it is, it's faint.*

"This is a room set aside for you to calm down in. The lock is so that nobody else can get in. So you know it's safe. Nora thought it would be best if I carried the only key." Zenny stood in the middle of the room, looking at me as I stood in the doorway. "I gave you the lock and key so that you can spend all the time here you needed and know that you are free to go at any time. We want you to feel safe here."

"Look at all the cute animals. I didn't know you liked cute stuffed toys," Evalana said from behind me.

"I only like to tear them apart," I growled. "So you created a space for me to rip things apart until I felt better. Why? Why can't I just go into the forest and take my frustrations out on the first animal I come across?"

"The dire boar should have been a lesson that the woods aren't as safe as you think they are. You aren't the apex predator." Zenny's face was emotionless. "We want you to be safe. Also, this is a lot less messy. No blood."

"Fine, but stand in a corner and don't leave," I said. I tossed the lock back to Zenny as I marched towards the helpless fodder.

Zenny smiled slightly. Without saying a word, she walked to Evalana and guided her to a corner away from me. Evalana closed the door as Zenny led her.

I grabbed what appeared to be a stuffed bear and ripped its

stomach apart with my claws. The linen holding the grass stuffing held no resistance to my claws, and grass flew everywhere.

There was an interesting surprise inside the stuffed bear: a tightly wrapped, small linen sack. I picked it up and cut it open to reveal a piece of dried jerky inside.

I looked at Zenny, narrowing my eyes.

She giggled. "That was my idea."

Without taking my eyes off of her, I plopped the meat into my mouth. *I hate that you know me so well. Why do you have to be such a good friend?*

I continued tearing toys apart and eating each little treat found inside each one.

I walked up to Zenny after the remnants of a dozen destroyed toys lay strewn across the floor. Evalana held a stuffed monkey in her arms as tears rolled down her cheeks.

"Did you fill each animal with jerky from the same animal?" I looked around and saw that most of the animals were horses, cows, pigs, and chickens.

"I hoped you would catch that," Zenny said as she smiled at me. "But there are a few rarer ones, like the bear, that we had to fill with something more accessible, like pig meat. Nobody hunts bears."

"I'm feeling a little better, thanks," I said, smiling at Zenny. "Let's go."

"Um, can I keep this?" Evalana said, holding up the stuffed monkey.

I grabbed the monkey from her hands, carefully opened up the back, and pulled out the meat from inside before handing it back to her. "Now you can."

"But you just ruined it," Evalana said, her voice choking up.

"I'll fix it for you." Zenny placed her hands on Evalana's shoulders. "I still need some practice at stitching wounds, so I can consider it practice."

"Thank you." Evalana grabbed Zenny and hugged her closely. "You're fantastic."

"She really is," I said as I nodded.

"You guys are too. I heard about your matches, and I know you're both great in your own way." Zenny looked at us with obvious admiration.

"You should have seen our fight." Evalana led the way out of the room.

"You guys are friends. You aren't supposed to fight." Zenny's face flushed, and her cheeks puffed out.

I waved my hand and shook my head. "Relax, it was for the tournament. Lestrana was right. Evalana was my opponent today."

"Oh." Zenny looked down. Her face was a bright shade of pink. She locked the door once we were all out. "So who won?"

"I did," I said, continuing to the medical wing. "We'll tell you all about it if your mom says you can come with us."

We walked back to the hospital room, where I had to apologize for my outburst and help clean up the door I'd destroyed. Zenny collected some thread and a needle before she asked if she could spend time with us. Evalana helped clean up the mess I made as some guys carried over a new door.

We all looked for somewhere to hang out and found a spare supply room close to the medical facilities. Evalana was still tired, and I wanted somewhere quiet. We used the crates in the room as our seats, and I used my gambeson as a cushion while Evalana gave hers to Zenny to use as one while we told Zenny about our fight.

"Wow, it sounds like you guys really went at it," Zenny said as we finished recounting the event and she stitched the toy monkey up. "They might still be cleaning up the field after that one."

"I never stood a chance. How can you have so much energy?" Evalana kicked her legs out in front of her as she sat on a crate.

"I just can. How tiring is it to use magic? Nora hasn't taught me much, so I don't know a whole lot about it." I sat on a crate across from Evalana, and Zenny sat on the floor in the middle of the room between us. "Also, you said you had magic fatigue. Is it different from normal fatigue?"

"It's hard to say, but it mostly depends on how good you are at using magic." Evalana supported her head with a hand as she stared off into space. "And magic fatigue is different because if I try to use magic now, I will fail and make things worse. I wouldn't be able to cast magic for the rest of the week. But if I rest, I'll be just fine." She looked at me, her eyes unfocused.

"The only thing we can do is make sure she gets lots of bed rest," Zenny said. "I'm done. Here you go." She tossed the stuffed monkey to Evalana, who snapped awake to try to catch it. She failed, and the monkey tumbled to the ground, landing soundlessly.

Evalana hopped down to pick it up. "Thanks, I haven't had a new stuffed animal in years."

"Aren't you a little old for toys?" I watched her return to her seat.

"Mom keeps saying that too." Evalana held the monkey close to her chest. "But my toys never tell me what to do. They never say that I'm too young to understand. And they always listen."

"Don't you have a bunch of friends?" Zenny asked.

"I want more friends, but nobody wants to be my friend." Tears fell from her eyes as she closed them.

"Aren't we your friends?" I asked. *Great. How come I always find depressed people to be my friends?*

Evalana sniffled as she wiped her tears. "You are, and it's nice to have friends who don't spend time with me just so they can ask for favors."

"Then what's the problem? Why would people ask you for favors?" Zenny asked as she stood up.

"It's because people want to get close to Daddy. He says that I shouldn't let people do that." Evalana held the toy even closer. "My brother is always looking out for me and protecting me. I want to do that for everyone. I want to protect everyone."

"So that's why you're participating," I said. *Idealistic and naïve. That's a dangerous combination. I feel sorry for her.*

"Yeah, but Mom and Dad didn't want me to. They said that my time would come later. But I had to prove that I could do this." Evalana's tears resumed. "They were right. I wasn't ready."

"Losing to me doesn't mean that you aren't ready." I hopped down and walked over to her. "You were right. If I couldn't beat you, all I would have had to do was outlast you. I can easily find bits of time to recover. While you take days to recuperate, I can do it in moments." I lifted her chin and smiled at her. "It's a perk of having the recovery aptitude."

Evalana's hazel eyes shimmered as she looked up at me. "Two aptitudes?" I nodded, and she cried and giggled at the same time, then started laughing. "I lost to a hero."

I think "hero" might be a strong word.

She continued laughing, and I glanced at Zenny and shrugged my shoulders. Zenny just smiled.

Slowly, Evalana regained her composure. "You had better win the whole thing and beat my brother while you're at it."

"Who's your brother?" I raised an eyebrow.

"Aurtour." She smiled.

"I'll try to remember that." *I've never heard that name before. Is it supposed to mean something?*

"So, do you girls want to do something fun?" Zenny shifted the mood. "I'm free for the rest of the day. Mom said I could go enjoy the festival."

"Let's go win more stuff." Evalana bounced and looked at me.

"Actually, I need to go hunt something." I lowered my head. The tugging at the back of my mind hadn't gone away.

Evalana stared at me with her head tilted and eyes wide open.

Zenny asked, "Okay, so do you want to try to find us after you're done?"

"Why do you need to go hunting?" I could hear the disappointment in Evalana's voice. "Didn't you hunt that rabbit the other day?"

"That wasn't hunting; that was me grabbing a meal." I slowly backed up. "And that whole bit of me tearing apart the stuffed toys didn't work. Sorry, Zenny. It's just a part of who I am. I get these irresistible urges to go out and hunt something every few days. If I don't..." The memory of the caged wolf in my dream flashed through my mind. "I just can't ignore them anymore."

"Promise me you'll find us once you're done." Evalana jumped to the ground. "Actually, could you make sure you clean off all the blood first?"

I giggled. "I promise. And, yes, Zenny, I promise not to get hurt." I gave her a slight smile. She stood still, her mouth open as if she wanted to say something, but I beat her to it. "It's almost lunchtime. Evalana, why don't you go and show Zenny those vegetable skewers that you tried to feed me? You're probably really hungry after puking your breakfast up earlier."

"Why did you bring that up?" Evalana glared at me, but the growl in her stomach agreed with me. "Oh well. You're going to love them." Evalana grabbed Zenny's hand and led her towards the door.

"Is there any broccoli on them?" Zenny walked with Evalana.

"Who eats that abomination?" Evalana said, hunching her shoulders and visibly shivering.

All of us laughed. *I'm glad that those two can get along. I just wish I fit in better.*

After I returned my gambeson to my room, I headed for the nearby forest. *Hopefully they killed that dire boar.* As I approached the tree line, a sense of dread crept up on me. I stared at the forest with a longing in my heart. *I guess I still feel that this is the dire animal's territory. When I talked to Allen yesterday, I should have asked if they'd killed it.* I followed the trees, hoping to find the edge of the dire boar's territory so I could hunt in peace.

How do I know that this is another animal's territory? I dove into the deepest recesses of my memories, digging for any relevant information. *Animals mark their territory using different methods. Rubbing scent glands to spread pheromones or using their pee and poop are the two most common methods.* I looked around for any signs of animal droppings. *None. Okay, so that means pheromones or pee.* I lowered myself to the ground and tried to let my instincts guide me.

Nothing happened until I just stopped thinking. A presence filled my mind. She didn't think the same way I did. Instead of words and pictures running through my head, emotions let me know what she was doing. My body moved as the wolf inside me willed me towards the tree line, sniffing the air. My jaw itched as it felt like something was missing.

Then fear filled me as I inched closer to the trees. The wolf brought an indistinct scent to my attention. *I can smell that? That's the smell of the boar.* My body froze as I made my realization. *Oh, I guess I took back over.* I noticed the ground was a few inches away from my face.

As I stood up, I brushed myself off and looked around. *I hope nobody saw that.* I focused on what my instincts taught me, then looked for where the scent weakened.

"Thank you so much for showing me this," I whispered to the wolf inside me. "I'll try to learn more from you later, but right now, let's hunt." I grinned as I found the direction where the scent was weaker.

Soon I lost both the scent of the boar and the feeling of dread from being near its territory. *Alright, I just need to avoid that direction. Then, if it is still alive, I'll be fine. But that thing better be dead and carved up. I want to eat some of it.*

When the sound of a bird flapping its wing above me caught my attention, I stopped looking for signs of potential prey. I glanced up and saw an eagle landing in a nest near the top of a tall tree. Drool pooled in my mouth as I wondered about the taste of eagles. *Do they taste like chicken?* I studied the tree and thought I might be able to climb it.

I began going up. *I know wolves aren't known to climb trees, but they don't have opposable thumbs, either. Although this might be much more difficult if I wasn't as strong as I am.* I dug my claws in whenever a handhold didn't present itself, but I used the branches as much as I could. Slowly and methodically, I made my way up, also making sure that the bird stayed where it was. I had to constantly swallow the drool in my mouth as I imagined how it would taste.

When I was two-thirds of the way to the nest, I made a mistake.

I looked down.

That's a long way down. Why did I think climbing this tree was a good idea? How am I going to catch the bird and then climb down with it? This was a stupid idea.

A sound interrupted my thoughts. I looked up to see the eagle looking down at me. *I guess the cat's out of the bag.*

The bird flew from the nest. *Well, I guess there goes lunch. It was stupid of me to think I could catch a bird.* I readied myself to climb back down until I saw the eagle diving straight for me.

"What?"

The eagle screeched at me as it drew back its wings and lined its claws up with my face. I attempted to move my hand between us, but I forgot to let go of the branch I was holding. The tree limb snapped, and I swung it at the bird, managing to hit the creature. But the extra weight threw my balance off, making my toe claws on my right foot slip out of the tree trunk, and I started falling. I didn't go far, as the branch below me caught me, but the impact against my arm and ribs was painful.

The bird got tangled in some branches too. The stick I'd been holding had hit the ground with a thud.

After the eagle freed itself, it took off with a screech. I watched it fly around the tree and dive in again. This time, I made sure my hands were free as I prepared to catch it.

The bird flew in, but before it got within my reach, it flapped its wings in my face. Brown feathers flooded my vision as I reached out blindly, and even though I felt my hand touch something, I couldn't grab hold of anything.

The feathers cleared from my vision, only for talons as large as my claws to replace them. I leaned back, trying to avoid being viciously clawed, but the bird scratched the left side of my face, the claw scraping against my cheekbone.

I screamed in pain and fear as I found myself falling again.

I tried to catch myself on a branch, but I succeeded only in smashing my fingers against it. I tumbled more uncontrollably after that. My world spun. I couldn't tell which direction was up and which was down. I fell through some smaller twigs before landing gut-first on a wide branch. Somehow, I reflexively caught myself on the limb. The impact nearly knocked the wind out of me, and I groaned in pain. Everything stopped moving as I stared at the ground. I was on one of the last branches I could have landed on.

I took a few breaths before stabbing pain shot through my back from what felt like eight knives, and I screamed with what little air I had in my lungs. I reached a hand back to grab the bird and was rewarded with it biting down on my thumb. My scream turned into a growl as my vision blurred.

If I'm going down, so are you, bird brain. I pushed off the branch and leaned back. The eagle tried to flap its wings from underneath me as we fell to the ground together.

I landed on the bird with a sickening, yet satisfying, crunch, and the eagle stopped moving.

I would have smiled at my victory if it weren't for the talons in my back and the sharp pain in my tail. I don't know how I had air to scream, but I did. The pain in my tail was unbearable, and the only thing I could do was roll over, cry, and scream in agony.

I screamed and cried until the pain lessened.

Nobody came to check up on me. Nobody came to help me. Nobody can hear me.

My mind slowly righted itself and rational thoughts returned. *What have I done? I could have died out here, alone. No one would have known. All because I had to hunt and all because I had to try to eat an eagle. I had no reason to think that was even possible. Now I'm here, lying on the ground, suffering, alone in the woods. I'm surprised another predator hasn't come up and tried to eat me. I probably wouldn't be able to do much to stop them.*

I rolled over onto my stomach. *I know I should listen to my inner wolf more since she can teach me all kinds of cool things I could do, but I need to guide her to more reasonable objectives.*

My tail still throbbed, and when I moved it, more pain shot through me. It felt like it was on fire. Tears kept falling down my face, but I couldn't scream anymore. I looked at the eagle corpse beside me. *You had better be the best thing ever. I almost died trying to catch you.* My back felt wet. *I'm bleeding. And my ribs could be cracked.* I looked down at my tail and saw why it hurt so much. There was an unnatural bend in the middle of it. *And my tail is broken.* I planted my forehead on the ground. *It's going to be a long walk back, assuming I even can walk with my tail broken.*

35

TASTES LIKE CHICKEN

kay, first thing's first. I looked at my tail. *I have to fix that.* Even though I knew what I needed to do, the pain that would soon follow would make me wish I hadn't. *Just think of it like ripping off a Band-Aid. Something that I haven't done in this life, but at least I know what I mean.*

I took a deep breath as I grabbed both sides of the unnatural bend in my tail. The burning pain caused me to clench my teeth. I closed my eyes and, in the fastest movement I could, straightened my tail. My eyes bulged open, and I screamed at the top of my lungs again.

Tears wanted to pour from my eyes, but those wells had long since dried up. I took a few deep breaths as I looked at my tail. *It looks correct now. Good start. If it weren't for the constant dull pain coming from it, I wouldn't have guessed it was ever broken.* Gingerly, I tried to wag my tail. As soon as I moved anything near the section that was broken, the pain overwhelmed me. *I need to put a splint on it. But how do I do that out here? I don't have any rope, and there aren't any vines.*

There were several holes and tears in my shirt. *I guess this shirt is done for anyway.* I then looked for branches on the ground that I could use and found several broken ones that would work.

As I crawled towards the sticks, I grabbed my tail to keep it from moving. I retrieved four branches, each about an inch thick, and stripped any excess leaves and branches off, then set them aside and cut three strips of fabric off the bottom of my shirt. I placed my tail in the center of the four sticks and used the fabric strips to tie them together. Even though it hurt more to do it, I bound them tightly.

I inspected my splint and wagged my tail. The splint held my tail stiff enough to move it, but the balance felt way different.

Now I feel really bad about what I did to that wolf. Is this some kind of poetic justice or just really bad luck?

A rumble in my stomach brought me to my next order of business. *How am I still hungry? Didn't I eat while I was with Zenny and Evalana?* I looked at the eagle corpse, drool trickling down my chin. *Whatever. This appetite of mine is getting out of hand.* I crawled to the bird, cut off its head with my claws, and ripped open its chest. After I removed the organs that I didn't like, I consumed the animal from the inside out.

I ate the organs in its chest, and while I chewed, I removed the rib cage. I cleaned off any meat that clung to the ribs with my teeth, and I pulled the breast meat away from the skin that had all the bird's feathers. After the breast meat was done, I moved to the legs, ripping them apart to get past the feather-covered skin and to my precious meat. Then I looked for dessert in the bird's bones, but I couldn't find any marrow.

Once there was nothing left to eat, I stared at the carcass. I let out a burp as I felt the food in my stomach settle just a little more. *I ate the whole thing.* The bird's main body was the size of my torso, with its wings spread out easily three times its height. Feathers, blood, and bones littered the surrounding area.

I looked down and saw my blood-coated fur riddled with feathers, leaves, and dirt. Blood coated my fur up to my elbows, and I imagined my face had plenty of blood on it too.

Wow, I kinda got a little carried away there. Eagles do taste like chicken, only with more chicken flavor. I contemplated if that was the right way to describe it as I mulled over the aftertaste in my mouth. *Either way, it was delicious.*

I looked up at the sky. *I have to get back. Salien needs to look at the wounds on my back. I know I heal quickly, but I need to make sure my injuries don't get infected.* A thought ran through my head. *Can they get infected? I have yet to get sick since I arrived in this world.* I shook my head. *Better play it safe. Infected wounds aren't something I want to gamble with.* I took my time standing up, very aware of my disrupted balance. I took a step and fell to the ground. Landing on the ground hurt a lot more than it should have, especially in my ribs.

I'm not crawling all the way back. I looked around and saw the branch I'd hit the eagle with. *That might be large enough to use as a walking stick. Hopefully it will be sturdy enough too.* I crawled up to it and stripped off any extra branches and leaves, then stood up again. It was easier with my new impromptu walking stick, and I took a few trial steps. *Alright, this is slow, but it'll work. Have I become too dependent on my tail?*

I limped back to the tournament grounds. The sun was getting close to setting once I finally arrived at the edge of the village.

People watched me, pointing and talking amongst themselves. *Does nobody want to help the injured beastkin? Can't they see that I'm obviously hurt and need help?* I glared at the people who just stood by before the sound of heavy footsteps running in my direction forced me to turn my head towards them. I saw a little elven child leading several female knights, all in matching armor. *Thanks, kid. You did something all these adults were too scared to do.*

Each of the women wore breastplates with metal pauldrons and chain mail sleeves and a white gambeson skirt. Some wielded spears, and others had bows and arrows.

"Lucia?" a familiar voice called from the knights. One knight broke away from the others as she ran towards me.

"Captain?" I asked, recognizing the elven woman. *What's her name again? I know it started with an "A."*

"What happened to you?" She stopped next to me, scanning me from top to bottom. "You look horrible. Here, let's get you to the medical room." She reached out her hand towards me.

I took her hand and allowed her to support me as I let go of my walking stick. "You should see the other guy." I smirked as I looked at her.

"Who did this to you? Where are they right now?" Panic filled the elven knight's voice.

I put my hand on my stomach. "Right here, where he belongs." The bird was still digesting, which left me feeling a little sluggish.

"You ate him?" She flinched in surprise. "Why?"

"I was hungry," I said flatly. "He tasted like chicken, only better."

"People taste like chicken?" The knight captain began to shake.

"No. Eagles taste like chicken." *People taste different. Each race probably tastes different. But I'm going to keep that bit of information to myself.*

The elf slumped her shoulders as she sighed. "Oh, you had me worried there for a moment." She turned to the knights that were following her. "Don't worry, I'll take care of her. There's no emergency." She returned her attention to me. "You really do look awful, and is that a splint on your tail?" She pointed at it.

"Yeah, it's a little broken. I can't walk very well with it like this." I gripped the lady even tighter. "Could you help me?"

"I can carry you if you'd like." Her voice felt caring. I nodded. "I'll be careful." She turned her back to me and lowered herself slightly. "Hop up." I placed my hands on her shoulders and lifted my legs into her waiting arms. She struggled to stand back up. "Wow, you're heavier than you look."

"I'm not fat. It's all muscle." I could feel my cheeks warming up as I blushed hard.

"I'm sure it is." The elf's voice was strained as she walked towards the arena grounds.

"I'm sorry, but I can't remember your name." I hid my face behind her shoulder.

"It's Aenwyn." Her voice was soothing.

"Thank you, Aenwyn." I turned my head and rested it on her shoulder as I closed my eyes.

"Did an eagle really do all that to you?" The concern in Aenwyn's voice was obvious.

"Some of it, yeah. But falling out of the tree did most of it," I whispered into her ear.

"Do I want to know what you were doing in a tree?"

"I would rather not talk about it." *How am I going to explain this to Zenny?*

Aenwyn carried me to Salien, who cleaned me up and stitched the wounds on my back. Salien also placed my tail in a proper splint and put bandages on my hand and face. She then moved me to a room away from everyone else because they were all giving me hateful stares, especially Lestrana.

The door to the room I was lying in flung open, and a shout accompanied the sound of the door hitting the wall.

"You big dummy!" Zenny's face was red as she marched towards me after slamming the door closed and dropping the basket she was carrying.

I didn't flinch because I had already covered my ears, ready for her outburst.

Tears welled up in her eyes. "You promised me."

"I know." I released my ears and turned away from her. "I'm sorry." *That phrase can't even begin to express what I really want to say, but even after all the time I had to prepare, that was the best I could come up with.* "I'm sorry for not keeping my promise. I don't know the words to tell you how rotten I feel for failing you."

Zenny ran and jumped on the bed, hugging me. She landed on my tail, causing me to scream in pain. Horror filled her face as she hurried off the bed. "I'm sorry. What did I do?" She held her hands in front of her mouth as she looked for something.

I shifted my tail to the other side of me. "My tail's broken, and you just jumped on it." The throbbing pain had almost disappeared before now, but it returned with a vengeance. "It isn't your fault. You didn't know and couldn't see where my tail was. It was my fault for leaving it on that side."

She returned to hugging me, but this time she didn't get on the bed. "I was so worried when Mom told me to go to your room to get some clothes. She said you had a little accident while hunting, but this looks like more than a little accident." She released me and waved to my face.

"I fell out of a tree," I tried to say with a smile and the happiest tone I could manage. "Who would have thought that wolves belong on the ground—that I belong on the ground?"

Zenny's face turned bright red as she clenched her fist and hit me on the top of my head. "You big dummy." I put my hands where she hit me. "What were you doing in a tree?" Zenny looked at me with a glare that reminded me of the one Nora had given me on multiple occasions.

"I was being a stupid kid." I looked away from her. The pressure of her glare was too much. "I saw an eagle fly into its nest, and the only thoughts from that point forward were about how to get to it. I never considered the consequences of my actions. The only thing running through my head was to eat the bird. I never thought about what I would do once I was at the top of the tree after I had killed it. I just acted on impulse. I know I shouldn't do that, but I couldn't stop myself." I couldn't hold back my tears anymore. "I just wanted that bird so badly. I'm sorry I couldn't keep my promise to you." I turned to look at Zenny. The tears in my eyes blurred her image. "Can you forgive me?"

Zenny wiped the tears from my eyes. "Of course, you big dummy. That's what friends do." With my vision cleared, I could see Zenny smiling at me. "Did you at least get it?"

I sniffled. "Yeah." I tried to put on a smile.

"How did it taste?" She walked to the basket she had dropped at the door.

"Like chicken."

Zenny giggled at my answer, causing me to giggle also.

"Now, what did we learn?" she asked as she placed the basket by my side.

"To stay out of trees," I said in a playful tone.

"Will you?" Zenny eyed me closely.

"Yes, ma'am." I saluted her.

Zenny doubled over, laughing. I then started laughing just as hard as she was. We continued for a little while before Zenny slowly regained her composure. I collected myself too. *Laughing that hard hurts, but I feel so much better now. I needed that.* She gave me a smile, which I returned with one of my own.

"Okay, you need to get dressed. You have visitors who want to talk to you." Her voice was full of seriousness.

"Who?" I asked as I went through the basket to put on the clothes she'd brought me.

"The beastkin ambassadors." Zenny gave me a worried look.

I pouted once I finished putting on my clean shirt. "I don't want to talk to them."

Zenny lowered her tone. "Your mom is with them, and she looks sad."

A sense of dread built in my gut.

I eventually finished getting dressed. "Do I have to?"

Zenny slowly nodded.

I sighed as I sat on the edge of the bed. "Fine," I said in a defeated tone.

Zenny walked to the door of my room with a solemn look. She turned to glance back at me. "You're my best friend, no matter what. I just want you to know that."

What's going on?

She left the door open as she walked away. I could hear her stop. "She's ready. You can go in now."

Why does she sound so sad? What didn't she tell me?

36

WHO'S YOUR ALPHA NOW?

I stared at the doorway as the two beastkin from earlier followed Nora into the room. The beastkin stood just inside the door, with the panther beastkin standing half a step in front of his companion. Nora closed the door before walking towards me and standing between the beastkin ambassadors and me, splitting the distance perfectly in half. The look on the panther beastkin made me extend my claws as I readied for a fight. His face had an enormous bruise on it, but despite it, he had a grin that was begging me to slash it off.

"Are you done running, pup?" His voice was as cocky as his expression.

"What do you want?" When I narrowed my eyes at him, I noticed the hare beastkin flinch backwards.

Nora's voice held no emotion as she said, "They're here with the blessing of King Ramos."

"That doesn't answer my question. What do you want?" I raised my voice.

"We're here to take you back to The Wild Kingdom." The panther's wide grin somehow grew wider.

"Lamso, maybe we shouldn't be so aggressive with her." The hare beastkin clutched the other beastkin's shoulder.

"Silence, I know what I'm doing," he whispered back.

She shrank back behind him, lowering her eyes to the ground.

"You should take her advice," I growled.

Lamso put a hand to his cheek. "You got lucky. You won't be able to do that again."

"You're right." My vision was slowly shifting to red. "Next time, I won't be so nice." *Why does his face make me so angry? Maybe he should stop smiling.*

"Lucia, please calm down. Ambassadors Lamso and Regimes are here to talk." Nora took a step forward to block our view of each other.

"Why do you care?" I could feel the adrenaline running through my system.

"I'm your—" Nora started.

"Guardian. I know," I interrupted her. My heart ached as I talked. "This is none of your business. You said they were here to talk to me. You've done your job. Now let me take care of my business." I watched Nora take a step back. Her eyes shimmered as she held back her tears.

"You will learn respect, pup." Lamso's voice carried a low growl as he took a step towards me.

"My name is Lucia," I growled back at him.

"You are acting like a pup, so I will call you a pup. Now, you're coming with us. You don't belong here." He stood over me.

I looked up at his towering stature as I stayed seated on the bed. "No."

Shock filled the panther beastkin's face, but it quickly faded as I watched him bare his teeth. "I wasn't asking." He reached with his right hand to grab my shoulder.

My vision finished shifting to red as I grabbed his forearm with my left hand, just past his armband. I squeezed as hard as I could, eliciting a cry of pain from the large man.

"Why you little..." He growled and swung his left hand towards my throat. I caught that arm too and attempted to crush the bones in both of his forearms, but Lamso flexed the muscles in his arms to resist me.

I stared at the fire in his eyes, and even though I held both of his arms in a painful grip, he just gritted his teeth and growled. He kept trying to close his hands around my neck, but I was too strong. Even though I was hurt, I was at full strength.

If you haven't got the idea yet, maybe this will get through to you. I loosened my grip just long enough to angle my claws to insert them in the space between the two bones in his forearm. His knees buckled slightly as I twisted my claws, feeling his bones cracking.

"Stop this." Nora moved to intervene, but the hare beastkin grabbed her.

"No, do not interrupt. This is part of our culture." Regimes moved in front of Nora. "There can be only one alpha. One must submit. This is how they must settle it."

"But—" Nora started saying.

"This isn't a fight. It's a contest of strength only. Lamso won't hurt her too much if he wins. He may be aggressive and brutish, but he knows the laws." Regimes' voice carried more certainty than before.

"That's not what I'm worried about," Nora said under her breath.

I kept twisting and prying the bones in Lamso's arms apart. He didn't scream; he only grunted and growled in response. I used the leverage I held over him to stand up. I still didn't match his height, and he continued to stare down at me defiantly as he again tried to reach for my throat.

With a flick of my right arm, I threw the beastkin's arm out wide. I grabbed his throat with my claws before he could reach mine. The fire in his eyes died out as he stood motionless. His arm hung limp as his breathing went from deep, full breaths to short gasps.

"On your knees." My voice seethed with every bit of anger I possessed.

He complied. Slowly, he dropped to one knee and then to the other, all while keeping his free arm out wide.

Pride filled my heart as he kneeled before me. But even while on his knees, he could still look straight at me. *It's not enough!*

I slammed the palm of my hand into the base of his throat, and he fell onto his back, choking. I held on to his right arm as I placed my foot on his throat. Lamso panicked and grabbed my foot, but I reached down and moved his hand. His claws scratched me lightly, leaving a few small trails of blood.

"I told you I wasn't going to be nice next time." As I growled, I bared all my fangs at him. I extended my toe claws into his neck, drawing a tiny trickle of blood. I wanted him to know that any mistake would only make his death more painful. "Any last words?"

"I submit," he wheezed. There was no rumble in his voice. No bravado. No courage. *Good. Know your place before you die.*

"Please spare him." Regimes' voice snapped me back to my senses. Everything returned to normal.

"Why should I?" When I looked up, Regimes was kneeling on the floor, her head resting on the ground.

Regimes replied, "Because he submitted."

"Because you know you shouldn't," Nora said at the same time.

"Now that he has submitted, you may make your demands of us." Regimes never lifted her head from the ground. "If they are within our ability, we will complete them. Just please spare my mate."

I looked down at the panther beastkin with surprise. *These two are together?* "Fine." *I shouldn't get into the habit of killing people.* As I stared into his eyes, I released his hands and held my bloody claw inches away from his face. "But I never want to see you again." I carefully straightened myself and returned to my seat on the bed. "Regimes, stay and answer all my questions."

Lamso scampered backwards. He only stood up to open the door and run out. Regimes never moved an inch.

"What are you doing?" Nora walked towards me, her face full of concern.

"I have questions that need answers. And since she can likely answer them, I'm just using the cards I've been dealt." I grabbed the sheet off the bed and used it to clean the blood from my claws.

"What has gotten into you lately?" Nora stared back at me with sadness.

I glared at Nora. "I couldn't stand the sight of his face. It put me in a bad mood."

"Let's go. She needs time to calm down." Nora reached out to pick up the kneeling hare beastkin.

Regimes shrugged Nora off. "I can't go. I have to answer her questions."

"This isn't the best time for her." Nora tried to lift Regimes again.

"Let her answer my questions. Don't you have questions too?" I interrupted.

"You're not thinking clearly." Nora stood up and faced me. "You're too emotional right now. You just had an accident."

"An accident that happened because I let myself get carried away." I clenched my jaw as I growled. "You don't know what it's like. Just go. Don't you need to be a guardian to the other kids too? At least you can relate to them."

"There's something wrong. I wish you would let me help you." Nora's voice was soft, and her lips quivered.

I glared at her. "Just leave me alone."

She walked out of the room, sniffling.

After a few moments of silence, Regimes lifted her head enough to look at me and asked, "Why did you say that to her? She only—"

"Wanted what's best for me?" I interrupted. "I know. But I don't know why I said that. Things are really confusing for me right now. I'd rather not talk about that with someone I don't know."

"Very well. What are your questions?" Regimes returned her gaze to the ground.

"Let's start with something simple," I said. "If I go with you, what will happen to me? Where will I go, and who will take me in?" Before she answered, I sighed. "And please sit up and talk to me. It's weird to talk to you like that."

Regimes raised her head and shifted her legs so that they stuck out to the side. "You will come with us to our village, and the leader will give you a job. You're on your own to find a place to stay. I can tell you that nobody will take you in, though. You're too old." Her voice was slow and consistent. "Thank you again for sparing my mate."

"He should be thanking you." I saw confusion creeping over her face. "You said that he wouldn't kill me. I've only killed people who were going to kill me or people around me. And you asked nicely." My mood improved drastically now that it was just me and the hare beast-kin. *Why did both Nora and that Lamso guy make me so angry?* "You said I would be given a job and left to fend for myself. What if I wanted to pick what I wanted to do, like be a hunter?"

"That isn't how it works. The elder gives you a job based on the needs of the village. If the village needs a hunter, then he might give it to you. But you need to do the job that he gives you, and if you do, food and clothes will be allocated to you." It sounded like she was reciting some religious doctrine.

"But no place to stay," I added.

She nodded. "Correct."

"You know that I'm still a kid, that I'm ten years old, right?" *They can't expect a child to be able to take care of themselves like that. Can they?*

"It doesn't matter." Her emotionless answer threw me into confusion. "These 'orphanages,' as you call them, are a strange concept to us. Any child that loses its parents, if they are strong enough, will find a way to survive."

That's taking the survival of the fittest a little too seriously. "Congratulations. You have just sold me on not going with you," I said as I put my head in my hands. "Let's move on to something more complicated. Can you tell me why I'm so angry all the time? Why do I constantly need to go out and hunt something?"

"How old were you when your parents died?" She tilted her head to one side.

"Four, but that doesn't matter since I was hit in the head and forgot everything before that moment." I groaned at my first memories of this world.

"Oh." Her ears drooped as she lowered her head. "I'm sorry. I wish I had known sooner. But we only found out about your existence last year."

"Well, blame the orcs that sacked my village for carrying me to this kingdom," I blurted out.

She perked up at the mention of orcs. She looked at me more

closely, almost as if she was seeing me for the first time. "What season were you born?"

"Wind, why?" I asked.

Her eyes grew wide. "You survived? You survived when everyone else in Gainhir was slaughtered?" She stood up and took a few steps towards me.

"I don't know what village you're talking about, so maybe?" *Does she know about my parents?*

"Silver fur, ten years old, blue eyes, lived in Gainhir six years ago..." She listed off facts, not bothering with my question, lost in her thoughts. "Lucia? As in Malcolm and Kendy's daughter?"

"I don't know." I shrugged. "How do you know if Gainhir was the village I used to live in?"

"Because that's the last village that was so thoroughly destroyed." Regimes took a closer look at me. Then her face lit up. "You are definitely Kendy's daughter."

"You knew my parents?" I watched her closely.

"Yes, Kendy was my friend growing up. After she met Malcolm and moved to Gainhir, we stayed in touch, sending letters to one another. You look just like her. She told me she had two daughters. But everyone thought you were dead." She kneeled in front of me and grabbed my hands, tears flowing down her cheeks.

"I had a sister?" *What should I do? What do I say?* I felt lost. Hearing names from someone else's life that I had taken over felt disorienting.

Regimes released my hands and gave me a hug. "I'm sorry. I'm so sorry." She cried on my shoulder.

I sat in shock before I pushed her out to arm's length. "Sorry for what?"

"Who else was captured with you?" Regimes asked.

"Nobody. I was their only captive," I said carefully.

"Did they do anything to you while you were their captive?" She gave me a look of worry behind her tears. "You must have been terrified for all those weeks."

"They didn't do anything. I blacked out and woke up just before some knights killed the orcs. A knight took me to the orphanage because I was alone." *Weeks? Was I in a coma or something? How am I alive? Did my recovery aptitude keep me alive for all that time?*

"I'm sorry that you've been in a strange land full of strange people who don't understand you." The hare beastkin tried to wipe the tears from her face, but more just replaced them.

"You have no idea," I mumbled absentmindedly. *No, I didn't mean to say that out loud.*

"Then why don't you come with us?" She was slowly regaining her composure.

"You're asking me to start over again." I looked into her puffy, bloodshot brown eyes. "I'm sure you and my mother were great friends, but even hearing her name, I feel nothing towards her. Yes, living here has been frustrating, to say the least, but I have a life here. I have friends, one of whom you met, Zenny. I know I don't deserve a friend like her, but if I leave now, I don't know what will happen to her. Also, the life you said I would have if I went with you doesn't sound like it would have much freedom."

"Okay, I think I understand." A smile grew on her face. She stood up and sat next to me on the bed. "Is there anything I can do to help? You said you had questions. I believe I can give you answers."

"That will help a lot. So far, I've relied on information I've read in books. I don't know how accurate they are." I looked at her with hope. "Why do I have these constant urges to go out and hunt? And why do I get so angry so quickly?"

"Well, the need to hunt is your instincts telling you that you need to get stronger. Don't worry, once you start your seasons, it will get much easier to handle. I had so many days where I would just chew anything I could get my teeth on." She smiled, showing her four front teeth. They were large incisors that barely fit in her mouth, slightly overlapping.

"So all beastkin children have something that their instincts drive them to do?" I asked.

"Yes, but primal beastkin have it worse." She smirked.

"Primal beastkin?" *That's something I've never seen in a book.*

"It leads me to your next question: why do you have the temper that you do? You know how your teeth are like those of a wolf's, right?" I nodded. "And mine are like a hare's. But Lamso has teeth just like a human." I nodded again. "You and I are what we call primal beastkin. Our diets and temperaments are much closer to the animal we resemble."

"Oh, I was told that classification was based on our diets: carnivores, herbivores, and omnivores," I interrupted.

"That's such a crude way to put it. Humans have to simplify everything." Regimes shook her head. "As a primal wolfkin, you can only eat meat. I'm sure you learned that quickly." I nodded, not wanting to remember the few times that I ate something that wasn't meat. "There are a few gifts primal beastkin have that other beastkin don't. For one, our senses are sharper, and we can also hear our instincts much more clearly." *I've already learned that through trial and error.* "But like wild animals, we face each situation with two major responses: fight or flee. As a primal harekin, I have a predisposition to flee."

"And I have the desire to fight," I said before she could continue.

"Right." She eyed me worriedly. "Other beastkin have similar reactions, but for us, it is much more..." Regimes struggled to find the last word before she settled on one. "Intense."

"I guess that explains more than a few things." My voice trailed off.

"What's wrong?" Regimes swung her arm around my shoulders.

"Being a beastkin is hard." I stared at the floor, drained of all energy.

"Sorry, sweetheart, but living is hard. It doesn't matter what race you are." She spoke with a motherly tone, and I gave a half-hearted laugh before she asked, "Why aren't you asking about your mother?"

"Because I'd rather not know about her," I said coldly.

"That's a little harsh coming from someone so young." Her disappointed tone didn't bother me.

"I guess if there's any general advice you can give me, I'll take that." I was feeling mentally fatigued. *Even though my body heals quickly, my emotions and mind do not.*

"Don't get pregnant during your first two mating seasons." Her blunt advice felt like a slap to the face.

"Wait, what?" I shook my head, trying to make sure I'd heard what I thought I'd heard.

"If you get pregnant during your first two mating seasons, there will be complications. The first year you have your mating season will often lead to a premature stillbirth." The sadness in her voice made me believe that her advice hit too close to home. "Your second mating season will often lead to one child, but the child is more likely to survive. Your third season will be when you have your normal two children and they will be healthy."

"I don't know which is more unsettling, the information you just told me or how open you were about talking about mating seasons." *She must be tired too. Yeah, that's it.*

"What's wrong with talking about mating seasons? You're a woman. You are going to have them. It's a natural cycle." She gave me a look like she was trying to figure out what I was thinking. "You said you were ten. They'll start in a few years."

I'm done. "I think it's time I headed to bed. I have a match tomorrow." *I don't want to talk about mating anymore. I never wanted to talk about it in the first place.* There was a small tug from my instincts. "Hey, Regimes. Would you mind if I asked you one more question?"

She smiled and tilted her head. "Of course not. You can ask me anything."

I flattened my ears. *Now, how do I ask this without sounding completely crazy?* "Um, do you have an inner beast?" The hare beastkin just stared at me. "What if I were to tell you I had an inner wolf? Is that normal?"

"No." She put her hand on my shoulder. "No. Is everything alright? Do you have a voice in your head telling you to do things?"

I shrugged her hand off as I stood up and headed for the door. *Great, now I sound crazy.*

"What happened to your tail?" Regimes shrieked.

I turned and saw her staring at my splinted tail. "Uh, I fell out of a tree,"

"What were you doing in a tree? How did you get up there?"
You sound worse than Zenny.

"I can use my claws to climb wooden objects. And I wanted to eat an eagle." I sighed.

"Did you get it?" Regimes shifted to the edge of the bed.

"It was delicious," I said with a toothy grin. "It tasted just like chicken."

37

CHILL OUT

I sat in my bed, staring out the window. *What do I want?*

I could see the sun resting beyond the horizon, but it had spread its light without showing itself yet. *I can keep asking myself that question, but it isn't going to get me any closer to answering it. Maybe Lamso was right. I don't belong here. But do I belong with them? Being told what I have to do for the rest of my life doesn't sound enjoyable. But if I stay here, I'll be different from everyone else. Hearing from Regimes that my urges will get more manageable as I grow up helps.*

The morning breeze rustled the trees in the distance. I closed my eyes and focused on their lulling cadence. *After hearing the names of my body's parents, I just can't feel anything for them. People keep telling me that I should be sad that my parents are dead, but I just can't feel anything for someone I never knew. Knowing about them won't do me any good. But why did I treat Nora like that? Was I just lashing out at her? I know that she cares about me as much as she can, but she has August, April, and Molly too. And after we're gone, she'll have more to replace us. She's done this for years before I arrived, and she'll do it for years after I'm gone. How can she try to treat us like we were her own children when she's going to have hundreds over the long*

294

years of her life? But if that's the life she wants, who am I to deny her that?

The sounds of conversations coming from the fairgrounds tainted the soft auditory massage carried by the wind through the leaves. With a heavy sigh, I started brushing my fur. *The Voice sent me here to help protect this world from the threat of the demon lord, and then I got this body. I was told I could live the life I wanted. But what life do I want to live? I know I said I wanted to be a hunter, but that was before I knew that my urges would become easier to handle. I guess I enjoy the feeling I get when I catch some prey, and I enjoyed myself as I ate that eagle. It is just that; is there a life for me here? I know Zenny is my best friend, and I just made friends with Evalana. Maybe I'm just looking for a place to belong. Maybe I just want a home.*

The light from the sun illuminated everything outside. There were no footsteps outside of my room. I was the last contestant on this floor. *There are only four contestants left. One of them is Evalana's brother, Aurtour.* I stared at the brush in my hands for a moment before placing it back with my belongings.

I collected my gambeson and stood up. *I might as well see this through to the end. Who knows, maybe my place is with a knight company. The captain of The Maidens—Aenwyn, I believe her name was—she was nice.*

I removed the splint from my tail and cautiously moved it around. *It doesn't hurt, but I should play it safe.* I replaced the splint since it helped with my balance and kept me from being tripped up too much.

The rest of my injuries weren't too bad. The cuts on my face and hand were mostly healed, but I couldn't examine the wounds on my back. *Since my match will be first, I'll stop and ask Salien to look at them after.* My ribs were uncomfortable, but not painful. *I really should be careful in my match today so I don't aggravate my injuries. It's kinda funny that I hurt myself more outside of the arena than in it.*

A growl in my stomach told me I shouldn't have spent so much time lost in thought and grabbed breakfast instead. *Maybe I can find something quick.* I grabbed a few coins and hurried out to the market. I tried to stay as close to the tournament grounds as I could, looking for the first stall that had meat. After finding one that served skewers of boar meat, I bought what I could afford and earned myself more than a few stares when I asked them not to cook it. I hurried to the equipment room while practically inhaling my food, and I put on my gambeson before I walked into the hall.

The other three contestants were standing around, silently avoiding eye contact with each other. I stepped over to the board to see if I could find Evalana's brother's name. I did, and it looked like I could face him in the grand finals. As I stood looking at the board, I heard footsteps approaching me from behind.

"Are you Lucia?" a confident voice asked.

"Who's asking?" I turned to see a human behind me. He stood several inches taller than me, with a body full of lean muscles. He wore a deep purple gambeson, heavy leather gloves, and the usual leather boots. *His boots look brand new.* He held a shield, and an arming sword sat on his hip. His bright-green eyes and lush golden locks looked very familiar. His face had a slight stubble to it, although it was hard to see because of its light color.

He never flinched from my aggressive stare as he replied, "Aurtour."

"Oh, so you're Evalana's brother." I relaxed as much as I could, given that I was feeling warmer than I liked.

"So she introduced me. Then let me first start by saying thank you." Aurtour gave a slight bow.

"Why?" My voice shook as I stared in confusion. I looked around the room and noticed the other two people staring at us. *Great, this guy is making a scene.*

"I saw what you did to the three contestants you fought in the preliminaries. I'm glad that you didn't do the same thing to her." He stood up straight.

"She's my friend. Of course I don't want to hurt her." *When is this thing going to start? I don't know if I can keep talking with this guy.* "She told me to beat you up, though."

Aurtour let out a short laugh. "She would say something like that, wouldn't she? But I'm glad to hear that you call her a friend. But if you will indulge me, why do you want to be a knight? Why are you here at all? I'm sure as a beastkin, there are other places you would rather be." He held onto his shield with both hands as he waited for my response.

"Honestly, I thought I knew what I wanted, but now I'm not so sure." I turned my gaze to the ground. "I'm an orphan, and I'm sure you know what that means."

"I do," Aurtour said with an almost regretful tone.

"So right now, I'm trying to find a place where I can have the most freedom I can get." I looked back at him.

"But why didn't you go with the ambassadors from The Wild Kingdom?"

"How do you know about that?" I shot him a glare and watched him closely.

"They talked to my father about taking the beastkin that was participating in the tournament back with them." He made it sound like that was the most obvious thing in the world.

Father? "They said they had the blessing of the king. Is your father the king?" He nodded. "If you're the king's son—a prince—that means Evalana, your sister, is a princess?" My jaw bounced several times as it hit the ground.

"She didn't tell you?" Aurtour looked at me with a confused look.

I shook my head. "No. I guess that explains a few things." I held back a laugh. *The announcer wasn't just grandstanding.*

"I have a hard time believing you didn't know that she was the king's daughter." Aurtour looked like he was examining me.

"I didn't know the king had kids until I heard about this tournament." I put my hand to my head because I could feel a headache coming. "And let me guess, you're here to interview me to make sure I don't plan on using our friendship to exploit the kingdom. Does that sound about right?"

"More or less," Aurtour said nonchalantly.

I sighed. "Are you going to do the same thing to Zenny?"

"Maybe."

At least he's brutally honest.

The crowd started cheering now. "It looks like things are about to start." I hoped that was the end of the conversation. "Do I pass?"

"For now," Aurtour said as he walked away.

"For our first match today, we have Lucia," the announcer called. I focused on the ground as I walked out, trying to ignore the sounds of the crowd and taking my position on the field. "After yesterday's performance, I imagine you're all hoping for great things from her. But her opponent is looking to freeze her hot streak and bring it to an end. Give it up for Farryn." The announcer motioned to the entrance, and an elf walked out and took his position opposite me.

He stood at the same height as me, which made him shorter than the average man. While Aurtour was athletic with lean muscles, this elf had bodybuilder levels of muscle on him. But I didn't get the same feeling I got when I saw Simyn for the first time. *So he's stronger than the average person, but he doesn't have the physical aptitude. I should be stronger than him.* His skin was a dark bronze, darker than I'd seen on most people, and he didn't have any weapons in his hands. *Another mage? How many are there in this tournament?* The orange hair that went down to his shoulders shimmered in the sunlight. He wore a blue gambeson, simple tan pants, and boots, but no gloves.

"Will Farryn stand up to Lucia's ferocious onslaught?" The announcer turned to face the crowd. "Will he even be able to stand after she's through with him? Let's see how wild this semi-finals match can get."

I'm beginning to think you're doing that on purpose.

The announcer stepped off the platform. "Begin!" he shouted, and the crowd went crazy.

As soon as the announcer gave the signal, I sprinted towards my opponent. Surprisingly, Farryn did the same. But as he ran towards me, I saw ice form around his hand, and in the time it took me to take a few steps, a flanged mace was in his hand. I panicked at the sight of such a dangerous weapon appearing out of nowhere. *Is a weapon like that even allowed?* I dug my claws in and came to a halt as I waited for him.

So he uses ice magic and fights with weapons he makes from it. How do I approach this? We didn't cover this during training. If he was a mage, I'd have to close the distance as quickly as possible and interrupt any spell casting. If he was a martial opponent, I'd need to stay just out of reach and wait for him to make a mistake like over-swinging. But he has a weapon and can cast spells. Do I go in or stay out?

My opponent noticed my indecision and charged at me faster. He ran up to me and swung his mace at my chest.

I stepped back out of reach. *At least he picked a mace, the easiest weapon for me to handle.*

When Farryn brought his mace around for a second swing, I stepped into his reach and moved to catch the haft just past his hand.

I grabbed his weapon, and the look of confusion on his face when his arm stopped moving brought a smile to my lips.

"How?" he whispered as he looked at me with a scrutinizing gaze.

"I'm stronger than I look," I said with a grin.

I spun around, pulled the elf over my shoulder, and threw him to the ground. He landed with a satisfying thud. I moved to pry the icy weapon from his hands, but I met no resistance. He let go of the mace, and I almost stumbled backwards. I looked down at him in time to see him raise his other hand and hit my face with a breeze.

I stood in shock. *Wasn't that supposed to do something?*

The look on the elf's face told me his spell hadn't worked the way he wanted it to. I noticed I wasn't feeling as warm and my gambeson was almost bearable. When I tried to ask him what he'd hoped to do, my jaw wouldn't move. I took a few steps back and placed my free hand on my lips, where I felt a cool, smooth surface.

Ice? He sealed my mouth shut with ice?

I used more force to open my jaw, and the ice shattered, freeing my mouth.

"Didn't that hurt?" the elf asked as he stood up.

"No, in fact, that felt pretty good. Could you do that to my gambeson next?" I looked at him hopefully.

He stared at me. "What are you? That usually leaves people screaming in pain."

That's rude. "I'm a wolf beastkin," I said as I threw the mace I'd stolen back at him.

The mace wasn't balanced for throwing. However, any object thrown hard enough can become a dangerous projectile. Farryn dodged to the left, and I followed his movements as I charged at him.

He tried to throw a punch at me, but I easily sidestepped and clotheslined him.

How did this guy get this far? Evalana was much more work to defeat than this loser.

Before he could get up, I stomped a foot on his chest, and he clutched his front as he groaned. I grabbed a foot and dragged him behind me as I walked to the edge of the arena.

This guy should feel bad. What kind of display was this?

Once I arrived at the edge, I swung the elf around to throw him out. But as he came around into my view, I saw that he'd encased my hand and his foot in the same block of ice. Panicking, I tried to halt myself as his momentum carried me towards the edge with him. I dug my toe claws into the ground and leaned back as much as I could, barely succeeding at keeping myself in the arena. I looked out and saw that he had a pillar of ice underneath him, holding him off the ground.

You little cheater. My vision shifted to have the slightest tint of red. *Fine, you want to play dirty. I can play dirty too.*

I yanked him back towards me. He cried out in surprise. I stared down at him and growled. "This is your warning. Give up."

"You don't scare me," he said with a grin on his face.

He conjured more ice and shaped it into a spear before he thrust it at my face.

I grabbed it and dug my claws into it for a better grip before tearing it out of Farryn's hand, then I stabbed it in between the bones of his shin, pinning him to the ground.

Farryn screamed as he lunged for his now-pinned leg.

Remember, I can't be too malicious.

I broke the ice that held my hand to his foot and walked behind him. Taking a deep breath, I crouched down behind him as he sat up screaming, trying to remove the ice spear that pinned him to the ground.

"Do you fear me now?" I said in a low growl.

He stopped moving and screaming in response to my question.

It would be so easy to just slide my claws across his throat. It would be so easy. Just one quick motion. Nobody will miss him. I shook my head. *No killing!*

I wrapped my arm around his neck, placing my elbow just under his chin. I then placed my other hand on the back of his head and performed a sleeper hold.

The elf flailed in panic as I squeezed. After a few brief moments, his movements halted and his body went limp.

I released him and stood up while waiting for the announcer to declare my victory.

"You killed him," the announcer said as he ran towards me. "Arrest her." He lifted a hand and pointed at me as several knights in a variety of armor came rushing towards me.

"I didn't," I growled at him. "He's still breathing. He's just unconscious."

As the knights ran onto the field with their weapons drawn, Farryn stirred. His movements were slight as he groaned, but he moved enough for everyone to see that he was still alive.

I crossed my arms as I stared at the announcer. "I told you so. He's fine."

The announcer guy stared at me with a glare that almost drove me into a rage. "Lucia wins." His tone carried no excitement, but I also had to guess that magic carried his voice so everyone could hear.

The knights put their weapons away and gave me a plethora of different congratulations. I didn't pay attention to any of them as I glared at the announcer, holding back the urge to rip his throat out before storming out of the arena.

38

YOU'RE A MONSTER

I opened the door to the medical wing. "Are you here to see Salien or Zenny?" an elven woman greeted me with a smile.

I don't know her name; I just know that she's a doctor from another town. "Oh. I'm here to see Salien," I said.

Most of the beds were vacant when I looked around the room. *One of these beds is going to be occupied soon.*

The elven woman nodded without losing her smile and walked out the door I'd just come through. *Yesterday, she wanted to take care of my injuries, but I wouldn't let her touch me. I really have trust issues.* I placed my gambeson on a bed and sat down as I waited for Salien. Shortly after my match, my back began itching like crazy, and it had only worsened with time. *I really hope it isn't infected.*

A pair of knights carried Farryn in and set him down on a bed. He didn't even look at me. The knights gave me another quick round of congratulations on their way out.

The elven woman who had greeted me returned and went to take care of Farryn, and Salien arrived shortly after. Her arms were full of fresh blankets. "Everything alright, Lucia?" she asked as she put her load down.

"My back itches a lot. Could you look at it for me?" I said as I lowered my voice and gazed at the floor.

"Do you want to go to the other room?" She placed a hand on my shoulder.

"No, you can just use a blind. It's just a little embarrassing that I come here because something itches after what I've done to send people here." I continued to avoid looking at Salien.

Salien pulled a curtain across to give me some privacy. "I'll admit, what you did to those two boys was..."—she paused as she sat down next to me—"a bit extreme. But what that girl received was more in line with what others have come in with so far. So don't beat yourself up over it." Her voice was quiet as she clasped her hands in front of herself. "Whenever you're ready, go ahead and lift your shirt."

I pulled my shirt up and turned my back to her. "How bad is it?"

Salien giggled. "I'll be right back with a knife."

"What?" I turned back to face her.

"Relax." She placed her hands on my shoulders. "I just need to remove the stitches." I sighed as I slumped my shoulders. "Your skin is growing around the stitches. If I don't remove them now, you're going to have them forever." She gave me a playful smile. "Watching you heal is spectacular. August's recovery aptitude can't be compared to yours."

I could feel the heat in my cheeks growing. *It might have something to do with the fact that this body may or may not have come back from the dead.* "Sorry I'm so jumpy." I turned my back to her again.

"It's fine," she said as she stepped to the curtain. "Cass, could you hand me a small knife?" There was the sound of someone walking towards us and then pausing for a moment before walking away again. "Thank you."

"Is this going to hurt?" I asked.

"It will be uncomfortable, but no, it shouldn't hurt." I could feel Salien sit down behind me. She placed a hand on my shoulder blade as she started cutting the stitches. "You know, Zenny is going to miss you."

I assume she's talking about me going back to The Wild Kingdom. "I'm not going."

"Don't you want to go be with your own people?" Salien sounded concerned.

"And be surrounded by people I don't know? Be told what I'm supposed to do? Start over and be left to fend for myself? No." I could feel a noticeable weight sitting in my stomach. "I'm too afraid to start over again. So I'll continue with what little of a life I have here. The devil you know, right?"

"Don't you mean demon?" Salien felt like she had finished cutting the last of the stitches. "But what about finding anyone who knows you? Maybe you'll meet someone who can help you."

Salien pulled the strings from my back, making me tense. *Oh, that does feel weird.* I tried to relax. "I don't want to meet anyone who might have known me. I don't want to disappoint them. Whoever I was before may not be who I am now, and I won't pretend to be someone I'm not." *I have trouble being who I am even as it is.*

"I guess I never thought about that. Almost done." Salien pulled another string, causing me to tense up once again. "Have you told her that yet? She spent the entire night crying."

"I haven't had the chance. Where is she now?" I felt Salien pull the last of the stitches out.

"She wanted to watch your match, so I let her go with Melody. If you're here, and with the lack of new injuries, that means you won, right?"

I nodded and put my shirt back on as I turned to see her smiling face.

"Then she will probably be on her way back. You can wait here if you like." Salien stood up and opened the curtain.

"If that's alright." My stomach was feeling a bit uneasy. *I know she'll be happy, but I hope she doesn't try to talk me into going with the two from The Wild Kingdom.*

"Of course it is." Salien returned to work.

I removed the splint from my tail and tried to gauge how it felt as I wagged it.

"I take it your tail is healed too?"

"Yeah, I guess I didn't break it too badly." I admired my appendage. Nothing hurt and it moved exactly how I told it to.

After sitting and waiting patiently for some time, the door to the hospital wing opened and Zenny walked in. She ran up to me immediately once she saw me sitting on the bed. "What's wrong?"

"I just needed my stitches removed. They were starting to itch." I put on a smile for her.

Zenny placed a hand on her heart and let out a long exhale as she sat next to me. "That's good. I thought he injured you during the fight somehow. Although I didn't see when he could have, other than the time he froze your mouth shut. Did that hurt?"

I giggled. "No, it felt pretty good, actually. Remember, I like the cold."

"A little too much sometimes." Zenny joined my giggling. Her face quickly turned serious. "When was the last time you saw August? Nora is looking for him everywhere, but she can't find him. She went out into town to search for him."

My heart ached as I remembered what my last words to him were. I stared at the ground. "Two days ago, just after I attacked the beastkin ambassadors and Midas." I lowered my ears and fidgeted with the fur on my tail.

"You attacked them? And they're still going to take you away with them?" Zenny flinched away from me.

"I'm not going with them," I said while holding on to my tail. "I'm staying here."

Zenny leaned forward and hugged me. "I'm so happy to hear that, and I want to talk about that more. But I'm worried about August. What happened when you last saw him? And where was it?" She ended the quick hug as she turned my head to look me in the eye.

"I may have said some harsh things to him." My guilt gripped my heart as I recalled that moment. "I was in my room and upset when he came in with a heart that Melody gave him to deliver to me. He left my room crying."

"Did you hurt him?" Zenny whispered.

"Not physically." I felt a few tears escape my eyes and roll down my cheeks.

"Let's go find him so you can apologize. You didn't mean it, right?" Zenny stood up and took my hand in hers.

"I don't know," I replied. My honesty surprised me as much as it did Zenny. "I don't know a lot of things lately. I'm just so lost."

"Maybe if we can find August and you apologize, you'll feel better." Zenny smiled at me as a single tear fell from her eye. "He may need our help. Maybe we can use this time to sort out what's bothering you."

"I know what's bothering me. I don't have anywhere I belong." I felt my tears free-falling down my face. "You have Salien, Evalana is a princess, and I have nobody."

"You have Nora." Zenny returned to her seat next to me and placed an arm around my shoulders. "She's as much a mother as anyone else."

"But she isn't my mother. She's my guardian. Looking after me is her job." I placed my head on Zenny's shoulder and cried.

"You know that isn't true. You're bottling up your emotions and jumping to conclusions again." Zenny held me close as she whispered in my ear, "I'll prove it to you. Once we find August, we'll talk to Nora and tell her about your feelings. You'll see that you're wrong."

"I hope you're right," I said as I attempted to compose myself. Once I wiped away my tears, I looked at Zenny's smiling face. "So, where do you think we should look?" I asked.

"I'll look around the stalls and games. I don't want you to get overwhelmed by all the people." She paused as she looked to be thinking. "Why don't you look around here? See if he got lost somewhere."

"Okay. If I find him, what then?" I stood up, ready to begin my search.

"Bring him back here. Also, if you don't find him before the end of the day, stop by here and we'll check in town together. If I find Nora, I'll bring her with me. That way we can show you that you do belong somewhere." Zenny smiled her infectious smile.

How did I ever get a friend like her?

We went our separate ways as we searched for August. With my gambeson in hand, I searched through the halls of the tournament grounds until I found some stairs that led farther underground. *I've never been down here.* I focused on my ears, hoping I could hear August long before I could see him.

The stairs led to a dark unlit tunnel, but I didn't have any trouble seeing through the maze-like structure. There were several storerooms, many of which looked like they'd had something in them but were now empty. I checked every room systematically until I heard, in the distance, an echo of someone talking. I couldn't understand the distorted voice, but I followed it.

Hopefully that's August and he's just really lost.

I followed the sound of the voice until it slowly became clearer. Eventually, it led me to a room with a closed door, but there was a light behind it. *These voices don't sound like August at all. But maybe they've seen him.*

I approached the door and opened it. Six very large elves in tanned leather armor sat on crates as they stared at me. Two of the men were sitting on a rather large crate with a small boy tied up and gagged in between them.

August!

Letting go of my gambeson, I dropped to a low stance. Growling, I prepared to charge the two elves flanking August.

One of the two sitting next to him drew a knife and held it to the boy's throat. "I wouldn't do that, missy, unless you want to smell his blood." He spoke with a strange accent, and he sounded like he barely, if at all, moved his tongue while he spoke.

I froze at the fear in August's eyes. I growled as I pulled my ears back and bared my fangs.

The other man who was sitting next to August spoke up. "You can bark all you want, little girl. But if you move from that spot, the boy's life ends." He had an eye patch over his right eye and spoke with a similar accent.

My vision started to shift to red, but I forced it back as hard as I could. *If I lose control, August dies.*

"What do you want?" I lowered my voice as I filled it with the deepest rumble I could.

"You're the beastkin competing in the tournament, correct?" The shortest of the elves, but the one with the most muscle, stepped up towards me. He had a very long sword on his back.

I nodded, and he continued, "Then it's simple. We want you to kill the prince in your fight with him today."

I heard footsteps heading in my direction. *A witness? Maybe I can get some help with these kidnappers. Time to stall.*

"That fight isn't until tomorrow." I made sure not to change my outward expression to give away that someone might come to help me.

"We were told that the fight is happening today," the elf with the long sword answered, grinning.

"Oh look, you saved me the trouble of looking for you."

I turned around and found whose footsteps I was hearing. The announcer guy stood in the doorway behind me, a devilish grin on his face. "We can speed this along, then. This makes things so much easier since you've done the hard part for me."

What's going on? He tries to get me arrested for murder but he wanted me to see this? I don't understand.

The announcer waved his hand towards the elf with the long sword. "He's right, though. You're going to fight the prince today. And if you want the boy to live, then you'll kill the prince."

I growled as I leaned forward, ready to pounce on him.

"Ah, ah, ah." He wagged his finger at me, then pointed behind me. I turned to look and saw two knives at August's throat. "You will do exactly what we tell you to do."

August shifted enough so that the gag slipped out of his mouth, and he cried out to me, "Lucia, help me. I'm scared. Save me."

His words tore at my heart as tears rolled down my cheeks. An elf walked up and replaced his gag, then tightened it.

I can't do anything. If I try anything, they'll kill him. But I can't just leave him like this. My mind raced through every option, and in every scenario, August died. I lowered my head, unable to think of anything I could do.

"Will you let him go?" I whispered.

"What was that?" the announcer asked.

"Will you let him go?" I repeated myself, this time staring at the bald elf. Tears cascaded down my face as I stared at him, mustering all of my determination. "If I kill the prince, will you let him go? Do you swear you'll let him go?"

"I will tell my men to release him." The announcer grinned at me. *I can't get any more than that, can I?* "I take it that means you'll do it," he said. I didn't object. "Fantastic. Let's go to the field now. The sooner the better." The announcer went to leave, but turned back to me and held up a finger. "You'll tell nobody about this, or the boy dies. You run away, the boy dies. If you return without me, the boy dies. Got it?"

I nodded weakly. "People have called me a monster. But what you're doing is monstrous."

"Sticks and stones. Now stay close, put on your gambeson, and follow me." He motioned for me to come with him.

I did as the monster said and followed. I was out of options. *Did I just say that I would kill Evalana's brother just to save August? How did this happen? I don't know if I can do it. Can I kill someone who's innocent to save someone else? Will they go through with their part of the deal? I don't have a choice. They were going to kill him. If I fail, he'll probably die too. There's no way that I can win this, is there? I can't get away to find Nora to save him. I can't save him by myself. I can't tell anyone.*

We arrived at the entrance of the arena. I kept my head down and followed him into the ring. *If I kill Aurtour in front of everyone, I'll be a criminal and executed as a murderer. There's no hope for me. There's no hope for August.*

39

AN UNWINNABLE FIGHT

I stared at the ground, shoulders slumped, tail limp, and thoroughly defeated. I stood on the opposite side of my opponent, the one I was to kill in exchange for the life of a child. *For August's life.* Tears soaked my face as I waited. *What choice do I have? I can't let August die like that. But can I kill Aurtour with everyone watching?*

"Since we had such quick fights today, we decided to end the day with the grand finals match. Are you excited? Are you ready to watch the match of a lifetime?"

An overwhelming wave of approval answered the announcer's questions. My ears hurt, but I didn't flinch.

"I guarantee that this match will go down in history. We have the tournament's prodigy, Prince Aurtour. He's won all his matches by using a different weapon style each time. This time he fights with twin gladius swords." He paused until the crowd's cheers died down slightly.

"His opponent has been a true dark horse in this tournament. Let's hear it for Lucia." The crowd cheered, but it was clearly less intense than when he introduced the prince. "Not only is she the first recorded beastkin to live in the capital city, but she's the only beastkin to participate in this tournament since its inception. She savagely tore through the preliminary match. She hounded her opponent into giving up in her first round. And in the last match, she overpowered her enemy with her beastly strength."

Each sentence stabbed into my heart, filling my vision with red. For a moment, I almost pounced on him so I could rip his tongue out.

But I can't. Not while August's life is in his hands. That doused all the fires of my rage. *I'll kill you the moment August is free.*

I lifted my head high enough to glare my unspoken promise at the elven announcer. He simply grinned as he saw my face. He slowly walked backwards until he was off the field.

I want to kill him, but not because my instincts tell me to. He isn't threatening me, and August isn't close enough for my instincts to care. I want to do it because he's evil. I want to kill him because he's manipulating me and using the life of an innocent to commit a horrible crime. I should kill people like him. But I can't, not yet. Not while he has August hostage.

The announcer gave us the signal to begin. I turned my attention to Aurtour. He held two blades, one in each hand. The swords were perfect twins, twenty-four inches of blunted steel.

Aurtour took several bounding strides toward me. I stood still. I couldn't find the will to fight him. He must have seen my unwillingness and charged.

Maybe I can make it look like I killed him, but not really. Can I do that? I fooled the announcer once with the sleeper hold. That won't work since people get back up too quickly from it.

Aurtour didn't give me any time to think as he lunged at me with the sword in his left hand. The stab was easy to dodge. I sidestepped to my right and waited for his reaction.

Aurtour planted his lead foot, attempting to swing the sword he had extended towards my chest. I caught his wrist with my right hand. Before I could pull him off balance, he brought his trailing leg up and kicked me right in the stomach. I released my grip as I stepped back, clutching my midsection.

I didn't have time to wait until the pain subsided as my opponent brought the sword from his right hand down low and swung it towards my face. I moved to my left to dodge the attack and took a step towards him. Aurtour took the sword in his left hand and stabbed at me from below his right arm, but I continued to circle around him, trying to force him to attack across his body.

Once he knew his stab would miss me, he took a step backwards and brought the right sword across his body in a defensive slash. I retreated out of his reach because he held the other sword ready to stab me should I move in.

I need to get within his reach. He picked shorter and lighter swords on purpose. He knows what I want to do. That's what I get for being so one-dimensional. Then again, I only had one season to learn how to fight. He's been learning his whole life. I need to change it up. I need to do something he won't expect.

I let him make the first move again. He led with a testing stab of his left sword, and I sidestepped it again. This time, I moved to my left. Aurtour bent the elbow of his left arm to drive the sword towards my torso, but I quickly reversed my direction and moved to duck underneath the attack. Aurtour brought his right sword down low for a slash below to follow my movements.

He trapped me.

I went in the only safe direction I knew—down. As I dropped to the ground, I felt the breeze above my head as the sword missed me by inches.

I can't keep fighting defensively. I need to force him to do something different.

I dug my claws into the stone underneath me and pulled myself towards Aurtour's shins. He jumped over me, and I sailed underneath him. I caught myself before I went too far. I heard Aurtour's boots collide with the ground, and I turned my head and kicked at the back of his legs.

Aurtour fell to his knees and caught himself with his hands, still holding both swords.

I pushed myself up first. I tried to jump on his back to force him to the ground completely. But as I took my first step, he swung his left sword around towards me. I caught his elbow this time. Aurtour lifted his right sword to attack my hand, but I pulled his left arm outward and dragged him into a semicircle around me. With no balance or control, his attack didn't even come close to hitting me.

Seeing Aurtour's legs sprawled out behind him and his left arm still within my grasp, I planted my foot right between his shoulder blades. His face hit the ground with a thud, and he grunted from the impact. I twisted his left arm back to keep him from rolling around out of my hold, and he dropped his sword.

Now what? Where do I go from here? I looked at the announcer and saw the grin on his face. *I have to do something. August is counting on me.* I stared at the back of Aurtour's neck.

It won't work. The moment they find him to be alive, August is dead. I can't save him on my own. Evalana can't cast magic yet, and I don't know where Nora is. August, Evalana, I'm sorry. I'm sorry, Nora; I'm sorry, everyone.

I pushed my arm into Aurtour's back, keeping him pinned. He struggled against my hold but wasn't strong enough to break out.

"I yield." His voice was somber as he relaxed. Tears flowed down my cheeks as I opened my mouth and placed my teeth at the base of his neck. "I said, 'I yield.'" Panic filled Aurtour's voice as he tried to move again. I held my teeth at his neck.

All I have to do is bite down, and August will be free. I'll be a murderer. I'll die, but August will live, right? I don't have a choice. I can't let August die just so I can live. I won't be able to live with myself. I held still while Aurtour continued to struggle and call out to me, but I couldn't let myself hear his words.

Just one bite. I promise it will be quick. You won't suffer.

"I'm sorry," I whispered.

He suddenly stopped moving, but I don't know if he heard me over the crowd. Tears cascaded from my eyes as my teeth rested against the prince's spine. It would have been easy, it would have been quick, but every muscle in my body seized up. Nothing responded to me.

If I kill Aurtour, Evalana will think I'm a monster. I'm not a monster. I can't become a monster to save someone. I won't be.

Once I removed my jaw from Aurtour's neck, my body moved again. Unable to continue, I collapsed on his back, releasing my hold on him. My body felt drained as I cried on top of him, and my tears soaked his gambeson. "I can't do it." I repeated those four words over and over.

Aurtour never moved. He just lay motionless underneath me, accepting my tears.

"What are you waiting for, you stupid beast? Kill him." The announcer marched towards us. "Or do you want that boy to die?"

Aurtour's muscles tensed.

"I can't do it," I repeated once more.

"Fine, if you want something done right, do it yourself," the announcer said under his breath. His voice shifted from his normal one to his magically enhanced one. "Ladies and gentlemen, let the main event begin! Now I have to kill both of you. Starting with the useless..."

I didn't let him finish. The moment he said that he was going to kill me, my vision shifted to the darkest shade of red I'd ever seen. I didn't fear it. In fact, I welcomed it. A deep, primal growl escaped my lips before, in one fluid movement, I pushed off the prince, turned around, and pounced on the announcer as he walked up to us. My jaw didn't have any trouble biting into his throat, and I savored the feeling of my teeth sinking into his flesh, the sweet taste of his blood, and the fear in his eyes as he saw the chunk of his neck in my mouth as we fell to the ground together.

My vision shifted to an even darker shade of red. Everything kept getting darker and darker. The crowd didn't exist. The prince didn't exist. Only the elven monster clutching at the blood pouring out of his neck did, and I wanted him dead. I slashed my claws across his face and reveled in the gurgling sounds of my prey. After revealing his skull, I tore open his chest. I ripped out his ribs, threw his lungs to the side, and crushed his heart. I scattered his entrails around as I moved in a fury until there was nothing left of his torso. He had one eye open when I looked up. Mocking me, the terror-frozen organ stared at me, unmoving.

I grabbed his head and smashed it into the ground.

His eye was still open even though his head was horribly misshapen. I continued to force his head into the ground over and over until his face and eye were a thin paste.

A touch on my shoulder caught my attention. It tried to pull me away from the monster. I shrugged off the intruder and jumped back onto the legs, shredding them mercilessly.

Again, someone tried to pull me away. I turned to see who was trying to stop me.

Aurtour's face was inches away from mine.

"It's alright. He's gone. He can't hurt anyone anymore." His voice was soft. Something about his face caused the red in my vision to wash away.

While breathing heavily, I turned to look at the announcer and saw my handiwork. *Did I just do that?* I stared at the pool of blood, organs, and bones. The grisly sight would have left even the most battle-hardened warriors feeling nauseous. But I felt no guilt, no remorse. The sight left me feeling hungry. *What was so important about him again?*

"August!" My shout caused Aurtour to jump and let go of me. "August is going to die now. Because of me, he's going to die." I dropped to my knees as I buried my face in my hands and found more tears to cry. I could hear something going on in the stands, but I couldn't accurately understand what was happening.

"Who's August?" Aurtour kneeled next to me as he placed a hand on my shoulder.

"He's a little boy from the orphanage where I'm from. Some guys kidnapped him and told me that if I didn't kill you in the match, then they'd kill him. That guy was their leader or something. Maybe it was all his idea. I don't know. But since I didn't kill you, and since I killed him, there's no hope for August." I barely looked at Aurtour as more tears fell.

"Why didn't you say anything?" Aurtour asked.

"Because they said if I told anyone, he'd die," I said in between sobs. "And I didn't have time. As soon as I found out, he dragged me here to fight."

"How many are there?"

"Six. Too many for me. I can't get to August and save him before one of them cuts his throat." I dropped my hands to my sides.

"How many do you think you need to take out to guarantee August's safety?"

"Two. Why?"

"How many can you take out?"

"One, if I have something to throw." I looked at Aurtour. There was a glimmer in his eye. I didn't know what it meant.

"I guess that means I have to take the other one out." The smile on Aurtour's face was almost infectious.

"Does that mean you're going to help me? After I almost killed you? Why?" I wiped the tears from my face.

"You didn't. In the end, you chose not to kill me, when you clearly could have." Aurtour spared a glance at the elven announcer's remains. I saw him try to stifle a shudder, but he failed. "Quite easily, too. They forced you to do this. The very least I can do is help you save an innocent child."

"In that case, I need something to throw," I said as I stood up.

40

SAVE AUGUST

Screams interrupted our brief planning session. I looked up and the complete lack of guards around us seemed odd to me. *I just slaughtered the announcer. Why didn't any of the knights try to stop me?* I looked up at the stands, and the ensuing pandemonium left me staring, eyes wide and mouth agape.

"What's happening?" I asked.

"I don't know." Aurtour sounded just as surprised as me.

People ran around panicking. Strange gangly, pale-skinned creatures jumped on defenseless spectators and attacked them.

"We need to save August right now." I grabbed Aurtour's gambeson and pulled him towards the armory.

"But what about everyone in the stands?" Aurtour's previous calm demeanor was nowhere to be found.

I saw some knights fighting off the odd creatures while others tried to herd people to the safety of the exits. "It looks like the knights have this handled. The longer we wait, the more likely it is that they'll kill August." I pulled Aurtour behind me as I ran.

"You're right. This situation looks like it's being handled." He followed me of his own volition. "You need something to throw, and I need to grab a bow. That will be enough, right?"

"Yeah, but what are you going to do for a weapon? I have my claws, but all the weapons in the armory are blunt. And I have a feeling that their weapons are sharp." We continued to run down into the hallway.

Aurtour held a dagger in his hand. "Don't worry about me."

How did I miss that? How long has he had it? "Where…"

"The master of ceremonies dropped it right after you bit his throat out." I watched him grimace as he recalled the moment. "But I still need to grab a bow. This dagger will be enough afterwards."

"What's your aptitude?" I said as we entered the armory of blunted weapons.

"Muscle memory. You?" Without looking at me, Aurtour walked over to the bows and arrows.

"Physical." My concise response earned me a quick look of surprise from Aurtour, but he chuckled. "I figured that. You're lucky I didn't learn any unarmed combat techniques. Our fight would have ended much differently if I knew what you were going to do."

"Now isn't the time for that conversation." I glared at him as he strapped a quiver of arrows to his belt. *You still would have lost.* "Those won't kill anyone."

"No, but a shot in the right place will stun them for a while."

I rolled my eyes as I walked towards him.

Aurtour held out his arms with the bow in hand. "Do you have any proper arrowheads that I don't know about?"

"Give me an arrow." I held out my hand, and Aurtour gave me one. I took my claw and shaved off the blunt head, then made four quick cuts with my claw to make a sharp point at the end of the wooden shaft. "We have to hurry. Give me two more arrows. Make them count."

"Where did you learn to do that?" Aurtour watched me intensely as he placed two more arrows in my hand and he took my modified arrow.

"I constantly gouge the wood floors at the orphanage I live at. I'm well aware of how sharp these claws are." After quickly modifying the two arrows, I handed them back to him. They weren't perfect points, but they now possessed what I hoped was a deadly enough tip. I looked at the small metal ball I'd removed from them. *That might work. It's not perfectly spherical, but if I hit someone's head, they shouldn't get up.*

"How do you keep your claws sharp?" Aurtour leaned closer to me, staring at my claws.

I glared at him. "That's personal information." I turned to leave. "Try to keep up." I gave my new partner a wink and a grin.

I took off to where August was held captive, but I slowed down once I heard Aurtour couldn't keep up. Even though all the wooden walls looked the same, I navigated them to the best of my memory until I found the room I was looking for. I stopped far enough away so we could approach quietly. It was more for Aurtour because I was afraid his boots stomping behind me would give us away. Also, after looking at Aurtour breathing heavily as he caught up with me, I gave him a moment to recover.

I placed a finger to my lips as I pointed at the door to the room where I'd last seen August. Aurtour gave me an incredulous look but said nothing as he took several deep breaths. "Once we get to the door, I'll take the one on the right and you take the one on the left," I whispered. *The fewer steps he takes, the better.*

I led Aurtour to the door, making sure his steps were as quiet as possible. As we approached, I could hear the elves talking.

"How much longer are we going to sit here with the brat?"

"I don't know."

"The boss said he had some grand plan to cover our escape."

"What about the mission to kill the king? Weren't we supposed to assassinate him?"

What? This is about killing the king? I hope Aurtour didn't hear that. He might do something stupid.

I turned and saw that his expression hadn't changed. *Either he didn't hear them, or is keeping it very well hidden that he did.*

"The boss said he thought about that too. He said there was something special in this room that nobody was supposed to find out about."

"How much longer until Ryo gets back? I've got to go."

Is Ryo the announcer's name?

Their voices sounded too similar to me to figure out who was saying what. But it didn't matter. We were setting up to kill them. They were prey. *And prey doesn't need names.*

We stood by the door and I held up a single finger before I pointed to myself. Aurtour nodded as he grabbed a modified arrow.

Since the door opens inward, I might be able to shock them by kicking it as hard as I can. For this fight, I want every advantage I can get.

I closed my eyes and focused on my emotions, specifically my rage and the feeling I got when my vision shifted color.

A familiar red shade greeted me as I opened my eyes. I took a step forward and kicked the door as hard as I could.

The door didn't swing open. It went straight into the room and tumbled to a stop in the center of the space. I stepped in, ignoring the surprised shouts of five elves. *Five? Whatever, one less to worry about.* Two elves were sitting next to August and jumped to attention at my entrance.

I threw my arrowhead at the elf half-standing to the right of August. It whistled before it struck the elf's forehead and embedded into a noticeable crater in his skull. He fell backwards from the impact. The other elf that was within arm's reach of August caught an arrow in his eye socket. His body stiffened before collapsing.

Two elves were standing on the left side of the room, and the last elf was on the right side. The two on the left went to draw their swords, but the one on the right drew a dagger and moved towards August, catching my attention immediately. I sprinted forward. Before the elf could get close to August, I let out a deep growl and pounced on him. We fell to the ground together as I bit into his right shoulder, but he caught himself before his face planted into the ground.

The leather armor prevented most of my teeth from digging into his flesh, but that just made me bite down even harder. The elf howled in pain and tried to roll over and grab my hair, but I rolled with him, throwing him underneath me. The sudden flattening of his shoulder told me his bones had just shattered.

The kidnapper collapsed to the ground, unable to support himself in his current state. His screams hurt my ears.

I released his shoulder and pulled his head back by his hair.

Don't grab my hair!

His cries shifted to a gurgling sound as I ran my claws across his throat. I slammed his face into the ground and severed his spine before I looked at what was going on around me.

Aurtour held both the announcer's dagger and one of the longswords the elves had been using. I also noticed that there was only one elf standing and fighting him. The other was lying in a puddle of blood, face-first.

More prey!

Aurtour blocked the last remaining elf's horizontal slash with his dagger and lunged with the longsword in his other hand. The elf side-stepped as he withdrew his blade from Aurtour's dagger. I stalked around to his back as the elf gave his full attention to Aurtour.

"Behind you," Aurtour said with a cocky tone. He made a quick pointing motion towards me with his dagger.

The elf turned around to face me.

You sold me out!

"What..." His words died in his throat as I pounced on him, my teeth digging into the soft flesh of his vulnerable throat. I bit and tore his neck out, then slashed at his face with my claws until he stopped moving.

"Why are you so excessive? He was dead after the first bite." I looked up to see Aurtour watching me, disgusted.

"You have a problem with a little blood?" I asked as I tried to return my vision back to normal. I opened my eyes to find Aurtour looking at me, clearly unamused. "Fine, I get a little carried away when I'm angry. It's just so hard to stop." I stood up and saw August shaking, still tied up and gagged. "Not like you would understand," I said under my breath.

I walked over to August so I could cut him loose. His eyes looked like they were about to pop out of their sockets. I heard footsteps approaching as I cut the ropes that tied August's arms and legs. He scrambled out of the bindings and backed away from me the moment he could move, flattening himself against the wall.

I was about to tell him to calm down, but he pulled the gag out of his mouth and pointed behind me. "Look out!"

But I was already aware of someone standing in the doorway. The person walked up and stopped just before August shouted. I turned and grinned at the newcomer.

I'm going to enjoy this.

The elven kidnapper looked at the bloody scene in the room before he looked at me, terrified.

"Go on, run," I said with a slight growl.

He turned and ran the opposite way we'd come. As I took off after him, my vision instantly shifted to a reddish hue. I didn't wait for Aurtour; I just chased the elf down like the helpless prey he was. His panicked cries encouraged me as I closed in on him effortlessly before I jumped on his back and tore him apart.

I'm hungry. Maybe one bite will be fine. I pulled out his heart and took a bite.

"Are you eating him?" Aurtour shouted as he came running towards me.

I growled at him and clutched my food to my chest. *Mine!*

"Let's go. We need to get August out of here." Aurtour pointed back towards the room. "He's the whole reason we came down here and killed those men, remember? And we need to figure out what else is going on too. What were those things attacking the people in the stands?"

I swallowed my bite and shook my head to return to my proper senses. "Right, August." As I stood up, I quickly ate the rest of the heart, then ran back into the room to see August looking at the corpses of his captors. "It's okay, August. I won't hurt you." I held up my arms, attempting to put the boy at ease.

"That was so awesome!" August shouted.

My consciousness skipped for a moment as I halted.

"I knew you would save me." He jumped off the crate and ran

towards me, avoiding the puddles of blood. He stopped just out of my arm's reach. "Why are you all covered in blood? Are you hurt?"

"None of this is mine," I said as I crouched down to his level. "Listen, I'm sorry for what I said to you. It was wrong of me to say that. Like the rest of us, Nora's trying her hardest to do what she believes is right." *I know you won't understand completely, but hopefully, I can repair the damage I did.* "I was upset, and I vented my frustrations on you."

"But you saved me. You're a hero." August looked at me with a smile on his face. "What's that other stuff you're talking about?"

I sighed as I slid my hand down my face, being careful of my claws. *He forgot the whole thing. I guess being kidnapped can traumatize someone. Maybe he's just shocked, and this is how he's coping. Yeah, that has to be it.*

I lowered my hand and saw the blood drip off it. *And that was just on my face. I'm a real mess.* "Let's go to the medical wing. You should be safe there. And hopefully Salien has some answers for us."

"Um, can you carry me?" August tugged at Aurtour's gambeson. "I can't run as fast as Lucia."

I offered a hand. "I can carry you."

August flinched and turned towards Aurtour. "I don't want to get all covered in blood. Mom might get angry with me."

Aurtour chuckled as he lifted August onto his back.

I can carry August and run faster. But no, he wants Aurtour to carry him. I'm covered in too much blood for him. I rolled my eyes as I turned to follow them. Something felt off and I looked back at the room one more time. An ominous feeling filled my gut as I saw pools of blood spreading across the floor. I hadn't noticed before, but there were strange markings on the floor in one of the corners. *It's probably not important.*

But when I went to walk down halfway, everything rotated slowly. I placed my hand on a wall to catch myself.

"Are you alright? Are you hurt?" Aurtour sounded odd.

Is his voice slowing down?

"No, I just feel a little woozy." I looked at my hands as I felt a slight tingle in them. "Was it something I ate?"

"I don't know. You started eating the heart. Is that normal for you?"

I giggled at his question. "Of course, I eat hearts all the time." *They're delicious.* "But wasn't that an elf's heart? That's a no-no. I shouldn't eat people." I continued giggling.

"What's wrong with you? What's so funny?" Aurtour looked worried as he set August down.

"What's wrong with her?" August took a few steps away from me.

"I was about to ask if you've seen her like this before." Aurtour looked at me closely before he reached to place a hand on my forehead.

I slapped his hand. "No. You don't get to pet me." I pouted. "You're very handsome, but I don't want to mate with my friend's brother."

Aurtour's eyes popped wide open as his face turned a pretty pink color. He blinked several times while staring at me. "We need to get you some help. You're acting like you're drunk. Hopefully someone can figure out what's going on. Can you walk?" He held out his hand to me.

"I can outrun a wolf. Of course I can walk." I took a step and nearly tripped. I leaned against the wall. "Why aren't you working right? You were supposed to move the other way," I scolded my tail.

"I don't think I can handle this for much longer." Aurtour grabbed me and wrapped my arm around his shoulders. "August, I'm going to need you to keep up."

"I can," August said with a wide smile.

As Aurtour lifted his arm, I could smell his sweat. "You stink. Take a bath." I fanned my nose so I wouldn't smell him as much.

Aurtour looked at me with the cutest hazel-green eyes I'd ever seen. "I'm not even going to go there."

I giggled again. "You're cute. If you wanted to, you could get yourself a girlfriend. Or do you already have one?" I leaned on him, barely able to stand.

"What's she talking about?" August asked.

"Nothing!" As Aurtour dragged me towards the medical wing, his face turned completely red. I couldn't stop laughing.

I can run much faster than this. All these halls look the same. Boring! Why didn't someone think to hang up some interesting decorations? Maybe some directions, or a cute little map. Oh, I can't feel my toes. Is it me or is it hot in here? Wow, I'm really hot. What's all that noise? Hey look, it's Salien.

41

PEACE?

"Hi, Salien." I flailed my arm around as I waved at Salien.

"What happened to you?" Salien came running as Aurtour set me down on the bed.

"She isn't hurt. But there's something wrong with her head. She hasn't stopped talking nonsense." Aurtour sat down on another bed, gasping.

"I wasn't talking. I was just thinking. Maybe you heard my thoughts." I tried to point my finger at him. "Stay out of my head."

Aurtour rolled his eyes.

"This is just like that time when that elf attacked us that one night. What happened?" Zenny grabbed Aurtour's shoulders. "What did she eat?"

"She took a bite out of a heart she pulled from one of August's kidnappers. They were a group of six elves." He looked at Zenny with raised eyebrows.

"Oh no. She's going to fall asleep, and we need to evacuate." Zenny grabbed my shoulders. "You need to stay awake. We need to leave."

"Wait. Give me a moment." Evalana's voice approached. "Something feels off."

"Come here, August. Have a seat over here. Let me take a look at you." Salien knelt down as August stepped towards her.

"You have the strangest friend." Aurtour smiled and nodded at his sister.

Evalana started jumping up and down, squealing. I flinched at the ear-piercing sound. "Yes! I knew it. Thank you." She hugged her brother.

I giggled.

"Oh, right." Evalana released her brother and straightened her shirt. "Lucia, can you use magic?" She stood next to me and leaned in close.

"Nope," I said as I smiled. "You're so beautiful. You know that, right?"

Evalana blushed. "Maybe now's not a good time. Can you hold still and tell me what you feel?" I nodded. She placed a finger on my chest, right above my heart. Countless feathers tickled my skin. I couldn't hold back the laughter as my skin tingled.

"Stop that, that tickles," I said in between laughs.

"She's been overloaded with magic. How did she do that when she can't use magic?" Evalana asked as she turned to Zenny.

"You know what's going on?" Zenny looked at Evalana with hope.

"Yeah, but I don't know how this happened." She turned to me with a sad look. "She has a surplus of unfocused magic. Since she doesn't know how to do magic, we can only wait for it to burn through her system normally."

"But why is she acting like she's drunk? You never acted like this when you were learning magic," Aurtour said as he lifted himself up to a seated position.

"I'm not drunk. I'm hungry," I said as I pouted.

"Because Mom taught me how to channel the magic so it wasn't unfocused, and she was there to control how much magic I handled. That's why you never saw me like this. But unfocused magic has many strange effects on the body and affects each person differently." Evalana never turned away from me. "But I can't help her. Once the magic is in her body, she has to use it."

"I might have an idea," Salien said as she moved Evalana to the side. She sat on the bed next to me. "Lucia, please forgive me. But this is for your own good."

Why does she look worried? If it's good for me, why would I need to forgive her?

"Do you need a hug?" I reached a hand toward her.

My head suddenly shifted to the right. *Where did Salien go? When was I looking at that wall?* I turned my head to the left and saw Salien standing next to the bed I was on. My left cheek felt warm and tingly.

"What?" I raised my hand to touch my cheek. Salien raised her hand and slapped my other cheek. My vision was blurred for a moment before I turned to look at Salien. "Hey, that tickled."

Aurtour pulled her back. "It's not enough. Let me."

I watched him pull his arm back and bring it forward. I didn't feel anything. But I think I fell asleep.

I stepped into the familiar, yet drastically different, cave. The cage nearly filled space, and the cave had shrunk even further. Even though the cage had grown, the space between the bars hadn't. The lattice of metal looked impossible to move.

Inside the cage sat another familiar sight. My inner wolf didn't look at me. I could feel the sorrow emanating from her.

"What's wrong?" I asked as I grabbed the bars.

She lifted her head and looked at me. A single tear rolled off her fur as it dropped from her eye. An image of Aurtour, mangled and bloodied, appeared in front of her. Beside Aurtour's corpse, August's body appeared, his throat sliced wide open. A feeling of confusion washed over me.

"You didn't know what to do when the announcer forced us to try and kill Aurtour, did you?"

She nodded and the images disappeared.

I looked at the ground. "Honestly, neither did I."

The silence in the cave felt slightly disorienting. But nothing more came from my inner wolf while I stared at the ground in silence.

"But it worked out in the end, right?" I tried to laugh, but didn't feel like I meant it. I looked at my wolf, and she rested her head on her front paws as she stared at me. "You want to protect everyone, don't you? All this time, there was nothing evil about you. You were violent and destructive because that's all you knew would get my attention. I wasn't listening. You're not my enemy. You're me, and I'm you. Isn't that right?"

She shook her head.

I tilted my head. "Then who are you?"

She walked up and pushed her nose into my chest.

I stepped back. "What does that mean? Can you tell me?"

She shook her head.

"Oh." I slumped my shoulders and flattened my ears. "Either way, I believe we started off on the wrong foot." I extended an open hand into the cage. "Peace?"

The wolf placed its snout on the back of my hand and, while standing up, pushed my hand against the lock of the cage. I grabbed the lock and pulled down hard. It shattered, and I opened the cage door and tossed the broken lock behind me. I took a step back to make room for the wolf.

She slowly walked out, never taking her eyes off me.

Imagining the cage melting into slag, I watched it slowly disappear from existence. *I will never make that mistake again.*

I turned my attention to the wolf I'd released. She stood towering over me before she put a paw on my chest and forced me to the ground. The wolf bared her sharp fangs inches from my nose as she growled and stared down at me, but she opened her mouth and licked my face. I couldn't help but laugh as her tongue tickled me.

"Alright, enough." I sat up and pushed her back. When I looked at the wolf, it felt like she was smiling as she walked away. "There's nothing wrong or evil about you."

The wolf stopped mid-stride and turned towards me.

I could feel that she was confused. "I promise never to put you in that situation again. There has to be a way we can both be happy. We're in this together now."

I thought I caught a strange expression in her eyes. *Is she amused with me?*

I watched as she left the cave, and something felt different. A bright light grew from where the wolf disappeared.

My face hurt, a friendly reminder of the moment before my little talk with my inner wolf.

"Alright, who hit me?" I sat up, ready to attack whoever had hit me until I blacked out.

"Waterfalls." Zenny jumped on me, hugging me tightly.

I shook my head. "Someone hit me. I'm allowed to be angry. I was just sitting here..." My voice trailed off as the memories of what I'd said and heard flooded through my brain. My face burned. "Ow. What happened? And somebody better start explaining why I needed to be slapped."

"I slapped you because the last time this happened, Zenny said that you fell asleep and all your injuries were completely gone, and Evalana said that you needed to burn the excess magic in your body. I thought maybe your body burned the excess magic last time by using your recovery aptitude." Salien shrugged. "And if that didn't work, slapping a drunk is one of the easiest ways to quickly sober them up. But nothing happened..."

"So I slapped you a little bit harder," Aurtour finished for Salien. "It wasn't my intent to knock you out. I thought with your physical aptitude it might take more to knock some sense into you. But why is she saying you have the recovery aptitude?"

"I have both. Get over it," I said. "But why did you slap me?"

"We needed to injure you to give your aptitude something to do." Salien gave me an innocent shrug. "It worked."

"It hurt," I grumbled. *I shouldn't be too upset.* Lying back in the bed, I sighed. "So how did I get this unfocused magic from eating an elf's heart?"

I watched as everyone exchanged questioning looks. But nobody answered.

"We don't know," Zenny said with a frown.

I stared back at the ceiling. *Great. Another thing to add to the freak show.* "You guys said something about an evacuation?" I looked at Zenny.

"There are demons attacking the tournament. Nobody knows where they came from, but there are so many of them." Evalana shuffled her feet as she held her hands together.

I leaped out of the bed. "Then what are you all still doing here?" I asked, ready to lead the way out. "Let's go!" *I've had one encounter with a demon. I don't want to repeat that. Not right now.*

"Farryn can't walk," Evalana said as she pointed to a bed at the back of the room.

I followed her finger to a familiar dark-skinned elf. "Oh." Bandages covered his leg as he lay on the bed.

"'Oh?' Is that all you have to say?" he shouted as he sat up.

I pointed my finger at him. "You were the one who made that spear of ice. It isn't my fault that you made it so sharp."

"This isn't the time." Salien blocked our view of each other and held her arms up. "Stop acting like immature children. Someone has to help Farryn. We need to leave as soon as we can. Everyone else has already gone."

"Lucia is the strongest person here. She should help him." Evalana waved her arm, directing me to the injured elf.

"No, noncombatants should assist him. I need Lucia up front and fighting." Aurtour's voice carried an air of authority I hadn't heard from him yet. He pointed to Zenny and his sister. "You two should help him."

"No, I want to help." Evalana stomped her foot.

"He's right. You're still recovering from your magic fatigue. You'll just be in the way." I felt a pulling sensation in my heart. "Out of everyone here, we're the only two who can fight."

"Not you too." A tear clung to Evalana's eye.

"You have magic fatigue?" Aurtour turned to face his sister. "Why didn't you tell me?" His voice lost all professionalism as he fussed over his sister.

"Because I knew you would act like this." Evalana lost the tear in her eye and pouted.

"You didn't know and you still put her in the back?" I looked at the prince. "What kind of brother are you?"

"I'll do whatever it takes to keep my sister safe." Aurtour faced me with his eyes fixed on me.

"She has to grow up sometime. You can't always be there for her,"

I said as I rolled my eyes. "Either way, grab Farryn and let's go. Though I'm not too opposed to leaving him here."

"Don't even joke about that." Salien used her mom voice as she narrowed her eyes on me.

I flinched as my instincts feared her.

"This time, try to be a little quicker with your kills. We don't have time to let you get carried away." Aurtour walked up next to me and drew the sword he'd claimed from August's captors.

"What are we up against?" I asked.

"Demons, lots of them," Salien said as she gave me a grim look.

"If there are lots of them, that means they must be fallen demons, the weakest type of demon," Zenny said as she jumped up and down with an eager look on her face.

I gestured for her to continue.

She stared off into space as she spoke. "Fallen demons are the weakest of all demons. They take down their opponents through sheer numbers. They aren't exceptionally strong or hard to kill. However, you shouldn't underestimate them. They aren't mindless swarms of animals. They are incapable of feeling fear or pain. So if you see one, look for more, or your death will only add to their ranks." Zenny shook her head slightly as she returned to her usual smiling self.

"Great," I said as I threw my arms up in the air.

Aurtour opened the door and gave me a slight bow. "Ladies first."

And they say chivalry is dead. Oh, wait, wrong world. This world has knights. Of course chivalry is alive and strong. Although I appreciate the sentiment, why am I the one who's leading this mobile food chain into a potential horde of demons?

"And why am I going first?"

Aurtour averted his gaze. "Because your fighting style is a little wild. To put it politely. I think it's best if I handle any that gets past you. Also, I can help you if you get surrounded."

Oh, now you've done it. "Wild?" I asked as I raised an eyebrow. "I'll show you wild."

I stormed out of the room, letting the shades of red fill my vision.

He just had to call me wild. I'm not wild. Short-tempered, excessively violent, moody, and easily distracted, maybe. But I'm not wild.

42

THE FALLEN

Everyone followed me out of the room as I led the way to the exit. The exit wasn't far away, and we made it there without seeing any demons. But as I opened the door to the outside, eight creatures stood in a pool of blood, eating three bodies.

So those are fallen demons.

Their skin was so pale it looked like there wasn't any blood in their veins. Long lanky limbs ending in pointy, talon-like extremities moved erratically as they shoveled flesh from the dead into their mouths—mouths that were far too large to be natural since they opened large enough to fit August's head inside. If it weren't for the adrenaline in my system, I would have panicked at the sight of a featureless face with no nose, eyes, ears, or hair.

Blood dripped from their mouths as strips of organs and flesh dangled from countless needle-sharp teeth. The moment I stepped outside, they looked up from their meal and stared right at me.

I guess they know I'm here. How?

They all opened their mouths, and the sound of bones rattling filled the air. The noise grated on my ears as they stood up. *You're ugly and sound awful.*

The sounds of everyone stopping behind me as the rattling noise ended reminded me I had a job. *I will keep them all safe.* I growled as I returned to my rage-fueled state. There was a tickle in the back of my mind. I wasn't alone. My inner wolf was there to aid us.

I sprinted towards the demons, ready to intercept them. They charged me, running on all fours in a gangling stride. They moved slowly, like they were moving through molasses.

I picked out the closest one and jumped to collide with it. I tackled it with enough force to drive it backwards and land on top of it. It reached for my face with its sharp fingers, but I grabbed its head and twisted it violently. A sharp snap and its limbs fell like a puppet that had lost its strings.

I looked up. Two more of the demons bounded off the ground, attempting to pounce on me. I rolled to the side and watched them land on the one I had just killed. One started tearing up the body beneath it, while the other turned to look at me. We lifted our hands at the same time. My claws slashed into its face first as I ducked its attack. I scraped the bone of its skull, and blood poured out of the wound I made. It didn't bleed red blood; it was clear and colorless. I didn't have time to be surprised at the sight. It lunged forward, opening its mouth inhumanly wide.

I drove the claws on my left hand up and slashed its throat vertically, embedding my claws inside its mouth as I punctured through its bottom jaw. Another fallen was running towards me, and I heard it leap upward to tackle me. I took the creature that was stuck to my claws and used it as a punching glove, hitting the jumping demon in the face with the crown of its head. The collision freed my hand as the two tumbled to the ground together, their skulls caved in.

As soon as I freed my hand, something collided with my left side, just above my hip. I hit the ground hard. My hip and shoulder sent out a dull pain, but I easily blocked it out. A fallen sat on top of me and was about to stab me in the gut with its talon fingers, but I grabbed its left arm with my left hand and rolled us over, pinning its arms together with one hand. Then I slashed at its heart and cut deeply into its lungs.

My right shoulder exploded in pain as the head of a fallen leaned into my vision. I released the demon below me and grabbed the head of the one that was biting my shoulder. I pulled its head forward, attempting to open its mouth farther. The teeth on its bottom jaw dug deeper as I pulled. Once its top row of teeth cleared my gambeson, I moved its head up. Its teeth gouged the back of my shoulder through my gambeson until its jaw snapped shut after I lifted it past my shoulder, my blood dripping from its mouth.

The demon below me stabbed my left bicep. Screaming, I used the head in my hands as a weapon against the demon that now had three of its four fingers in my flesh. The crunching sound of skulls cracking and one of them splitting was enough to convince me they were dead. The claws in my arm slipped out.

I didn't get a moment to breathe. I could hear more running from behind me. As I stood, I tried to give myself a chance to recuperate by taking a few steps away from the demons. I could see Aurtour running towards me, but he was still a long way off. *Did I really run that far ahead of them? Or is he that slow?* I turned back around to face the immediate threat.

Three remaining demons spread out evenly in a semicircle about an arc away from me.

A fire burned in my shoulder as my blood poured out, dripping from my arm as it soaked my fur. *It isn't looking good for me.*

The sound of all three demons jumping demanded my attention. One demon leaped at my legs. The second one went for my hips, and the last aimed for my head.

I moved to intercept the one going for my head.

The demon tried to tackle me, but I caught its arm and dug my claws into its ribs, pulling on it and twisting to change the direction it was going. I spun around like a top for one and a half revolutions before I released the demon, throwing it as far as I could.

I didn't have time to admire my throw because the two other demons hit the ground and pounced at me again. This time they didn't aim for different heights, but for my left and right. I slid under them and grabbed hold of one demon's ankles, slamming it into the ground. I heard a few cracks come from the impact, but the creature still moved. Before it could scramble to its feet, I ran to its head and stomped on it with everything I had. My foot broke through the monster's skull, and it stopped moving.

The demon that I didn't impale raised its claws and slashed at my face, but I caught its wrists and nearly fell to my back as I lost my footing. I turned my attacker around and felt an extra weight on my right foot as it dragged the corpse of the demon.

My attacker leaned forward, snapping its vicious jaws inches from my face. I released its arm and pulled its head down to expose its neck, but the creature stabbed my side before I dug my teeth into it. I still bit down hard, crushing the vertebrae and severing the spinal cord. The demon went limp instantly.

I dropped the corpse in my hands and spat out the meat in my mouth. The sulfurous taste caused me to gag slightly as I tried not to vomit. I lifted my foot out of the skull and tried to shake the brains off my toe claws.

Gross, that is so gross.

I heard footsteps and looked to see Aurtour charging past me. He ran straight into the last fallen, sword-first. The demon clawed at his gambeson but didn't get a good hold. After a few moments of struggling, the creature slumped to the ground.

"Took you long enough." I took a deep breath between each word and returned my vision to normal.

"You don't stop until you've won the battle." Aurtour flicked his sword towards the ground, sending most of the blood to the dirt. He looked at me with an expression I couldn't read. "That was both the most terrifying and amazing display I have ever seen."

"Glad you liked it." I collapsed to my knees. "I can't do it again." My vision slowly shifted out of focus. *I think I'm losing too much blood.*

"Easy there." Aurtour sheathed his sword and knelt down beside me. "I've got you. You did well. You should be proud."

I turned to look at everyone else that was following us and smiled. Evalana and Zenny carried Farryn together, while August held Salien's hand.

I did good. I kept them all safe. Now we can all get away safely.

Aurtour scooped me up and carried me towards them. My vision went in and out of focus with each step.

"I'm so tired." My voice barely escaped my lips.

"It isn't time to rest yet. I need you to stay awake. The doctor will fix you right up," Aurtour whispered in my ear.

"She will?" *Is it me or is he really a nice guy? Is he single? I doubt it. Whoever he wants to marry will be one lucky girl.*

Salien sprinted towards me, leaving the kids behind. "Set her down. How much of this blood is hers?"

Aurtour gently set me on the ground. "She has several deep wounds from what I can see," he said as he carefully removed my gambeson.

"Easy," Salien said. "You don't want to make things worse."

My arms screamed in pain, my side ached, and my shoulder burned. "Am I going to die? I don't want to die again." My thoughts didn't stay in my head, but nobody reacted to me as they worked.

Salien pulled out rolls of linen and a sewing kit from the backpack that she wore. She placed the back of her hand on my forehead. "She's warm but not feverish. I don't even know if she can recover from this. I can feel her getting colder." Salien's trembling voice scared me. "I'll do what I can, but we don't have anyone who can use healing magic. And even then, I don't know if it would be enough."

Aurtour folded my gambeson and made it into a pillow for me as he propped me up. "What about that thing you said about her using excess magic in her body to increase her recovery?"

"Do you see any elves for her to eat?" Salien started with my side, stitching it up and wrapping the linen bandage around my stomach. "Besides, she doesn't look like she can eat. The fact that she's still awake is a miracle. She must be in unbearable pain."

I wasn't in pain; I'd lost all feeling a short time ago.

"I'm not letting her eat any part of me." I heard Farryn's voice in the distance.

"Sis, can you give her any of that unfocused magic stuff you were talking about?" Aurtour's voice seemed quieter.

Where's everyone going? Don't leave me.

"I can't. It's still too difficult for me to do any magic. Mom said I have to wait until at least tomorrow before I even try." It was even harder to hear Evalana's muffled voice. "But you can."

My eyelids became heavier, and I really wanted to go to sleep. *Aurtour said I need to stay awake. But a quick nap won't hurt, right?*

"Why would I do that? She stabbed me in the leg."

Everyone's voices became so distant I couldn't distinguish who was who.

"She just risked her life to save yours. The least you can do is help her, since my sister can't. She also went easy on you in your match. This isn't the time to be petty. She's worth more than you ever will be."

Who's saying such nice things about me? I guess I can ask after my nap.

43

DO YOU NEED A HAND?

W*hy does my shoulder hurt so much?* I lay still, not opening my eyes as I felt more and more pain in other parts of my body. *What happened to me?* I tried to open my eyes, but blinding white light forced me to slam them shut. Everything felt weak. I groaned as I tried to roll over.

I felt a hand on my chest. "No, don't move. It's okay. You're safe now," a soothing feminine voice whispered to me.

Wait, the demons! My body shot up as adrenaline spiked through my system.

Several tearing sensations decimated all desire to move. As my eyes came into focus again, I saw Salien with her arms placed on my chest, trying to push me back down. Zenny jumped away from me, and I started falling. I hit the ground, and if something wasn't hurting before, it was now.

"Lucia, you're awake." A less-quiet Evalana came running towards me.

I tried to figure out what happened after I fell asleep. I noticed I was lying on the ground next to a litter. It looked like it was made of sticks and a tied-up bedsheet.

I looked to see who'd dropped me—a knight in white armor with a scar that ran down the left side of his face. He was a knight that I hadn't seen in years, but he greeted me with a smile.

"Hello, little miss. Long time, no see." His deep, soothing voice confirmed his identity.

"Hi, Drue." My throat protested by holding most of my volume back. *It's nice to see he doesn't have any new scars from when he rescued me from the orcs years ago.*

"Are you okay?" Salien knelt down next to me and inspected my shoulder and side. "Does anything hurt?"

"Everything," I said as I gave up moving. I stared at the sky, trying to figure out how long I'd been asleep. *The sun has only moved a little. I guess they've only just started taking me somewhere.*

"Sorry about dropping you like that. Your movement surprised me," Drue said as he placed a hand on the back of his bald head. "You ready, Your Highness?" Drue bent back down to pick up the litter.

"Yes." Aurtour's voice sounded behind me. "Let's get moving before more demons show up."

More demons? Did I not get them all?

After Salien rolled me back onto the litter, she and Drue lifted me off the ground and started walking.

"I'm so glad you're okay. You had me worried." Zenny looked like she was on the verge of tears. "Why were you so reckless?"

I looked at Zenny's moist eyes. "I wanted to protect you." A single tear fell down her cheek. "I kept you safe. Because you're my friend."

"Who's going to keep you safe, you big dummy?" Zenny's tears flowed down her cheeks.

"I don't need anyone to save me." I smiled. "I can take care of myself." My voice slowly returned, although it was still scratchy.

"Not if you keep hurting yourself like this." Zenny waved at my injuries.

"I heal quickly. It'll be fine. You'll see." I gave her a thumbs-up.

"You almost didn't survive this time." Salien's tone grew dark. "If Farryn hadn't helped you, it's likely you wouldn't have survived long enough to heal. But even I'm surprised at how fast you're healing. I can almost watch your wounds close."

"What did he do?" I looked at Farryn. He was being helped by another human knight who I'd never seen before. He wore one of those cloth armors with plates underneath it. *I need to learn what that armor is called.*

"He sealed your shoulder in ice to prevent further blood loss, then infused you with some unfocused magic to aid your recovery." Salien glared at me. "You should say 'thank you' to him. This is why you don't leave anyone behind. Everyone has something they can contribute."

I blushed as I turned away from Salien. I couldn't handle her stare any longer. *Okay, I guess he wasn't completely useless after all. I still don't like him.* "Where are we going?" *Not that I have any say in the matter.*

"We're evacuating everyone to the headquarters," Drue said, slightly turning his head to talk to me. "Unfortunately, we have to go all the way around the tournament grounds to reach it so we avoid the fighting. Everyone else is trying to kill all the demons. I don't know how so many showed up so quickly. And without warning too."

"Don't worry, we're almost there," Zenny said, still sniffling. "You can get rested after we get there."

"I'm feeling a lot better now." When I lifted my arms, I felt a slight stiffness where I saw bandages wrapped around my bicep. "I think I might be able to walk after some food and drink."

"I think I've got something for you." The knight who was helping Farryn handed a small metal canister to Evalana.

Evalana removed the leather stopper before handing it to me. "Sorry, I don't have food for you."

I sniffed the metal canister and could smell water inside. "This will help a lot. Thanks." I gave them a nod before downing the entire contents. The water made my throat feel better and helped me cool down a little. "I want to try to walk. I promise I won't slow us down."

I started rolling off the litter.

"No, you stay right there, young lady." Salien's tone was harsh as she pushed me back on. Everyone stopped walking when I started moving. "You've done enough. Let others help you. You need to rest."

"But I'm feeling better," I said as I flattened my ears and gave her my saddest face. "If I sit still like this for too long, my tail will go numb."

Salien sighed. "It isn't much further. Can you wait until we get to the knights' headquarters?"

I shifted so that my tail was a little more comfortable. "Fine. But where's Nora?"

Salien flinched slightly. She looked like she was about to say something, but took a deep breath first. "We don't know."

"There were reports of a large-scale magic battle going on at the edge of the festival grounds," Drue said. "I would put a season's salary on her being involved with that."

My heart skipped a beat. *Is she in danger? I have to help her.*

I grabbed the edges of the litter, eager to jump out, but something sounded off. A slow, rhythmic thumping noise caught my attention.

"Do you hear that?" I flicked my ears around to locate the source.

"Hear what?" Zenny looked around frantically.

The thumping sounds grew louder and came more frequently. "That."

I continued narrowing down where the source of the sound was. "There, it's coming from there." I pointed to where I thought it was coming from. I followed the direction my finger pointed and saw a flat wooden wall.

Now I look like I'm crazy. Of course they can't hear it. My hearing is way better than theirs. But Zenny and Salien should believe me.

"There's something happening on the other side of that wall," I said hurriedly, as everyone turned to look at me.

The moment I finished my sentence, the wall exploded. Shards of wood flew out in all directions as everyone shielded their faces. The litter I was on tipped over, and I fell out. Before the shrapnel from the wall reached our little group, a heavy shock wave struck everyone and knocked us down. I hadn't hit the ground yet as the shock wave came towards me, and I watched as the ground moved underneath me.

This is going to hurt. The dirt rose to meet me, and the moment I touched it, I tumbled uncontrollably.

I leaned into the roll, trying to gain control of my movements, and eventually stopped. Once my vision quit spinning, I looked to see what had happened. Everyone was on the ground, and there were two more people that weren't with us before. I didn't have time to figure out who they were because there was a massive, ugly creature standing in the brand-new hole in the wall.

A massive purple cyclops stood triumphant, without a care in the world that it was completely naked. A single black horn grew from its cone-shaped head above its eye, which was a large black spot in a sea of white. It was hard to tell where it was looking as it opened its mouth, where three rows of perfectly aligned triangular teeth ran in circles. Watching its mouth, I didn't see a neck. Either it didn't have a one or it was just so fat that it blended together seamlessly. As I looked further down at the creature, I figured he was just that fat.

A deep laugh that sounded like it came from a cave, complete with its own echo, assaulted my ears.

"What have I found here?" His voice was no less deep, but it sounded like he was trying not to drown himself in his own saliva. "I was thinking I had only found snacks. But it looks like I found enough to almost make a proper meal." As he laughed, all of his disgusting girth rippled.

I wish someone could remove that sight from my memory forever.

I tried to stand up. My legs were shaky, and I hadn't completely recovered my balance. Everyone started getting up except for the two people who'd arrived with the repulsive creature. They weren't moving. A pool of blood grew under each one.

Farryn and the knight who had been helping him were the closest to the cyclops, and they were still trying to get back to their feet.

The cyclops walked up to them and lifted a round, flat foot over Farryn, slamming it down on his waist. Everyone stopped to witness the elf scream in agony. The knight next to him reached for his sword, but the purple creature slapped him with a hand larger than the knight's head. The knight's head was on his shoulders one moment, and then it was flying past me, completely detached from its body, the next.

My instincts screamed at me to run. I wanted to, but as soon as I saw Evalana run at the creature, I couldn't.

"Get off him, you monster!" Evalana screamed as she ran into the creature's massive body.

Her entire height didn't even reach the cyclops's elbows. She bounced off the monster, barely causing a ripple in all of its fat, and landed on her butt. She stood right back up and pulled her hands back.

"I said, get off him!"

No, she can't use magic. What is she thinking?

The ground next to her shifted until it became a spear point, aimed at the creature's rotund belly. The spear was large but didn't launch towards the purple cyclops. Instead, it stayed frozen in place, protruding out of the ground threateningly.

Evalana caught herself as she collapsed.

"How cute." The creature looked down at her with a wide grin. "I always enjoy eating mages. They tingle on the way down."

Thick fingers grabbed Evalana and lifted her up. She screamed as she held out her hands to keep the monster's mouth away from her.

I pulled myself towards her. *No! Not her! Not Evalana!*

I summoned every bit of rage I could muster. My vision easily shifted to the red I desired, giving me the focus I needed to move faster. The pain in my back and arms didn't slow me down anymore. I stood up and sprinted forward, one goal in mind: to kill this creature who had dared to touch my friend.

"I will kill you!" I screamed.

Evalana squirmed in the cyclops's grip, trying her best to stay out of the dangerous mouth. From the look in the creature's eye, it was letting her think her struggling did any good. Her right hand slipped from the monster's lip and entered his mouth. Before she could retract her arm, the creature snapped his jaws shut. Evalana screamed even louder as the cyclops cleanly cut her arm through the middle of her bicep. She flailed around more wildly than before, and the stump where her arm used to be sprayed blood everywhere.

"No!" both Aurtour and I screamed simultaneously.

I passed Aurtour, who was running towards the cyclops too. Evalana's screams didn't drown out the sounds the monster made as it chewed on her arm.

It opened its mouth to take another bite, but I leaped towards it with every bit of strength I possessed, jumping high enough to reach its head. It paused its attempt to take another bite from my friend to look at me as I released a scream, and it looked dumbfounded as I plunged my claws into its eye.

The cyclops bellowed as it dropped Evalana and reached for me. I pulled my hand out of its eye so I could jump down and cover my ears, my vision blurring as I did.

The cyclops pawed at its now useless eye. I turned to see Evalana in Aurtour's arms as he carried her away, and Drue drew his sword to charge at the disoriented creature. Farryn stopped screaming and didn't move once the giant cyclops no longer had a foot on him.

I guess he didn't make it.

"Go! I'll hold it back while you escape," Drue shouted at me.

I watched Salien grab Zenny and August and run in the direction we were going before the cyclops showed up, and I ran to catch up with Aurtour. Evalana's skin was pale, and she'd stopped screaming. She wasn't moving much at all.

I looked at her arm and saw that the blood now trickled out instead of spraying.

"Set her down," I shouted as I grabbed Aurtour's arm.

"No, not with that thing so close." Aurtour shrugged my hand off.

"If you keep running with her like that, she'll die!" I grabbed his gambeson and pulled him to a stop.

Aurtour's face contorted into horror as he stopped and looked at me. I turned to see that Drue was cutting at the cyclops's legs while avoiding its wild movements.

"What do we do?" Aurtour sounded distant as he gently laid Evalana on the ground.

"We need to deal with her arm," I said as I examined it. It was cleanly cut, with no bone shards or torn skin. *That thing has sharper teeth than me!* "We need to stop her from losing more blood." *There's so much blood. Too much blood.*

I salivated.

Eat her! a thought that wasn't my own, in a voice I'd never heard before, commanded me.

44

GLUTTONY

"Who said that?" Everything around me slowed down. "Who's there?"

Eat her. The same voice repeated itself inside my head, flat and grating but impossible to ignore. The words didn't sound like they originated from anywhere around me. **You're weak. Eat her.**

I heard a faint growl behind me. But it was too far away from me to be a concern.

"I won't eat my friend. I shouldn't eat people." I slammed my eyes shut, trying to block out the voice.

Do you want power?

A second growl danced behind me.

"I am strong." I shook my head. "Get out of my mind. I need to save Evalana."

If you want to save her, you need power. A power I can give you.

"How can I have the power to save her if I eat her? You're contradicting yourself." I wanted to stare at whoever was talking, but everything around me was frozen in time.

It doesn't have to be her. You can eat the boy.

I growled. "Her brother isn't any better."

This time there was a howl. It wasn't loud, but it felt like something was trying to reassure me.

I touched Aurtour and tried to shove him to see if it had any effect. I couldn't move him. I could feel him, but nothing I did affected anything. It was like everything was in some kind of stasis. *Or am I the one in stasis, staring off into space while Evalana dies of blood loss?*

You were about to eat the boy earlier. You didn't eat him because there were so many people watching. But what about now? There's nobody around to see you do it. The girl won't live long, and the man will be easily dealt with once you have the power I give you.

"You're wrong!" I slammed my eyes shut again. Anything to help me ignore the voice.

The howling became harder to ignore. For some reason, I didn't want to ignore it.

I dug my claws into the dirt. "I didn't kill him because I'm not a monster. And because I'm not a monster, I won't go around eating people just because you told me to."

The girl will die soon. You can't save her. Eat her and grow stronger. You are weak and hungry. You can't save anyone in the state you're in. Take her life so you can save others.

"I will save her." I turned to look at Evalana's motionless body. My stomach gurgled, and then I felt a pang of hunger like I'd never felt before.

Feed. Feed and join me. I will show you great powers that will make those you have seen look insignificant by comparison. Feed and grow strong. Sate your hunger. It's easy. You've done it before.

I have done it before. Those elves tasted sweet. Molly's blood was tangy. I wonder if all human meat tastes just as tangy. As I kneeled next to Evalana, I licked my lips. There was another growl, it was much closer this time.

I looked at her pale face and shook my head. Footsteps behind me forced me to turn around. I saw a massive wolf with silver fur.

Something radiated from the wolf, a feeling. *Remember? Remember what?*

The memory of what I almost did to Aurtour replayed in my head. "No! I won't do it. I am not a monster!"

Give in to your sin. Everyone does eventually. Why not get something in return for doing so? Succumb to your gluttony.

"No, get out of my head!" I shouted. A snarl from the wolf joined my shout.

You brought me here. I'm here because of you.

"What are you talking about?" I looked at my wolf. *That's right. I'm not alone. There's nothing I need from you. I have all the strength I need already within me.* "It doesn't matter how you got here. You don't get to tell me what to do." My voice seethed with my rage. The large wolf let out a bark behind me.

You can't ignore me forever. I am gluttony itself. You can't keep lying to me or to yourself. You will submit to your sins, and I will be there waiting for you.

It's almost like it doesn't know the wolf's there. Why doesn't he see her?

I stood up and stared at the cyclops. *Haven't I seen a powerful being appear naked out of nowhere before? That's right, that day in the basement five years ago.* "You're a demon, aren't you? Specifically, a sin of gluttony." I bared my fangs as I growled. "Well, I don't care who you are. You won't get me to eat my friends. How about I eat you instead?"

My inner wolf stepped next to me. Her growl was so deep my body vibrated. *She's livid. And so am I.*

You can't hide. I will follow you until you die. And you will die today as I devour your flesh, drink your blood, and savor your bones.

I turned to my inner wolf. "What do you say we shut this walking meat sack up and make him pay for what he did to Evalana?"

My inner wolf just growled and bared her fangs as she leaned closer to the ground, ready to pounce. *I'll take that as a yes.*

Consuming a gluttonous mortal like you will be a treat I

haven't had in a hundred years. Your soul will belong to me before the day is out.

"We'll see who eats who!" We charged at the cyclops.

Everything went black for a moment before I was suddenly sitting next to Evalana. It was like nothing I just saw happened.

"Lucia!" Aurtour's shout sounded distant.

Did none of that just happen? Or was that something the demon did to put me in a dream-like state?

I turned to Aurtour and saw that he was wearing a belt to carry the scabbard for his sword. *Right, priorities.* I grabbed his belt and pulled him towards me before I cut the leather with my claws.

"What are you doing?" He struggled against me as I pulled his belt off and threw his sword at him.

"Saving her life." I noticed that my vision was still red.

"You dare defy me!" the cyclops bellowed behind me. "I have seen your sin. You won't escape from me."

I have to hurry.

I looped the belt around the stump of Evalana's arm and pulled it as tight as I could. The leather bit into her soft skin, ceasing all blood flow. *I'm sorry.* Guilt threatened to slow my movements and dissolve my red vision. I turned to Aurtour. "Go. Get her out of here. I'll deal with this demon." I turned to face the cyclops.

"But what about you?" Aurtour placed a hand on my wounded bicep. I felt a slight stab of pain but ignored it.

"I've bought her time. You need to get her some real help now." I shrugged out of his grip. "Besides, this thing wants me to eat someone, so I'm going to eat him. Let's see how he likes it." My vision turned to an even darker shade of red as I turned and faced the demon. "You hurt my friend and then told me to eat her. You're going to wish I killed you quickly."

The cyclops ceased his flailing and ignored Drue as it lumbered towards me. Drue had inflicted many deep cuts, but the demon continued, not flinching as a fresh wound opened up courtesy of Drue's sword.

Adrenaline fueled my rage as I dropped to all fours and sprinted to keep him as far away from Evalana as possible. I drifted towards the building, and the cyclops followed.

Drue ran to keep up with the cyclops but looked back to see me running towards it. "What are you doing? I told you to run!"

"It wants me. So it can try to catch me," I growled as I ran along the wall.

I jumped onto the wall, ready to launch off of it as soon as I saw an attack.

The cyclops swung his meaty fist at me, and I pushed off as hard as I could and led with my claws. The punch sailed above me and crashed through the wall, but my claws stabbed into his fleshy gut.

Although my claws pierced the skin easily, it felt like I was hitting solid brick. My arms folded as the rest of my body kept moving, and my face hit his stomach while my legs curled up to my chest. The cyclops's skin felt clammy as I removed my face from his belly and unfolded myself to stand on the ground.

The demon grunted and extended his other hand to grab me. Removing my claws, I ducked under his limb and moved to get behind him as Drue drove his sword into the back of the cyclops's knee.

Wood splintered behind me, and, as I turned to face the monster, I saw him dragging his fist through the wall. He removed his hand, causing a shower of debris, and threw a punch right at me. He tried to turn, but with the wound to his knee, the leg buckled, and he lost his balance. I dove out of the way, barely avoiding the demon as he hit the ground.

The sin of gluttony really wants me. But if he's anything like the sin of wrath, then he'll have some kind of trick up his sleeve. I just need to be ready for when he uses it. Whatever it is. But how can he see me?

"You can run and hide, but I will find you no matter where you go," the demon roared. "I've marked you and will follow you until I have you."

I ran towards his head as he scrambled to reach for me. Drue charged in and drove his sword into the demon's rib cage. The sword entered down to the hilt as Drue put his entire weight behind it.

The demon pulled his arms back and hit Drue with his tricep, knocking him back a short distance. Drue landed on his back with a grunt and slowly moved to get to his feet again. The cyclops had also snapped the blade at the hilt, and I saw the hilt lying on the ground next to Drue. The monster fell to his hands and knees, and I pounced in its moment of weakness.

I clawed at the spine, looking for a way to immobilize the demon, but the sin of gluttony straightened up and launched me off of him. I easily landed in a four-point stance, ready to pounce on him again. The demon shouted and flexed his muscles as he started radiating heat.

Every open wound was quickly closed and vanished in front of my eyes. I couldn't help but stare in disbelief. The sword Drue had embedded in the demon was slowly pushed out through the same wound it went in. With a simple thud of the blade hitting the ground, the display was over. The wave of heat and the cyclops standing up told us how much trouble we were in. Every wound had sealed shut and restored itself, including his eye that I'd destroyed.

My vision returned to normal as I looked for any sign of a lasting injury. I didn't find any.

"How do we kill him?" I turned to look at Drue, hoping he had some answers, but his pale face, bulging eyes, and open mouth told me I was on my own for this one.

I turned to look back at the demon and found him grinning. *What do I do now?*

"You should have joined me when I gave you the chance. You have no hope of outlasting me."

His voice caught my attention. *Wasn't his voice deeper before?* I turned to look at the wall where he had recently punched a hole. Instead of being at shoulder height, the hole now sat level with the cyclops's eye.

He's shorter.

"Did you just heal yourself and, in exchange, get smaller?" I blurted out. *No, I'm not supposed to let him know that I know.*

"Knowing won't save you. Now you see the hopelessness of the situation you're in." His grin grew as he leaned forward. "You had your chance. Now you will fuel my power."

I grinned. *Thanks for confirming that for me.*

"Why are you smiling?"

"Because I know something you don't," I said before I sprinted away from the building.

The demon roared as he charged to intercept me. *That's right, follow the wolf into the forest. I want to play a game. Besides, Drue isn't in any state to help me. I don't want him to die for or because of me. I don't know whose field we're running through right now, but I'm sorry.* Sprinting towards the tree line in the distance, I led the cyclops on a chase to the woods.

"Why are you running? Are you that scared to die?" The demon's breathing showed that he couldn't run as fast or as long as I could.

Interesting. That's going to make this much easier for me.

"What's the matter? Don't you like fast food?" I stopped and raised my arms as I taunted the cyclops. "You look like you could use the exercise."

The demon squinted his eye as he ran even faster. The hunger I felt earlier returned, only this time it was much worse. I doubled over from the pain.

Must eat something.

The thunderous stomping of the cyclops must have alerted all the wildlife, because I heard something scurrying behind me. I turned to see what it was and saw a rabbit running through the crop. Without hesitating, I sprinted after it and scooped it up. I quickly and poorly skinned a section of the creature as it kicked in protest, then took a bite out of the rib cage, bone and all. As the flavors washed over my tongue, I felt the hunger become almost manageable.

"I told you. You will succumb to your gluttony eventually." The demon's voice was much closer than I remembered. Once I'd swallowed my bite, I returned to my senses, and I turned to see that he'd almost caught up with me. "It's been a long time since I've eaten a wolf. This will be something to remember. I always eat my marks."

I placed the rabbit in my mouth before I dropped to all fours and sprinted as fast as I could. Based on the sound of his footsteps, I knew I was outrunning him. I made sure I ran to the edge of the forest before I turned to make sure he was still following me. The demon wheezed as he continued towards me.

I figured he was out of shape, but wow. But I guess I can't be too hard on him. I'm feeling a little tired too.

"I hope you don't mind, but I'm going to finish this while I wait for you." I held the rabbit up for a moment before I went to work, quickly removing the largest sections of meat.

He would catch me if I stayed still too long, so I only ate the largest pieces of meat and ignored the organs.

The demon roared even louder as he clenched his jaw and ran even harder.

"Are you jealous? I thought you were gluttony, not envy."

The air around the cyclops distorted slightly as he sped up again. This time, he sped up more noticeably as I watched him shrink a bit. *I must have touched a nerve with that one.* After standing still for a little while and eating the rabbit, I felt much better.

Okay, I'll admit it. My recovery speed is quite incredible. Although, is it still supercharged from the magic Farryn gave me? Either way, I'll put it to the test with this plan. I really hope it works.

45

NO BEASTKIN LEFT BEHIND

T he cyclops continued his unrelenting charge as I waited for him. *It's time to start.* Once the demon was within one arc of me, I ran into the forest.

"Hiding won't work. I know where you are at all times." His voice was less harsh on my ears as he tried to sound as triumphant as possible.

There's something missing here. Where's the boar's territory? Oops, I forgot. A bunch of knights already went out and probably killed it. I guess I'll have to make this up as I go.

I scooped up a rock off the ground. "Who said I was hiding?" I asked as I threw the rock at his giant eye.

The cyclops flinched at the sight of the projectile heading for him. He tried to raise a hand to protect his face, but my rock hit him directly in his large pupil. It seemed his eye was quite the sore spot to strike. He shouted and flailed around, just like the last time I took out his eye, the demon charged blindly and ran into a tree and bounced off. *That tree was almost as large as the cyclops, but he broke through the wall with ease earlier. Is he weaker? I think I might have a chance. I need to injure him continuously without making a mistake. It's hard to tell how strong he really is.*

As he turned to rest on his hands and knees, I jumped on his back. I frantically clawed at his spine, hoping to force him to use his regeneration again. The demon reached around to grab me, but I avoided his awkward attempts.

The cyclops flailed around, trying to dislodge me from his back. He succeeded, and his elbow clipped me in his thrashing. I tumbled away from him until I hit a tree. My shoulder where he'd hit me didn't feel broken or dislocated, but it definitely hurt.

The demon stomped towards me, yelling something incomprehensible. The volume alone forced me to cover my ears.

I growled as I shifted my vision back to its red hue in order to ignore his bellowing and concentrate. The cyclops jumped towards me, ready to flatten me as he sailed through the air, arms and legs spread wide. I rolled my eyes as I stood up and dodged the heavily telegraphed attack. But as he landed, I watched the dirt ripple, and the shock wave launched me backwards. I flailed my arms and legs pointlessly in my panic.

I heard the snapping of tree branches and soon saw the branches that I'd broken. Desperately, I reached for any branch that would hold me, but every one I touched broke. Some of the larger branches slowed my descent, but I was still helplessly falling to the ground. I changed tactics once I'd run out of branches. Instead of landing on my back like last time, I twisted my body and got my legs below me, readying myself to roll as soon as I landed.

I braced for impact, and once I hit the ground, I let my legs buckle as I leaned forward. *It worked.* After rolling to a stop, I looked down at myself, noticing a few new scrapes and cuts, but I was largely unharmed.

Wolves don't belong in trees. I belong on the ground. This wasn't my fault, Zenny.

I looked for the demon and saw that he was standing up again with steam rolling off his body. When I saw that his eye was open and not bleeding, I felt a touch of hope. *That's right, keep healing yourself. You'll run out eventually. And when you do, you're mine!*

I growled as I leaned forward to charge. But when I took my first step, everything suddenly became heavy as an unimaginable weight pushed down on me. I looked behind me to find the source, but I saw nothing.

Maybe it's an invisible force pulling me to the ground instead. Is he manipulating gravity?

"Now you've done it. You're almost not worth the trouble." The cyclops sounded nearly normal. "There's no escape for you now."

Every bone in my body protested the weight. I pushed against the ground with every muscle I had. The force pushing down on me vanished when I stood on all fours, and I grinned. "This is getting old. Proving you wrong, time and time again."

The demon ran at me. My weight seemed to correct itself, and I was free to move again.

He's as tall as Nora now, maybe a little shorter. I growled as I charged him.

The cyclops led with a fist that I ducked under. As I ran past him, I slashed at his gut, opening up four deep wounds. The demon swung his fist back around towards me, but I was already well out of his reach. I skidded to a stop and prepared to continue my hit-and-run tactic.

I waited for the demon to launch an attack, but he didn't. He stood there, looking at me and waiting. It was difficult for me to control myself and not just run at him, no matter how much a part of me really wanted to. So I walked around him, keeping a set distance, trying to get him to do something.

The cyclops stood stationary the whole time. I stared at his back, unable to restrain myself any longer. *I won't get a better window.* As I dashed forward, the demon didn't move. Instead, an incredible force pulled me to the ground. I tripped and stumbled forward. Unable to catch myself, I landed face-first.

Once I hit the dirt, the demon moved and looked down at me. He lifted his foot and tried to stomp on my head.

I threw every muscle to my right to roll out of the way. His foot hit the ground behind me, and I felt the earth quake from the impact. The force pulling me to the ground disappeared. I turned back around and stabbed my claws into his leg as I bit into his shin. The demon brought his other foot forward and kicked me in the gut, knocking the wind out of me and sending me rolling. I didn't stop until I collided with a tree, cracking my ribs.

A burning pain shot through my side as I struggled to breathe. Every inhale took monumental effort and summoned more pain. It was almost enough to convince me I should just give up and die. *No, I will not die, not like this.* I forced myself to breathe as deeply as I could, focusing on pushing out my stomach. As I took another deep breath, I clenched my jaw and held back a scream. I could hear heavy footsteps heading my way.

The cyclops was strutting towards me as I turned to look.

"I hope you enjoyed your little struggle, but this is where it ends," the demon said as he stood over me. He held up his arms and waved them around. "It's a shame you have to die out here alone. It would have been a treat to see the faces of those who would have seen me devouring your broken and beaten body. I imagine their despair and sadness would taste just as sweet as your blood." He finished with a toothy smile.

All his grandstanding accomplished was to give me more time to catch my breath and get it under control again. "My blood is more tangy than sweet." I put on a grin for him.

The demon looked at me with what I thought was pity. "You don't know when to quit, do you?"

"Nope."

The demon lifted his foot over my chest and brought it down. I caught it in my hands, but I didn't have time to admire how his foot squished as he leaned forward to put more of his weight on me. I pushed back harder. I couldn't shove him away, and he couldn't lean down any further. We'd reached a stalemate. I was afraid if I moved, I would lose all my leverage and get flattened. I think maybe the demon realized that if he let up even just a little, I would throw him off.

We stayed locked there. My breaths were short and sharp, my arms burned, and I could feel the tendons in my wrists wanting to give up.

Then I heard shouting. "There it is. Kill the demon!"

Help? Someone came to help me?

The demon turned his attention away from me to see who was yelling. Several arrows struck him in his torso and arms, and a ball of fire slammed into the cyclops's eye, engulfing his entire head in a heat that I could feel down on the ground. Despite all the attacks the demon took, he never abated in his attempt to crush me. He just closed his eye as charred skin covered his face, then roared as he activated his healing power.

Wave after burning wave rolled over me. Steam flowed off the demon, filling my lungs as I breathed. My fur kept most of me safe, insulating me, but my eyes weren't so lucky. Neither were my lungs as I breathed the steam in. I screamed in pain as the demon roared. Every arrow that pierced the demon's skin was forced out, and each of them fell to the ground one by one.

As quickly as the heat arrived, it dissipated. Everything was slightly blurry, but I could still make out most details.

For a brief moment, both the cyclops and I realized we weren't pushing against one another during the time he was healing himself. The demon tried to crush me again, but I held his foot back. I even found the strength to move him back. The surprise on my enemy's face was priceless.

More arrows showered the demon's body, and he stumbled backwards as another ball of fire struck him in the chest. This time, the fire burned a small chunk of flesh off. The demon fell to the ground on his back.

I rolled over on my hands and knees; my lungs and face burned. A stinging pain emanated from the pads on my hands. *Is it over?* I turned to see if the cyclops was still breathing as he lay on the ground. He activated his healing again. I leaned against the tree and put an arm over my face for protection. He shrank only slightly this time.

Is it done? Is that the last time he can heal himself?

I turned to see who was shooting at the demon and saw Drue with a collection of eight other knights and another familiar face.

Midas? What's he doing here?

The cyclops attempted to get up. *That demon doesn't know when to quit either.*

I crawled over to him and saw that he was huffing. I watched as he stood one more time, and another hail of arrows met him once again.

"I told you I was going to eat you," I whispered.

I summoned whatever energy I had in reserve and jumped on the demon, who was as tall as me now, and forced him to the ground. The arrows that were still in him made a cascading wave of snapping sounds before I bit down on the demon's neck. My jaw crushed his vertebrae and severed the spinal cord with little resistance.

The sin of gluttony went completely limp.

I spat out the flesh and bones in my mouth since he tasted like flavorless globs of cooked fat. His body warmed up, warning me that he was going to heal himself again.

Oh no you don't!

I continued to bite piece after piece out of his neck. Each bite was hotter than the last, and it was quickly becoming very painful to touch his body. But I kept biting. I was determined to make sure he didn't get up again. Each moment brought more pain, and each bite left more blisters in my mouth, but after the last bite, his head fell to the ground, completely severed. The body cooled down immediately once the head hit the ground with a sickening plop.

I panted as I looked at the demon's face, permanently contorted into a grimace.

That was for Evalana. You shouldn't have harmed my friend. And by the way, you taste awful.

Footsteps came running towards me as I crawled away from the demon. Every breath was painful, every movement was just as agonizing, and I was thoroughly out of energy. My arms and legs gave out as I collapsed to the ground and stared at the treetops. *I did it. I kept everyone safe.* The image of Farryn's crushed body flashed through my mind. *Or, at the very least, everyone I care about is safe.*

Drue walked up to me and stared down with a huge smile on his face. "Are you still with us?" He knelt down next to me.

"Yeah," I said as my voice slowly started to fade.

"Take it easy, kid. We'll get you some help. What you did was nothing short of heroic." Drue gently picked me up.

"We'll dispose of the body. Get her to the headquarters as soon as you can." Midas's voice was as flat as ever.

My consciousness was slowly fading, but I had one last burning question. "Why did you come back for me?" I looked up at Drue's scarred face.

"In the Brilliant Crusade, we don't leave anybody behind. That includes beastkin." Drue gave me a mirthful smile. "Besides, I could never live with myself if I had to tell Allen you died because I ran away."

"Thanks for coming back for me," I said as I closed my eyes.

46

SILVERBREEZE

Everything felt warm and comfortable as my consciousness returned. My eyes flickered open, but I was blinded by the light of the sun. I lifted my arm to shield my eyes enough so I could see where I was. *How long have I been out this time?*

As my arm moved, I felt extra resistance as my body protested against me. Soft cotton sheets hugged me as they also held me down to the heavenly bed. *I must have slept fantastically last night. Why else would I be so stiff?* I sat up while still shielding my eyes as they adjusted to the light.

Once my eyes adjusted, I looked at the bed I was in. *This thing is large enough for three people to sleep comfortably.* I tried to imagine how people wasted entire days lazing around, supported by such softness. *As tempting as it is to join them, I should figure out what happened.*

Several wide wardrobes were spaced out around the room and made of dark timber that reflected light with its waxy protective finish. I looked around and saw that everything was constructed with the same materials. A rectangular window filled with glass let the sun in. The light-blue painted stone walls took me by surprise.

I've never seen a room made completely out of stone like this. I've also never seen stones painted like this. Some of the buildings in Aquittemia had stone outer walls, but the ones I went inside still had wood on the inside. I haven't been inside the majority of them, so perhaps some of them were more like this one. Well, I guess I'd better figure out where I am now.

Sliding out from under the sheets filled me with a pang of sadness. *That's a really nice bed.* I checked to make sure my wounds were still bandaged, but I didn't have any dressings. My injuries were completely healed, and I couldn't find any trace of ever having received them. *Seriously, how long was I out?* Someone had put me in a loose-fitting white silk nightgown. *This feels nice, too.* I looked at my fur and saw it needed a good brushing, so I looked around the room for a brush.

I found one sitting on a desk with a round mirror next to all kinds of small jars and paint brushes. There were a few larger bottles, each filled with a different-colored liquid. When I opened one, it smelled unbearably pungent. *Is this some kind of perfume? And if that's perfume, then is that makeup? Whose room am I in?* I opened the wardrobe and saw a plethora of silk dresses, shirts, skirts, and other clothing items. *Whoever lives in this room is definitely a woman.*

I heard footsteps as I brushed my fur back into order. They sounded almost like someone was walking barefoot on the stone, but it was too muffled for that. *Oh, they must be wearing a pair of soft-soled boots like the ones I found in the wardrobe. Wait, maybe the owner of this room is coming in.*

I stood still, watching the door and listening to the footsteps. I breathed a sigh of relief as the footsteps didn't stop but kept going instead.

After brushing my fur, I thought about the clothes in the wardrobe. *I can't keep wearing a nightgown, but I don't have anything else that has a hole cut for my tail. I don't see my stuff.*

I looked around the room some more and saw a chair sitting next to the bed with a flat, folded piece of cloth resting in the seat. The strings wrapped around it and tied into a simple bow made the cloth look like a present. I picked it up and noticed that it wasn't just a piece of cloth, but a neatly folded silk dress. I cut the strings and unfurled the piece of clothing. The dark-green silk garment looked like it was fitted to my exact size, with a small bust and a hole in the backside near the waist. Short sleeves and intricate lace hems told me it was expensive.

Someone wants me to wear this. But why something so formal-looking? It isn't like I'm going to see the king or anything. Or... I looked at the window, then at the bed, and then at the wardrobe. *Evalana is a princess. I just might be seeing the king.*

I put the dress on but struggled to tie up the back so that it stayed up. After several tries, I succeeded and looked at my reflection in the mirror on the desk. *It looks good on me, but something feels wrong. I don't like it. But I don't have anything else to wear.*

I sat down on the bed, trying to figure out why I didn't enjoy wearing something so nice. *Don't I want to look pretty? I guess I'm a girl who likes something a little more practical. A girl who likes to get her claws bloody, sink her fangs deep into her prey's throat, and roll around in the snow. I take good care of my fur, and I'm filled with a small sense of pride each time I look at it. But I could never be a princess like Evalana, all prim and proper. To everyone else, I look like I'm too wild for civilized company, partially because I have this overwhelming need to fight anything that resembles a threat. And if anyone tries to intimidate me, I take that as a personal challenge, a challenge that I must answer. If I'm in a knight company, then at least I can explain it to everyone and we can work something out. And that's just one of the many reasons I couldn't be a princess. My lack of patience after that would—*

"A coin for your thoughts?" a familiar, gentle voice interrupted my inner debate.

"Ahh!" I jumped, turned around, and tried to stand up all at the same time. All of my limbs went in every direction, and instead of landing on my feet, I fell off the bed and landed on my butt.

"Oh no. Are you alright?" Nora ran over to the other side of the bed, where I fell. Her footsteps were far quieter than I remembered.

Why is she covered in bruises? And is she limping?

"What happened to you? Are you okay?" I stood up, rubbing my now sore butt. "How did you sneak up on me like that?" *Are there more injuries that I can't see under her clothes?*

Nora sat me down on the bed. "I'm sorry for scaring you. I didn't mean to." She sat down next to me. "I knocked, but you didn't answer. I thought you were still asleep, but I wanted to check up on you. But I'm alright."

"Where did you get all those injuries?" I lightly touched her bandages. "What happened to you? Why didn't you help when the demons attacked?"

"These are just some minor cuts, bruises, a couple of hurt ribs, and a twisted ankle I got while fighting some mages who ambushed me to keep me away from the tournament grounds." Nora removed one of the bandages. There was a light-pink line where a cut was healing. "See, nothing bad." But her tone changed. "I wanted to help and be there for you and the others. But some people were following me. Apparently they knew I was looking for August in town and the rest of the grounds." Her voice sounded melancholic.

"Why?"

"I imagine they were part of the group who summoned the demons, kidnapped August, and tried to force you to kill the prince." She turned and gave me a forced smile. "But we put a stop to their plans. We did what we could. I defeated those mages and helped with the clean-up of the remaining demons. I'm just glad Melody was able to keep everyone else safe."

I stared at the wall straight ahead. *That's right, we did it. August was saved, we evacuated, and I killed the sin.*

"But usually I can't get anywhere near your room without you knowing." Nora turned my head to look at her. "I know this isn't what you're used to, but are you okay?"

"I didn't realize I was that distracted," I said as I looked down at the floor.

"What's bothering you?" Nora put her arm around my shoulders.

A lot, but I should start with something small. "I'm sorry," I whispered.

"What for?" she asked as she pulled me closer.

I rested my head on her shoulder. "I've been difficult lately. I guess with everything that happened with the demon, I finally have some perspective. Something happened to me when I saw August held hostage by those men. I didn't just want to save him, I *needed* to save him." I rambled on, unable to stop myself. Every word I said came out faster than the last. I couldn't hold back any emotions, and I didn't want to. "But I couldn't kill Aurtour like they wanted. I know now that they were never planning on letting August go in the first place, though I guess it didn't matter once the demons started attacking. But after we saved August, leading everyone as we evacuated, I felt the same feeling. I needed to protect everyone. Well, not everyone. I didn't care about Farryn. And when I killed all the fallen demons I saw outside, I'd never felt more satisfied with what I had done. They were safe, and that's all that mattered. And when the sin of gluttony showed up and bit off Evalana's arm, I almost lost control. I led him away from everyone so that they were safe. Believe me, I really wanted to kill him, and I did, but making sure Evalana made it to safety just felt more important."

"Wow." Nora loosened her grip on my shoulders. "First, I'm sorry, but that was three days ago." Her tone was sorrowful. *Have I been asleep for that long? That explains why I don't see any of my injuries.* "But you don't know how proud I'm to hear that you did what you did. Aurtour and Drue told me everything."

"Even after all the things I said to you the other day..." I turned and grabbed Nora in a hug as tears trickled down my cheeks. "Here you are, listening to my rant like nothing ever happened. I'm sorry."

Nora returned my hug. "I told you, if you ever need an ear to listen to you, a shoulder to cry on, or a hand to hold you, I'll be there."

I cried in her arms, soaking her dress, and she stayed still until I finished and collected myself.

"Feel better?" She scratched behind my left ear.

I wagged my tail. "Yeah." I wiped my face on my arm. "I have some questions."

Nora smiled. "I'm sure you do, but I know of a few people who want to talk to you. They might answer some of your questions." My stomach woke up with a loud growl. "And I think you are overdue for some food." We giggled at my stomach's cries.

Nora stood up and offered her hand to me. I took it and walked out of my room with her, then through wide stone hallways lined with heavy wooden doors. There were several other people walking the halls, too. Most of them were guards, but there were some others who I guessed were workers who maintained such a large building. They ignored us beyond their initial glances.

I lost track of how many rooms we passed and hallways we traveled until we reached a much-larger pair of doors that went all the way to the ceiling. I could hear voices talking on the other side, but there were too many to parse out what people were saying.

A large stone building, personal guards, a cleaning staff, and expensive clothes. Am I in some kind of castle? Yeah, no doubt about it anymore. I'm on my way to meet Evalana's father, the king.

Nora opened the doors with a flick of her wrist, and all the people I'd heard earlier stopped talking and turned their attention to me.

I froze. My heart raced as I stared back at the crowd of very colorfully dressed people.

Nope.

I released Nora's hand and dashed out of sight, then put my back against a wall.

Nora turned to look at me, then closed the door with another wave of her hand. She walked up to me and wrapped an arm around my shoulder. "Are you okay? Do you need a minute? Or are there too many people?" Her voice was as soft as her touch.

"Too many people," I said between panicked breaths.

"Alright." Nora gave me a quick head pat. "You're going to want to cover your ears for this one," she said with a smile.

I did as she suggested and watched her go back into the room. She closed the door behind herself. "All of you, get out!" Her voice was painfully loud.

I'm covering my ears and I'm on the other side of a stone wall and large wooden doors. How loud is she yelling?

"I don't care who you think you are. I told you to leave. No, you can't see Lucia. She doesn't want to see any of you. I said, 'out.' Now!" The ground and walls shook as she shouted.

Sometimes it's easy to forget she's a powerful mage. That reminds me: I should ask her about the unfocused magic that I somehow absorbed.

I released my ears to listen to the shuffling of feet and uncountable murmurs of discontent. *I guess being a hero of the kingdom lets you get away with ordering others around.* Once I couldn't hear any more footsteps, I walked up to the door, opened it, and cautiously poked my head in to look inside. I entered now that there were far fewer people.

Nora turned to look at me with a smile on her face, and she gave me a slight nod as she waved for me to follow her.

I entered and looked at the massive room. While most of the building's stones had been unaltered in the halls, in this room every stone received a color. They were painted in a three-color pattern that originated in the center of the room. Starting with red, then white, then yellow, the pattern repeated until it reached the walls of the round room.

While the floor was painted, banners of all different sizes and shapes covered the walls. Only one banner was repeated, the Kingdom of Rophmna's banner—a blue flag with five stampeding horses. The version hanging here was far more detailed than the ones decorating Aquittemia's stone walls. But other banners hung alongside them in different colors and sizes, differing wildly from each other, and none were identical. I only recognized two of them. The first was the same symbol on Aenwyn's armor on a gray banner, and the other was the image on Allen's banner, a blazing sun resting on a pillar with a white background.

Those must be all the different knight companies. Wow, there's a lot of them.

Four rectangular stone pillars in the center of the room stood in a square formation. They were painted white to match the color of the floor where they stood. The distance between each pillar was about two arcs, and there were two lit oil lamps on each, providing light to the windowless room. There were several other oil lamps burning, providing enough light to keep the area very well lit. I also saw two long and narrow wooden tables. They looked just like the furniture in the room that I'd woken up in today. One table had papers, ink pots, books, and quills scattered over it in a disorganized mess. The other table had only three candelabras on it.

A set of double doors sat in each of the four cardinal directions. The set I'd entered from was the largest of them. To my right and left, each side had its own large single door. At the far side of the room sat the smallest door, which was barely visible as the throne in front of it demanded my attention.

Six wooden rods grew from the back of the throne. Something was carved into them, but it was too difficult to see from where I was. Each pair of rods was the same height. The tallest pair were in the center, and the shortest pair were on the outside. They grew out of the solid back of the chair, which came up to just below the shoulders of its current occupant. An anatomically correct stallion standing on its hind legs made each armrest of the throne. Cushions on the back, sides, and seat of the chair cradled the king. A sword in its sheath sat propped up next to his left armrest.

I gawked at everything as I slowly made my way to the center of the room behind Nora. On the large, expensive chair on the raised dais, the king sat and stared at me with tired green eyes. He was easily almost as tall as Nora. His jaw was square, yet his smile felt inviting. His sandy brown hair, perfectly straight with gray roots, fell to just below his ears. *Both Aurtour and Evalana must get their hair from their mother.*

He wore a purple surcoat over his black tunic that fell to his knees and parted at his waist. Clean leather boots climbed halfway up his shins. I stared at him as he sat lazily to one side, holding his head up on an arm wedged between the armrest and his head.

"So you're the famous beastkin my kids have told me so much about." His voice carried throughout the room without the usual tingle of magic.

He's the king, but I don't remember his name right now. My heart quickened. "That's probably because I'm the only beastkin your kids know," I said with a forced smile.

A slight grin crept across his face. I shifted my weight from one foot to another as I stood waiting for him to do something.

The king chuckled for a moment before he straightened his posture as he spoke. "I've had so many conversations with people over these last few days about you. But I'm curious as to why Nora just cleared out my throne room without my consent. Would you like to explain?"

"I don't do well with crowds," I whispered as I turned to look at the ground.

"She's just woken up and is likely very hungry." Nora stepped between me and the king. "Lucia gets easily agitated, more so when she's hungry. So I believed it was in everyone's best interest to remove those pointless nobles and their babbling." Nora crossed her arms.

Hungry doesn't even begin to describe me right now. My stomach roared to agree with me and prove Nora right.

"Those pointless nobles have influence." The king closed his eyes as he talked. After a brief pause, he opened them again. "However, I believe we can do something about that hunger of hers." His smile widened. "Please bring some meat for Lucia."

"Right away, sir," a man who I hadn't noticed before said as he moved to leave through the door he'd been standing by.

"Also, please inform my daughter that her friend is awake." The king's voice softened and became far more gentle than I would have thought him capable of.

"Yes, sir." The man performed a quick bow in the doorway before leaving.

"I've heard a lot about what you've done. Both my children vouch for you. You also have two heroes of this kingdom vouching for you." The king folded his hands together as he leaned forward on his throne. "And as a father, I can't thank you enough for what you've done for me." I thought I saw a shimmer in his eyes. "But as your king, I can reward you as best as I can. I've recently read many reports about you from Aquittemia."

I stepped behind Nora to use her as a shield.

369

"None of them are bad."

I relaxed and poked my head out from behind Nora.

"There's a name that people use when they talk about you. I believe it's a beautiful name for a beautiful young woman. So from now on, introduce yourself as Lucia Silverbreeze."

Do I have a last name now? I looked up at Nora. "What does that mean for me?" I asked with more enthusiasm than I wanted to let on. *I know not everyone has one, and that it's a privilege of sorts, but I don't know the details.*

"It tells everyone that you've done a great service for the kingdom. Once people know that you have a title, they'll show you respect," Nora said as she kneeled down, placed a hand on the top of my head, and scratched. "You're not just any beastkin now. You've done something worthy of merit, and now the entire kingdom will know it."

I turned towards the king. "But what about Drue? He was with me most of the time. He even saved me. Did he receive a reward too?" My tail slowly wagged behind me.

"He's already received his reward," the king replied. "We're here to discuss you, not him."

I heard footsteps approaching behind the door I'd entered from. When the door opened, I drooled as I smelled the sweet and savory scents of meat. I turned to see six men and women carrying large steel platters with lids, and I wagged my tail vigorously, my eyes following the food as they headed to the table with the candelabras. They placed the trays down, and one by one they lifted the lids, revealing lamb ribs, roasted boar legs, whole rotisserie chickens, strips of pickled bacon, a whole tail of some reptile, and a pile of hearts.

I didn't wait for the people to step away or for permission. I sprinted to the table and jumped on it. Nowhere in my mind did I remember that I was in a throne room in front of the king as I attacked the platters of food like a starving animal.

After I stuffed an entire heart in my mouth and picked up the tail to try it, I heard Nora clear her throat. I looked at her without letting go of the food.

"Where are your manners, young lady?" Nora put her hands on her hips.

Oh, right. "Thank you, Your Majesty," I said with a mouth full of heart.

Nora slapped her forehead before groaning.

47

MAGIC FIXES EVERYTHING

"At least get off the table," Nora said as her hand slowly slid down her face.

I stopped shoveling food in my mouth for a moment and jumped off the table out of reflex. I saw another person bring in a large mug of water. As soon as they placed it down next to me, I quickly swallowed the food and drained the contents of the cup.

I still don't know what kind of lizard has a tail that large. But whatever it was, it was delicious. Kinda salty though.

"Please forgive her lack of decorum, King Ramos."

I turned and saw Nora bowing towards the king. *So that's his name. I need to remember that one.*

King Ramos chuckled. "You must be starving. There's nothing to forgive. Please eat until you're satisfied. I hope it was all cooked to your liking." He waved towards the platters of food.

Now that the food had registered in my stomach, I could think rationally again. "Well, it doesn't taste too bad." I looked at the food. "It would have been better if this was all raw." *And not spiced.* But it tasted decent. Even though they'd cooked the meat, it still had a pink center. Unfortunately, the spices distracted from the taste. But I was too hungry to be picky.

Tomorrow is going to be a bad day. All these seasonings are going to give me diarrhea.

"You eat raw meat?" The king sat up straight, his mouth agape as he looked at me.

"Didn't Evalana tell you?" I asked as I grabbed a roasted boar leg, the last meat I hadn't tried yet.

And speaking of Evalana. I could hear her talking to someone as she moved down the hall. Her footsteps were irregular, making it difficult to tell if she was walking or running.

"Here she comes now." I pointed to the door that she would come through.

The door opened, and Evalana walked backwards into the room, pulling another woman in. "You'll really like her. Aurtour said she's alright."

There's something different about her. Did she do something with her hair?

Evalana wore a long-sleeved yellow dress with a decorative white lace belt. One sleeve was tied off at the stump where her arm had been severed.

The woman Evalana dragged in looked to be an inch or two shorter than me. She wore a light-blue dress with dark-blue embroidered patterns of teardrops on the skirt. Her hair was gray, and the wrinkles around her eyes and lips made her look even older. Even though Evalana was pulling her along with one arm, the woman walked with such surety that there was no doubt she was the queen.

"You need to stop these childish actions. People won't respect you if you keep acting like this." Her scratchy voice made me straighten my back, put my feet together, and bring my elbows in.

Evalana stood, not fazed in the slightest. "Lucia and Zenny don't care that I'm a princess. They treat me like a regular person. They want to be my friends. And not because they want something. That's what I want." She moved like she was going to cross her arms, but found that it was impossible to do with only one arm. She put her hand on her hip instead.

My appetite died as I stared at her stump. I put my meat down before I spoke. "I'm sorry I didn't get to you in time." My words didn't feel satisfying to say.

"You're the one who saved my daughter's life?" Evalana's mother asked as she took a few steps towards me.

"This is Lucia." Evalana jogged up to pass her mother.

"Not anymore. Go ahead, introduce yourself." Nora extended a hand to me.

I stepped out from behind the table before I put my feet together and bowed. "Hello, my name is Lucia Silverbreeze." *It feels so weird to say that. Yet it also feels, I don't know, right, maybe?*

"Greetings, Lucia Silverbreeze. I am Besseta, queen of Rophmna." The woman's voice was flat. "So, why are you friends with my daughter?"

"Please don't do that, Besseta," King Ramos said before I could respond. "We've talked about this. Just let her be. She saved Evalana when it would have been easier to do nothing."

"See, listen to Father," Evalana said while pointing at the king. "If you want to get to know her better, teach her magic, just like you taught me. That way, you'll spend all kinds of time together and see that she truly is a great friend."

Queen Besseta turned to look at Nora. "I take it you're here because she's your charge?"

Nora nodded as she walked towards me.

A smile spread across the old woman's lips. "It looks like she has a more qualified teacher than me."

"Who could be better than you?" Evalana looked at Nora.

"Meet Nora Stormleaf." Queen Besseta waved to the other woman.

Evalana's eyes grew larger as she stared at Nora. "Really? You're that Nora? The hero, Nora Stormleaf?" She vibrated as she asked her questions.

Nora simply nodded.

Evalana squealed as she raised her arm in the air and ran to cut Nora off from standing next to me. "I wanna be just like you when I grow up. You're so powerful that you can save everyone. I wish my magic was even a fraction as powerful as yours. Can you teach me magic too, please?" Evalana bounced on the balls of her feet with each word.

I stared at the scene, blinking.

Nora leaned forward a bit and placed her right hand on Evalana's shoulder. She whispered, "I don't think you need me to teach you magic. You're quite an accomplished mage already." Nora turned her head towards me, and Evalana did too. "You should go to your friend and do something better than I can."

Evalana turned back to Nora and waited for instructions.

"Put her nerves to rest. She's feeling guilty about what happened to you. Cheer her up." She turned Evalana towards me and gave her a gentle push.

Evalana took a few steps towards me. Her frown was too much for me to look at, and I couldn't look at her arm because I couldn't handle the guilt. I lowered my head and stared at my feet.

"What's wrong?" Evalana squatted down and moved into my vision to look up at me.

"I couldn't save you in time. Now you have to live with only one arm," I said as I turned away. My throat tightened as I held back my tears.

I felt something coarse grasp my shoulder, and I saw sand shaped like a hand. It pulled and turned me around. Evalana stood smiling at me. I looked at the sand arm and saw that it connected to her stump. "A little thing like losing an arm won't stop me. Besides, I know something you don't."

I stared at her, confused.

"I'm not right-handed," she said with a wink.

"Magic, of course," I said with a sigh. "It must be nice to be able to use magic." Seeing her have a replacement arm lifted most of the guilt from my heart.

I hope she never loses that optimism. She was so quick to forgive me. I wish it was that easy to forgive myself.

Evalana's sandy arm detached from the stump and flowed down into a metal canister that she plugged with a stopper. "I can only use it for important tasks right now, but once I get better at it, I'll be able to use it all the time. But you can use magic too. You'll be able to learn how to do all kinds of cool stuff."

I looked up at Nora. "Is she right? Can I learn magic?" I wagged my tail in anticipation.

"Yes," Nora said. Her face held a gentle smile as she walked up and started scratching behind my ear. "I'm sorry I didn't see it the first time. I can't sense magic around me like your friend here. After the night you were attacked, I should've started teaching you. But I'll make up for it and start teaching you once we get home. How does that sound?"

I leaned a little to my left so Nora would start scratching the sweet spot behind my right ear. As she continued scratching, I nearly melted. "I can't wait."

Evalana giggled at my euphoric display. Then something about her bothered me.

"Are you taller? How did you grow"—I looked at her bust— "everywhere? And your face, it looks more mature, I think?" I leaned away from Nora's hand to concentrate on Evalana's appearance.

"I was hoping you wouldn't notice," Evalana said as she drooped her shoulders. She took a deep breath as she stood up straight again. "Don't get mad, but I'm a few years older now."

"How?" I whispered.

"It's a side effect of receiving healing magic," Evalana said as she scratched at her chin with a single finger and looked away from me.

"Healing magic makes you older? How old are you now?" I didn't hold back my surprise or my volume.

"Best guess? Sixteen, about three years older." She waved her hand dismissively. "But that isn't important."

The weight of the world crashed down on my shoulders as I fell to my knees. *Three years? My failure shortened her life by three years. And that doesn't include any complications that may arise due to missing an arm.*

I felt someone grab my shoulders and shake me out of my thoughts. "Stop it. Don't blame yourself." Nora's face was inches away from mine. "Yes, she's older now. Because of the situation, healing magic was the best course of action to take. You need to remember she was alive and able to be healed because of you." She wiped my cheeks with her thumb.

When did I start crying?

"Yeah, I'm still alive because you saved me. I don't think that monster was going to let me live for much longer." Evalana turned from me to her mother. "Besides, it was my foolishness that got me into that situation to begin with. I wanted to save Farryn so badly that I ignored my magic fatigue for one moment. I'm lucky that all I lost was an arm. If I have to lose three years to spend many more alive, I'll happily take that over death." She looked back at me and waved her hand down her body. "Besides, I think I turned out quite beautiful, if I may say so." She performed a slow twirl as she displayed herself.

"How do you do that?" I asked with a sniffle. "How do you keep being this positive?"

"Why are you so negative? Don't you want to be happy? What's happened can't be changed. Being happy is much better than being sad." She stood staring at me.

"If you're okay with everything, that's what matters." I tried to force a smile. "I got him. He bit your arm off, so I bit his head off."

Evalana shivered.

"Evalana, please take Lucia somewhere else. While it warms my heart to see you have a genuine friend for once, I do have business with everyone Nora forced out earlier." A wide smile sat on the king's face as he watched us from his throne.

"Do you mind if I take a couple of hearts?" I asked as I looked at the unfinished platter. "They may not be perfect, but I'm still a little hungry."

"Of course, they're yours. Do what you wish with them." King Ramos waved his hand towards the table of food. "Oh, and one last thing. I saw how you defeated my son. Consider the prize money collected against your debt."

Well, that's the best I could ask for.

I grabbed three hearts and turned to look at Evalana. "So, where are we going?" I started eating a heart. *Ah, pig hearts. Classic. Too bad about them being cooked.*

Evalana shivered as she watched me eat. "How about we go

outside and sit in the sun? It's a wonderful day out. Nice and warm." She stared up at the ceiling with a wistful look.

Ugh, the fire season is almost here. What's nice and warm for most people is annoying and hot for me. But if she can be in such bright spirits even with everything that has happened to her, I shouldn't let a little heat bother me.

"Alright, but can we find a place with a lot of shade? Oh, and no people too." I held up a finger.

"Only the best for my hero," Evalana said as she walked ahead of me.

I wish she wouldn't call me that.

"Go on ahead without me," Nora said as she walked towards the throne. "There's something I need to take care of. I'll find you after I'm done."

I shrugged my shoulders as I followed Evalana. I finished the last of the hearts. As Evalana led me down the stone halls, there was a question on my mind.

"Does it hurt?" I whispered.

Evalana grabbed the stump of her arm. "Yeah, sometimes it feels like it's still there. Also, trying to keep my balance is much harder now." Her voice sounded choked. "I know what I said in there, but it was all just so my parents wouldn't lock me away for the rest of my life. Sometimes the pain can be too much to handle." She stopped moving and hunched over.

I hugged my friend. "I'm sorry. It's my fault that you have to live with this pain for the rest of your life. I wish there was something I could do."

I turned her around and gave her a tighter hug. She hugged me back with her one arm. I let her cry, refusing to let the guilt build again. *She doesn't need me to break down in front of her. She needs someone to lean on right now.*

Evalana cried for a little while, and once she slowed down, I wiped a few tears from her face.

"If you ever need a hand, I will do everything I can to help." *Did I just say that to her? No!*

Before I could apologize, Evalana giggled as she sniffled. She squeezed me as hard as she could. "I accept."

After we enjoyed our hug, Evalana continued to lead me through more stone hallways. She never second-guessed where she was going and led me to a simple, heavy wooden door.

And in front of it were an old man with slicked back hair and a certain hare beastkin.

"Can we talk?" Midas asked.

48

I'LL DO WHAT I WANT

A growl resounded in my throat as I stared at the old reincarnator. "What do you want?"

Regimes stepped in front of Midas. "I asked him to talk to you." Her ears drooped slightly. "We heard about what you did. Facing a sin and defeating it—that's incredible."

I crossed my arms. "It was the right thing to do to save my friends."

"Well, Lamso and I were wondering..." Regimes turned her head slightly as she touched the tips of her pointer fingers together. "If you wanted to come with us to The Wild Kingdom, we could take you in. You know, give you a place to stay and talk about making sure you're a hunter."

I raised my eyebrows. "Why couldn't you do that before? What's changed?"

Regimes winced. "We didn't know how special you were."

"What does that mean?" I extended my claws, and the hare beastkin flinched again. "It wasn't enough that you were my mother's friend; I had to prove myself by killing a demon."

"Lucia, calm down." Midas pulled Regimes back while stepping forward. "It's just a proposition. You're free to decline. There's no need to be upset."

I glared at Midas. "And why do you care?"

He pointed behind me. "You're scaring Evalana."

I turned and saw Evalana holding the skirt of her dress in her hand. Her face was slightly red, like she was holding something back.

I snapped back to Midas. "She's not scared. And you were the one who asked if we wanted to talk. What do you want?"

"I'm interested in you too." Midas didn't flinch or show any emotion. "I won't lie. I hope that you won't take them up on their offer."

"What if I don't?" I narrowed my eyes at the old man. As I asked, I could hear Evalana exhale a heavy sigh.

The old man didn't move, he just stood as still as a statue. "Then I would offer you something as well."

Oh great. I can't wait to hear this one. I gave a slight shake of my head and motioned for him to proceed.

"Come and apprentice under me."

Evalana didn't bother to hide her gasp. I turned and saw her covering her mouth with her one hand. Her eyes looked like they were about to tear up.

Is she happy or sad? I can't tell.

I closed my eyes and growled. There was a long moment of silence before my words echoed in the stone hall. "No. Not now. Not ever. I'll never go with you."

Midas blinked several times. "Would you at least tell me why? I know what you've been through. I can help you—"

"No!" I extended my claws and raised them at the man. He still didn't flinch. "You have no idea what I've been through. You don't know what it's like for me. And you never will." I looked back and forth between Regimes, who was cowering behind Midas, and the old reincarnator. "You two didn't care about who I was until I earned my title. Each of you has plans for me and what you think is best for me. Everyone seems to think they know what's best for me. Well, I don't care. I'll do what I want." I doubted our conversation was private with the yelling I was doing.

"And what do you want?" Midas's voice shook ever so slightly.

I turned to look at Evalana. "To be your friend. To be Zenny's friend. You two were my friends before you knew what I could do and cared about me for who I am, not what I've done."

Evalana let go of her tears as she took a step towards me and wrapped her arm over my shoulder.

I turned to face Midas. "I want to protect them. And I'll do it my way: as a knight."

"Thank you," Evalana whispered.

"So, if you're done, my friend and I are going to go spend some time together." I kept a rumble in my voice. "Now leave. Us. Alone!"

Regimes ran past us, tears streaming down her face. Midas bowed but didn't say anything. The look on his face bothered me. It was emotionless, but it seemed like he was still thinking about something.

"Sorry about that." I gave Evalana a light hug. "You want to lead the way again?"

"Sure." She skipped to the door, but she paused as she held the door handle. "I know what you just gave up. And to hear you say the things you did, it means a lot to me."

And I meant every word.

She opened the wooden door, and a beautiful garden greeted me with flowers of every color and smell as I walked out. It was almost as good as Molly's garden back at the orphanage.

The more I looked around, the more I saw the true expanse of vegetation. Someone could get lost out here. And we weren't the only ones enjoying the colorful display.

Aenwyn stood with her face pressed up against a bush full of blooming purple flowers, completely ignorant of our presence. I watched her as she leaned back, her eyes closed and a wide smile on her face.

"What flower is that?" I asked.

"Oh." Aenwyn jumped at the sound of my voice. "These are purple grails." She caressed the flower petals gently as she admired them. "They're my favorite. My mom had a bush of these by every window and door, so our house would always smell like them. Even after a hundred and fifty years, I never get tired of their smell."

"It must be nice to have something to remind you of home," I mumbled.

"I see you're doing very well for someone who was on the brink of death three days ago." She turned and glared at me. "You didn't tell me you had two aptitudes. Keeping secrets like that isn't nice." She stepped away from the flowers and towards me.

"One, you didn't ask. Two, do you tell every stranger everything about yourself when you meet them?" I returned her glare with one of my own. "And finally, you haven't shared your aptitude. Sounds like a double standard to me."

"I see your point." She stopped walking, and her face softened. "My apologies. My aptitude is math. I'm very good with numbers of all kinds. And I can understand why you would keep your second aptitude hidden. You don't want the attention, do you?"

"That's an understatement," I said as I crossed my arms.

"Why don't you like the attention? Don't you want people to like you?" Evalana leaned towards me.

"The moment you found out I had two aptitudes, you called me a hero. At the time, I never thought I could do anything heroic. I don't want people to have that expectation of me. But since the tournament, I've learned that, like you, there are people I want to protect." I stared into her eyes. "You're one of them. I would rather have just one of you than dozens of faceless people who 'like' me." I turned my head to look at Aenwyn. "You said that you were almost willing to invite me to join your knight company. Is that offer still available?"

"Absolutely!" Aenwyn's sudden excitement surprised me. "With everyone knowing what you did, and you requested to join my company? I didn't have to ask. I'll rub it in all their faces." She hunched over and rubbed her hands together.

"Wait, everyone knows what I did?" *Am I famous now? I don't know if I can handle all the attention since crowds and I don't agree.* "What do you mean?"

"A bunch of knights who brought you to the headquarters demanded you get immediate attention," Aenwyn said matter-of-factly. "And once all of the demons were slain, some knights got a little drunk, including the large guy who carried you in. He told the entire story of how you killed the sin of gluttony. It was certainly an interesting story."

Thanks, Drue.

"I should also tell you something else. I can join when I'm fifteen," I said, and watched Aenwyn's face shift to confusion. "As a beastkin, I mature physically faster than a human or an elf. I'll be full-grown when I'm fifteen. So, can I join you then?"

"That's something." Aenwyn didn't hide her shock. "Of course, when you're ready, we'd love to have you. And don't worry, we'll take good care of you." She held out her hand. "Welcome to The Maidens, Lucia."

I wrapped my tail around me and held it. "It's Lucia Silverbreeze now." My voice squeaked slightly. I reached out a hand to shake hers while still holding my tail.

"That's a lovely name." Aenwyn's warm smile helped calm me down. "So how about you tell me a bit more about yourself, like which of these flowers is your favorite?" She wrapped her arm around me and guided me to some of the colorful plants.

Evalana followed us, humming the entire time.

49

COOL DOWN

Nora caught up with us later and told me it was time to go. I said my goodbyes as she readied our travel supplies so we could leave. Melody and the other kids were already back at the orphanage. Zenny and Salien had also returned home. Nora had been the only person to follow me back to the king's castle so she could take me back after I recovered.

Nora drove a horse-drawn cart with all of our belongings that had been collected from the tournament grounds before they took me to the castle. It was a two-day journey back to the capital city from the king's castle, so on the first night, after we set up a tent to sleep in, Nora sat me down.

"Alright, now is a good time to figure out what magic you can use." Nora sat cross-legged in front of me. I sat with my legs out to the side, and I wagged my tail as I leaned forward. "I need you to do exactly what I tell you when I tell you, without questioning me. Got it?" She held up a finger as she gave her instructions.

"Yes." I didn't bother holding back my excitement.

"Alright, I need you to concentrate and give me your hand. Do you know what it feels like when other people use magic on you?" Nora said as she extended her hand to me.

I placed my hand, claws up, in hers. "I think so. It's like a tingling sensation."

"I want you to concentrate on that feeling and let me know if you notice any changes." Nora grabbed my wrist with her other hand. "It might help if you close your eyes for this. Fewer distractions." She smiled as she winked.

I did as she suggested and relaxed as I closed my eyes. It didn't take long to feel the familiar tingling sensation.

"My hand tingles," I said without opening my eyes.

"Good. Now concentrate on that feeling," Nora said.

The harder I focused on the sensation, the stranger it felt. It slowly permeated throughout my hand before it shifted to surround it.

Is that magic? It feels like I can touch it.

I wiggled my fingertips to touch it, and it felt like I'd stuck my finger in something soft and malleable. "It feels spongy." I fought the urge to open my eyes.

I want to do this, and Nora said that closing my eyes would help.

"Do you feel something in your hand?" I nodded. "Try to move it. It doesn't matter where or how far, just move it."

"How?" I focused on the strange feeling on my palm and tried to squeeze it with my fingers.

"You have to will it. This is the hardest part, but I know you can do it. Make the magic move how you want it to." Nora's voice somehow made everything feel possible.

"Will it?" Alright, I want you to move up. The feeling in my hand didn't change, but I could feel something else in me move. I focused on that and tried again, this time more forcefully. The resistance from the magic felt like I was trying to push a building with one hand. I pushed more, trying harder and harder. A growl escaped my lips.

You will move up now! My hand got colder, but I continued to push with every ounce of willpower I had. I could feel energy leaving my body, entering my palm and making it colder.

"It's getting colder." I pulled on the energy leaving my body and threw it at the magic in my hand.

"That's good. Don't fight it. Just let it happen." Nora sounded excited.

I could feel the resistance in my hand lessening. *Maybe if it's colder, it will be easier to move. Now how do I make something colder? Ah, why can't I remember? It's getting harder to remember everything from my last life. I'm forgetting too much. Whatever, let's try Nora's way, just will it to get colder.*

I focused on the cold sensation and imagined it getting colder. It didn't take long for the temperature to drop. As the temperature lowered, so did the resistance in my hand. *It worked?* I continued to make the magic in my hand colder until I felt no resistance at all.

"Stop!" Nora shouted.

I opened my eyes to see a layer of frost on everything within arm's reach around me.

Nora shivered as she smiled. "Congratulations, you can use ice magic," she said through her chattering teeth.

I jumped up. "Yes!" I screamed at the top of my lungs. "I can use magic."

I ran around the area while jumping and laughing. Nora warmed herself by the campfire, smiling the entire time.

I stopped and stared at my hand. *Can I do it again?* I retraced the steps that Nora had walked me through. I felt the tingle in my hand and pulled the energy from inside me and wished for it to get colder. A fine mist slowly formed in my palm as I watched. *How cold can I make it?* I continued to watch as the mist thickened. Everything around me felt more comfortable.

"Stop, Lucia." Nora stepped towards me and raised her hand.

Before I could stop, it felt like I tripped on something, except it was the energy inside me that stopping. The sudden change felt like something lurching.

The feeling of the magic was gone as I stared at my hand. "What happened?" I watched as the mist disappeared and everything slowly started warming up.

Nora stopped and relaxed. "Congratulations again, you have successfully magically fatigued yourself in record time." Her disappointed glare drilled into me.

"I'm sorry—it—I just—I got carried away." I drooped my ears, tail, head, and shoulders. "It just felt so... I don't know how to describe it." I lifted my hands to look at them.

"I know, honey. It's exciting to learn you can use magic." Nora walked over to me and hugged me. "I know how you get when you're excited. This was eventually going to happen. I guess sooner's better than later." She led me to the tent. "We were going to see if you could use any other magic, but I guess it's time for you to go to sleep. No magic for a couple of days. Using magic while magically fatigued is dangerous." She opened the tent flap for me.

On the way to the tent, I noticed that everything looked brighter, and Nora practically glowed. "Why are you glowing now?" I asked as I sat down in the tent.

Nora's eyes popped open. "That was fast." She calmed down and smiled. "You can see magic much more easily now. Once someone starts using magic, it makes it much easier to see magic. What you're seeing is that all elves are full of magic. It's what makes it so difficult for me to see it in others. Everything looks like it has some magic to me." Nora sat down in front of me again. "My guess is that's how you absorbed all that unfocused magic by eating the elves. Finding an elf that doesn't use magic is almost impossible, but sometimes you'll find one, like Evandol, who can't. But it's only the elves from Rophmna. The elves in Osarin always have some magic, some in a greater capacity than others."

"But how do I channel unfocused magic so I don't get all loopy again?" I tilted my head.

"We needed to learn where to put that magic first," Nora said as she poked my nose. "Once you recover, we can figure out if you can use any other magic. We know you can do ice manipulation and that ice is your primary element. Even though I'm unique because I can use all kinds of magic, air manipulation is my primary one. So get some sleep. You need it." Nora stood up and started to close the tent.

I put my hand in the way to stop her. "I can't sleep right now because I'm too worked up. Physically, I could go for a quick hunt. I feel the need to go hunting growing." But there was a distinct feeling in the back of my mind. "It's hard to describe, but it feels like my mind is tired and completely awake at the same time." I stood up and exited the tent.

"If you need to go hunting, let's do it quickly. But please, if you feel anything wrong, tell me immediately. Even accidentally using magic is dangerous, especially now that you're fatigued."

I turned around. "You're coming with me?"

"After your last hunting stunt?" Nora put her hands on her hips. "You will always have someone go with you, even if they can't keep up with you the entire time. As long as they're close to you, it'll be good enough. Understand?" Her mom voice forced my tail between my legs, and I nodded. "Good. Which way are we going, and how far back do I have to be?"

"It mostly depends on how loud you are." I relaxed. "I'll let you know when something is close."

Nora followed me while I hunted. It didn't take long before I caught a porcupine. We took it back to our campsite, and she let me eat half of it before going to sleep. *I never expected porcupines to be so fatty, but they're surprisingly tasty. You just need to be careful that you don't poke yourself with their quills.*

After a quick meal and satisfying my urge to hunt after having spent several days in bed, we settled in for the night. When I woke up, a certain feeling was missing. I turned and looked at Nora as she rolled in her bedroll next to me.

"Guess what?" Nora looked at me, confused. I focused on making the area around my hand cold and created the fine mist again. It was much easier this time. "I've already recovered." I grinned.

Nora rolled her eyes as she lay back down and stared at the top of the tent. "Alright, now I'm jealous of your recovery aptitude."

We started laughing together as I stopped channeling the magic. We spent the entire morning trying to see if I could use any other type of magic, and, after a lot of trial and error, we learned I couldn't use any conjuration or enchantment magic, and I could only use ice and water manipulation magic. While I could barely manipulate water, it became much easier to manipulate when I turned it into ice.

Magic is so cool!

50

HOME

I watched the sparse snowflakes slowly flutter to the ground where a thin bed of snow welcomed more flakes. A human couple stood watching me while I carried the crate of August's things to the wagon.

All the fake smiles people give me are getting on my nerves.

I gave the two a passing glance as I loaded the crate for August. After I walked back to the entrance of the orphanage, I saw him looking back and forth between the two humans—who were his new parents—and me.

I gave him a polite smile.

He probably wants to say goodbye. I approached the steps and sat down on the top one after wiping away the snow. "Come here, buddy." I waved the boy over. "What's wrong?"

August sat down next to me, not bothering to clear the snow first. "I'm going to miss you." He stared at the ground, his voice distant.

"I know, but this is good for you." I wrapped an arm around the boy and pulled him close. "Don't you want to have a family who's ready to love you?"

"You're always so warm in the ice season," he said as he wrapped his arms around me. I let him hug me. *He needs this.* "I wish I could be just like you."

You don't know what you're wishing for. I carefully placed a finger under his chin and lifted his face to look me in the eye. "And why would you want that?"

"I want to be strong, just like you. If I'm not around you, how can I do that?" August looked at me with shimmering eyes.

I smiled at his innocence. "You don't need me to be strong."

"But you're the best at everything. You can use magic, you can run really fast, and you're super strong." August's praise tugged at my heart.

"I can't do everything," I said. "Yes, I can do those things you said, but there are things that I can't do, and I have my flaws too." *Too many to count. But I need to forget about them right now. I need to cheer August up.* "Remember, there will be times when you will fail and fall down. Remember that you can always get back up. Sometimes you'll try to do something that everyone says you shouldn't do or can't do, and there will be times when people will tell you how you should act. Don't ignore them, but you don't have to listen to them either. Be who you are and do what only you can do. But there's something you can do that I can't do, something nobody else can do." I leaned in close to him before I whispered to him. "Do you know what that is?"

His eyes grew wide. "No." He leaned closer to me.

"I can't be August," I said with the largest smile I could make without showing my fangs.

"But I'm August." He started bouncing as he sat next to me.

"And do you want to know something?" I waited for him to finish nodding before I continued. "August is great too." I tapped his nose with a fingertip.

"Really?" he asked, his voice filled with energy.

"Yes, and I can see two people who are ready to see how great August is. Are you ready to show them your greatness?" I gave his new parents a quick look. They stood huddled together in their heavy cloaks, watching us.

"Yeah!" August jumped from the steps and almost took off

running towards his new family. He turned around with a worried look on his face. "But will I still get to see you again?"

"If your parents say it's okay, I'll visit when I have time." I leaned forward, resting my forearms on my knees.

August turned towards the couple. "Can Lucia come visit?" he nearly shouted as he practically vibrated with excitement.

The couple looked at me. *I know that look. They want to say no, but they can't.* "Of course she can visit you anytime," the man responded.

August turned to look at me again. "Did you hear that? You can visit us anytime." His shouting hurt.

I flattened my ears. "Volume, August," I said with a sour look on my face. He covered his mouth after he realized what he'd done. "Yes, I heard. Remember, I can hear a lot better than you. So if you can hear it, I can too." I relaxed and tried to put on a smile for him. *I really wish I didn't need to keep reminding him about that. But he's five, and this is a big day for him. I can give him a little leniency.* "Now go with your parents to your new home," I urged him.

He ran to the couple, who lifted him onto the wagon to ride in. They led the horse that pulled the cart away from the orphanage without looking back, but August turned and waved at me. I returned the gesture until he was no longer in view.

"Did you enjoy the show?" I asked as I lowered my arm.

The front door to the orphanage opened up, and Nora stood smiling at me as a tear rolled down her cheek. "You sounded so grown up." She extended a hand to help me up. "Though I can't help but wonder, who was that little speech for?"

I took her hand and stood up. *At eleven years old, I'm sixty-nine inches tall, and I still have to look up at Nora, but I'm getting close. How am I still growing so much? And if I keep growing like this, how tall am I going to get? The two beastkin ambassadors were tall. Am I going to be that tall too?*

I grinned. "Does it matter?"

"I guess not." Nora shrugged. "I know you like the snow, but please come inside. I need you to do something."

I walked inside and shook off the snow in the entryway, then began walking through the now nearly deserted orphanage. "Actually, can you answer a question first?" I stopped after taking a few steps.

"Sure. What do you want to know?" Nora closed the door and walked up next to me.

"Since the tournament, you've found a home for almost everyone. Molly, I understand couldn't you couldn't find a home to adopt her before she turned seventeen, but you found families willing to adopt everyone else. All year, you've worked to find homes for not just April and August but all the new arrivals who lost their parents during the demon attack. Everyone except me, that is. Something's changed in you. What is it, and why?" I turned to face Nora.

"I thought about what you said during the tournament. You planted a seed of doubt about whether I was doing the right thing." Nora looked at me. She had a few more tears running down her cheeks. "Maybe I was being selfish, and I wanted to be a mother to everyone all at once. Once we got back, I resolved to change what this orphanage was about. It isn't about forcing a family to happen. I want it to be a place that gives everyone the family they deserve. So I've been finding people who were indecisive about adopting and helped them come to their decision." Her expression slowly changed to one of determination as she spoke.

"I guess that means I'll be stuck here alone. Everyone talks about how they accept what I am, but nobody wants to adopt me. It's fine. I came to terms with it a while ago." I slumped my shoulders as I walked towards the hallway. "So, what did you need my help with?"

"I need you to pack your things," Nora said.

"Why?" I slowly turned back to her and watched her movements closely.

Nora smiled. "There's someone who wants to adopt you."

"I doubt that. Where are they? And why haven't I met them?" I straightened up and crossed my arms.

She held out a folded piece of paper with a wax seal. I took it, and, with a single claw, I broke the seal, unfolded the thick paper, and read it. With each line, I could feel my eyes growing. Once I got to the end, I couldn't hold the paper any longer. It fell to the floor as a single word escaped my lips.

"Why?"

"You deserve the same as the other children who have walked through those doors." Nora pointed to the front door. Her voice had never sounded more welcoming than it did now. "You deserve a family that will love you for who you are. And over the last few seasons, I just can't see you as anyone else's daughter but mine. I love you too much. I want you to be my first daughter. Maybe I'm being selfish again, and if you don't want to, I would understand. But I want you to know, no matter what happens or what you do, if you ever need a home to come back to, I will always accept you. I'll always be here for you." Nora held her arms out, welcoming me with a hug. "So, do you want to be adopted?"

I didn't know when the tears started; I didn't care. I grabbed the elven woman without hesitation and cried. "Yes, yes, yes, yes." I repeated the three-letter word until it became lost in my tears.

The tears that rolled down my cheeks were the happiest I'd ever shed. And each new one was happier than the last. Nora, my mother, simply embraced me. I could feel tears falling from her face too. After we spent forever crying our eyes out, we continued to embrace each other.

Nora broke the silence first. "You know this means that you don't have to join the knights anymore. You're free now, free to hunt to your heart's desire." She broke our hug and looked me in the eye.

"I still want to join The Maidens," I said, wiping the tears from my face with my arm. "Not because I have to, but because I want to. Being a knight is the best way I can think of for me to do the most good. I'm really good at killing, and maybe as a knight I can use my predisposition for violence to help protect people." With a playful laugh, I continued, "Besides, I liked Aenwyn. She was very nice."

Nora chuckled slightly. "Remember, it's Captain Aenwyn to you now," she said as she waved a finger in my face. "But before all of that, you need to pack. We're going to live somewhere else." Nora turned me around and gave me a light shove towards my room. "I think you're going to like the place. It's right outside the city and a short distance from the woods."

My tail wagged behind me as I collected my things. I packed my clothes, brushes, mirror, and toy unicorn. Before placing the wooden toy in the chest, I held it in my clawed hands.

I've kept my promise. No one has died for me, and I've saved those closest to me. The memory of the day in Nick's shop played in my head again.

Once the memory finished, I created a small cylinder of ice as thick as my forearm in the palm of my hand. I crushed it, letting the shards of ice fall to the ground.

I dare the Demon King to show up. I will kill him. This is now my world, my home, and I will protect it.

www.ingramcontent.com/pod-product-compliance
Lightning Source LLC
Chambersburg PA
CBHW060221030726
47499CB00004B/1132